MW00463308

...from a Dead Queen's Hive

This is a work of fiction. Specific names, characters, places and events are either the product of the author's imagination or are used fictitiously, and any resemblance to actual persons, living or dead, businesses, companies, events or locales is coincidental.

ISBN-10: 1679990756
ISBN-13: 978-1679990755

Printed in the US by Amazon.

...from a Dead Queen's Hive

A Novel

by Doug Sweet

"We've been torn from our soil,
ripped from the sun-caked earth
...angry bees from a dead queen's hive."
  Larry Barrows, 1967

Chapter One

Southern Oregon: April, 1974

*Great apocalyptic dreams of America: hamburger stand to the heavens,
gas station to the galaxy—running out of fuel. Deeply chiseled headstone
to human endeavor.*

*Eighty percent of her children grind down their teeth faster than they can be filled.
Only dentists know, and they're afraid to say for fear of declining business and unpaid
mortgages. But get one drunk sometime and he'll spill his guts. Behavioral Sink.
Guilt-churning stomach acid.*

*"Most of the damage is done during sleep," he'll admit, sloshing some Chivas on the way
past his pearly whites. So much, then, for the great dreams of the country, gnashing
through the darkness, subliminally fearing the dawning.*

And yet despite a tangled network of short-circuited confusions
jamming the world's airwaves, what seems like some out-of-kilter
pitch-n-yaw in the inner ear of the earth that's hooked-up to the
phases of the moon and consequent rising of tides; despite global
glaucoma and OPEC embargos, Chinook salmon still manage to come.

Mobilized by instinct, they merge into a swelling pilgrimage
through the ravines and canyons of the ocean floor. Swirling in
multilevel, mazelike schools to weave open-eyed through the softened
and frayed underwater carnage of centuries, man-spilled from the
surface. Unsalvageable wreckages of Man O' War or Galleon mixed
with the gutted, bullet-pocked bodies of Spitfire, Corsair, Zero, Mig
and Phantom, joined by re-entry blackened first stage rocket boosters
that fall back as so much acid rain to the earth again. Chinook are

spurred by genetic drives to play hide-n-seek with the fallout of history—all this sea bottom clutter—threading their way through shuddering seaweed fields, moving on currents unseen from the surface, steady deep watery breezes that undulate the kelp beds.

The fish leave the ocean depths and crowd up against the ledges of the Pacific continental shelf that juts out onto the sea floor. To form voluminous pools offshore or in tidal bays, waiting for their signal to head inland. To travel sometimes hundreds of miles up rivers, up smaller, intersecting streams, even up tiny creeks in a thrashing frenzy of reproduction. Sea lice and a manic death drive accompany them to their final, pent-up orgasm after their vertebrae-rending, crashing, leaping, cell-searing struggle to find their sandy bottom birthplace—a conjugal visit lifetime delayed. Not every species of salmon dies after spawning—many can come and go from sea to river numerous times. But here on the West coast, from northern California to Alaska, each Chinook through a counting gate is one that won't be coming back except as decomposed, slurried particulate in downstream runoff.

Despite the camouflage of the sea, these salmon are not really hidden. Conglomerate fishing fleets from dozens of nations that have been bracketing the globe for mullet and shad and herring, cod and hake and tuna, are now in hot pursuit, tracking the schools with sonar and depth charts, maps of undersea topography. Until the weather and time finally dictate action and foreign-tongued men curse the cold, water-shrapneled wind in Finnish or Norwegian, Russian or Japanese as they haul dripping cables from the brine below. The tanker-sized trawlers lower their net booms to tilt outwards from the gunwales of the ships, resembling the slanted metallic arms of the newest Navy missile launchers.

In this dim dawning, fogged and sea-breathed light from Oregon coastal towns like Nehalem and Manzanita and Brighton, Kinceloe Point and Netarts, Wecoma Beach and Tierra Del Mar, Florence and Gold Beach—from such European named places—you can see the

2

ships outlined against the horizon, bristling above the corrugations of the currents and the milling fish below.

Roughly uttered shouts are windswept across slippery decks to mingle with the whirring of the engines and hoists as the metal-cased city heaves with diesel effort through the ocean foam, frantically trying to snare its prey. Because when the coastal river's drooling into the sea becomes epileptic, when enough fresh water has diluted the salinity of the water offshore, some strange and elemental chemical reaction takes place, described by scientists as electron flow and alkaline levels in the slimy layer of placentic membrane that surrounds each fish, but described by those who watch from the banks as sheer mayhem...(*If you really want to get a notion of it to last imprinted on your memory, travel up the Oregon coast on highway 101 to the North Umpqua and head inland about fifteen miles on the twisting, tree-tunneled river road to the tidewater at Scottsburg, where a rag-tag collection of RVs and pickups have been drawn, like iron filings to a magnet, to every scrap of ground flat enough to park on. Join the hundreds of fellow harvesters in hip waders and down vests, baseball caps and hair curlers, country music and Blitz Weinhards or Luckys in their hands, who hold scoop nets and old landing nets and chicken wire funnels so that they look like mutated gargantuan hands as they stand in two feet of water and January's brittleness, looking seaward. Until someone yells, "Here they come!" and you see an invasion of tiny silver smelt that roils upriver like a hurricane storm front, like a 50's science fiction movie of gigantic army ants overrunning thatched African villages, or locusts devouring Utah. Plunder, you might call the harvest if you'd never seen it before. But to the local river-waders, the yearly event means buckets and tubs of wriggling smelt headed for home freezers, driers, or smokers. It happens on regular intervals, but there is no time for considered thought once the run begins. It's only later that you might reflect on what you experienced and wonder whether there was any plan to it all, or whether you just got caught up in the frenzy yourself, took your cues from the smelt's own actions*)...because Chinook sense destiny in the same way and charge upstream with a fury and abandonment

3

which has become legend in the few parts of the world they can still run.

Along with the rain.

With worms struggling through soggy channels to seek the air again, to die in solitary pools as alluvial leavings of the earth's constant shedding.

With glacial erosion and human grieving. Cleanly understandable as concepts but cold, complicated and malignantly dirty up close.

With the water beading on the bracken and sword ferns, running minor causeways along the lines of each frond's ribs.

With the dark and spirited columns of rain that have marched inland from the sea; have mobilized themselves to scale ocean side cliffs in relentless pursuit of territory; have fogged out over the beachheads as so many hulking and scrambling soldiers, photographs of smiling children and wet-eyed wives tucked beneath the fold of their uniform shrouds.

Soldiers of the rain mustered from their tidal society to be carried and catapulted upon the unsuspecting fir tips standing sentinel above the crashing, spraying watershed creeks. Government timber for miles of clear-cut, 2-4-D'd and partially replanted forest. Back over the Oregon coastal mountain spine, miles now from the widespread seascapes, back to where rivers run rapidly and narrowly through geologically young canyons. Back even further into creek valleys where the rain continues to dive behind a constant wind, kamakazi-ing down like maelstroming lightning, striking highest points first, dripping off in steady overflow, sluicing audibly through a base soil of pine needles and skunk cabbage. Falling so steadily as to inundate the trees, so that they cannot possibly absorb it —the banzai rain — until streams swell with runoff, forge new tributaries. Hillside clinging ferns nod heavily, dropping down just as a wrestler relaxes under the weight of an opponent, using his own mass as fulcrum, a pivot point, losing his adversary. With each plant's gentle dip, water picks up speed, running faster in frothy channels so that swarms of

4

insects hiding under rocks are overcome with the funneling, lower-seeking water...

His wipers are clicking in rhythm, smearing semicircle arcs across the glass. He blew the smoke of his cigarette hard against the windshield where it flattened before the heater vents dispersed it to the back of the VW camper. *Father?* He glanced at the crimped roach in the dash top ashtray, looked out at the dark and festering sky and downshifted into third for the hill ahead. He'd just come through Ruch, the last what-you-could-call-town on the river, where the north and south forks of the Applegate join — or split — depending on your direction.

The bus labored and whined up the half-mile grade. As soon as he crested to start down the other side, he could see people in the creek. From that distance, he couldn't tell more than that they were standing together in a wide bend just below the new house. He knew the place well enough, having driven past it sometimes twice a day, watched its construction, modular though it was. Wondering, with each passing — the way a snapshot retrieves a consistent memory — wondering who these people were. Who had erected a Boise-Cascade prefab veneered ranch-style gone suburban on one of the half-acre lots chopped out of the Sandusky homestead with Preacher creek frontage. Had graded a square plot into the hillside, smoothed out a patch big enough for their double garage. Then had the consummate audacity to put their name "Halverson" on the quaint gingerbread barn mailbox by the road so he'd be notified, with each passing, that this was their dream home in the country. *Bastards aren't escapin the city, just carpetbaggin it out here in handfuls. Wonder if they know nothing's stable, that we're spinnin around at 700 miles an hour, that earth's orbital speed through space is 67,000 miles an hour? Wonder if Dad sold em the fuckin property?*

Most days, he preferred to look on the other side of the road, to see how many rabbits were in their wire pens next to the bus stop shack that advertised them as "Rabbitts for Sale." But today? What with sucking down beer at The Alibi since morning and all the weed, and the burying of his father this afternoon...*and*...he mentally added the emphasis...the fact that these men were standing mid-calf in the tributary, he kept his focus on the tiny gathering as the scene flashed in and out of the alder, twisted and tangled willow and vine maple that lined the banks. As he came down the hill and relaxed the gears into fourth, he could finally see what they were doing.

There were five of them in rubber boots—three with pitchforks— hard at work trying to flip salmon out of the shallows where water spread thinly over the new sand bottom the last flood had sifted against the near bank. He could see the sweeps of pitchforks plunging, one followed by an upward jerk that sent a twisting, pirouetting fish flopping onto the grass behind them, left to squirm with others already gasping there. A man in a road-crew yellow slicker rushed up the slippery, matted bank to kick one that was sliding sideways back down toward the water.

It's Friday, he thought, as his bus leaned around the corner past the spear-fishermen and he caught one last rearview flash of oblique rainfall hitting a river surface already roughly turbulated. *But it seems more like a Sunday. Funerals are religious ceremonies, after all. Otherwise, we'd just dump corpses in the ground and get on with it. Nothin in the box but dead meat, regardless of how many scripted prayers are offered up to Christ the Savior. Now that I think of it, JC must'a been nailed up on a Sunday. And Babylon destroyed. Sodom struck by lightnin. Carthage leveled by Scipio's army, stab em from any direction you can. Rasputin murdered after nine tries, rolled under the Neva ice in a rug. Martin Luther spinnin out from paranoia while peasant blood ran rampant over unplowed German fields. Ich bin nicht? Maybe man cast from Eden in the fairy tale? And Pearl Harbor? That was a Sunday, after all. What about Nagasaki? Hiroshima? Remember Birmingham Sunday church-blown children? Bloody Sunday? Sunday, sabboth, death. He thought the three identical. End of pain? Protestant reward? Cotton Mather and the Blue Laws? Malleus Malificarum? Savonarola roastin in the piazza? If life is pain and death is the* *end of breathin, then…no, that's just the weed talkin now. But certainly that's all she wrote. Sunday, the last day, Omega, the end. Humankind can't take the finality of it all, have to make up stories about immortality where every petty, back-bitin relative miraculously becomes fuckin nice, enlightened, transformed. All that medieval shit, the ritualized mess. Like when I was an acolyte and used to hear em nearly chantin, the priests. Comin back off the communion rail…*slicing across the altar draped in purple and gold tasseled skirting to where a thirteen-year-old Zane LaRoux sat looking at the blood red carpet in his freshly butch-waxed hair, with a mouthful of braces, wearing an expression fully serious for the occasion as his nostrils twitched with the incense of high-church Episcopalian and he wondered with pinching guilt whether Father Jamison, the old priest who had always smelled of Vicks *Vaporub*, whether he could see him masturbating now that he was dead and supposedly in heaven. Not that Zane really believed in heaven like that: Jesus coming down on a rainbow, arms out, palms up, beseeching. A picture on the wall at summer church school he remembered from when he was seven. Something absurd about it even then, if he could have known the word. The tightest bind of these church things was that no one alive ever really knew. You had to die first.

But that had been then.

Now his father was the dead one, and plenty of the Catholic relatives had shown up, even if it was an Anglican burial. *So who were you really, Dad? Laurence Ernest LaRoux? Ernest? Jesus! Earnest to get over on whoever you could.* When Zane tried for a fix on his dead father's features, it all went hazy, came apart. He could distinctly smell the cigarette smoke and *Lavoris* on his father's breath, but couldn't recall many details of his face. *Who were you? Surely more than that straight smile, hard to figure stare I always got? Or the perpetual sarcasm, the racist jokes, the pickin at everyone's scabs, the continual abuse. Have absolutely no idea from the get-go what was happenin behind your eyes, how you thought. Only got the prepared statement…the voiceless violence.*

7

He could see the arrangement of aftershaves on the medicine shelf growing up: *Skin Bracer, Brut,* some Avon duck that smelled like insect repellent; when he thought of objects—shoes jumbled on the closet floor, green and yellow golf spikes, slippers from some past Christmas never worn, the smell of grass clippings locked into the knit fabric of the faded blue deck shoes—these he could get a handle on, could remember with extreme and ruthless clarity.

He was on his way back upriver from the funeral and already he'd forgotten what color his father's eyes had been. *Blue-gray, sort of. But what exact hue? I should know somethin as simple as that. Like how you felt when you were slappin me around. Why you had a pathological need to lie about the most mundane things, make up those ludicrous stories. Where'd all that come from? I don't know. I mean KNOW, capital letters. UNDERSTAND. REALIZE. Shit! Just more goddamn words. I mean, you should KNOW somethin about him; he was your own flesh-n-blood father, wasn't he? Not like knowin there's a war goin on, or knowin seventeen thousand Bangladeshis starved this month, but KNOWING from inside. Never saw you when you weren't on stage performin. Even huntin and fishin you were playin a role, always had an audience. I know what you thought, I guess, but I never knew any 'why's'. Like I could see the patterns, the shapes, but never knew why that's what I was lookin at. Mortal coils and all that. If I'd ever had a clue what scared you, maybe I'd of had some...might'a had some notion of who you were. Was pushin real estate till you dropped dead the expression of your inner being? Probably the jive, gettin over on people. Throwin your weight around. Constantly tellin me I was some kind'a fairy with my nose in a book. If no one was around you'd give me one of those fake backhands, the one's I'd flinch at every time—your power to inflict. Other than that you didn't do anything you liked that I could tell, not after the lake.*

Diamond Lake. Known for all his twenty-six years and well before that as just "the lake" to his extended family. Ninety miles from Medford and, as his dad always clarified in the same pedantic baritone, "ninety miles from Bend and Roseburg, too, equidistance. The gem of southern Oregon." Up to high school, he'd considered

Diamond Lake his own private being-left-alone paradise. In his earlier years, his family owned the massively timbered lodge, thirty-two steeply pitched roof cabins, the stores and gas stations at either end of the lake. Aunts, uncles, cousins, friends: they all worked at the lake. Weekends from early May to mid-October and virtually all summer Zane lived there too, exploring the shore, floating wood chip boats down one of the feeder creeks, catching frogs to pet and put in a shoebox under the lodge, amazed the next morning that they weren't still there.

The year he started second grade, his family sold out of Diamond Lake Resort, and his dad immediately signed a ten-year lease with the Forest Service to maintain and manage the public campgrounds that lined the eastern side of the lake. The western shore, for as long as he'd known, was dotted with summer homes owned by valley orthodontists and car dealers. He'd learned that before he was born his family had also owned a summer cabin, up until they bought into the lodge. So it seemed natural and normal to him that Diamond Lake was somehow in his blood. That it was his piece of the world, where he could disappear most of the day without attracting attention. He'd had the run of the campgrounds, learning to hike deep into the surrounding woods and find his way back. Taking the half-day climb up Mount Thielsen to the base of the top rock tower by himself, fantasizing Nazis behind boulders, dug into the slanted forest floor, potato mashers ready. Gave him a weird tingling at the base of his spine, being squeezed way deep inside.

Until his teens, he'd catch grey squirrels, "go-downs," because, as his father would invariably tell anyone listening, "every time you look at one, it goes down its hole." He'd keep them for a month or so, tame enough he could feel around on their claws and scratch their throats while they shelled peanuts, until seeing them in the cage got to be too much and he cut them loose out behind the crew dorm, a wood-floored tent with deep thickets of blackberries pushed right up against the back canvas wall. His own green pole tent, complete with a tightly stretched cot and footlocker full of books and clothes, was pitched amongst some lodgepole pine opposite the crew's quarters. Each night he'd lie in his sleeping bag accompanied by the sputtering hiss of a Coleman lantern, reading *Ripley's Believe It or Not*, or gutty combat stories of infantrymen in Italy, or jets streaking out of the sun over the Yalu river. "Bogies at three o'clock." Sunny days, he cruised for hours in the fiberglass outboard with its tiny cabin, fore and aft steering wheels, covered and open. He'd troll flies, patrolling close to the banks to scope out campers and spy on the summer home families playing badminton. If he had any money on him, he'd tie up at the marina dock and walk up to the lodge for pie and coffee. Chocolate cream or huckleberry. It was all about being seen wearing his deep forest green Diamond Lakes Camp, Inc. shirt with insignia. His mother told him he'd lived at the lodge since he'd been born, and the familiarly layered wood smoke smell of the lobby kindled warm memories every time he went in.

Once he hit thirteen, other than being on the water, he lived mostly for wood haul every afternoon at four. He'd climb up the side rails of the beat up two-ton truck, dig himself a hole in the mountain of wood against the cab, and go along for the ride. At each campsite, they'd toss out a few chunks into the powdery lifting dust. The first sight of a girl who wasn't too young, he'd clench his jaws and put on a determined frown, pretending that he wasn't there just for fun, that he belonged. Returning to headquarters in the empty truck bed, he'd admire the crosshatched scrapes and scratches on his arms, splinters in his hands. Gave him a sense of accomplishment, of adultness. Something a little aristocratic about it, like he was a notch up from ordinary. At least Zane could remember how his father looked in those years: green work pants and shirt, a uniform, every day the same. That was before the Forest Service took back the lease or, in the language of the times, "declined to renew" it. *Once he lost his place at the top of the feedin trough, the old man quit fishin there cause he said there were so many goddamned boats on the lake you couldn't fart without someone else sayin, "excuse me."* For a couple of years, his parents had kept a small vacation trailer at the sheltered South Store mobile park, across the highway from the lake, even paid to moor the boat. Zane figured that all those years as the man in charge didn't settle well with the role of being just another paying customer, as eventually his dad towed the trailer into town and stowed it beside the garage under a room-sized canvas tarp. And that was the end of talking much about "the lake."

Even your love of the place looked a lot like lust, didn't it? Bein the boss. Everything scheduled on your time, down to the nightly poker games. You, Mom, Lee and Daisy laughin through the smoke and tinklin of highballs in the front of the trailer, playin poker while I read back on the bed with hot chocolate and the warmth from the propane light on the wall. Snug as a bug. You think I never found out later you'd been bangin Daisy all along? You think I didn't know that? Your own goddamn brother? No wonder things went tits up. And I had to find out from Mom when I got her stoned my last year in college, one of the few times she ever talked about anything more important than her women's club. But I didn't know any of that when I was a kid. And what I thought I knew eventually turned out to be bullshit. Flat out. All your military stuff. Ranger brigade on Utah beach at D-Day war stories. Mom also told me all you ever did was run movie theaters in R & R camps. Jesus! All those lies about climbin cliffs under fire, all your stories nothin but lies. Like threatenin to take me down to the enlistment center to sign me up cause that's the only way anyone would ever make a man outta me. Tough guy playin the army hero. But what I remember as that kid readin on the bed wasn't real, even at the time. Wasn't what was really happenin. I was outside lookin in alone. Curse of the only child.

He accelerated at the first of only two straight stretches of the Applegate highway, by the junction with Little Applegate Road, and realized he'd covered four miles since the spearmen, had lost track of his thoughts again. Driving on autopilot in a pelting rain with the wipers keeping time. He jerked the sticky driver's side window back a crack since the heater vent blew right in his face. *Can hardly see outta*

11

the windows. It's all too dismal, this repetition of things long gone, this flashin déjà vu.

Because he and Sasha had been at the lake just last summer. They'd stopped on the way back from one of Sasha's college friend's wedding in Prineville. A rare two-day excursion into the dress-up country club world, even if it was just the dusty dry Prineville golf course, and even if dress-up just meant he had to wear a tie. He only owned one, a day-glo Mr. Natural number, sole of shoe lifted high. "Keep on Truckin." Sasha wore a skirt and sweater he'd never seen before, just a touch of make-up. Dazzling him anew with her olive-skinned elegance, conditioned as he was to well-worn jeans and t-shirts or sweatshirts from the Britt Society Thrift Store in J-Ville.

The two-story house with outbuildings on the Applegate where they lived required their near constant presence since Zane had hired out to his landlord Lester in return for rent; they seldom got away for more than a day. As Lester had told him when they'd shaken hands on the deal, "When the cattle need feed or the cows need milking, don't do no good to be off in Medford shopping. If 'n you get what I mean." Lester had a peculiar mannerism of squinting and smiling at the same time, a perpetually brown stained home-rolled Bugler hanging limply out of the corner of his mouth, his face deeply lined. "We run on farm time out here; it's something you just have to get used to."

Heading west out of Prineville in the early afternoon the day after the wedding and reception, they'd hit Highway 97 at Redmond, driven through Bend towards LaPine and Crescent on the back roads to Medford. By 7:30, after stopping once for food, they'd only managed as far as Tokatee, the California and Oregon Power Company's transformer complex just north of Diamond Lake. They could have made it all the way back up the Applegate in another three hours or so when Sasha said she was tired and wanted to stop. Stress lines furrowed her forehead when she talked, her voice a hint raspy.

He was tired too, but wasn't about to say so; after being mostly invisible at the country club while Sasha mixed with her collegiate friends, Zane had slid into a tetchy funk, fueled by an open bar. By the end of the night, he'd given up trying to socialize, had parked himself on a bar stool and wondered how he'd devolved from SDS organizer on the road to this two-bit, *Prineville for christsakes*, nagauhide and formica, unemployed DJ for music country club. The next day fallout was that he hadn't said much of anything while driving.

He'd turned off the highway at the entrance to Diamond Lake Campgrounds and lined up behind some California cars that inched slowly forward. He saw that the check-in hut he'd helped carry two-by-fours to when it had first been built still looked pretty much the same, save for a few extra coats of paint. When he'd pulled up to the open window, some summer-work coed leaned out to tell him...*Told me, mind you, me*...who, from age ten on could have explained the different flow patterns of Squirrel Creek, Skunk Creek or Porcupine Creek, and by twelve could almost guarantee a limit of trout any day, depending on what the bug hatch was or whether the moon had been out the night before, or literally which way the wind was blowing...*told me*...whose family had built its own compound of trailers with cement foundations and wood decks. Two of his father's brothers, Lionel and Leland—all seven kids in the family had names starting with "L" (Lionel, Leland, Laurence, Lois, Lucretia, Luella, Lucille)—worked summers at the lake, along with a couple of his dad's army buddies and a few assorted friends. *All of them workin for Dad, that part was always clear.* The headquarters was fenced off from itinerant campers with split rails and boulders blocking the dirt roads. *We even had our own private docks, just like the summer homes, five boats tied up like vacationin celebrities...told me*...whose earliest childhood memories were of lying on the black bear rug in front of the six-foot wide fireplace in the lodge, running his tiny fingers over the exposed teeth and glass eyes in the bear's head, poking the silicated tongue. Who, when he could navigate around on his own, would crawl into a leaky rental boat down at the marina every so often and push himself out into the lake until one of the crew or the state cop in residence motored out to tow him in…*told me I could have space L-3, like I was just another flatlander without a clue. Probably a goddamn sorority girl, judgin by the heavy mascara and whiney sincerity.* But he didn't know where L-3 was—they'd never had an L-anything—and he had to check the mimeographed map to see it was located in what he'd always known as "the wilderness." At least that's what everyone called the near mile of lakeside his father had refused to develop, reiterating often that some of the land should be left untouched. This stretch of lakeshore had sported filigree stands of aspens next to the water, and out on the lake after dark all he had to do to get back to his dock was aim just a little left of the light patch they made on his horizon. That night, as they bounced along the gravel road that'd been dozed into the soft volcanic soil, he came to see why his father had protected that whole section of land for so long. It had been a buffer, a barrier between Diamond Lake Camps Inc.'s nerve center and the hordes of campers who were their all too often needy clients. That night, he'd come face to face with the reality of being just another paying schmuck.

They'd found L-3, despite its newness and despite the darkness, because when the prisoners made the signs at the penitentiary in Salem, jig-sawed wood into the shape of the state, routed out the letter and number so L-3 was cut into the wood, the cons poured silver paint into the grooves so the signs would blink to life, neon-like, at the approach of headlights.

I should'a seen things comin that night. Should'a put the two an' two together then, instead of waitin for the hammer later. She kept it all a secret for two months. And it wasn't but a couple weeks later she had it done. I should'a figured it out then, that night, at the lake…driving around what used to be his own private playground. The long wait in line mixing with his resentment at having to cool his heels in Prineville. Sasha speechless beside him. Zane remembering his father's attempts to hold onto the campground as though he were making a final last-ditch stand against time; and as his headlights swept across a collection of aluminum lawn chairs and bikes strewn around a well-lit camper on the newly poured concrete pad that summer night, he'd seen the results of his father's plans. "Nothing," he'd thought then. As if the Forest Service, in developing the wilderness, had destroyed not just the ground as he'd known it, but had also wiped out a chunk of his own life like a minor cost override in a department budget.

He shook out another cigarette from the pack on the seat. The rain had let up considerably, swollen purple clouds having taken the north fork of the Applegate back at Ruch. He was headed upstream on the south fork, up into the Siskiyou mountains where the highway he was on shrunk down to a one-lane dirt road that dead-ended just inside the California border. Lester's working farm, and their neighboring house lay in the river valley about seven miles from the state line, surrounded by federal BLM land, in the last open pastureland on the Oregon side. Upstream, only old man Perry's mining claim and cabins a mile and a half away, and then another three miles to the Copper store, which was also the post office for fifty or so families strewn through the foothills as well as school bus drop for kids going into Ruch. *Like livin at the edge of civilization, thank whoever the fuck's twistin the dials. At least until they put the dam in and the land grab heats up. Until then we're safe.*

Doesn't matter if it was love or greed that drove you, Dad. I saw last summer that the lake was gone, turned into another asphalt holding pen. Just like I waited ten years to be one of the crew, and when I finally got legal age to run the saws and drive the trucks, it was over. Done. Gone. Yanked out from under me. No more goin to the lake. No more gettin out of the valley in the sweaty summer. No more freedom. You worked outta the house in town, in the garage remodeled into an office, so I had to put up with your narrow eyes on me all the time. An' if I wasn't gettin your dismissive glares, callin me a snot-nosed ingrate, it might be a quick slap on the side of my face, another shove into the wall or some furniture. Only did it when it was just the two of us. That's why I couldn't stand bein alone with you, even after I

15

got too old to smack around, after I broke your ankle with the hardball by mistake on purpose. But you're one dead motherfucker now. So, even if I once thought you might have had some small streak of real human feelin when I was too young to know different, it doesn't matter anymore. Buddy Holly. Light's out. Show's over.

They're lying on the deep purple Indian print of interlinked mandalas that covers the bed of the VW bus, facing each other without a lot of room between. Sasha's dark hair is piled up on her head, skewered in place with black enameled chopsticks, her bare midriff above the jeans showing smooth olive skin, as she's propped herself against the bus windows. The light from a lavender-scented, homemade three-wick candle perched on the narrow ledge behind the front seat threw her shadow high onto the camper ceiling. Van Morrison was being painfully reproduced on a battery-operated cassette player, the "Moondance" tape floating thin and tinny, violas and cellos and violin weaving with the threads of marijuana and patchouli that spiraled up from the ashtray between them. She was reading Hesse, having just come out of her *Alexandria Quartets* phase. Zane was scribbling in his gnawed little spiral bound notebook where he tried to keep track of his best lines. "We live in a society in the last desperate gasps of cardiac arrest and all we know how to do is take its temperature." He hated aphorisms written by anyone else, but thought his own stuff was worth keeping. For the most part, at least, since he regularly purged lines that had lost their ring. "Rivers don't flood twice with the same water volume unless they're damned," he'd printed the week before in block letters at the top of the page he was on. This time, he'd written in his cramped, backward slanting style. Now that he'd finished, he was waiting for Sasha to ask him what he'd just come up with, but she was buried in *Steppenwolf*. When the Van Morrison cassette clicked off, he hit the stop button and the top half of the machine flipped open.

She looked up from her book. "Aren't you going to play the other side?"

"I dunno. I'm kind'a tired of it."

"Then play *Ladies of the Canyon*."

"What about Cary get out your cane?"

She frowned. "That's on *Blue* and we don't have it."

"And we don't have it," he mimicked in falsetto.

"You jerk." She smiled when she said it, batting half-heartedly at his arm with loose fingers, a southern belle gesture if he'd ever seen one.

"Let me tell you somethun" He swept his left arm in front of him, grabbing the cigarette pack and lighter in one motion, scattering ashes.

"What? You going to make me listen to one of your sayings?"

"They're epiphanies, not sayin's." He lit a Pall-Mall and blew the initial cloud upward. "An' I can see it'd be pearls before swine right now."

Sasha shifted her weight slightly, the ashtray sliding a few inches closer. "You're just mad I had such a good time with my friends and you weren't the star."

"Yeah, right. More like you abandoned me to a coven of insurance salesmen."

"They weren't all sales*men*," she emphasized. "And they sure as the world weren't a coven…"

He interrupted, "I misspoke on that part."

"…and you've got a lot of nerve to talk to me about abandonment. How often have I had to feed those damned cows? How many nights have I spent out there by myself in the last two years? Mary Jesus."

He didn't respond immediately, since he'd traded his cigarette for the stubby joint and was sucking loudly on it squeezed between his thumb and index finger. He was screwed; she'd nailed him. Said "Mary Jesus," so he knew better than to put up a fight. She was a thin, 5-10 Greek goddess with waist-length black hair and a slow fuse,

17

but whenever he heard the "Mary Jesus's" she'd picked up from her mother, he knew it was time to switch gears.

"Ok. *Ladies of the Canyon* it is, then." He slid the cassette into its cradle and snapped it closed, pushed play. Joni Mitchell's voice, when she finally came on, seemed threadbare and gnawed—the tiny player reducing sound to a dissipating echo. "I wish you'd been able to see this place before the Forest Service got their hands on it again."

"I'm not talking to you," nor was she looking at him. Joni Mitchell soprano-ed about "rogues" in the closed-in air while Sasha patted her bun of hair, avoiding the chopsticks.

"But look." He stopped there, waiting for a reaction.

She pointedly flopped *Steppenwolf* face down with a small, exasperated sigh and stared out the window next to her head, seeing a spattering of vague lights from other campsites, his distorted reflection on the inside of the glass.

"Diamond Lake used to be full a' kamloop trout. Beautiful soft-mouthed, tricky to hook fish that we drifted flies for, me and my uncle Lee. Kamloops came from Canada; somewhere in the thirties someone dumped them in the lake and this place became famous, folks came from all over to fish for kamloop. They spawned like salmon, had a bigger head than a rainbow, got much larger. I grew up starin at the twenty-seven pounder mounted over the lodge fireplace. Anyway, Lee and I would wait till the sun hit the top of Mt. Baldy before we went out, and we'd fish till it was pitch dark. When I was seven, and Dad had leased the campgrounds after he'd sold the lodge, the whole lake was shut down for a year to get rid of the chubs which were chokin out the kamloop."

"What's a chub?" Her voice was flat, mouthing an uninspired question.

"Just a little trash fish that multiplies incredibly fast, kind of like the Snopes family in Faulkner novels. There's even one specie that's indigenous to Oregon, called Oregon-ick-thees, or somethin like that. So, anyway," he swallowed, "they had to poison the lake to kill the chubs off. Problem was, they also killed off all the kamloop. So when they replanted they decided to stock with rainbows cause they were easier for tourists to catch and they already had millions of them on hand in the hatcheries. Anyway. Whew...I'm gettin a little off track here..."

Sasha still doesn't look up, "I know you can't tell a story straight, Zane. I'm used to that by now."

"...like I was sayin, they poisoned the lake that year and no one could camp or fish, the lodge and all the stores were closed that whole season. But bein's we had the lease on the campgrounds and Dad knew everyone—all the Forest Service people and the cops—we came up durin that summer cause the family was markin out the spot for camp headquarters, layin foundations and buildin wood decks for the trailers. This one time I was wanderin around the shoreline with a coffee can for catchin frogs when I saw this really big kamloop way in close to the bank, just swimmin back and forth. I picked up a rock and hit it on the head, jumped into the water and grabbed it by the tail, coiled it in the coffee can. I ran back to the trailers where everyone was sittin outside in the sun round a fire: Mom in her 50's style two-piece bathin suit and Dad with his khaki fishin cap full of flies, Lee and Daisy and a couple others I don't remember. I showed them all my prize. Dad asked me if it'd been swimmin or floatin when I hit it. I said it'd been swimmin of course, cause floatin would have diminished my good aim with the rock. Dad said it was probably floatin since the lake had just been poisoned a month before, but I said it'd been swimmin for sure. The capper was that Dad decided to fry it up and he tried to get me to eat some of it. I didn't want to 'cause all of a sudden I wondered if it'd really been swimmin, or if it was full of poison..."

"Is this story going anywhere? I'm missing the point."

"...ok. The whole absurd thing came down to me cryin cause I thought, maybe it'd been floatin after all so Dad would die and it'd be my fault. I didn't know then that the poison used to clean out lakes is

Rotenone, which just hits the nervous system; paralyzes the gills so the fish actually drowns, but doesn't have any residual effects. The poison doesn't get into the fish's system really. Course I didn't know that then. I thought poison was poison, so I was cryin. Then everybody else starts laughin at my cryin which only got me to doin it harder and louder..."

Sasha fingered her book with a slightly bemused expression, stoned smile but distant. "Is that the story?"

"No...well, the point of the whole thing is that I'll never be able to find that piece of shore anymore. It was in the wilderness, and now the wilderness is gone. I could remember exactly where I hit that fish for years afterwards, could take you right to it. But now it isn't even there for me to find what with these campsites every twenty or thirty feet and the shore so trampled down it all looks the same. The aspen grove I used as a guidepost is even gone, cleared out. Like the whole little kid frantic thing that meant so much to me then, that whole string of minutes, like they never existed at all. Never did. An' my old man won't even fish here anymore, says the place depresses him. Depresses me right now."

"So what can you do about it? Change it back?" She's told him before that he dwells on the past far too much. "You're always talking about stuff being gone, lost. What about here and now? What about trying to live in the present?"

"I don't know what to do about it. You always want some simple fuckin answer. I'm just sayin things've turned to shit." His voice was rising, already too loud for the confined space of the bus, drowning out the music. "It's just a story I thought you might understand. But forget it."

"What I don't understand is why everything is so dark with you. Negative, negative, negative," Her eyes narrowed as she spoke, hardened, sighting-in. "We're not a 'we.' We're you wallowing in how miserable everything is, and me trying to figure out why I have to hold the world together. I sometimes wonder if I signed on for this. I

20

mean, did I say I wanted to spend my life trying to persuade you to have a reason to care?"

"Is this about gettin a full-time job?"

"That too. But I'm not going to let you make me feel guilty about your own lack of responsibility, or maturity." Joni Mitchell giggled at the end of her song. Zane cringed. "And it matters now more than ever. I'm pregnant," she said dryly.

He tried to sit up with a jerk, but hit his head on the roof of the bus, sagged back down on the bed, scattering the ashtray's contents. "Jesus. Are you sure? How do you know?"

She nodded, watching her finger trace the pattern on the cover of her book. "Two months."

"Jesus," he repeated, putting cigarette butts back in the ashtray, "bringin another kid into this world." He waited a beat. "Who's the father?"

He watched her fumble with the sleeve of incense, and could tell she was trying to draw out another stick. *She's tryin to keep her hands busy so she won't cry or hit me.*

He swung around the corner by the turkey farm, its inhabitants seated like white fuzz on some miniature bleachers. *Yeah. I should have figured it out then, last summer. Cause we never went back to the lake. Too overrun with people. I should'a seen she'd never have that kid. Should'a known it then.* He did know he only had four more miles to drive, four miles to maneuver the increasingly stubborn bus around the tight turns of the Applegate highway, and he hoped he'd be able to make it all the way before he passed out. It had been known to happen. Especially on this road. Especially when Vince still lived out by Jackson Park and the two of them would drive back from the Blue Max in Medford after Vince had cleaned and closed the bar. Spinning down the river road at three in the morning, smoking joints and drinking cheap red wine. Celebrating the end of one day and trying to hold off the beginning of the next while they fantasized about buying

21

some old house in town with Vince's Indian money, turning it into a gourmet restaurant they could all run together, growing their own herbs in oak barrels on a well-sculptured back patio.

In those days, Vince still had Herman, the green Triumph roadster, before Soapy presented him with first one daughter and then another and he traded Herman off for Pussy Blue, the Ford pickup with diamond upholstery that had a better head for driving the river and slower acceleration. Just the thing for a family man.

Better him than me, I guess. He catches his eyes in the rearview, half-sagged, red glazed. They tell him that, in addition to all the other flaws in his character, he's a lousy liar.

...the water moving through ivy and vine maple and laurel and alder, pine and fir, larch and maple. Funneling through each tangle of chokeberry and salmonberry and blackberry. Sliding around each fungus and moss-covered tree corpse disintegrating in the constant blanketing of rain, feeding the earth from which it came, until each and all becomes part of the water's progress and the overflowing of the one adds to the advance of the whole. The water now springing into arpeggios—music of the streams—syncopated with tree echoes and the reverberations of mid-channel rocks. The orchestration becoming more harmonic as, against the fabric-like greenness of the hillsides, the water flows contrapuntally, branching continuously down to the soft carpet of the valley pasture floor, draining then into the brassy, Stan Kenton big band sound of the river.

Chapter Two

Peter Pan has finally reached puberty and found the world vastly altered from what he'd expected. In the process, he's become painfully aware that his age has chased after and caught him with ten-megatonal precision.

Tinkerbell can't get airborne anymore, haunting the darker downtown streets of LA, looking for a fix. Wendy volunteers much of her time to help out the local D.A.R chapter, waving plastic flags at returning aluminum caskets.

And Captain Hook—we mustn't forget Captain Hook, as much as we'd like to...
he's been running the country.

Sasha opened the firebox of the kitchen woodstove, brushing her hair back as she poked another chunk of split fir onto the glowing coals. The dark green ceramic stove with inlaid chrome fittings and double warming ovens was wedged crossways into the cramped space between the foot of the stairs and the half wall that cut the kitchen off from the large living room. They'd found another wood stove for the big room, a trash burner without its shell. Both were vented into the brick chimney that rose two stories through the middle of the structure to emerge just below the peak of the roof on the stream side. The same stream that ran down through the V of the converging ridges behind the house and had eaten a deep channel through the front pasture to the Applegate. The same no-name drainage creek that became the third-base foul line when everyone from town came out to play softball.

With a couple folded white towels, she drew bread from the circulating oven. She'd been baking all day, beginning right after Zane left for the funeral in Medford that morning. Of course, she hadn't gone with him. Couldn't stand his dad Larry, a florid faced, watery eyed, misogynistic bully. As soon as she'd seen the "Don't Californicate Oregon" sticker on their bus's back window wobble across the rickety wooden bridge over the river, turn left and disappear behind the roadside row of Scots pine, she'd tuned in the Ashland FM station. Friday morning blues except for the news every hour. Nixon released the White House tapes. Expletives deleted, she heard the buttery-voiced DJ say. Eighteen minutes conveniently missing. *Thank God he's gone; this would send him into a rave. He'd start waving his arms, preaching, and would end up going on about the Army Corp of Engineers and the new dam.*

She'd begun her morning sifting, stirring and kneading dough and the house smelled pleasantly of yeast and burning wood. After she'd put the first loaves in the warming oven to rise and wiped her floury hands on her hips, she decided to straighten up downstairs. She and Zane had finally gotten past the Planned Parenthood abortion last summer, she thought. Sasha could never have told him why she'd decided to abort. That she didn't trust him to be around, that she saw herself alone with a child in a dead-end, downward spiral. And after she'd gotten the embryo sucked out, Zane began acting like he was the injured party. All his trying-to-be-subtle jabs, niggling expressions of displeasure. *No bodily contact. Made sure nothing touched, slept on his side, back to me, on the edge, as far away as he could get. Months on end.*

They'd finally defrosted things before Christmas. Began talking to each other without pronounced undercurrent suspicions, fewer heavy exasperated sighs. Managed to make love again, to laugh together, seemingly past the clumsy self-consciousness from a long period of emotional separation. Until the first Saturday in February when they'd gone down to Brooks and Aurora Gervais' compound of buildings on the other side of Ruch for an Aquarius party.

Brooks was considered a successful artist whose deep space paintings—vast black canvases with mauve and chartreuse planets looking lonely—hung in banks, law offices, medical clinics and hotel lobbies all over the state. The Gervais family had homesteaded on the Applegate just west of Ruch five generations before, though now Brooks was the last in a long line, his parents having disappeared in

1968 while fishing for ling cod off Ketchikan. Neither they nor their boat were ever found, and Brooks inherited the three houses plus outbuildings after probate.

He'd turned one of the houses into his studio, bashing out walls and installing massive skylights. The Aquarius party had begun there before eventually spreading out to the main house as well as the smaller guest cottage. Probably fifty people had shown up, not including dogs and kids, and Heavy Duty—team catcher, ex-marine sniper and former University of Washington doctoral candidate in molecular biology—lovingly distributed hits of mescalin to as many of the adults as he could find. Duty had caught Zane and Sasha as soon as they arrived, telling them to "open up" before popping gelatin capsules into their mouths, giving each a slug from his bottle of Aquavit to wash them down. *That was two months ago and we haven't recovered from that night yet. Zane's cut himself off again, distant and cynically cold. He's been pouting and slouching around since the party. Then his dad dies and he goes completely into the tank. It's not like he lost his best friend. Larry was overbearing and cruel, from what I could tell. Father is such an empty concept for me in the first place. Nothing there, never has been. Uncle Andreas and Kostas tried, I know. I never suffered for lack of attention, but they had their own kids. After Mom died, I was just an extra plate at the table, another present under the tree. So 'dad' is an empty box. But even if I'm foggy on the concept, I do know Zane absolutely couldn't stand him. So I don't get it.*

She'd watched him prepare for the funeral most of the week, drinking *Vino Primo* or Gallo *Hearty Burgundy* every night until he staggered up to bed or passed out on the living room couch. When he was awake during the day, she'd find him sitting sullenly by the front window, staring out toward the river or dejectedly working through the stack of *Oregonian* crossword puzzles his mother Shirley had carefully cut out and saved for him. When they heard Lester's truck pulling around back every afternoon, Zane grudgingly dragged himself out to help with the cattle. Sasha didn't need to be a shrink to recognize depression; it lay like a thick, sticky fog in every room. Just listening to Zane's musical choices could send her into a downer on its own. Phil Ochs, Cat Stevens *Tea for the Tillerman*, Janis Ian, Tim Hardin, *Madman Across the Water*; one depressing song after another.

In these moods, Zane chain-smoked until the abalone shell ashtray overflowed. He was his own weathervane in that respect. After more than four years, she could see the warning signals before he ever sent them up. Generally starting with sulking inactivity, a moroseness that seemed to ebb out of his pores. Until he'd eventually erupt with a sharp tongued bitterness that reverberated through the air. *I'm still clueless where it all comes from, the morbid self-absorption. I know the pattern, though, can predict his next move. He's a Cancer, moves sideways. When he withdraws and isolates I think he believes he's punishing me, but he's the one who suffers most. Cringing and weak. Acting guilty to the core. So much different from when we met.*

She'd been attracted to him when he was in action, radiating intensity, and had found herself inexplicably drawn to his swimmer's body—broad shoulders but slim figure—his black hair lifting in the wind, his voice deep and rich like dark chocolate that even the under-powered PA system couldn't mask. That first time she'd ever laid eyes on him as he stood at the microphone on the stage, she was aware that people around her were responding to him, paying attention—that he exuded a presence. *Felt like a groupie, panting after him like some brain dead naïve nitwit. But he was fascinating to watch. Still is when he's on, when he's plugged-in.*

It was November of '69. The 2nd Moratorium march against the war when close to three million turned out to protest in cities across the country. In Portland, raucous shouting crowds filled Broadway Avenue from Burnside at the bottom of the hill to the park blocks next to Portland State where the march ended. She'd ventured from her apartment to check out the demonstration, but couldn't have explained why. She tended to avoid large groups of people, wasn't any kind of party girl. And though she certainly understood the

26

reasons people were protesting, her nature was more geared to quiet conversation than loud displays. But she'd come out that day anyway, without any premonitions of how alarmingly magical it would be.

Can still feel my skin tingling.

After she'd set the two loaves of honey-wheat bread on the counter by the sink and put the last uncooked loaf in the oven, she checked the firebox of the stove again to estimate burning time. She squinted at the wavering, glowing coals and the flames that were already funneling upwards around the piece of fir she'd just put in. Heat lapped at her face and she paused, bent over, listening to B.B King lamenting that the thrill was gone. As she banked up the fire and closed off the damper, she decided he wasn't singing to her. *Not gone yet. Not completely.* Wiping her hands off on her jeans while she straightened back up, she saw her Himalayan cat sleeping on the landing at the top of the open stairway. "Such a life, Erasmus. You've got it pretty cozy out here, don't you? Varmints to eat and a wood stove to bake your brains. And no Shirley sprinkling perfumed powder on you." The cat's left ear twitched as though it were shaking off a fly, twice, then twice again, but he didn't open his eyes. "I know you hear me, you ungrateful beast. You beautiful big baby."

She feared she was developing neurotic habits when she found herself checking the fire one more time before pulling Zane's green army coat off the nail by the back door and slipping it on. The FM sent melodic waves of The Who's "Magic Bus" from the living room as she opened the back door off the kitchen. She wanted to be outside, in the now gently misting rain.

Closing the back door behind her, she breathed in the familiar air. Damp cattle and the river, that faint fish smell combined with moss and green algae sponge deposits on the banks and rocks. A hint of pitch from the fir and pine that loomed high above her on the converging hillsides behind the house. Growing things everywhere.

She stepped off the broken planking of the back porch, stained white and green with chicken droppings since the hens roosted in the rafters at night. Her feet left small, rapidly filling pools behind her in the loamy ground, water trickling in each footprint as soon as she lifted her heel. Still hearing music from the house, though muffled and muted so much she couldn't identify what it was, who it was—she was aware how deeply she'd grown to love living in the country. *Not many straight lines, sharp corners. More like a webbed tapestry. Smells overlap and blend, yet somehow remain distinct, noticeable. Sounds of cattle and birds, the river and creeks. Shades of green thatched together everywhere I look.* The rain was almost caressing her, misting and mixing with her heat-penetrated body, her music-mellowed thoughts. *Nothing like the rain in Portland, city rain.* It ran gray and brown once it hit, she remembered, flowing down debris-littered gutters and choking its way through overloaded drains. Flooding low-lying intersections with muddy water. It wasn't like that here. *Quieter here,* she thought, as a blackbird called out from somewhere up the ridge to her right. *Quieter here than when Zane's around, even if he's not talking.* And immensely different from the third story apartment they'd shared in Portland, when they lived above an all-male bar on Montgomery near downtown. A converted office building: toilets down the hall, sharing mildewed shower space. A leggy sculptress was the only other resident of their floor, a frizzy-haired women in her thirties who wore as many bracelets, chains and necklaces as could fit on her body. Who dressed or draped herself in different combinations of paisley and hippy cloth. Who Sasha had never seen without a wineglass in her hand and who played Dylan albums day and night, flipping the stack over, again and again, until the order of songs burned into Sasha's consciousness. She could have recited what was coming next the way bible freaks could run through all the books in order…fast.

Finally, unable to tune out the Dylan brain worm eating in her head, she'd gone down the hall to see if she could request a change in music. Before she could make her case, however, she'd gotten sucked into a dizzying swirl of storytelling where she learned the chain woman's name was Endora. *Of course that's her name. Where's Samantha*

28

and Tabitha? I can smell hashish and jasmine; she must be loaded all the time. Probably why she keeps playing the same records. She's too stoned to notice. After a few minutes of very one-sided conversation, Endora had eventually launched into a rather loose-jointed stream of invectives about world affairs, insights into the power of mystic visions and testimonials for the undeniable benefits of Ginseng. Sasha had left the incense permeated apartment that day with her own heavy lump of gray clay wrapped in newspaper and Endora's chain-jangling well-wishes to let her spirit out. Sasha's artistic spirit, however, only came to her poking the lump into a kind of bowl shape and calling it an ashtray/incense burner.

In that first year they were together, after both had graduated from Portland State—she in Sociology; he a year earlier with a double major of English Lit and Political Science—Zane sporadically wrote edgy political articles for *The Willamette Bridge* under the pseudonym of d'Artagnon, but spent most of his time doing on-the-ground organizing, while she worked four nights a week cocktailing at Snow's Library Lounge by campus. She didn't have a solid fix on what kind of organizing he was up to, as he wrapped himself in the secrecy of "it's better if you don't have details." Even though she had firsthand evidence he was friends with one of the Chicago Seven defendants and knew the rest of them; even though she'd accompanied him to Minneapolis where he'd met with a whole slew of folks to plan demonstrations, she wondered whether all the smoke screens he set off that first year in Portland weren't really to cover his tracks where other women were concerned. *Strange I can think of it like that: "where other women are concerned." So objective sounding, when I mostly just sensed him covering things up.*

She didn't have a destination in mind when she left the house, and couldn't have come up with one now, but kept walking toward the V of the ridges behind the narrow back pasture. She wondered, as her memories spun their way out, whether a good part of Zane's current aimlessness didn't stem from him turning his back on political activity

29

when they'd moved to southern Oregon. At the time she'd made it pretty much an ultimatum, after all, having decided she didn't want to spend most nights alone.

She passed through the fence line's wobbly gate, stepped carefully across the twin-rutted, water ditched path Lester's pick-up had worn in an arc at the back of the property, between the fenced pasture and the converging slants of hillside that came down abruptly to the creek.

Lester's farm was behind the high wall of timber that formed the right side of the V. Though she couldn't see any of the buildings, she often noticed the thin twisting fiber of chimney smoke reaching up above the trees. If Lester honked his horn down by the barn and it wasn't raining very hard, she could pick up the faint sound. Behind the sloping hillside on the left was government timber all the way up to old man Perry's mining claim where Zane's high school friend Eamon McGregor lived in a one-room log cabin. No-leg Richard lived downstream, on the other side of Lester's, in a barn-like open house that accommodated his roller board and wheelchair. In effect they had no immediate neighbors, no noise except an occasional jet overhead or the cattle bellowing for feed, an unmuffled vehicle on the Applegate highway. The semi-isolation of the house, practically hidden in amongst the trees, sold her on the place the first time she laid eyes on it. *Such luck we had, despite the way it looked.*

They'd gotten the tip on the property from a guy Zane played darts with at the Fish n' Chips in Medford, while they were living in the trailer next to the garage at Zane's parents' house on Summit street. His dad had moved out to a condo across town a month after they'd shown up. Tension in the house; Zane stayed in the trailer if Larry was home. Sasha thought Larry used them as an excuse to move out by himself. She was sure he wanted to do it anyway, but saw his chance after they'd come to stay. Shirley pushed them to share the house with her, but they'd preferred to sleep in the mobile where they could come and go without raising eyebrows. Erasmus had run of the place, Shirley pampering him with canned tuna and nightly brushing.

This arrangement worked pretty well for about eight months; they used the house for most everything except sleeping, or smoking dope. Right away, Sasha picked up a fulltime job as a cashier/customer service person at Payless while Zane talked about painting houses. Mostly, she knew, he spent his time at The Alibi tavern with his buddies, or up a river fishing. Once again, she was the only one with a stable income, the breadwinner. Not that he was a complete sponge; he managed to finish some paint jobs and once actually did cut firewood for a couple weeks. She couldn't help but notice, though, that when he earned money he thought he ought to be able to spend it any way he wanted. Mostly, she knew with some resentment, she worked while he fiddled.

Since they didn't have to pay rent while they stayed with Shirley, Sasha had squirreled away close to two thousand in a savings account she'd started with her mother's very meager insurance payout. She'd been day-dreaming about quitting her job at Payless and letting him worry about where the money was going to come from, was damned well his turn. Just in time, the stars swung into alignment, and she could trace it back to one of many nights spent with Zane throwing darts at "Ye Olde Pub Fish and Chips" while she sipped box white wine and fended off the not-so-subtle advances of Stan the drycleaner.

Stan had made a big deal out of telling her he'd clean her ankle-length, white leather lamb's wool coat for free, her graduation gift from uncle Andreas. Stan kept going on about it, so she finally let him take it. From then on, when he'd had enough to drink, he'd whisper "How's about you and me getting together," watching to make sure Zane was busy at the dartboard. Stan wasn't much of a prize, over fifty with an ill-kept white beard curling over acne scars—a squat wife named Rosie who'd usually be somewhere on the premises, smelling of vanilla. Both Stan and Rosie played on the dart team, and Sasha couldn't help feeling sorry for the bubbly round wife who always smiled, but rarely talked much. She thought perhaps she was

31

projecting her own circumstances, the feeling sorry, having had plenty of experience being on that side of the fence.

One night, out of the noisy combination of juke box Tammy Wynette, beer-soaked laughter and loudly shouted dart scores, Stan let it be known that he knew someone who had an old house for rent with some acreage on the Applegate. "When you get to mile marker 31," he'd winked at her with uplifted eyebrows, breathing Guinness in her face, "it's the next right. Bridge over the river. Follow the driveway. Guy's name is Lester; wife's Adeline, that means noble, ya' know. You'd like her." *Sasha. Not short for Natasha. Just Sasha. Means nothing, ya' know. All us Croatians in Thessalonia, mixing for generations, according to mom.*

A few days later, they'd driven through Jacksonville, taken the left fork at the Ruch Y and followed the river road out. The VW bus windshield provided a wide panorama, as they passed the new vineyard a couple miles beyond the junction and then watched the houses seem to slink back away from the roadway, fewer and fewer the further they drove. Just as Stan had said, they saw the 31 marker and immediately found the gravel road and the sturdy, newly timbered bridge over. The driveway ran almost up to the base of the high hillsides, dividing narrow flat pastures dotted with cattle. They pulled in next to a dirty and dented red and white Ford pickup while Sasha gaped at the huge log house with rock foundation, the steeply-pitched cement barn that looked a block long, stretching out behind. She kept seeing cats everywhere.

Not just a single cat here and another there, but in couples and groups: on the front railing, on the porch roof, on the ground, on the woodpile against the log wall. When they got out, a tortoise shell started rubbing against her legs before she could even walk around the front of the bus. She had leather boots on and nearly stumbled trying to avoid kicking the mewling creature. Two black labs appeared from around the back corner of the house, wiggle-wagging their way up to them, tongues flopping.

"They won't bite," a throaty woman's voice from the open door, but Sasha could only see a dark shape inside the screen, "Come on up. Don't mind the cats; they'll move." By now Zane was rubbing both dog's heads as they crowded around him while he tried to walk.

"You Stan's friends?"

"He gave us directions," Zane said, as they entered the house.

"I'm Adeline," she looked them straight in the face with crows-footed smiling eyes.

"Lester's out in his cabin, but I'll get him," as she waved them through a front room packed with sagging couches and deep cushioned armchairs, cats on every flat surface, smell of cold wood smoke. A Russian Blue was curled on the fireplace mantle, all four legs dangling.

"How many cats you got?" Sasha thought Zane sounded a bit indignant.

"Forty-six right now." Adeline had pulled a gray phone off the wall next to the archway that led to a linoleum kitchen. "Lester. Come home," was all she said, and didn't wait for a response as she replaced the phone. "He's got a squawk box in the cabin. Now come in here and sit down," gesturing to the oval table with straight rail-back chairs. Cats leapt from the seats, but a huge Tabby watched unconcerned, stretched out on a worn tablecloth. Adeline called it Josh and told him to get down, but he just closed his eyes. "Oh, please," Sasha said, "he's all right," as she sat and began stroking the cat's back. Zane stood stiffly until Adeline put a hand on his shoulder, "Anywhere's fine, sit yourself."

Within ten minutes, all three of them were laughing because when Adeline opened the cupboard for coffee cups, a Siameze-looking shorthair calmly climbed out. "That's Nora. She's always in there."

"Do you know all their names?" Zane was scratching under Josh's chin.

33

"People ask that all the time. Wouldn't you know the names of your kids?" Adeline poured coffee for Zane and herself. Sasha had asked for tea. The kettle rattled on the gas stove, beginning to hiss.

"You want *Constant Comment*, honey? Or will *Lipton's* do?" Sasha thought Adeline looked like a washed-out purple pear-shaped bag. "Ruch Mercantile Store" sweatshirt over a stained skirt that hung in broad pleats to the floor. Sasha liked her. Her stringy dark brown hair straight off the top of her head, two equal halves. Her round face with a mole on her cheek, her warm brown eyes came across as soft and inviting. She seemed like someone in a perpetually good mood; that's the sense Sasha got from the start. "Whichever's closest," she answered.

Sasha was beginning to wonder if this Lester was ever going to appear, when Adeline responded to her unspoken question. "Lester's got hisself a cabin on the other side of Lobster creek, out behind the barn. Built a bridge over so he could get away from all us women. Had to put up with the two daughters and me for quite a while. He built it when the girls were high-school age. Said he had to have some privacy. So he's got a bunk bed in there and an easy chair, wood stove he can make coffee on. Old refrigerator that used to be in here. Portable TV, of course, so he can get his football games. He hides out from time to time."

"Sounds great to me," Zane said, rubbing Josh's head.

"Works out for me, too, you know. I just don't tell him that."

"Tell me what?" A scratchy male voice from outside. Sasha flinched at the gruffness behind her, turned half-around to see him coming through the back screen door. He hitched himself up the step and into the kitchen, nearly shuffling, stooped and bent. Looked like a painful task to take three steps and sag into a chair.

"That you don't move as fast as you used to." Adeline set coffee in front of him. "This is Zane and Sasha," she held his eyes with a determined stare. "They're gonna take care of the house," she said evenly, never breaking eye contact.

34

Sasha glanced at Zane, who was smiling like an idiot. Entranced and vapid, all at once. Open-mouthed. She reached over the cat to touch his forearm, gave him a "what's up?" face. He snapped out, closed his mouth, ran his hand through his hair. "We came to see if we could rent," he said, looking at both of his hosts, or trying to.

Half an hour later, they were all filing out the kitchen door, dogs they now knew as George and Martha jumping around excitedly. They were off to see the house that Adeline had already said was theirs. When Zane had tried to return to the question of rent, she'd shushed him. "You two make the house livable, agree to help out Lester sometimes. That'll be rent enough. I speck we ought'a get on over there and see what we got, though, don't you?"

Sasha wondered if Lester had any say in family business. So far, he'd only been smoking home-rolled cigarettes and squinting at them across the table. She decided his semi-closed eyes were a permanent feature of his face, like the deeply tanned and wrinkled skin that hung in little folds down his cheeks, like waves of icing on the side of a cake. Crammed in the front of the pickup, Sasha folded up on Zane's lap and, having to keep her head tipped at an angle, they went back across the river to the highway. Lester turned right and, thankfully for her, only drove down the road about thirty seconds before he yanked them roughly to the right again, down a small, steep hill and across a spongy, sagging bridge. They bounced down a rutted driveway, and from what she could see pinned to the headliner, they were driving next to a wire fence. Lester jammed the truck to a stop without warning, Sasha barely able to see past Zane's head, as she jolted back and forth.

"Looks like the house of Usher," she thought, when she'd finally extracted herself off Zane's lap and stepped out of the truck. Her back hurt and she stretched, head tilted skyward for a few seconds, hands on her hips. When she focused on the looming side of the house in front of her, she thought it looked as though the ground were reclaiming it. Brown/green muck had soaked into the lapped boards.

No foundation she could see, stains reached upward from the muddy ground in jagged patterns that looked like lie detector scribbles. With Adeline leading the way and Lester hobbling along behind, they'd entered the tall box of a building with a roofed porch. She felt they were walking into an enclosed junkyard. Smelled like sour milk, dust and rotted meat. Every room littered with garbage. Broken crockery. Ripped clothes. Empty food containers: cans, bottles, cartons and pizza boxes from town. Chunks of wood. Someone's residential detritus. Their footsteps sent up geysers of motes and fur into the dank air.

Up the incredibly narrow and dark walled-in staircase to a small landing, and then another set of stairs to the second floor hallway. Four doors set into the walls. Each room, more of the same. The far left-hand door wouldn't open more than a few inches at first, until Zane put his weight behind it and pushed the obstructions back a bit. Amongst the mountain of debris, they found a torn down slant V-6 engine (according to Lester), piles of children's clothes that seemed laminated, layers stuck to each other with mold. A litter of dead kittens under a mattress.

Adeline was breathing heavily through her nose, shaking her head. "Damn, Lester. I had no idea. This place ain't fit for chickens, way it is." Lester squinted and smoked, but said nothing.

"Let's get down outta here kids. You must be ready to scoot."

Zane and Sasha assured her they were fine, but exchanged looks of disbelief. Frowns and raised eyebrows. Back down the creepy stairway to the kitchen, Lester pulled open a drawer under the counter; it was full of dirty fluff and rat droppings. "Somebody's been livin here," he grinned. Adeline headed for the door and didn't slow down.

By the time they'd finished off Adeline's "leftovers," a ham, potato and cheese casserole, a deal had been struck. They would clean and inhabit the house and could live there as long as they paid the electricity, kept the place up, and helped feed the cattle when asked.

Adeline had already adopted a maternal air, putting her hand on Sasha's arm to tell her how much better she felt knowing they'd be making use of the house, that it wouldn't be sitting empty anymore. Lester didn't say much, except for asking Sasha if anyone had ever told her she looked a lot like Jane Fonda. "In the face, I mean, Missy." Sasha had shaken her head slowly, hesitant to guess Lester's opinion of Hanoi Jane. Zane had just one question before they left.

"How did someone manage to fill that room upstairs right up to the door, so it wouldn't open?"

Lester replied succinctly. "Ladder in the window." Zane nodded dumbly, and she could tell he was aware he'd asked the wrong question and wasn't about to try to follow it up.

They moved from Shirley's two days later, first week in August, in spite of her syrupy entreaties to stay. They slept in Zane's canvas umbrella tent—the one he'd kept from Diamond Lake—until they'd cleaned enough space downstairs, made it somewhat livable. Attacked the front room and kitchen first. The house already had a round-shouldered refrigerator with a shoebox freezer. Under the stairway in the kitchen, a door opened to a water heater with no water lines and a toilet that only flushed if they poured a gallon of water into the tank before they used it. The gravity-flow pvc water line from a rain barrel fed by an underground spring two hundred yards up the hill only connected to the kitchen faucet. No bath or shower; they used the river and a bar of soap in the summer, canners of stove-heated water the rest of the year. Starting from scratch, like having a homestead of their own. She thought fondly of how connected she and Zane had been three years ago, laughing often as they worked together to make their home in the country. Seemed another lifetime to her in so many respects.

By now the rain had quit. She was standing next to the creek at the bottom of the hillside slant, where across the running water the land took off upwards in steep, bushy undergrowth. She could hear the creek splashing somewhere above and beyond, up the ravine at the

37

notch of the two ridges where she knew a series of beaver dams formed deep pools. She'd been up there many times in the summer when those pools shallowed out to a couple feet deep. Then, the little glade the creek bordered on one side was full of grasshoppers springing and flitting in the shafts of sunlight the forest let stream through. She'd taken a blanket one day and lounged in the glade reading *The Master and Margarita*. As peaceful a day as she could remember. Now, she had to stop at the bottom of the slope where the creek fanned out into a minor delta, the current pushing against three small vine maples suctioned from the bank, bobbing slowly, pulsating in the swirls. She peered into a backwater behind the nodding logs, looking into the slower moving but still frothing, percolating creek. She thought she saw fin movement, waving fish tails signaling her to look deeper beneath the surface reflections, trying hard to catch a glimpse…

…Crowds were separating and unraveling, but hundreds stayed to hear anti-war speakers in the light, drizzling rain. A small bandstand was tucked into the upper corner of the park, one large white banner stretched overhead, the black omega Resistance sign in a red circle. A handful of organizers were milling around on the stage as she held her paper cup of mint tea with both hands for warmth and blew steam softly across the top, watching the soggy, straggling last lines of marchers beginning to disperse.

She almost left during the second speech, a frightening-looking, spike-haired girl draped in black who harangued the crowd for ten minutes in high, screechy "mother-fucker" this and "fucking fascist" that's. Rain curled in under her collar and she could feel her socks getting soppy, since she'd only worn tennis shoes, hadn't planned on staying out long. In fact, she'd already begun worming her way back towards Broadway and home when Zane started speaking. She didn't know who he was, of course; she wasn't up on her local college radicals, so damned many of them. Not that she wasn't sympathetic to causes, but she'd spent the bulk of her time hunched over an open book, chewing on her pen. She didn't have time for martyrs with persecution complexes—what she thought of the self-appointed student activists she'd seen around campus. When she heard his voice, though, echoing off the adjacent office buildings, she turned around, began inching between people back to the stage. Felt drawn to his sound, like a bassoon, throaty and intense. The soft hair on her arms stood straight, her spine tightened all the way to her tailbone. She realized she was transfixed. Completely out of character for Sasha Kristapouli, who knew her good looks attracted men, always had, but who had no time for leering, testosterone-fueled idiots who wanted to paw her. She wasn't a virgin, and she certainly wasn't frigid, just that the rampant casual sexual encounters of a college campus seemed so much sweaty fumbling to no good end. She preferred solitude and the control it gave her.

She couldn't explain her intense, visceral attraction to this man whose words hooked and blended into each other. Seemed to make sense in purely harmonic ways. Somehow, his voice was rubbing all her raw spots, like the Roberta Flack song about Don MacLean, softly killing. He looked like Anthony Perkins, she thought, sinewy forearms beneath the rolled-up sleeves of his blue work shirt, his hands carving the air with long fingers and an intriguing grace of movement. She threaded her way even closer to the stage. *Something about him. Some vibrancy. An orgasmic energy? What's going on with me?* Her own trade winds had been in the horse latitudes for quite some time, she knew. Not just becalmed, more like paralyzingly dull. But something about his voice kept drawing her forward. When he'd finished speaking and stepped off the back of the platform, she was already waiting close by.

To say that she'd gotten caught in an emotional whirlwind would be to understate her own very active complicity. She was keenly aware of what she was doing that rainy afternoon. She'd blatantly sought him out. No way around it. She'd heard the stories about people feeling they'd been hit by lightning or blinded by passion; that's certainly not how she experienced their meeting. For her it was more like a Gestalt, an unfolding, promised blossoming of intriguing possibilities.

Sasha waited while he finished a conversation with a small group, heard him say they needed "a friendly sea to live in" before he turned. She knew she was on unfamiliar terrain; he could ignore her, walk on by. But he didn't. He stopped, made direct eye contact for a good five seconds. Smiled. *Holy shit. What happens now?* she wondered.

They had a couple of drinks at Snow's, though she had no idea how they'd gotten there. It was a dream fugue where they moved without walking, more like gliding, with a soft light embracing the two of them, rendering everything else dim and out of focus. Twelve blocks to her apartment above Rubisch's corner grocery, where he bought a liter-and-a-half of Almaden claret and Mrs. Rubisch gave her a conspiratorial smile before they headed for the stairway.

"...Look at what happened last year. McCarthy and Kennedy galvanized millions of supporters. Then Bobby gets shot, McCarthy gets ignored and we end up with Hubert fuckin Humphrey." Zane was speaking quietly, breathing out smoke from his cigarette with the words. His voice a bit hoarse, high tones cracking. Sasha's apartment was a bedsit: one open room with a tiny bath closet, no kitchen. They were sitting on her bed on the floor, drinking wine out of coffee cups. "It's impossible to talk about any kind of democracy when the country's been at war since the '40s. I mean, our whole economy's geared to defense spendin, arms production. Think about it: Berlin. Korea. Lebanon. The Dominican Republic. Vietnam. We've never stopped. That and the urban police campaign against black men pretty much defines how decisions are made, whose interests get served."

She poured the last of the wine into their cups. "Seems you're tilting at some pretty high windmills."

"Fuck yes," he said, "that's the point."

She watched as his face tinged red, his voice rising half an octave.

"And remember the urban riots." He leaned towards her, keeping eye contact. "After King's murder, over a hundred riots erupted in cities all over the country. But those cats didn't loot guns and ammo; they weren't part of any kind of revolutionary movement. They took TVs and *Miss Clairol* steam mist hair curlers. Refrigerators and toaster ovens, for christsakes. They just wanted more of what white culture valued. Jesus!" He stopped, locking eyes with her. His shoulders sank as he exhaled noisily. "I'm sorry," he said, shaking his head, eyes to the floor. "I just don't know how to come down from these damn things."

"But to your point, I've always thought that if you don't confront structural racism you're not really taking things seriously," she said calmly.

"What's your name again? I like the way you think." She didn't speak when he reached for her.

And later, while they lay together with the bedspread over their legs, their clothes strewn around them, under them, she traced a daisy on his cheek with her fingernail. He'd kissed her forehead and whispered her name. She felt she was hearing it for the first time as it found her Achilles heart.

The steam from the coffee pot on the hot plate was condensing on the window just above the bed, obscuring the fire escape railing outside. Several candles put out a diffused, softened light. Blinking neons from the street below cast colors through the room, the occasional car headlight splashed across the ceiling.

They'd already gone through each other's obligatory "life story in ten minutes," though they'd laughed afterwards when Sasha pointed out that they'd each changed their voices for the ritual. She'd asked him why she'd never seen him around campus before.

"I graduated a year and a half ago, and I've been workin out of state most of this year."

"Doing what?" she asked. "What kind of work?"

"Organizin."

She'd propped herself up on one elbow to see his mouth move when he talked, gathering evidence that mattered to her sense of harmony. "People pay you to do that?"

"Not so's you'd notice. Slow busses, hitchhiking, sleeping on couches—that sorta thing."

"So you're not doing it for the money. You're one of those outside agitators, stirring up things."

"I confess," he said. "I'm guilty on all charges. You gonna make coffee before all the water boils away?"

She sat up, cast him a backwards semi-frown which she hoped he wouldn't take seriously. "Isn't that a little sexist? I'm supposed to make the coffee?"

"I'm the guest. And I'm naked."

She pulled a folded yellow sweatshirt off the pile of clothes at the foot of her mattress on the floor bed, ducked into it, pulled it down so it barely covered. "It may be instant, but it's Antigua," she said, as she was free-pouring the granules into an aluminum percolator without the guts. When she looked down at him, he'd suddenly gone somewhere else, was staring blankly at the throw rug next to the bed. "Black," she asked?

"Is beautiful. Yes, please." When he raised his eyes to hers again, she thought of how piercing they were. She knew, in that glance, he was going to complicate her life terribly, that she was already entangled, ensnared, probably enraptured. And whatever drug he was pushing, she was already hooked. Her years of making sure she was in control of her life, that she definitely didn't need someone else, seemed ludicrously hollow to her now. It wasn't as if she was infatuated with this person on her bed; she wasn't starry-eyed or head over heels, but she was very sure she wanted him.

"So, if you grew up in Fresno, how'd you get up here in the great rainy northwest? It'd be tough to find a place more different from Fresno." He reached for the cup she extended, sat up looking around him like he'd lost something. "Please don't take this badly, but I've got to put some clothes on. I'm feelin kinda helpless like this."

He gyrated into his jeans without standing up, as Sasha folded her legs beneath her, sitting on the edge of the bed. They were only a couple feet apart and she fought to keep from running her hands through his chest hair. *Like my uncles'.*

They sipped steaming coffee quietly for a moment. Zane dug his cigarettes out of his pants. Lit one, staring at the red Pall Mall pack. "Look what it says here, right under this picture of two lions with their dukes up. 'Wherever particular people congregate.' What a load of crap. Washed-out alkies in every dive bar I've ever known smoke these things. Real 'particular' people." He twisted his head, taking in the MC Escher prints and a large poster of Albert Einstein that hung on the walls. "Love what you've done with the place."

She laughed from deep in her throat. "Thank you. I put a lot of work into it." They were still sitting, legs touching, and she reached out her hand to brush his lips with her fingertips. She was aware of an internal tug, a need to touch him, to linger—so much to learn. She felt, she knew somehow, at the fraying, disjointed edges of her consciousness, that he was emotionally dangerous. Complex. An intriguingly strange mixture of confidence and vulnerability, strength and softness. With layers and layers between.

"So you told me about livin with your uncle...what was his name?"

"Andreas."

"...Andreas...and your mom died when you were in high school..."

"...Cancer..."

"...but you didn't say anything about your father."

Her head jerked back as if she'd been threatened. "My father? Geez. I haven't thought of him in a long time. I never even saw him. Mom left Greece while she was pregnant with me."

"Why?"

"Well, Andreas and Kostas—that's my other uncle—had immigrated right after the war, ran a bakery in Fresno."

"So you were born there? Sounds like a country-western song. Born in Fresno, But why did she come here in the first place? Why'd she leave your father?"

"She said he left us."

"Fuckin men," he wagged his head slowly, smiling slyly.

She refused to react, was determined to have this piece of her past over and done with. "I've had to put the story together myself, since neither of my uncles or my mom ever just sat down and explained. Always hurried little bits of information, then they'd change the subject." She drank some coffee. "You sure you want to hear this?"

He nodded. "Please."

"So you know Greece was torn apart by civil war right after World War II ended." She sought his eyes, looking for a response. He tilted his head forward and sideways. Acknowledging.

"Well, my father took off into the hills to join the leftists, the communists. Mom said she never heard a word from or about him from the day he left. Seems the government had instituted a program of essentially kidnapping the kids of those who'd left to fight. They put them in indoctrination camps, re-education centers, nursing barracks, even took babies. Mom told me she was afraid. She was six months pregnant and on her own, so she decided to join her brothers here in the US. They paid her passage, I guess, cause she had nothing."

"And she never knew what happened to him? Ever?"

"None of us."

Sasha decided she hadn't seen a fish after all, just the movement of the water deceiving her. She began walking back toward the house, digging both hands into the pockets of the Army jacket.

Zane is like a feral cat, wild and cautious at the same time. Helps to remember that, that I know that. If I get some distance, I do see him as a wounded beast. In his stronger moments, he can reach out with intense kindness, can be disarmingly loving and compassionate and tender and oh, so very wise. I need to force myself to look beyond the surface, his sluffing off of everything, anything getting too close. His hunched, negative, self-contained and distant stance that lingers too long. But when he's in some kind of action, even intellectually, he's truly remarkable and lovely. Notices and remembers everything; can quote something he's read back verbatim, from memory. He doesn't know those times when an electric charge shoots through my stomach and down my legs and I'm devastated, smitten by his strength and power. He can fill me up in so many ways. Can wrap his arms and legs around me and I don't care about anything else. Moments when I wish I had the personality to interrupt him and kiss his neck or find soft and feminine words like the lace I could never wear since I was always a "big" girl and one who never knew joy or comfort or praise from a father's lap. Or someone to say the words that told me I was cute or precious or lovable because of who I am. Moments he doesn't know and I can't tell him.

She'd been staring at the top of the ridge between them and Lester's place, focusing on each separate tree tip in relief against the gray, mushy sky. Wonder who he'll be when he gets back from the funeral? She thought the trees towering above her were standing sentinel in some way, or were like the rails of a child's crib, protecting her. She drew in a deep, deeper breath, focused on calming down, regulating her breathing.

Damn! The bread,

45

Chapter Three

Typso Tyee led the small band of Applegate Indians who had broken off from the Siskiyou tribe and retreated to the headwaters of the river, high up the western facing slopes. When General Lane summoned all the Rogue Nations to Table Rock—the uplifted rock mesa just east of Gold Hill—to witness the peace treaty in June of 1853, the Applegates refused to come down out of the mountains, told Lane's Indian interpreter that they were "here, and here's where we're going to stay.

Lane recruited a renegade band of Shastas to go upstream to the Applegate's camp and propose a feast to Typso Tyee. The Shastas promised fresh meat, claiming they'd captured a steer from one of the farms outside Jacksonville.

In truth, the US Army had picked up the tab for the side of poisoned beef which rendered the Applegates helpless to the Shastas' knives.

When the renegade band reported their success to General Lane, he had them arrested and sent to Yreka, in northern California, guarded by a well-armed patrol of out-of-work miners. None of the Shasta braves arrived with the patrol in Yreka; they'd all been shot trying to escape. Months later, one of the miners told anyone who'd listen that his fellow patriots had tied the Indians' hands behind their backs and forced them to run for it. They'd turn two or three loose each evening and made wagers on who could shoot them as they ran.

George Cruikshank twisted the glass of his Jack Daniels on the rocks, looking through the tinted, windowed wall that opened the airport lounge up to the runways. Further across the valley, nestled at the base of the eastern foothills, he could see the glowing red tips of wigwam burners from the lumber mills on highway 52. Lifeblood of the Rogue valley, he thought. *Lumber mills, plywood mills, molding mills. Smell of burnt sawdust always in the air. Medco, Kogap, Georgia-Pacific, Timber Products—all of them running three shifts. Thank God there's no paper mill. But we still smudge the pears every year. Burn black oil or old tires, laying a dark gray smog from Shady Cove to Ashland to Grants Pass, covering the whole valley.*

George had grown up outside Eagle Point which was just off 52, on a twenty-acre working livestock farm. In such rural locations during the fifties, farm kids enjoyed considerable lenience when it came to school attendance. Not that anything was down in writing, but most school officials lived in their districts. Couldn't avoid running into parents at stores or gas stations or church; they were part of the fabric of the communities, so certain policies handed down by the state simply weren't enforced. Particularly when the valley's other world famous export crop of pears began to bud in the spring and high school boys got called in by orchards at 11 pm or 1 am, if the forecast said frost, to light the pots under each tree, and would keep the pots burning until dawn. *Was great. All through high school, we got out for harvesting, hunting season, planting season and mornings for smudging season. Which was fine by me, getting there at ten or eleven, smelling of coal tar. Shortened the misery of banging my knees—those cramped wooden desks on rails.*

He was sitting at the bar of the Medford terminal on a Saturday morning, waiting for Colonel Walter Hustad of the Army Corp of Engineers, who was supposed to be on the scheduled 10:17 United flight from Portland. George didn't know exactly what to expect; he'd never met the colonel in person, had only read the pseudo legal language of his numerous letters whose inflated yet sterilized words gave no hint to the character of the person writing them. *Probably a secretary anyway. Colonel's dictate, don't they?*

As if he weren't intimately aware of how bureaucracies worked. After twenty-some years at the Bureau of Land Management—BLM for most people in Oregon—he'd witnessed plenty of overt demonstrations of how the chain-of-command drizzled shit downhill. He'd survived this long in the Bureau mostly because he'd learned early on that it wasn't a place to look for friends. Not that making friends was his long suit anyway; he could count them on one hand without needing his thumb, as long as he didn't use his left hand which was missing half of its first two fingers. Souvenirs from Korea. Along with his starkly and prematurely white hair, which he kept crew cut short. Thought it wasn't quite so obvious that way.

He was nineteen when the brown bleached out. First Battalion, Seventh Marines at the Chosin Reservoir when the Red Chinese sent their entire 9th Army across the border. Withering artillery barrages: bodies blasted apart, entrails steaming, stench of bowels blown open. As soon as the artillery lifted, hundreds of bugles sounded, announcing the flood of infantry. Outnumbered three-to-one for seventeen days and nights of sub-zero, howling wind through the Toktong pass.

Everything froze: fingers, toes, ears, morphine, plasma, rations, firing pins. Fixed bayonets for hand to hand combat up and down the line. Shrieks, screams and curses, the clang of metal on metal. Malignant moans of dying men. Sporadic gunfire, most rifles and pistols froze too. Just nineteen when his hair went white from visceral sustained terror. Considered himself lucky, really, only losing a couple fingertips to frostbite. Even if it wasn't enough to get him shipped out. Buddies started calling him Casper.

He swirled the Jack in his glass for a moment, then drained it in one long swig. *Yeah. I know something about chain-of-command. Assholes with oak clusters.*

"Jackie?" He held his empty glass in front of his face. "I've got time for one more." *He won't be here for at least half an hour. Don't know why the Corps didn't arrange someone to pick him up. What I get for working in an office instead of out in the woods. District manager or not.*

After he mustered out at Camp Pendleton, with eleven hundred dollars in his pocket, he caught a Trailways north for the long, jostling trip to Medford. 1953, July. The bus was sticky hot, and the reeking toilet combined with passengers' sweat pushed him to the verge of nausea the whole trip. At every dismal little sun-baked stop up the gut of the San Joaquin valley, George bought stale sandwiches, candy bars, and gulped down a couple beers if he could get them. Then back into the slick vinyl seat for more bumping hours on highway 99.

When the bus cleared Siskiyou summit, just north of the state line with California, he could look down to see the upper reaches of the

Rogue valley by Ashland and realized he was finally home, pretty much intact, if he didn't count his recurrent nightmares. He knew the war that was never called a war had shattered whatever he might have thought of as plans for a future. George Cruikshank, strapping six-foot-two farm boy from Eagle Point, had returned from combat missing large chunks of his emotional life. Adrift and alone, and in no mood for making nice with civilians who pretended they'd been behind him all the way.

His parents, ever closed-mouthed and stoic, naturally assumed he'd pick up where he left off working the farm. George took a good look at them one morning in the kitchen, a couple of weeks after his return, and saw washed-out, plain and homely people. Not evil, and seldom harsh, more an overwhelmingly tattered dullness. Faded clothes and trivial conversation, when they talked at all. He'd never seen them embrace, much less kiss. Not once. And the farm meant sloppy, wet, stenching routine: forget a vacation or a break. Meant that every time he drove into Eagle Point he'd have to pass old man Hendrick's two homemade billboards that fronted the highway, next farm over. "Get US out of UN" and "Impeach Earl Warren." He didn't know why those crudely painted signs wound him up so. Wasn't as if he had deep-seated political agendas himself. More like he saw all such rampant preaching as suspect, as someone trying to get over on him.

So, he didn't need to do a lot of tallying up of pros and cons to convince himself he couldn't stay on the farm.

Once he focused on his parents' drabness, he couldn't see anything else, couldn't get them out of his head. Just as years before he'd decided his girlfriend at the time looked a lot like an Afghan dog with her bleached blonde hanging hair, angular sharp tanned face. And that was all it took. He could never *not* see it. In the same way, he knew he had to escape. If he'd learned anything cringing in a frozen foxhole, every muscle in his body tightened, shaking and shivering uncontrollably, he'd seen that the light could go at any second. Whatever all this was, could end in the space between heartbeats.

He'd made use of his GI Bill that September, enrolling in Forestry at the state university in Corvallis. Nothing more complicated to him than that he loved being in the woods and thought he might as well find some occupation that would let him work there. He hadn't, at the time, considered what he was doing in terms of any career. He just thought of himself as headed in that general direction. Didn't see any need, and had no desire, to plan anything rock solid.

His fellow undergraduates were a few years younger, but miles behind in being alive, certainly in seeing men killing each other. Hadn't been splattered with the sticky, dripping brains of someone who'd just been talking to them. Hadn't lived in granular, cellular terror awake or asleep. Seemed mostly interested in pep rallies, pizza, beer, Beaver football and sex. His crew cut fit the college trend, but George's white hair and missing fingers marked him up front as someone apart. He wore khakis with a plaid Pendelton shirt usually. No white shirts with thin black ties. Hush Puppies instead of Penny loafers. Few talked about Korea, as though it never happened, which rubbed him wrong at first but eventually proved to be a godsend. He wasn't prodded or put on the spot to spin out war stories. No one wanted to hear them; like wanton infidelities, the war never came up in mixed company.

"Ladies and Gentlemen," a monotone male voice spoke from the speakers on the walls, "United flight 167, scheduled for 10:17 is currently experiencing delays. Please see a representative at the United desk for further information." George caught himself staring at the speaker hanging above the double wide glass doors that led to the open auditorium-like terminal. Thought the small box looked like the grill of a '56 Pontiac. He'd been halfway through his second drink before the announcement crackled and blared. Been watching Jackie's shapely ass as she moved up and down the bar. *Looks just like a catcher's mitt. Spalding. Rawlings.* She was wearing tan slacks and a tightly revealing pink V-neck sweater. Her dark brown hair hung to her shoulders where the ends flipped up. She was also wearing a wedding ring, but George knew she flashed that around for show, to keep obnoxious lounge lizards at bay.

They'd spent time together a few years back. Seven months to be exact. One of a long string of short, intense relationships George seemed to cultivate like dandruff. When Jackie's ex had the kids on weekends, George stayed over at her clean carpeted house just down the hill from the Rogue Valley Manor. Overlooking Harry and David's world-renowned pear packing plant outlined against the western hills. No way in hell he would have invited her to his place, a ratty threadbare three room apartment tacked on to the rear of the Jacksonville Tavern with back alley view of dented garbage cans and overflowing dumpsters.

They'd gotten along well enough, he remembered, sexual buddies for a while. Both liked Patsy Cline, Jim Reeves and Vodka martinis. She loved sex, laughing and football. Hadn't suffered any kind of dust-up at the end that he could recall. No shouting, no theatrics, no tears. She was real, didn't put on airs. What you saw, and all that. He often wondered whether she was too transparent for him. No place to hide, no secrecy. Perhaps all that was just too much for him to handle? At any rate, they'd drifted apart on different currents. Even now he couldn't remember why their love fest ended. Did she find someone else? Or had he hit a wall with boredom, as was usually the case? He smiled to himself that she'd once told him he looked like Burt Lancaster in *The Birdman of Alcatraz*—white hair did it. Her two boys were probably in Junior High by now, he calculated. *But she's still looking good. Aging well.*

She lingered in front of him, arching her eyebrows so her eyes grew wide. "So," she stretched it out. "How've you been, George?"

"Surprised to see you here. Last I knew you were working at that Blue Max joint on Barnett."

"Same owners. I work where they need me," giving him a warm smile. "So what're you doing here on a Saturday morning?

He exhaled dramatically for effect. "S'posed to pick up some bigwig Colonel from the Corp of Engineers. That flight they just said was delayed."

"You still with BLM?" Staring over his shoulder as she scanned the handful of customers sprinkled around the room to make sure no one needed anything.

"For the duration," As he watched her eyes sweeping the lounge, he wondered if he ought to drop a hint he'd be up for a repeat performance. She knew what to do with her body, that much was vividly memorable. He'd lost track of how long it'd been since he'd last broken a sweat on tangled sheets. Decided he couldn't decide whether to try. His ambivalence sucked him dry, like dropping a weighted curtain on the show. *I'm a waste of time. A mishmash of maybe, maybe nots. AND, I have this goddamned Colonel to see to.*

Jackie turned to draw another beer for the sallow, suited man at the end of the bar who'd stuck up an index finger, like he was waiting to making a point, and held it there until she reacted. George bristled when he looked over, thinking he'd like to break the guy's finger off at the stump for being such a stuffed-shirt prick. Instead, he stood up, laying a five on the bar.

"Gotta go, Jackie. You take care." He caught her eye for a second as he walked behind the finger-pointer on his way into the terminal proper. She didn't look the least bit broken up that he was leaving.

Zane awoke Saturday morning to sunlight slicing through scattered clouds, hitting the wet pasture, turning it into a glistening mosaic. He'd built their bed up on four by four posts with plenty of bracing so their pillows would be level with the double-sashed window. When he opened his eyes, he was already looking outside. He lay still at first, feeling blood pulsing into his temples, his ears

53

buzzing, whining: another pounding hangover. Cotton mouth. Dehydrated. Sasha was playing Judy Collins downstairs, the sound coming up through the floor. The *In My Life* album. The one where she's lounging on wrought-iron patio furniture with a slim cigar in the ashtray on the table; she's holding a hand mirror.

> "Marat we're poor,
> And the poor stay poor..."

A chorus of voices swelled behind Judy's, rising and falling like a surf. He'd always thought this particular selection must have come from a musical: interludes, different tempos, repeated refrain. He smelled coffee, wood smoke and his own sweat, stale tobacco and alcohol wafting out his pores. *Jesus! Why'd I stop at Richard's? He pulled out some hash and everything after that's hazy. Was on his roller board, zoomin around, hair stickin up. Don't know how I made it back. Remember Sasha's face, but don't know what we said. Fuck me runnin.*

He rolled out of bed, pulled on his jeans, caught his image in the wall mirror to see that his moustache was splayed out, plastered to his face, hairs going in all directions. Looked like that old guy on TV who's always drunk, mispronouncing words, slushing his voice. *Doctor somebody? Professor somethin. Irwin? Now I'm gettin them all mixed up.* He ran his fingers through his shoulder length hair, still checking the mirror, and spit on his hand to...*Corey. Professor Irwin Corey, but that's not the one I mean...*press his moustache back in place. *Christ, I'm a rat brain. Negative drug reaction.* He hummed a different song, thinking the lyrics that went with the tune. "But it cleans me out, and then I can go on." *Jimmy Buffett. AIA.*

Erasmus was curled in his spot on the landing, and Zane stepped over him on his way down the stairs. Wondering how Sasha was going to react to last night. Raw voice, high-pitched and scolding? Long suffering existential angst with sagging shoulders? Ramrod angry and silent? He knew he deserved whatever he got. He also knew from experience that nothing could get him off the hook faster than a good crisis, and banked on the funeral earning him some slack.

"It's alive." She carried a small plate with bread crumbs over to the sink without actually looking at him. From the living room, Judy Collins was finishing up as Sasha deposited the plate in the sink, turned around, leaned back against the kitchen counter and gave Zane her full-on, sizing-up, amoeba in the microscope attention.

"Alive, my dear, is a matter of immense conjecture," he said, pouring coffee from Sasha's dented pot they'd hauled down from Portland. Sipping cautiously from his cup's chipped rim. Eying her just as cautiously. She had him pinned in front of the radiating stove, and as much as he wanted to sit down, get off his shaking legs, he'd have to turn his back to her and leave the room to find a seat elsewhere. An old habit. Walking away in the middle of a conversation when he felt trapped. Not a conscious decision—he didn't plan flight instead of fight—it just happened. Some time ago, she'd let him know, with flushed face, trembling hands and welling tears, that his behavior was degrading and cruelly dismissive. That got him. Flashed him back to standing in front of his father, small and victimized, trying to disassociate.

"You going to tell me about it?" she asked, "the funeral?"

"Not until I sit down somewhere." Cup in hand, he headed for the living room where he sagged down onto the couch. Sasha remained standing in front of him, on the other side of their hatch cover table strewn with ashtray, empty saucer, Pall Mall pack, baggy of Mexican dirt weed—stems and seeds aplenty— ZZ Top papers and a small pile of stick matches. He added his coffee to the collection. "Are you gonna sit down darlin, or are you holdin the floor?"

She pressed her lips together, narrowed her eyes a bit, and sat on the front edge of the wooden-armed chair by the front window. They were eight feet apart on opposite sides of the room. Their front room woodstove ticked with heat at the end of the couch, the only ambient sound now that the stereo had clicked off. She'd sprinkled some curry powder on the stove earlier so the living room smelled sweetly. Sasha put her hands on her knees, leaning forward slightly, looking at him expectantly.

"So whadda' you want to know first?" he asked, lighting a cigarette.

She shrugged, staring at the Ansel Adams poster of Half-Dome at Yosemite that Zane had thumb tacked to the walls of old barn wood just after they'd nailed the boards up together. She remembered when he'd hung the print, and that she'd squinted to better tell him which corner needed lowering to level it out. "It's your story," she said finally.

"Ok then. Well, first off, I didn't bother with the church service. Went down to The Alibi instead and watched Jeopardy at noon with Fat Jack. Won eight thousand. Final question was *The Wasteland*, which was too easy, although only one of the contestants got it."

"What was the clue?"

"Twentieth-Century Literature. Gave us a quote: 'This is the way the world ends. Not with a bang but a whimper.' Easy, like I said."

She was leaning back in her chair now, crossing her knees, holding onto one foot. Her green eyes looked much lighter to him than usual, as if tinged with a reflected yellow. Sunlight funneled into the room from the side window, making a shaft across the wood floor, diagonally slicing across the rug in front of the table. He could see she was mentally tying things together, engaged and serious but not seemingly upset. Weighing her words. "Didn't you think Shirley would have appreciated your help at the service?" Her voice didn't have any edge, wasn't accusatory. And her face was open and smooth.

"What help? I'm pretty sure she wasn't on the verge of faintin or collapsin with grief. Besides, you know how I feel about churches, religion, all that crap."

"I was only thinking about her. But you know her far better than I do."

Zane rocked his head from side to side, spewing cigarette smoke in a stream. "I'm not so sure. I don't know how she could'a lived with that fuck all those years." He was moving stick matches around on the table like he was working a puzzle, using both hands, his head tilted back, the cigarette hanging on his lips. When he looked up, Sasha was watching his hands move. Then she caught his eyes and pushed her head forward a little, nudging. "Whaaat?" he whined.

"Is that it? You stayed at the tavern all day?"

"I went up to the cemetery when they dropped him in the hole. Wanted to see that, for sure. You know he plastered those Elk's club "Love it or Leave it" stickers all over this car." His voice dropped to matter-of-factly. Hands moving the matches, keeping his head down, cigarette between fingers.

"Who came to the gravesite, then? Who'd you talk to?"

"Didn't talk to anyone. Wasn't exactly at the graveside. I watched from up the hill, leanin under a tree outta the rain." He stabbed the Pall Mall into the ashtray rather dramatically, breaking it in half. "Ok?" He stabbed that out, too.

"Zane?" Sasha had dropped her chin, eyes pleading, eyebrows arched like she was looking over the top of her glasses, except that she didn't wear any.

"Ok. Listen," he said, swallowing dryly before he could continue. "This could take all day at this rate. I don't know why I'm makin you pull everything out of me, really I don't. I'm gonna have to do it all at once... After I get more coffee." *Feel like I'm slidin down a steep slope with no way to stop. Like that kid who cartwheeled down the side of Mount McLaughlin at Scout Camp. Ron Knight leapt up in the air and grabbed hold of the guy. Saved his life, but both of them broke bones. Feel like I did then, watchin.*

Sasha wondered what twisted, convoluted story he planned to spin as she watched cattle graze in the sunshine out the side window, birds fluttering and swirling above them. *Please don't jack me around. See if you can be straight for a change.*

57

Zane came back with the aluminum pot which he set on the floor by his feet after refilling his cup. His hands were shaking, his heels bouncing out a staccato, alternating rhythm. *This is different*, she thought. *He doesn't normally look so nervous, Especially when he's trying to run something by me. That's when he's usually at his smoothest, most in control.*

"It's too quiet in here." He rose off the couch and walked over to the stereo that rested on a cinder block and barn wood shelf under the side window. Albums on the floor overflowed from the space under the shelf, unruly stacks leaning against the outside of both ends. His body blocked the sunlight for a moment when he straightened up with *Blues and the Abstract Truth* which he dropped onto the turntable and switched on. He twisted the volume dial way to the left so the music was barely above a whisper when "Stolen Moments" began, flute and saxophones harmonizing.

"Ok," he said, returning to the couch, sitting back down. "I'm gonna tell you somethin I've never told anyone." But then he fell silent, watching light refract off the revolving record. Sasha wanted to grab his shoulders and shake him, do something, anything, to get his attention.

"Earth to Zane," she said. "You've got your coffee, got your music. I'm here listening. What's holding you back?"

Freddie Hubbard's trumpet squealed in the background, as he cleared his throat, spoke deadpan, as detached as a telephone operator. "He used me as his own personal punchin bag till I was seventeen," eyes still locked on the stereo. "Whenever no one else was around. Why I did everything I could not to be alone with em. Soon as I was old enough I got away."

"What? Who?"

"Good old dad. From as long as I can remember. As a little kid."

"He hit you?" She leaned forward, hands gripping the arms of the chair.

"Hit, slapped, cuffed, elbowed, kneed, kicked. Fucker had an expansive repertoire. My earliest memories. Bruises."

"My God, Zane. I had no idea…"

"Never talked about it."

"But all these years. You never thought you could let me in on it?"

"Too risky. No matter how I did it, I'd end up with the short end. Like King Lear, yellin in the storm. It's not rational, I know, but from the beginnin he made sure I kept quiet. Had his ways."

"What about Shirley? She didn't ever intervene?"

"I always assumed she knew when I was young. Figured that meant I deserved it somehow. Later I decided she was just clueless, which pissed me off in a whole nuther way. Like she didn't protect me. A betrayal." A new song started and Zane held up his hand, signaling for quiet. "Dig this one. 'Hoe Down.' Man, it's great." He wiggled his fingers in time with the melody, scatting along with it, "1. 2. 1-2-3-4. Da. Da. Da-da-da-da."

Sasha held her left hand with her right, abstractly contemplating her nails. He could switch gears so suddenly; she chalked it up to psychic defense mechanisms. He was following the base line of the music, pinching his fingers up and down to mimic the individual notes. She couldn't get her head around how easily and naturally he could do so many things, like writing smart columns for the *Willamette Bridge*. He could grow things, build things, argue philosophy or politics convincingly, could get out of his own way most of the time when confronting problems. And above all, she learned so clearly their first day that he was a gentle, patient yet passionate lover. She'd felt viscerally and intellectually met in a manner she'd never imagined. *A gentleness so contrary to his other moods, his craziness, which I can begin to understand now, his fury. Like a whole dirty, secret life. A constant hurting. Explains how he always sees himself as guilty, acts that way. Mary Jesus, It's no wonder.* As she looked at him across the room, seeing him bounce around on the couch, gyrating to the music, she wanted to wrap her arms around him to still the movement, quiet

59

him. But she knew that wasn't in the cards; she had to let him…what? *Process? God, what a bloodless word.* She had to let him be. See what came next.

Truth be told, when he'd started in, she'd feared another con job coming. But this made sense, felt right. *"And,"* she thought, it explained so much. In fact, as she watched him sway in rhythm, she realized she might need to rethink the major stumbling block to their relationship, what she considered his dishonesty, evasiveness, unwillingness or inability to be straight with her. What if this meant a sea change in their lives together, this confiding? *What a relief it'd be not to feel like the enemy, not to second-guess his motives. Not to suspect he was playing me cheap. Makes me giddy just thinking about it.*

'Hoe Down' ended and Zane stopped moving. "Now I've spilled my guts about lovely Larry, you want to hear yesterday's saga?"

"Please."

"I called Siskiyou Memorial Gardens from The Alibi and found out the internment was scheduled for two. Soapy had dumped Vince off on the way to her Bunco game. You know their house on Modoc is only three blocks from the cemetery, so I gave Vince a lift home, left the bus in his driveway, walked on over. Vince had scrounged up about half a pint of gin, stuck it in my jacket pocket. So, well-fortified, I camped out under the tree and watched everyone file up to stand around the grave. All my not-so-close Catholic relatives, the LaRoux clan. Obviously, I was too far away to hear anything, but could tell what was goin on…"

"They didn't see you?"

"Naw. Too busy starin at their feet. Tree branches hid me anyway."

"And you did all this why?"

"'Cause such a joyous occasion was only gonna happen once, an' I knew if I had to listen to any of his brothers or sisters yammerin about how sad they were, I'd lose it. Now that *would* cause Mom some grief." He pinched pot from the baggie, dropped it into the center of the saucer, started rolling it around with his thumb. "After everyone drove off, the ground crew pulled the tarp off a Bobcat that'd been sittin there disguised, and started pushin dirt into the hole. I walked down the hill and right up to the grave. The guy not runnin the Bobcat, who was leanin on a shovel, told me I wasn't allowed to be there. I said 'hell with that. I'm the son' and tossed the gin bottle into the wet mud on top of the casket…"

"Zane! You didn't!"

"Yep, I did. Then I flashed em a peace sign. Did my best impression of a military about-face, and left. Last I saw, the stringy-haired guy was tryin to retrieve the bottle with the blade of his shovel. I walked back to Vince's." He had formed an earthworm-sized rope of pot and began wrapping it with a gummed paper, ran his tongue along the edge and pressed the joint into shape.

The sweet smell blended with the toasted curry air, creating a complexly layered aroma with wood smoke, patchouli, peppermint soap, and cigarettes. Once, early on, they'd gotten a block of orange castile soap from the food co-op in Ashland. After a week or so, they'd realized the whole house, upstairs and down, reeked of the stuff, as did bedding and clothes. As an occasional scent, it wasn't unpleasant, otherwise neither of them would have been fool enough to buy it, but when it permeated everything, seemed to breathe out of the house, Zane had resorted to his own form of capital punishment. He'd buried what was left in the pasture, next to the phone. It still took a couple weeks for the house to air out.

He much preferred Sasha's recent obsession with curry powder. Went well with wood, he thought, though his favorite so far was half ginger/half curry. Heating and odorizing at the same time made harmonic sense to him. Cold, rainy days meant both stoves going. They could cook on the kitchen stove while they were heating the house: bake, boil, fry, simmer, and warm all at the same time. The front room stove could keep tea water, coffee, soups or stews hot. When they'd opened up the dingy, mildewed, closed in stairway by cutting the kitchen-side wall off at each stair tread, heat and scents naturally funneled upstairs, filling any room with an open door.

Summer was a different story: chopping wood and firing up the stove to boil water for coffee made no sense, so they lived out of a square electric frying pan and percolator which Shirley had insisted they take. Any serious cooking was done outside on a metal ironing board balanced on the edges of a rock fire pit in front of the house. Boiled crawdads were a summer staple—Lobster creek having been named for them—fresh picked salads with chilled crawdad tails. They'd both be lean, wiry and tan by July; limited red meat after May.

Zane caught himself re-running some scenes from two years earlier, when they'd taken out the dividing wall between two identical box rooms upstairs to make their expanded bedroom. Sasha turned one corner into her sewing-macrame' space: wooden bins stuffed with yarn. They'd built a sort of daybed out of a mattress on a plywood stand under the other window. The long wall was crammed with stacks of books, hundreds of them haphazardly balancing. During the construction phase, they'd made good use of the daybed and Zane remembered dozing on it one afternoon after Sasha had initiated a tryst that left him sapped and sated. When Lester's pickup honked for him to come feed the cattle, Zane had thought how good he felt, how much he genuinely loved life on the river with Sasha. After he'd jumped into the bed of the pickup with sideboards, more than half full of hay bales, Lester would drive in lazy loops through the three different pastures while Zane kicked the bales off after cutting the twine holding them together with his pocketknife. The cattle would line up in their regulated order well before they'd get there, telling time in some extraordinary cattle psychic way, falling into place in herd hierarchy. Just then, he remembered what he'd wanted to ask Sasha ever since he'd been in Medford yesterday.

"So, Miss Petrovsky, did you read Veblen's *Theory of the Leisure Class* in your sociology studies? Do you remember the 'theory of the French lawn'?"

"Certainly do." She had shaken her head when he'd offered her the joint and was now watching him gulp down smoke like a grouper inhaling guppies. Changing her mind, she got out of her chair, slid around the table and sat next to him on the couch, taking it from his fingers. "Why?"

"Walkin to the cemetery and back from Vince and Soapy's, I had this epiphanic moment."

She lifted her eyebrows, approximating wonderment. "Epiphanic again?

"Exactly. So, how would you characterize Herr Veblen's lawn theory?"

She put a hand on his thigh, as she passed the joint. "Medieval France. Feudal system in full flower. Serfs are starving and richest landowners come up with the truly obscene idea of letting land around their estates go fallow. Fenced off big squares around the house. No grazing, no planting, no growing anything except grass. A place to play croquet. A way of demonstrating power and affluence. Status. Became a cultural habit."

"And," he jumps in, "imagine bein one a' those starvin serfs, havin to look at that lawn every day of your miserable life. Like, you could feed your family on that ground. Grow onions and potatoes, tie up a goat. But instead, it's just gonna sit there, mockin you. A status symbol based on the death of others."

"Ratified by the church, of course."

"Sanctified you might say. So land use is political warfare, in a way. That's the epiphany I got yesterday. That the houses I walked past each had their little fences separatin em, and their neat little patch of lawn. Wonder how many of those lords and ladies today know what airs they're puttin on all over suburbia? What kind of statement they're makin?"

Sasha was mesmerized by Zane's thigh muscles she could feel through his jeans. And that reminded her of the time she'd asked if she could hold him while he peed because she wanted to know what it felt like. Made her twitch a little inside—not altogether unpleasant. She sensed something important had just happened to them, but couldn't say exactly what it might mean. She could feel him tightening his leg beneath her hand; he was sending out signals.

"One other thing," he said, squashing the roach. "Gifford came into The Alibi when I was there and said everyone was comin out tomorrow for softball spring trainin."

"Tomorrow? There's still cattle out there."

"I'll have to get Lester to help me move em," he said, sliding his right hand up under her sweatshirt, fingering her nipples as they stiffened.

"Umm."

When George Cruikshank left the airport bar, he'd laughed quietly to himself. The announcement had specified he should see the United representative. *Shouldn't be too hard to find.* United was the *only* carrier serving the Rogue valley; in the high-ceilinged, roomy terminal the one neon-illuminated booth squatted like an isolated island against the runway side wall. A blue and gray uniformed middle-aged woman with curly, peroxided hair was staring vacantly from behind it. "Barb" he read from her nametag when he'd stopped next to the flight insurance vending machine that stood at the end of the counter. $2.50 for $5000 of coverage. Quarters only.

"That flight from Portland," he began.

"167," Barb smiled.

"Sure. When's it getting in?"

"It hasn't left Portland yet, so arrival time hasn't been posted."

He splayed both hands out on the countertop, leaned forward slightly. "I need to leave a message for one of the passengers."

He'd scribbled a brief note on an official United Airlines memo pad Barb produced with a solicitous air, as though she'd been waiting for just this opportunity. George hadn't wasted many words: "Time conflict. Couldn't wait any longer. Yellow Cab can take you to

Medford Hotel." What did this colonel expect anyway? That having absolutely nothing better to do on a day-off Saturday, George would be at his beck and call? Would be cooling his heels like some mindless lackey? Fat chance. He had half a mind to go back into the bar, chat Jackie up. Who knew where that might lead? Well, actually, he had a fairly good idea where. He was convinced, on no palpable evidence other than how good she looked, that Jackie had recalibrated her sights on younger men, younger than him, at least. *I'm old and in the way.*

He drove his dark blue '68 El Camino from the airport to Ross Lane which left highway 99 and took him between two different plywood mills on the way across the western flats of the valley to Jacksonville. He'd long relished the sensations of driving between the plants, like passing through a blast furnace—the hot, burned air from the mill dryers—where plywood panels, thin glued "skins" of compressed wood sheets, were baked into shape and solidity. Didn't matter what was going on in the world, didn't matter what time of day or what season or what the weather was. Always smelled and felt exactly the same on this stretch of Ross Lane. Had since he'd gotten his first car in high school and been able to cruise Rogue valley back roads.

He knew dozens of little ponds strewn through southern Oregon, places he could catch blue gills, crappies, bass or catfish. Knew tiny creeks that weren't on any map but held brook or brown trout under bank overhangs. Knew which orchards didn't spray pear trees with residual poisons so the wild asparagus growing around the tree trunks was edible. Knew where to find morel mushrooms sprouting up through thinning snow on mountain ridges. He thought of himself as an organic survivalist, able to live off the land if needs be. Not the kind of survivalist that had been attracted to the Rogue valley back in the late '50s when *Time* or *Newsweek* or some other nationally-read magazine had printed a map of the United States that showed Jackson county and some little part of Maine as the safest places in the country from radiation fallout.

In the midst of the Cold War frenzy to build bomb shelters, hundreds of families had migrated to the area seeking sanctuary and solitude. They were the real survivalists, as far as he was concerned. Early in his time at BLM, George roamed the forests in a department pickup surveying and marking cutting lots and had run into several such outposts hidden in the backwoods. He'd never once felt like a welcome visitor when he rounded a narrow, rutted, dirt road curve to find a collection of buildings, chicken coops, goats, barbed wire and water tanks that constituted some reclusive family's fortress against a nuclear future. More than once, he'd been met by unsmiling men holding shotguns at their chests. He figured he knew better than most how many isolationists lurked on the fringes of valley society, hidden from sight, rarely emerging from the woods.

Although George could certainly comprehend abandoning so-called civilization, living on the edges since he carried the same strain inside himself. He couldn't swallow the "chosen people" attitudes he'd picked up from the few he'd heard speak. He saw them as paranoid and strangely aggressive considering they were supposedly living exactly where and how they wanted. Why were they so angry? Like all zealots, he thought, anyone who didn't agree with them had to be the enemy, had to be defeated. A classic case of siege mentality: paranoia and/or grandiosity shrouded in self-sufficient anger. He'd met a few zealots in Korea and he'd learned quickly that believers who had any authority, any power, were extremely dangerous.

Didn't matter what the belief system was, really, because the consequences, the results, were always the same. *Sucking hind tit while big boys played with models in some strategic war room.* George had no time for people who professed they alone knew the "answer" or the "way." One thing he'd learned in the midst of mass slaughter was that no one was special, that feeling superior was a fool's game, a fast track to disaster. *Wonder how the colonel's doing?*

He's also wondering how much flak he's going to catch at the office for abandoning said Colonel. Seated at one end of the long, deeply cigarette scarred oak bar of The Jacksonville Tavern, George can't help but hear Lloyd the owner holding forth on how lucky he was to have escaped that "jigaboo jail" of a high school in Torrance where he taught driver training for twenty years. Complaining about those "animals in LA" was Lloyd's favorite topic whenever he could catch the ear of a customer who hadn't learned to tune him out or change the subject. Although he had been known to set out a free beer from time to time to keep an audience.

Lloyd liked to rub his back up and down on the sharp corner of the beer cooler, talking, relishing his place in the spotlight, having the stage to himself. He used both *Vitalis* and *Jade East* copiously, wore polyester Hawaiian shirts from Sears or K-Mart and combed his oiled black hair straight back from his forehead, the comb's teeth exposing whitish-pink lines of scalp. He sprinkled his stories with the usual southern Oregon verbal standbys: "nigger, spic, fag, gook, queer, dyke, chink"—that's the way he talked. In the eight years George had lived in the back of the building, only once had he seen a customer take issue. A pot-bellied, middle-aged guy with expensive glasses and a carefully clipped beard, in a crew collar burgundy sweater-vest, clearly a tourist, piped up that he was becoming "uncomfortable" because of the language. Lloyd had swung his arm so that his body pivoted a few degrees and he'd pointed to the "Right to Refuse Service" sign taped to the bar mirror above the cash register. "That applies to you," he'd said. "Get out," throwing two quarters from his tip dish onto the bar in front of the offender. "Beer's on me."

George remembered the look of astonished fear on the sweater guy's face. The trapped man's eyes had swept the barroom. Maybe a dozen men of indiscriminate age in baseball caps, smudged by various shades of dirt, paint, sheetrock or sawdust, playing shuffleboard or pool, some staring at him. A smattering of worn-out, pasty gray faced skeletons hunched over their wine, paying no attention. Seeing the lay of the land, that he was alone, he reddened a few shades and kept his head down all the way out the door, leaving

67

the quarters which Lloyd returned to his dish before launching back to the story he'd been telling. No one in the place acknowledged that anything had happened. Done deal. *Welcome to Jacksonville*, George'd thought at the time.

Today, nursing a beer in his usual spot clear around the end of the bar where he wouldn't have to see himself or anyone else in the mirror, and mostly out of range from Lloyd's banter, George couldn't shake loose from thinking about the colonel. It'd been a high school stunt to pull, he knew, skipping out at the first excuse. *Japping out, we used to call it. You japped out, but you jewed in. Army Corp jews in on my turf, and I jap out on the colonel. Now I'm sounding like goddamn Lloyd.* George was aware of a familiarly dark current flowing through his synapses. And wasn't that the way it always happened—he'd be hopelessly stuck in the blackberry vine before he even noticed it had thorns. He didn't know if Jackie had set him off, or it was the flight being delayed. Or that he resented like hell being rustled up as a servant for the colonel. Whatever sparked the flow, he could feel a stubborn, aggressive numbness spreading through his body the way morphine circulates in the blood, deadening nerve endings, but leaving him crimped in a foul mood every time. Sunday dinners at four-thirty in the afternoon at the farm affected him the same way.

Until recently, the last couple years, George had faithfully scheduled a Sunday visit to his parents about once a month. He did it out of guilt, of course. Subjecting him and them to four hours of painful attempts to converse with each other seemed a sin, as if he believed in such things. George thought the only missing piece to those monthly enactments of an eternity in hell was a Lawrence Welk soundtrack with audience applause. He had no way of knowing what his parents felt, or thought. Never had, he'd eventually realized—and how many years had that taken him? He'd inherit the farm someday and when the time came he might quit BLM...and do what? That was the real question: who did he want to be? Not a federal employee until retirement and then a general, inevitable decline until pneumonia or prostate cancer picked him off—of that he was quite sure. *Damn sure. Didn't join the Bureau to have a career exactly. An' yet here I am. Forty-three. Nothing and no one to cling to. As if I knew anything about that, the clinging, the needing someone. Slept in separate beds for as long as I can remember. No touching. No sweet words, patting, smiling. Always felt I'd somehow been dropped at their doorstep. They just exist in the same place like they've been imprisoned together. Defeated. So what could I have learned about love or loving from them?* He smiled; one of those grim, peel-off-my-flesh-if-you-must smiles of sardonic sufferance favored by Hollywood heroes. Testament to a steely, steady, solitary character. Shane or Cool Hand Luke. *So is this it? Living in back of a tavern, spending my time drinking cheap beer and listening to idiots spout crap, day after day? I need to find something to look at instead of myself. And I won't find it at the Bureau, that much I do know.*

In his earliest years at BLM, George had no office; he worked outside, in the forests, staking out timber for cutting, tying ribbon around tree trunks. Surveying. Checking up on logging operations after contracts had been let to verify that state and federal regulations were being observed, negotiating with surly loggers when they weren't. Going back again after the crews had left to make sure they'd cleared and replanted. Kept him busy, sent him to the farthest edges of the district, down the narrowest skid roads, back up the tightest canyons. As a consequence, George knew the Rogue valley better than he knew himself, places didn't change their location. He could find some obscure, out of the way BLM road whose identifying signs were missing and know where he was. But as this morning at the airport reminded him, he had precious little grasp or control of his own desires or motives. As his job had dulled into paperwork and committee meetings. He seldom got to breathe forest air anymore and his sense of self had followed suit, had flatlined to a menacing mental hum.

For the last six years, as a district manager, George has been tied to a desk, trying to ride herd on a couple dozen campgrounds, eleven points of interest, six historical sites and he wasn't sure exactly how many mining claims. All fell under Department of Interior authority and were administrated by BLM. What had once been, if not friendly, at least a congenial work environment had morphed more and more corporate in its structure. He'd kept his eyes and ears open, had paid attention, watched a steadily more bureaucratic, almost military hierarchy become the norm. Put George off to the point that he no longer offered his opinions in meetings, kept silent even when he knew something that could help.

Everything's a competition. Verbal combat. Trying to one-up the guy next to you. See who can make who look bad. Weasels and ferrets, pointy faces and beady eyes. Straight from college. Never spent one goddamned day working in the woods. Didn't know a Peavey pole from a potato fork. Learned business management—whatever the hell that is—and don't know squat about what they're managing. I came the other way, from corks on the ground, Homelite in the truck, walking the forest. Barked shins, slivers, sprains. Poison oak, ticks, fleas, carpenter ants. Jesus! My first job was new guy clean-up the shit. Riding in crummy stuffed with rednecks who didn't go to Korea or to college. They tried their damndest to break me down, scare me off. Everyday I'd find horse hairs in my sandwiches or a curly pubic hair in my thermos. But they gave in soon enough. I was young and fit, sliding down sixty degree slopes to find a claim boundary. I just outworked 'em. Kept my head down an out of anyone else's business. And just look at me now. I'm a corporate shill with varicose veins bulging out of my shins.

George realized he was preaching to himself, the same old song. Whining and moaning, while Lloyd was braying about Nixon's tapes with missing minutes to two unemployed mill workers at the other end of the bar. George knew they were unemployed the same way he knew that Lloyd had voted for Nixon twice.

For the last eight years, since '66, he'd lived in the J-Ville Tavern. If he wasn't at work or out fishing, he was most likely in his back alley apartment or sitting on this very same bar stool, wondering where his

70

life was going. *No place fast,* he thought, as a loud cackling erupted from the out-of-work mill hands. Another hit for Lloyd.

Chapter Four

Ku Klux Klansmen and their allies in the Oregon legislature easily passed a bill prohibiting ownership of land by aliens in 1923. Aimed primarily at Japanese and Chinese immigrants, the law also banned public schools from using any textbooks containing negative remarks about the Founding Fathers or American heroes, regardless of context or intent.

On September 9, 1924, Ashland residents lined Siskiyou Boulevard three deep for a Ku Klux Klan parade. Red, white and blue bunting hung from storefronts, undulating softly in a whisper of a breeze as 300 men in full regalia, led by the Ashland Concert Band, marched in formation down Main Street to Lithia Plaza. That evening, in an adjacent open field lit brightly by a two-story burning cross, nine men took oaths of purity and temperance to officially join the KKK.

While townspeople enjoyed ice cream served by the Ladies of the Invisible Empire, a bi-plane towed a cross of electric lights overhead, weaving across the sky in wide circles. The Ashland Daily Tidings reported, in its next issue, that the march was "splendid, with its illuminated crosses and Klansman's robes." No one in attendance would have been the least bit uncomfortable around the robes and pointed hats.

A little after seven Sunday morning Zane had driven over to Lester's house. He knew his landlord would have been up since five or so, and predictably found him down at the huge, cinder-block barn that Sasha called the Taj Mahal, where he was forking hay through an opening in the wall to the horse stalls. With his permanently hunched back and stiff, jerky movements, Lester looked like a gnome or troll in overalls, Zane thought. The labs, George and Martha, were snuffling around on the cement floor, poking their heads into corners, under shelves and workbenches, slinging saliva. The pungent ammoniated air quickly burnt the back of his throat and bits of hay floated in the diffused, ambient light inside.

"Well, glory be. It's the professor," Lester's grating voice echoed a bit in the high barn, half filled with hay bales. He'd been calling Zane 'professor' ever since he'd seen their front porch filled with stacks of books when they were remodeling upstairs. Zane wasn't enamored with the name, as he was sure Lester had picked up on. Didn't stop him saying it, though. Lester's "edge" Zane called it. Like the twist of a knife in the wound. Or a back-handed comment that belies whatever nice things might have just been said. Zane figured it was Lester's way of making himself feel good, but he'd have to admit that even after three years he hadn't made many inroads into Lester's thought processes. As someone who prided himself on reading people fairly quickly, he was often stymied by Lester's terse comments, couldn't get a hold on what lay behind them. But he was sure of the undercurrent, and felt equally sure that, if it weren't for Adeline, he and Sasha would be homeless. Not that Lester was antagonistic, more like he'd rather just keep people at a distance, that he was suspiciously solitary by nature.

Lester quit with the hay, stood the pitchfork on the floor, leaning on it enough to slightly bend the tines, squinting at Zane. "What's got you out so early this morning?"

"Folks're comin' today for softball, and I hoped we could move the cattle."

Lester flicked a lighter to the stub of his home-rolled. "S'pect so." Smoke streamed. "Back the pickup in here. Keys're in it."

By the time Zane barely missed knocking off the side mirrors as he backed through the opening because the truck's high panels blocked his view, Lester had five bales on the floor, stacked neatly. Three on the bottom, two on top like the beginnings of an igloo, offset seams.

Zane lifted and shoved the hay into the pickup bed and climbed in the back, sat on the bump of the wheel well, leaning back on the side panels. Lester hoisted himself up onto the bench seat and ground the gears before the pickup crawled out of the barn. Cattle had to be shunted between pastures a few times each year, so Zane knew the routine. They'd dump feed out where the stock was supposed to go, then Lester used the truck to herd them in, with Zane walking, arms outstretched christ-like, whistling and shooing.

From his position in the back of the jolting and swaying pickup, Zane watched the barn jerk from side to side, the twin-rutted driveway bounce up and down. The inside of the barn a dark square rapidly receding, wobbling away into the white wall and then becoming a small smudge against the plaited greenness of the nearby looming ridges and the jagged line of the snow topped Siskiyous to the south. He thought of Sasha's face yesterday morning, remembering it half lit diagonally by the sun through the window as he'd cracked the flood gates he'd been guarding since childhood. Didn't know why he'd done it, the opening up. Telling her how he'd lived in constant fear of being assaulted.

Her eyes had widened and softened at the same time in an intimate and gentle caress—a look he'd never seen before—he did know that. Some fundamental reaching for, was what he thought. But who was he kidding? He hadn't actually been terrorized after age thirteen or so, had resigned himself to his father's slaps and punches. Learned to just get through whatever it was, come out the other side, burning with hatred.

After their urgent, open-mouthed sex on the couch yesterday morning, Zane spewed forth a steady stream of 'for instance' vignettes for her, painting one picture of childhood trauma after another. They kept coming. Of the Christmas he'd been sent to his room with a backhand to his ear for dropping the tinsel on the tree instead of placing it carefully. He wove a pattern for her, describing a chaotic collection of insoluble moments that could never be watered down. His dad throwing pitches at him, starting when he was ten. Getting him in the back yard with a worn through, bulky, oversize catcher's mitt. Larry was Rogue Valley Fast-Pitch league's only knuckleball pitcher and Zane caught most of the evening workout balls off his forehead or shins or chest or groin. He never knew where the ball was going and he had no catcher's gear for protection. If he complained, loving Dad would fire his hardest fastball at him with teeth bared.

Call him "a whining baby." Real uplifting and supportive—why he'd stuffed down all those moments.

One particular day stood out to him for its complete ordinariness. He'd been helping build a backyard fence while suffering a sinus attack. His dad, frustrated with Zane's constant snuffling, told him to "for christsakes" blow his nose. Zane had turned toward the house but was immediately yanked around by the arm. "Where do you think you're going?" his father had snarled.

"To get a Kleenex."

"Don't you know how to blow your nose outside?" Instantaneous with a slap to his face that splattered mucus and blood down his front. "Jesus Christ you're a sniveling wimp."

He'd kept quiet about all of it because of deeply tendriled shame at being victimized, and because of a twisted notion that no one could betray him, use his own history of weakness against him if they didn't know it. Strange how this worked. He made up stories about how he got bloodied or bruised, played up being accident prone and reckless. Never once thought about telling anyone else because he knew, without doubt, that eventually he'd have to be alone with his father again. And that knowledge shattered any fancy fantasy scenario he constructed, a certain knowledge that he was condemned to a battered servitude.

Being the object of physical violence and near constant verbal belittling had somehow convinced him that, despite all reason, some warp in his very being invited and deserved punishment. Often, after physical violence, his father would say "Look what you've made me do." Convinced him that whatever he got was because of who he was, a logical consequence of his weak and sniveling character.

Or, as dear Dad loved to reiterate often, the best part of him got tossed with the afterbirth. A thought that lingered, unwanted but as present as a swollen gland.

In the back of the pickup, Zane was pressing his two big toes alternately against the bottoms of his well-worn Adidas in a regular patterned rhythm, as Lester veered off the river road and onto their long, narrow, bumpy driveway. Even being jostled on the wheel well, he realized he was tapping his toes, his normally unconscious tic now front and center. *Left. Right. Left. Right.* Alternating. Keeping track. While he simultaneously bounced an index finger off of each knee to count fence posts passing by. The same way he marked guard rails, highway reflectors, driveways, mailboxes or on-coming vehicles while he drove, as though doing so pinpointed his moving position, calibrated his being. As long as he could remember he'd had these nervous habits. Like blinking in time to his pulse when he was alone.

A hot/chill adrenaline rush flashed up his spine, his heart suddenly skipped to beat double: two quick, close together pumps. He hyperventilated, couldn't draw air for a couple seconds, which scared him every time it happened. But nothing stopped his conscious counting. So acutely conscious that he'd long ago decided that he did it to create order, like simple A is to B and B is to C logic, or like addition or subtraction. He was fixated by beats and rhythm, with marking his time. How many knife strokes to cut the carrot. How many steps to the smokehouse. How many stair treads. How many swallows when he drank…four. *One, two. Three, four. Two sets of two.* Squeezing fingers. Pinching skin with a cadence. Habitually counting in his mind.

He could feel the terror attack coming like regurgitation: constricted breathing, sudden clammy chills that radiated from the base of his backbone in acidic waves. Scenes of destruction flashed through like slides from a carousel projector on automatic feed. One pustular image after another. Not hallucinations, but vivid imaginings of asteroids or missiles filling the sky, raining destruction. A cold steel conviction that he was physically dying, could disappear as a being in a snap. Into nothingness. No oneness. He'd visualize the tops of the Siskiyou mountains on the horizon exploding in his face. Was convinced cancer gnawed his bones or lurked in one of his vital organs. Always multiplying. Each scene catastrophically fatal, a yawning blackness reaching out for him. Until he'd fear that the puny surface bubble of experience was all there was, that betrayal and then oblivion surrounded him like a vast, deep sea. A waiting noose and a mumbling parson. As if he were not only facing imminently impending death alone in a structurally hostile world, but also had to know that anyone who might appear helpful was most likely just setting him up.

He'd learned that too through years of personal experience. When panic struck, his mind spun and echoed a recurrent mantra of variably moving connections and linkages, inexorably leading to a grim, malevolent fate of being chained, like Prometheus, guts ripped out, crows yanking at his organs and eyes. In his terror, his thoughts would snap and spark in frenzied, feverish attempts to coalesce into something he could see clearly, could recognize, could organize. But faded snapshots and future fears tumbled with one another in a dizzying display of emotionally-charged flashes on free-spool, always leading back to that same sickening understanding of civilization as the story that never changes, knowing that every society there ever was had played the same tune. A knowledge that sat like a leaking tumor in his bowels. *Whether it's the Sumerians tucked into the crotch of the Euphrates and Tigris three thousand years ago, or the Indus spread over the sub-continent and southeast Asia for more than a thousand years. Myriad dynasties flourishin in China. Shaka Zulu overrunnin the lower half of Africa. Blood cults in the Andes. Royal families dividing up Europe, cousins against each other. Doesn't matter. Always the same over-riding narrative, the same pattern. God. Emperor. Priest. Boss. Dad. Authorities, judges, the relentless line of watchers and minor rulers who organize themselves into Lion's Clubs, Elks Clubs, Moose Clubs, Eagles. Rotary, Kiwanis and Chambers of Commerce. Men with power spoutin institutionalized propaganda so everyone can pledge allegiance to something. An elaborately devised system held together by complexly incestuous webbings. Mirror-images of itself weavin religious myths, social lies and what amount to historical sight gags into a story that keeps grindin on.*

Millennia of well-fed mouths swearin that certainty and justice are possible only by followin their rules, buyin their line, while untold millions starve, are enslaved. The story calls itself culture or tradition or natural fact and gets taught in schools as gospel, becomes a ground of being. Unbelievably, those who suffer most from its tyranny are often its most vehement supporters, who willingly stay in line, march to the gas house—that's the beauty of ideological programin. Hobbes was right. Nasty, brutish and short. Or just plain ludicrous. Five hundred old men, women and children shot to ribbons and left to rot in a My Lai ditch, a Son My rice paddy, and yet Dick Van Dyke stumbles over the same hassock every day at 4:30. Reruns. Baudelaire's Spleen. The night Bobby was shot and the "Lost in Space" actor enunciated Yeats, "what rough beast slouches," staring straight into the camera at 2 am. Black, bottomless absurdity waitin to close over my head as I sink without leavin a fuckin ripple. I can't breathe.

These episodes of hollow dessication, of staring into the existential abyss, though occurring daily, had a short shelf life unless he was tripping. He'd learned to hold on and ride it through. He never knew when the mental and physical panic would erupt, could only sense first symptoms. Hot flash followed by cold chill. No air to breathe, his interior world reduced to cardboard cartoon cut-outs held together by gallows humor.

A lifetime of trying to cope had taught him to be still and let the fireworks burn out, however uncomfortably frightening that might be. His life at stake. And not a single day went by that he didn't face the demons of his own consciousness as they moiled and shoved to get at him, telling him nothing was ever fair or meaningful. *Breathe deep and even. Work through it.*

For now, it was over. He'd lived through the panic.

His thoughts slowed, catching entirely unexpectedly on dog-eared images of Kierkegaard pining away from lost love at some Copenhagen street café, scratching out sad idealist aphorisms. *Either/Or. Fear and Trembling.* Zane's pulse quit skipping beats; tight, raspy breaths slowed and broadened. As always, leaving him drained and sweaty and, for a few minutes, decidedly weak.

Out the back now he could see the front pasture stretching to a smattering of vine maple and birch that lined the river's bank. The morning sun diffused through scattered wispy clouds above the mountain tops that hadn't really exploded. This time. He often wondered if others suffered his panicked dread, went through this wrenching fear, but he knew no one he could comfortably ask.

Soon their house would emerge on his right as Lester followed the worn and flattened truck path around the house to the pastures. The algae, moss and fish smell of the river had been replaced by cattle droppings and still damp alfalfa. Closing his eyes, he could smell where he was by the different odors that hung, like micro-climates, in the narrow valley.

Sasha and Erasmus were together by the front porch when they swung into view. She'd tied her glossy black hair into a pigtail, was wearing a forest green PSU sweatshirt; Erasmus wound a tight slalom figure-eight between her feet. She was looking his way, backlit with weak tea sunlight. He stuck up a hand in a feeble attempt at a wave, holding it upright like some B movie Indian chief, or like he was being sworn in. *So help me God.*

The truck slid into a deep rut that threw him off the wheel well and onto his back on the hay bales. He relaxed, lay there without resistance, watching the sky wiggle above him, and got sucked into the fact that he couldn't conceive of infinity, *goes forever? that there is a forever?* Made no sense to him.

The only stellar expansion he knew was the ever-widening ozone holes, eating outward like paper burning from a flame held beneath. *Right Guard* and *Old Spice* and *Secret*; *Easy/Off* and *Raid* and *Desenex*. All those fluorocarbons sprayed heavenward, congregating at the poles. *Scientists have isolated molecules of the Sphinx's nose floatin in the effluent of the Amazon. Butterfly effect. Saw that somewhere. Eighteen missin minutes on White House tapes. Nixon's in a mess again. Silent fuckin majority indeed.*

Lester stopped the truck at the double-wide aluminum gate that led from the back pasture to the front, a thin but steady stream of smoke crawled out his open window. Zane swung himself over the closed tailgate to the ground and pulled the iron pins from each top corner, dropping it flat before heading around the front of the pickup. He pushed the pasture gate inward and walked it open while Lester drove through. They didn't need to talk, which was fine by Zane, who pulled four bales off the back, cutting their twine and kicking each one apart. The fifth bale was for scattering over cow pies in the ball field.

Lester nearly stalled the pickup trying to weave back out of the pasture as the space was filled with cattle. They'd bunched up tightly, bumping each other to get to the hay, complaining loudly. Zane didn't need to shoo any in; all twenty-some had made a beeline for the unscheduled feeding. He only had to wait for the stragglers to clear the gate before clicking it shut behind them. *Easy smeazy.*

Of course, Lester exacted his pound of flesh for having gone out of his way, for doing a favor. A constant Zane could rely on. Lester always made him pay. Tit for a bigger tat. Zane understood that he'd signed on as quasi-indentured servant in exchange for rent; he didn't begrudge helping. But he ended up with much more than just feeding the cattle. So many jobs needed doing.

This morning, he found himself roped into re-stacking hay bales that were strewn around the cement barn floor; irregular piles had to be picked up and fitted back into the wall of hay. All the while Lester slouched in his overalls, squinting at him over his saggy home-rolled like a chain gang trustee minus the shotgun, asking one question after another about how he and Sasha had come to be together. Where they'd lived before. What they did for fun. What friends they'd had. *What's got his juices flowin?* Zane wondered. *Three years we've lived here and just now he gets curious?*

Lester kept an easy smile and tumbledown face to the world, but Zane wasn't buying it. Something else was going on, some hard as flint edge or core or alter-ego that hung in the shadows. A threatening after-image lurking. A pith of antagonism Zane only saw in microscopic flashes, feelings. But it was there, he was sure. He responded to Lester's questions primarily in monosyllables, chopped and half-dropped words, long pauses. Eventually, Lester seemed to get the hint and busied himself straightening nails on the workbench, hammering at them against a table-top anvil.

Zane didn't get back home until nine, and as soon as he came through the front door, he saw that Sasha had been busy cleaning and straightening while he was gone—no baggie of weed or paraphernalia on the hatch cover. Step one in getting ready for the crowd. Anything they didn't stash was likely to disappear. People coming in and out of the house to use the toilet, get beer, hang out, eat. Paw through their records. He could see she'd washed the ashtray, swept the Persian carpet they'd liberated from the attic of West Main Presbyterian Church in Medford with Heavy Duty's help. Duty had donned a blue boiler suit with "Luke" embroidered above the pocket for the occasion. He'd walked straight through the church annex, up the attic stairs, and come back down with the 10 by 12 carpet in a roll on his shoulder. Now the carpet covered most of the living room floor, looking fresh and clean, brushed up. Spiraling *Blue Nile* incense and Bonnie Raitt's "Since I Fell For You" filled the room, along with the ever-present undertone of cold wood smoke that hung in the air downstairs.

Sasha came around the corner from the kitchen, drying her hands on a dish towel decorated with rows of stitched blue chickens. "You know, don't you, that Brooks and Aurora are likely to show up today." She draped the towel over her right shoulder, put her hands on her hips, held his eyes.

"We're bound to run into them sometime anyway." Zane broke eye contact and stared at the floor by her feet.

"But they'll be here. At our house."

"Yeayah?" He stretched it out, lifted lilt at the end.

"Are you saying it's no big deal?"

Zane moved past her to get a beer from the frig, popping the tab and sucking foam off the top of the can as he headed back to the living room. "Let's have some Sons of Champlin, *Loosen Up Naturally*."

"Don't be a jerk. I'm serious. Have you even thought about this? About how we're all going to act?"

"I've conscientiously tried not to." He lifted Bonnie Raitt off the turntable, replaced the tone arm onto the new record and stood watching it until the Son's horn section came in, jump-starting the album with a Tower of Power-like chorus. Sasha hadn't moved except to drop her hands from her hips, blue chickens still rippling down her front. Her eyes narrowed, green shading into gray.

"It's not exactly a secret," he said. "Everyone knows."

Sasha knew he was right. The folks who were coming for softball considered themselves all part of "the family," that was the way they talked about themselves. People who in high school wouldn't have spent any time together because they were in different years found that age didn't matter as much anymore. Their family, then, was comprised of people who'd never left Medford after high school, vets who'd returned from active duty, and others who, for a variety of reasons, had ended up back in the Rogue valley after college.

They weren't a Charlie Manson family, not a guru-inspired clinging together around some self-proclaiming prophet, not a repetition of their own experience growing up in the post-World War II patriarchal world. Bouffant hair, Pedal-pushers, and Dad's the breadwinner. This family was a loose and fluid assortment of friends who spent most of their time with each other. Movies, camping, going out to dinner and most anything else they did were all group activities. So much so that hardly anyone who lived in town ever ate dinner alone. People dropped by, joined in. All hours, and in any condition. When someone showed up with a steelhead or salmon, string of trout or bucket of catfish, word spread exponentially, growing from 2 to 4 to 16. So Sasha knew Zane was right. By now, nine weeks after the fact, everyone would have heard about the Aquarius party and how they'd swapped partners.

"Besides," Zane added, "I'm sure it's old news. People have other things to talk about."

"Until they get here and are reminded, you mean?"

"We certainly can't do anything about it now. What's done is done." Through the front window, he watched the cattle milling around where they'd moved them, in the pasture closest to the river where sunlight raised steam from the soggy field like ground-hugging fog. "I'll bet half the folks who show up today were at the party anyway. And remember," he smiled, "two days afterwards Patty Hearst got herself snatched by those Symbionese Liberation cats. I doubt our little soap opera is on the top of anyone's mind."

"Anyone except Brooks and Aurora?"

"Who knows? We'll just have to make the best of it."

Sasha didn't know what that meant. She couldn't fit her own deeply clinging sense of unease into the parameters of making the best of it. The "it" alone wasn't clear to her. *Did I initiate what happened? Did Zane's fawning on Aurora push me onto Brooks? Was it all a conscious choice, or a drug induced delusion? Mary Jesus! He had a mole on his left hip, wore tighty whiteys. I only remember him looming, hovering over me. Talcum smell of the sheets. Moody Blues as background. Him above me, breathing cognac sweetness. His tongue in my mouth. My God.*

Dredging up that night for the umpteenth time brought waves of icy nausea, constricting cramps like after the abortion. Gnawing disgust that she intuitively knew was unnecessary. She could rationalize her actions easily enough, not being weighed down with phony morality or some male-based behavioral standard. But no amount of self-knowledge could relax the knot that cinched tighter every time she replayed waking up next to Brooks the morning after. How frighteningly damaged she felt. How she'd fumbled into her

84

clothes, trying to be quiet, and gone looking for Zane; found him drinking coffee by himself in a too bright yellow-tiled kitchen. How both of them had acted as though nothing were out of place. Pick up the pieces and drive back home, an unspoken, tacit agreement to stifle and stuff any immediate recriminations. A quiet but intensely painful ride upstream, the silence itself shouting that they were both culpable, had each denied the other, violated a relationship already fraught with tensions and doubts. *Even after nine weeks, I don't know how to make something warm and fuzzy out of our mutual fiasco. Don't want to go through it all again. Want it gone, not in my living room with everyone making nice. Aurora playing Sparkle Plenty with her glittering eyes. Brooks touching me while he talks, fingers on my forearm, he's always done that.*

In fact, to her great relief, Brooks and Aurora didn't show up for softball after all. Sasha had eyed every arriving vehicle. And even though she hadn't seen the couple's Audi bumping down the long driveway, she couldn't relax until she was sure they hadn't squeezed in with someone else. At least a dozen cars and trucks were still nosed against the post and wire fences on either side of the driveway. A truly motley collection of junkers, beaters, fishing wagons, dented pickups and some VWs, a couple of motorcycles. Heavy Duty's white Ford van was parked next to their house, "Military Industrial Complex" stenciled in bright red on both sides. No-leg Richard's new black Mustang with hand controls was half hidden on the far side of the woodshed. Gifford's maroon '65 Impala, shiny and waxed, had turned around in what passed for their front yard and was headed back to the highway, leaving early. Sasha waved to Rochelle in the passenger seat just before Gifford—his jaw thrust forward—gunned the engine, showering rocks, dirt, and thick dust behind him.

Earlier, Rochelle had confided that Gifford was crushing up cross-tops so he could snort them instead of having to wait for digestion to send the dexadrine through his veins. He worked long shifts at the One-Hour Photo kiosk in the Big Y parking lot and never seemed to be in a good mood. Zane had said Gifford suffered from little man complex and Sasha knew from experience how he'd get testy and pushy at The Alibi, taunting even his friends once he dosed himself with beer and pot.

So Sasha never heard anyone moan about Gifford leaving early. The general tension level seemed to drop as soon as he fired up the Impala. Reminding her of junior high garage parties in Fresno summers when the bored chaperoning parent finally went back inside. Changed the vibes immediately. *Twistin' the Night Away. Earth Angel. Bobby Rydell. Gene Pitney. Isn't very pretty. Kissing games with lookouts. The Ventures. Crepe paper streamers, red bulbs in the ceiling. Stacks of 45's on the record player. The Fleetwoods. Mr. Blue. Tragedy. Lilian's mother Wanda never came out to check. She liked TV game shows, stretch halter tops, and Hamms by the half-case. Steve and Edyie albums.*

She surveyed what was left of the...she couldn't call it a game or even a practice...nothing as organized or as marginally productive as that, despite the banner Heavy Duty had strung between trees. Hand-painted with black drips: "Chicago Bears Spring Training." *Not too likely*, she thought, *the training part. THC, testosterone and alcohol more like it.* But what did she know about supposedly grown men who seemed committed to prolonging their adolescent love of games, the male strutting, puffed up chests? Darts, football, basketball, softball, pool, hunting and fishing: all about men/boys trying to prove things.

She found it hard to imagine, for instance, that Heavy Duty was ever a soldier, much less a sniper. Couldn't imagine him burrowing into some rice paddy muck to wait for a clear shot. Couldn't visualize him squeezing the trigger. Or ever doing it twice. Didn't seem at all in his nature, the executioner role. None of it computed. Duty put out soft feelers to other people; he didn't use his two hundred and fifty pounds to threaten folks. The Gentle Giant. An overused expression, she thought, since she'd never known anyone who better fit the image than he did. Was stand-in babysitter for the whole family. Played

86

Santa at Christmas. Santa with a face like a young Charles Laughton. *Quazimoto in the belfry. Heavy Duty on the ground.*

As if on cue, Duty appeared from around the back of their house, four little kids trailing, hanging, affixed to him like puppies. For some reason she couldn't begin to fathom, she found herself wondering where the phrase "night cap" came from. Scrooge wore one in the movie, with a tassel yet. So how did it come to mean more drinking? It was a shabby mental chase, she knew, given the ubiquity of alcohol at every gathering, but that didn't dampen her interest in word origins.

Lately, she'd been looking around the corners to the end of things. It shattered her, for instance, to think that Erasmus would eventually be gone from her life. Especially since she'd felt connected to his spirit ever since a humid and stuffy early June night in '70 when they'd camped next to one of the myriad lakes in Minnesota. Full moon flooding down as Erasmus crawled into her lap, head up, blue eyes reflecting.

She'd never yet been able to fully explain what happened that night. Not to herself, and certainly not to anyone else. Like a Mr. Spock mind meld tapping into the cosmic airwaves, she saw vivid magentas and violets sparkling in interwoven cyclical patterns, heard voices that were unrecognizable yet strangely familiar. Visions of an inevitable aloneness splintered her consciousness, deep down; back to her mother's last days in the Fresno hospice when she, Sasha, had tried to find vestiges of her own being in what was left of her mother's face. Drawn in cheeks. Sunken eyes glassy from a pain killer drip. And—this happening, she was sure, because Erasmus was funneling the experience, a kind of medium on her lap—in this vision, the woman who shared the room had suddenly screeched in a raw, indignant voice: "When will this be over?"

Venus, the evening star, winked back at Sasha on that starry Minnesota night. Erasmus had grown restless, had bolted up the nearest spindly tree, and she'd been returned to the reality of Zane cooking dinner on the tiny hibachi, a pencil joint pressed between his lips. They'd remodeled the VW camper. Taking out the eighth-inch, rivet-screwed veneer installed at the factory, they built a stable bed out of 4 x 6's and three-quarter inch plywood. Walls of the bus were lined with the kind of restrained shelving one sees in a boat cabin. Everything in its place, unable to fall out. Snap locks on drawers. A huge storage space under the bed. Purple print spread over the mattress.

Zane had Country Joe and the Fish going on the portable cassette player balanced on the ledge behind the bench front seat. "Not So Sweet Martha Lorraine," twanging away in near-oriental quartertones. "What's up, Miss Petrovsky? You look a little peak-ed."

"I swear to Joan Baez that Erasmus is a medium. I had visions with him on my lap."

"Visions of what, exactly? An don't say 'Johanna.'"

She laughed. "Oh God, Zane. Endora, the Dylan Lady on Montgomery street."

"Bringing it all back home." He handed her the remnants of his joint.

"It was some kind of celestial explosions and then I was my mother in the Hospice."

"Sounds Freudian to me. Castration complex, no doubt."

"Hand me that knife and we'll see." She bumped hips with him while passing the roach.

"Don't get me started. I'm trying to provide sustenance here in the land of lakes and cheese. Ever wonder how easterners see the country?" He asked, after a moment of dead air, dumping chopped onions and garlic into the sauce pan on the hibachi where they sizzled loudly. "After fifteen hundred miles of mountains and deserts, we're now in what they call the mid-west. That's pretty myopic geography."

She hadn't been listening then, not tracking words exactly. Was more conscious of frying onions and garlic, a sweet smell with olive oil. More like she'd been sucked into a swirl of contradictory emotions, thinking that being on the road with Zane and Erasmus on their way to Minneapolis for a National Student Convention at Macalaster College was as wild of a thing as she'd ever done. Pulling the bus into state campgrounds, or rest areas, or mall parking lots to sleep. He'd told her she'd be meeting some of the Chicago Seven. Zane was going there to help plan a May Day demonstration in DC scheduled for the next year, and they'd been stapling up flyers along their route for The People's Army Jamboree in Portland in August. Zane had warned her that once they got to Minneapolis, he'd be going to meetings without her. Too much at stake. Too many informants. The atmosphere too paranoia-inducing for her to be included.

After the mind-bending experience she'd just gone through, helixes rotating on moving axles, exotic locales fluttered at the edges of her consciousness, beckoning. She knew, in that moment, intimately and rigorously that she needed to see Kathmandu and Angor Wat. Wanted to float down the Nile and roam Patagonia with a mate *bambilla*. She'd rarely dared consider such possibilities, but traveling across the country had expanded her notions of what was possible, in a way she'd never known before. Zane was opening doors for her, but she was well aware that other, different options were not being chosen.

Sasha was brought back from their trip by Heavy Duty with kids in tow from the house. Two of them belonged to a friend of Greg's ex-old lady Darcy. She didn't know where the other two had come from, but that, in itself, wasn't unusual. The family's fringes were fluid and generally amorphous. Folks came and went, she knew. Watching Duty leading the kids past her into what, until half an hour ago, had been the playing field.

She looked back behind her to see waning sunlight filtering off bottles and cans strewn under the tree line at the back edge of the pasture, about ten yards behind home plate. Silver insides of potato chip bags flicked light. Sasha squinted to blur and soften visual edges, fantasizing Victorian clothes on her friends, or were they antebellum? Billowing gathered dresses, cinched in tight at the waist. Soapy was tending to her girls, two and four. Sasha imagined them twirling frilly parasols. Pumpkin sat with her Down Syndrome kid Sarah, a stocky, perpetually good-humored five-year-old. Sasha didn't know who'd come up with Pumpkin for a name, but it was a rounded-off way of meaning Jack O' Lantern, given Pumpkin's missing and widely gapped front teeth. *What's her real name? Darlene? It's always been Pumpkin. Never heard her called anything else. I admire her strength, what she has to deal with: two other kids and no father in sight. Somehow she holds it all together, laughs a lot. Works two waitress jobs.*

Zane and some friends were hanging out under a tree just up the hill a bit to her right. She could see—from waving arms and pointing fingers—that they were in an animated conversation.

"Man, it's 1974, for christsakes, why would anybody speak German? Must be Amish or somethun." Eamon MacGregor, called Greg, his wild tangled hair, curly beard, eyelashes, eyebrows, hair on his arms and legs, all the same blend of light brown and faint red. He was squatting on his haunches next to Zane, Richard and Vince under a wide-spread oak tree at the bottom of the steep hillside that shot up from the back of the pasture to tower against the sky. Richard reclined on the ground, his jeans sticking out in front of him in a straight V, prosthetic legs and shoes, all one piece with no knee joint; his aluminum wrist-clamping walking sticks lying next to him, reflecting late afternoon sunlight that penetrated the oak in wavering shafts. Both Vince and Zane were sitting on rocks in the shade, legs folded below them in lazy lotus fashion.

"What're you talking about?" asked Vince, scissoring his index and second finger together to Zane in the universal request for a cigarette. Zane tossed him one out of the pack at his side.

"Fuck, man. I'm tellin ya I walked into the Copper store the other day an Gus was speakin German with these two guys. They all looked startled when I came in, quit talkin, and the two guys immediately split."

"Maybe they were some of those Hessians?" Vince offered.

"They weren't bikers, I can tell you that for sure." Greg slid to the ground, putting a hand down for balance, "but they didn't have long beards or weird hats, so I guess they weren't Amish either."

"These mountains are full of strange folks," Richard laughed. He was lit, his light blue eyes sparkling and shimmering from the beer, wine and weed he'd been consuming all day. "I grew up here, ya know, an you wouldn't believe some of the stories I've heard."

Zane immediately thought of *Deliverance*, of Ned Beatty sodomized by the guy in overalls with bad grammar and Burt Reynold's thigh bone sticking out. John Voight fussing with his arrows. Then, he thought of himself. *If I saw his car in the driveway when we turned the corner it was like all the air got sucked out of me. I'd be at his mercy till Mom got home from work. One outta five times, he'd be in a good mood and I was safe. Never knew ahead of time, had to listen to his voice and watch him closely when I first got home to see what kind of mood he was in. "This place is a pig sty," he'd half-shout an I knew I was in for trouble.*

Chapter Five

By spring of 1853, enough souls had been captivated by the lure of placer gold and cheap land to create Table Rock City—what was later to become Jacksonville—the first permanent settlement in the Rogue valley and county seat before any such county existed.

Miners aimed hydraulic hoses at mountainsides until they disappeared, the run-off choking streams and creeks that fed the Rogue, the Applegate, the Illinois. Salmon and steelhead spawning grounds bubbled brown and silty. Anyone versed in Biblical disasters might well have marked the fish die off as the breaking of a seal. The gigantic mining operations sent deer, elk and small mammals that made up the bulk of the Rogue Indians' diet fleeing through the fingerling valleys where settlers decimated their numbers with muskets and snares.

Farmers dug up brush, trees and meadows with their plows, which also destroyed grass seed, acorns and camas, pretty much condemning the native people to starvation. Flat pasture or farming land was quickly grabbed up by clerks with families from Omaha and roustabouts from Tennessee. Such was the shape of civilization.

It's not just arrowheads that are plentiful in the foothills of the Cascades, human bones find their way to the surface in a regular and mocking tribute to the pushing of the nation's western edge.

Around ten the next morning, Sasha and Zane gave Greg a ride back upstream a mile and a half to Perry's mining claim. Greg had passed out on their front room couch the night before; Sasha had stuffed a pillow under his tangled head, draped an army blanket over him. The plan this morning was for Zane and Greg to fish with hand lines for trout in the deep hole round the upstream bend in the river while Sasha talked to old man Perry. No one knew how old Perry actually was. He claimed not to know himself, though he suggested on occasion that eighty was somewhere in his past. Which was easy for Sasha to believe, looking at his prominent, lumpy nose centered in a sea of deep facial wrinkles, lapped like fish gills. His zinc white eyebrows reminded her of pictures she'd seen of United Mineworker president John L. Lewis, flagrant and unruly. But his brown eyes watered by age seemed to ooze a distant but distinct reaching out.

Perry had taken an obvious and immediate liking to Sasha from their first meeting more than three years previously when they'd engaged in a long conversation ranging from the Russian mystics Ouspensky and Gurdjieff, whom he greatly admired, to the *Book of Mormon* which he found fantastically absurd. At the time Sasha hadn't read any of them and sat mesmerized by Perry's rambling, though insightful analyses. She liked Hesse, even Kahlil Gibran when she was younger, so mysticism and esoteric theories appealed to her in general, these in particular.

This day-after-softball began in the same laid-back, take twenty minutes to get out the door kind of mood that permeated their lives on the river. Town time, country time. Everyone knew the story. Townies looked on lateness as a fundamental character, or at least certainly a doing-business flaw. Country folk tended to relish their drives back home as though fleeing from clouds of toxicity. Generalizations, of course, but Sasha had seen and heard enough interactions of the two life forms to essentially buy the stereotype. *It's only a stereotype because it fits. Ok, but there's always a place where the shape takes over, dictates, frames. That's the fear. Not noticing you're being run by the shell and not the meat.*

Like two days ago when Zane was purging, telling her why he'd buried the phone first thing upon moving in. Oddly, she'd hadn't brought it up at the time. Having no phone didn't bother her; she rather preferred it. "I hate em," he'd said. "If one rings, I cringe, figure it's someone to rag me, or some emergency. If I hear the door slam, I assume you did it on purpose and immediately try to figure out what you're pissed about. It's like, you know, if someone tells me 'we gotta talk,' I know from the get-go it's not gonna be good news."

"Is that the way you see the world?" She was biting her lower lip softly, becoming a habit.

"It's the only way I know," he tried for helpless eight-year-old, missed badly.

"That's bullshit, Zane. You, of all people, are aware that ideas change all the time. You can always think differently."

"My rhetorical triangle has fallen over, so I don't know what I know."

She laughed. "That's not all that's fallen. What happened to your unquenchable thirst to learn, to uncover, that attracted me so much?"

He hadn't answered her question, instead launching into more horror stories of Larry's viciousness, her disgust of which had kept her soft and accepting all of Saturday.

By this Monday morning, she'd filed the issue away, thinking they'd return to it eventually, even if she had to be the one to resurrect it. *Got to get him moving again. And I've got to start taking care of myself emotionally. I'm frayed, I'm afraid. Ha! One sick lil' puppy.*

She and Perry were drinking alfalfa/mint tea in front of his fireplace where a small pile of embers glowed with wavering, rising heat even though the front door was wide open to the sunny meadow outside. Perry's moccasin feet were nearly in the firebox, his legs crossed at his ankles so that he was perpendicular to the fireplace itself. Sasha was resting her elbows on the small wooden table between them, holding her face in her hands.

Perry was trying to explain existentialism. "All you really have to do is look at the title of Sartre's big book—*Being and Nothingness*—that pretty much sums up the whole philosophy right there. That metaphysical systems make no sense when human life is transitory. When nothing lasts. And you can take that in two equally accurate ways. When nothing lasts."

"But doesn't...isn't The Fourth Way you talk about a metaphysical system?"

"Yes, of course, I'm not saying I agree with Sartre; I'm just saying what I think the thrust of the thinking is, young lady." He luxuriated in saying 'young lady.' She could tell from the twinges at the corners of his mouth as he said it. Having fun with her, but nothing cruel. And it wasn't sexual.

Sasha knew Perry had gone monastic in the fifties. Well, maybe not monastic as such, but he told her he'd quit devoting any time or energy to that part of his psyche. Sasha wasn't sure the psyche had control of what seemed to her to be animal appetites. Not animal and therefore necessarily bad, she didn't think, but just animal as in what we are, what she'd learned to accept as behaviors of a species more than as a feature of nationality, religion, or race for that matter.

"Many say that existentialism is about as far as philosophy can go, in terms of a theory of the subject, the person, existing...being. If I were a materialist, then I could kick the metaphysical in the teeth. But I can't help having a thread of a sense that some spark or synapse is common to all, maybe it's an ability to learn I'm talking about. I haven't worked it all out quite yet. But, no, I wouldn't swallow the existentialist line totally. What they say about alienation and personal obligation, however, about being responsible for consequences of your decisions, that makes perfect sense to me."

The fireplace end of the cabin was round river rock, floor to ceiling, with a wide, flatter rock mantle filled with stacks of books that spanned from side wall to side wall. Perry's voice was coming back to her off the stone and mortar, as he watched the fire while he spoke.

"More importantly, what do you think?" He inclined his head her way.

"I'm afraid of totalizing systems. You know, one big answer."

"Sure. Too easy." He waited a few seconds before continuing. "If you say, right now, 'let's go outside,' seems a simple statement. But 'outside' is nothing less than a chaos of possibilities, any of which could be reduced and examined down to all kinds of active systems and relationships to other things. Animals, plants, dirt, pine needles: all those are in constantly changing relationships to each other, and more. Changes in the air around them."

Sasha perked up. "And we haven't even gotten to Freud yet."

Perry turned his angular face to her, smiling broadly, showing two off-center missing bottom teeth. "Youth. It's all sex and excitement, isn't it? Eamon is like that. I can tell when he's about to take off for town. He loses focus and concentration on anything but escaping to J-Ville. Like he's intoxicated, or like he's already in rut."

Sasha thought of mescalin and Brooks on her and in her and Zane's own habits, his constant need for altering, adjusting, hiding behind substances. *And I am not blameless.*

Perry had quit staring at the fire and was looking at her directly. She felt pinned against a felt board. "I think you ought to take a look at the *Baghavad Ghita* if you haven't read it ..."

She shook her head.

"...because you'll get a deeper sense of the oriental or eastern mind, how it organizes the world. Much different than our western commercialized American dream."

Lulls in their conversations could take minutes, as Perry would return to contemplating the flickering fire. Sasha used this one to admire his handiwork in building the cabin. He'd crafted plenty of bookshelf space all along the south wall and there weren't a lot of gaps in the rows of books. His quilted bed with storage below was wedged into the corner behind the open door, and further down that wall his double warming-oven wood stove with two water tanks took up considerable space. The end of the room opposite the fireplace housed a network of shelves, drawers, cupboards and bins. All hand built, from Perry's bed, up to and over the doorway, clear to the corner. All in use. From her first visit, Sasha had relished the smells of candles, kerosene and corn meal in Perry's living space. Gave her a sense of well-being, of simple comfort. The only hanging decoration in the cabin was the MC Esher print of waterfalls that Sasha had given him last Christmas and that he'd affixed to the log wall on the right side of the woodstove. The optical illusion print of flowing water seeming to fall uphill fit well with Perry's soft, almost droning voice that relaxed into a way of sliding out of words with numerous tonal inflections.

In the beginning, two and a half years ago, Perry had regaled her with long and convoluted, switch-back stories of his career on the railroad. Of how he'd engineered on the Sally Rand freight run from Chicago to New Orleans for more than two decades working for Illinois Central. Sometimes, he'd be shuttled over to the Eastern Rocket which left New Orleans for Potomac Yard, Virginia. He lavished accounts of accidents, freak weather and labor problems on her, never raising his voice while he recited long gone IWW songs without singing: *Joe Hill* and *Whose Side Are You On?*

She hadn't spent much time with truly old people, but those she could remember seemed to live in ever tightening spirals, where horizons kept shrinking closer and closer to themselves. When's dinner? Not so with Perry, at least in terms of his constant reading. He appeared to be branching outward at the tail end of his life, thirsting for new ideas, new ways of explaining what he'd been looking at all his years. For her, visiting Perry had become an indispensable part of living on the river. He compensated for some of the human contact she'd lost by their semi-isolation. Gave her a solid grip on learning to live in the country to the point where she was honestly growing to prefer being alone, except for Zane.

Perry had answered her question, a couple of years earlier, about how he'd gotten attracted to all this reading, all this thinking. "Engineers on the railroad aren't typically interested in literature, philosophy and political science are they?" she'd prompted.

"Well," he'd drawled, imitating and emphasizing a rural and rustic tone for her benefit. "That's the thing, now. You're naturally assuming that certain forms of labor squash any possibilities for mental betterment. I'd call that a bit of arrogant elitism." He'd watched her frown. "Oh, don't take this personally, please. I'm talking in social terms, in the way culture weighs individuals by what they do for a living. A system, I think, that tells anyone who's not a university professor or a government scientist or a big company researcher that they've got no business treading in sacred or secret waters. That so-called normal people shouldn't bother themselves, shouldn't waste their time going after what they're not equipped to handle; they're like a dog chasing a car that way. It's what representative government means, after all. Someone else is making decisions for me. My bony ass is not allowed, much less encouraged, to interfere. The whole thing turns on the idea that someone else can speak for me better than I can. 'Cause, after all, I'm not smart enough to do it myself."

As Sasha remembered that day, she studied Perry's profile and thought he could have been some medieval churchman or member of an obscure flagellant order. His prominently hooked nose was what did it for her, cast its own shadow so to speak. But she was sure she really spun such webs because of his measured deep voice. Easy for her to accept his ways of seeing things; she left these conversations much calmer than she'd ever arrived. He had that power, oddly enough, without seeming to recognize it.

Zane and Greg were basking in brittle sunlight on a large rock that loomed out over a deep channel in the river, just upstream from Perry's swinging footbridge and trolley. Perry could move goods from the highway clear up to his cabin without having to carry anything. He'd put supplies in the trolley, and walking across the footbridge he'd pull the trolley along with a lead rope. On the other side, Perry had pulleys and cables stretched all the way up the slope to the cabin. He could walk up the trail, again pulling the wooden basket by a rope. From where they were sitting in the sunlight, looking downstream, the swinging bridge and trolley appeared magical, built by Hobbits and run by gnomes. Zane could visualize them scurrying around in a loose pack.

Neither of them had fishing poles. Greg's method of choice was to wind line around the neck of a beer bottle. Then, holding the hook with grasshopper and small Gremlin weights in his right palm, he'd point the bottle where he wanted to cast and toss the business end of the line as close to the spot as possible. Zane, on the other hand, or foot in this case, held a spool of line in his right hand, running said line between fingers of his left hand and down his leg to slide between left foot toes. Initially, he too would throw the bait into the bubbling water at the head of the deep channel beneath them, letting the grasshopper swirl down out of sight. They both knew that the beauty of their respective systems was the grasshopper; they'd remind each other time and time again that no grasshopper ever came back intact, hit every time, without exception, as long as fish were in the channel.

"So what were you trying to get us to pay attention to yesterday afternoon? Goin on about Germans or somethin." Zane squinted as Greg's face was indistinguishable, no more than a bright smudge, the sun still in the east and blinding Zane full face on.

"They were speakin German to Gus at the store."

"Who was?" He pulled in his line. Top half of his grasshopper was missing.

"The two guys in sweatshirts and Oakland A's caps."

"An he was answerin back in German?"

"Seemed like it to me."

"German? Sehr interesting, indeed." Re-baited, he flipped his line back into the water.

"No shit. Who knew Gus spoke German, or that someone I'd never seen before would come by to talk to him in it?"

Jesus, Greg. Stumble over some syntax why don't ya? "You're making it sound like some kind of conspiracy. What's got you cranked up?"

"I dunno. Somethin's not right. Did I tell you Wade Perkins showed up at the cabin last week? Nosing around without really saying what he was up to."

"Wade Perkins? Jackson county's Barney Fife?"

"You got it."

"What's the Forest Service have to do with Perry's minin claim? Isn't even the same federal department. Claims are BLM, and BLM is in Interior. Forest Service is in Agriculture...Geez! Did you see that hit?" His line had yanked sharply.

"Yeah, but he knew my name. Seemed to know a lot about me. Reminded me of the time I spent at the county a few years ago on a driving-while-suspended."

"Weird."

"That's what I thought, too. Don't know if he went over to talk to Perry or not. I stayed in my cabin while he was snoopin around. Seemed an official visit. Had his uniform shirt on."

"So, we got Barney Fife out of his jurisdiction and a couple of Germans at the Copper Store. What's it all mean?"

"That's what I'm asking." Greg pulled a ten incher from the river and knocked its head against the rock. It shuddered, sunlight catching the slight vibration of the rainbow's painted sides. "Two more like this an Perry an I'll have dinner."

Zane cocked his head, lifting his ear away from the constant churning of the water to pick up a far away high-pitched drone. "Do you hear that?"

"What?"

"Hold on a minute; it's getting closer."

Zane could tell there was more than one siren coming up the river road. The twists of the highway muted and then amplified the progressively clamorous whine of squad cars in full throat. Like a handful of yodeling banshees. Each cruiser's siren hit a different pitch, four-part harmony as it turned out.

The two of them stood as the shrill klaxons materialized. Four police cars slashed by above them on the highway. Two sheriff 4 x 4's packed with deputies, one state police cruiser and even Jacksonville's iconic police chief, Frank Carver, with a cigar stuck in his mouth. They all flashed through in an instant, their sirens wailing away behind the next turn. Flashing lights disappeared as fast as they'd rushed by.

"I forgot," Greg turned to Zane, " I heard in town yesterday that Bud Abbot just died penniless."

"Who's on first, then?"

Chapter Six

General George Crook presided over a town gathering in Klamath Falls late in 1853, coming away from the boisterous meeting well aware of the settlers' commitment to "exterminate "the Indians left in a handful of spotted encampments along the Illinois, Rogue and Klamath rivers. We know this from Crook's own autobiography, where he also scratched out on vellum with a nibbed pen that "it was of no unfrequent occurrence for an Indian to be shot down in cold blood, or a squaw to be raped by some brute. Such a thing as a white man being punished for outraging an Indian was unheard of. It was the fable of the wolf and the lamb every time."

In Requiem for a People, *we can read that "When the miners were left idle by the enforced January layoff, nineteen men from Sailor's Diggings decided to attack the snowbound Indian lodges along the Illinois River. They stormed one village but found only seven women, one boy, and two girls. They shot a pregnant woman nine times and murdered the little girls. Then the men retreated to the mining camp to arouse others to help them finish the massacre."*

1853. That same year the first burglar alarm and the first spring-loaded clothespin were granted US patents, as was a process to commercially manufacture potato chips.

When George Cruikshank parked his El Camino in his reserved slot behind the Post Office, he dreaded having to show up for work. As he walked across 10th street and approached what he called the melodramatic façade of the Courthouse—columns that didn't support anything—he struggled with an agonizingly juvenile impulse to keep walking, to call in with a phony cough and take a sick day. *Colonel Walter Hustad. It's been two days since his flight, so he's probably forgotten, or at least got the edge off me not waiting for him. This is a case of me thinking myself into trouble. Probably doesn't remember my name, or even that it was me who was supposed to get him.*

What George didn't know was that the Army Corps Colonel had already stirred offices on the floor below George's. Sensitivities were rising in the hallway outside the State Police office as the Colonel railed about not having an office dedicated to the "Corps project," as he enunciated sharply. About being abandoned at the airport upon his arrival, left to his own devices to get settled in. About no one contacting him since that arrival to see if he needed anything, to say "Glad to have you," or "Welcome to Medford." Anything. He was delivering all this to whomever would listen; a few office staff had looked up and appeared to be plugged in.

It was Captain Dave Brereton of the State Police who intervened, took the Colonel literally under his arm—the policeman was well over six feet while the Colonel probably didn't quite reach five-nine—and guided him down the worn, yellowed, pale green linoleum hallway to his own office with the view of the library across Oakdale street.

Brereton didn't exactly come out of central casting. Tall and painfully thin, his face was marked by a childhood pox, cheeks crisscrossed with lines. His right eye wandered just a bit when he got excited, but he'd learned to compensate at the firing line so it had never been a problem. His uniform hung from sharp shoulders, bony wrists protruded from his sleeves. But the pistol at his waist, his tear gas canister and handcuffs clipped to the wide, black belt spoke of undeniable authority, even if his basic appearance was less than overpowering.

Colonel Hustad stood at the window, his back to the state patrolman, his hands clasped behind him like Trevor Howard in *Mutiny on the Bounty*. Brereton could sense the colonel was fussing and steaming, out of sorts. His thin, straggly hair was combed over the top in a not-too-successful attempt to hide his baldness. His brush moustache was woefully out of date; his arms and legs seemed stunted somehow, giving him a dwarf-like quality. Certainly not an imposing figure in civilian clothes, and Brereton wondered if he might not look like a boy scout when in dress uniform.

But Dave wasn't one to put too much stock in first-off impressions. Growing up out on the Applegate near Provolt, towards Murphy and Grants Pass, he knew that often the most unlikely, ungainly looking steelhead fisherman could have two in the box before anyone else got a strike. All a question of knowing what you're doing.

Of course, he would have liked to cast a more leading man image, something like Rock Hudson before everyone joked about Jim Nabors. But he'd learned that power can come from being one step ahead of most people and he'd realized early on that mental acuity wasn't exactly a societal strong suit. He liked to think he took advantage of out-thinking perps, criminals and most everyone else.

Dave made the first overture. "So, Colonel Hustad?..."

As his visitor had turned from the window, Dave saw that he'd misread everything. The diminutive man's eyes were flat, his body language sagging. "Call me Walt, please. This military stuff never attracted me."

"Sure. What can I do to ease your way here? I've only been in this building for a few months. Our new State police headquarters is almost finished. That's why I'm billeted here. But I've been in the valley for years and pretty much know everyone."

"I'm not even sure what I need." He'd pulled his hands from behind his back and was examining his outstretched, splayed fingers like he didn't know who they belonged to. "I'm afraid I acted like a diva this morning. I don't know what came over me, except that I have to say that Medford Hotel is a bit of a dingy establishment. The shower never really got hot and my breakfast must have been made in a Radar-range."

"But it *is* only a block away, so I'm sure that played a big role in sticking you up there." Dave had indicated a straight-backed chair in front of his desk and slid himself into his office chair which could roll around the office on its wheels.

And he waited a good ten seconds before breaking the silence. "So, Walt? Is your being here an indication that the project is finally on a roll? We usually have a pretty good network, but no one seems to know anything down here as to when this damned thing is going to get going."

"In a perfect world, the contractor would already be breaking ground. You know, I'm sure, that logging off the timber comes first for everywhere that's going to be underwater. I'm here to finalize the acreage and let out bids. Once those contracts are granted, the major contractor can start. They're ready, I know. We've never worried about 'if' with this one, only 'when.'" Walter Hustad's voice clipped words off sharply, meticulously. Halfway between soprano and alto, he sounded like a minister to Dave, who had spent a childhood of Sundays listening to the same quality of voice at the Four Square church his parents dragged him and his sister to each week. "Sin and damnation" was what he remembered most from that timbre of voice. Except that everything in Walt's manner told him he wasn't looking at any fire and brimstone preacher.

George lingered in front of the glass case of the first floor newsstand. Arnold, the blind news agent, was filling him in on how next year's Oregon Ducks football team would certainly not go 3-9 as this year's had. "They've brought in some players from the LA area, so we're finally gonna get some speed on the field. We're gonna get our own coons. Shake up the Pac-8." Arnold wore regular glasses with cloudy lenses and hissed his breath out of the corners of his mouth, his teeth together in a fixed smile.

"Yeah?" George was just filling time. *Another redneck voice heard from. Wonder why the guys in Court House newsstands are often blind. Like YMCA massagers. Is it like a job requirement?* "Listen, Arnold, I got to get upstairs. Some of us have to work for a living."

Arnold bowed his head, his sign of release and relinquishment. George was nearly smacked in the face with an immediate, as in "right now" understanding that everyone, every consciousness, was the center of its own world—that was the nature of consciousness itself. Cut him a lot of slack in the sense that he didn't necessarily have to think badly of himself for seeing the world through his own experience. He didn't know how he could do it otherwise, seemed to just be the way things were. His eyes he was looking through. His memory stitched together all the stories. Why he was wrapped up in this thinking, in this moment, he couldn't say for sure. Most likely survival instinct, knowing he was going to take some kind of flak for his abandonment of the Colonel. Trying to firm up the ground he was standing on.

By the time he'd rounded the stairway on the third floor, heading up to the fourth, "Primrose Lane" was playing in his head. *Life's a holiday...on Primrose Lane.* He didn't remember that he'd ever liked the song in the first place, so wondering why it was a bug in his brain now was just another distraction. Maybe that's what he was looking for? Distraction. To be distracted from the overpowering smell of Lysol and floor wax that hung in the building's air. Along with deodorants, after-shaves, colognes and perfumes, which was why he walked up stairs instead of cramming himself into the one small elevator car that positively reeked with swirling, cloying chemical scents and the occasional lingering sour smell of sweat from someone headed to court.

As he negotiated the final set of stairs to the fourth floor, George's memory elbowed its way in, replaying a frozen moment from Korea. A windswept, scrub pine, ice and rock hillside outside Incheon when the splintered sunlight refracted off the snow, catching tiny slices of battle, fixing them in his mind. A colored Sergeant from Company B stood illuminated. His ammo man and loader was dead, so he'd pushed the rocket into the back of his bazooka himself and then, settling it on his shoulder, he patted his own helmet to give himself the firing sign. The next instant he just wasn't there anymore, nothing but wispy, lingering blue smoke. George remembered how, in the heat of combat, he'd thought how surreally strange it was to see the guy pat his own helmet. A moment etched forever. *Crazy sonofabitch.*

He walked halfway down the hall to the glass doors with the BLM seal. Pushing through, he saw the office secretary Heidi Logan scurrying back to her chair behind the reception counter. Heidi had worked for BLM since she was in high school, over twenty years ago. As a member of DECA, the Distributive Education Club of America,

107

she'd worked afternoons her last two years in school. As was usually the case, if George really wanted to run down some piece of vital information or double-check legal codes, Heidi was the one he asked. To see her short, squat figure hurrying as though caught red-handed away from her desk brought a smile to his face.

His reaction wasn't based on any sense of entitlement. As a district manager, technically everyone in the office worked for George, who'd never wanted to be a so-called executive in the first place. Didn't need to order people around in order to feel big himself. Thought of it was a negative, in fact. That he had to counter the inherent suspicions and stereotypical gossip about being the boss. His three man department consisted of Eugene, Raymond and Jeffrey. Each of them had worked there at least ten years, and in Raymond's case, more like going on sixteen.

George reflected on the fact that everyone in the office had some kind of Jones going on, everyone had their crutches and it seemed they were all oral. Heidi, for instance, kept a supply of Sweet Tarts and Red Vines in her drawer and dipped into it regularly.

Eugene drank cough syrup, sipping it on the sly, or at least he thought that was the case, but everyone in the room knew what he was doing. George suspected that Eugene might hang out at the Brave Bull on the weekends. Seeking out stretch pants with sequins, and lots of piled up hair. High-heeled cowgirl boots.

Raymond kept an ever-present bottle of Coke open on his desk which he used to wash down Snickers bars, Junior Mints or some other source of sugar. Exceptionally skinny, he compounded the impression by wearing thin black ties on short-sleeve white shirts. Pocket protector with scribbles of blue ink.

George thought Jeffrey was probably an alcoholic, given his frequent Monday illnesses, and given that he often became progressively more jovial as the day progressed. *A maintenance drinker*, George thought. *I know so many. It's what I live around.*

At 10:06 the call was logged in the Sheriff's dept. in the sub-floor basement. The news quickly came up through the building like rising water, spreading confusion and rumor: Gary Fausen's entire family missing on Applegate. Gary's father Cleatus said he'd driven out to the campsite on Carberry creek, a mile or so past the Copper store, because they hadn't shown up at the Fausen home in Ruch as scheduled. The elder Fausen claimed that the family had just disappeared, leaving everything at their campsite. Gary, his wife Clarise and their five year-old boy Gary Jr. and baby girl Eva were all gone. Their little terrier, Snoopy, was still on leash in the camp and their Chevy pickup was parked next to their cabin tent.

According to the father, Gary's wallet and truck keys were laying on the picnic table, along with open food containers, a half-filled glass of milk, two partial cups of coffee, Gary's pack of Marlboros with lighter. Cleatus Fausen reported that the campsite looked completely normal except that the family was missing. Gary would never take off with his wife and kids and leave the dog tied up, he'd said, or leave all their belongings out in the open unattended like that. Or go off without his cigarettes. Something was drastically wrong.

By the time the BLM office got the news, two Sheriff's 4 x 4's and Dave Brereton's state prowler had already pulled out of the parking lot, sirens and lights going full tilt. Of course, the story that made it up to the fourth floor had the qualities of a movie. Family snatched out of the woods. No real clues. Just vanished. Damnedest thing they'd ever heard. The facts, what there were, had been veneered with gossipy detail. As if everyone below them in the building had chipped in with what they felt were honest addendums, descriptions, ascribing of motives to hypothetical agents. Whole families don't just vanish, so someone or ones had to be responsible. How could anyone even gain control of three people and a baby, enough control to take them without any visible signs of struggle? Maybe put a gun to the wife's head, get the man to follow orders? Or grab the son to render parents docile? Rumors were rampant. Surely one person couldn't have done it. Maybe the biker gang?

George knew exactly where their campsite must have been; he knew the terrain of Carberry creek, on the road from the Copper store that went over the mountain and became Thomas road, down the other side to the town of Applegate. Not a town, actually. Store with eight seat lunch counter, gas pumps, bulletin boards, six or seven houses within sight, a Grange hall down the road back toward Ruch. George wondered whether police had sealed off that back door, or whether they were just racing pell-mell to the campsite, warning anyone within hearing from a long ways off. But so much time had already passed. Whoever had them could be long gone. With that thought, he experienced an icy snap of adrenalin. Not that he knew anything—he'd heard the same wild theories as everyone else—but his bodily alarm system told him this story wasn't going to end well. Grimness surged through. Scattered trash and human deformity. *Just a feeling. Rob Minter dropped a Doug fir on himself up above Carberry at Cougar Gap, wind took it. Six or seven years ago. Working gyppo. Wasn't an open casket.*

About half an hour after the police cars left the underground garage, George was at his desk in the only private room in the office. Staring through the glass top half of his door, he watched a short, slender, almost effeminate-looking man walk up to the reception desk and begin talking to Heidi, who swung her chair around, pointing to George. *What's up now? Who's the munchkin? But I think I know.*

He watched the man approach on a beeline to his office. Pushed himself out of his chair and opened his door before the guy had a chance to knock. George absolutely hated the sound of knocking. Didn't know why, that's just the way it had always been. Knocking was an interruption. Pissed him off like a noisy neighbor.

"Mr. Cruikshank?" A plaintive voice, he thought.

"George."

"Walt Hustad, Corps of Engineers."

110

I was right! He hesitated, thinking he was stuttering even though he hadn't spoken yet. "I guess I should apologize for not picking you up…"

Hustad waved his hands back and forth in front of him like an umpire calling 'safe.' "Not to worry. It *was* a Saturday, after all. I wouldn't have wanted to spend my whole day waiting for someone I didn't know, either. I did some spouting off here this morning downstairs that I don't feel particularly proud of. Especially now with what I heard happened out on the river. Am I wrong, or was this family that disappeared camping near the dam site?"

"No, you're right, Colonel. Carberry creek runs into the Applegate just upstream from where Schumann Brothers built their sluice pond, which I was told would be on the downstream side of the dam."

During this conversation, George had pointed Hustad into the visitor's chair and regained his own seat, rocking backward as he spoke. He took in what he could of the Colonel without fixed staring. *Looks like an old Noel Harrison with a British moustache. I liked The Girl from U.N.C.L.E. Stephanie Powers. Great lips. Leo G. Carroll got paid twice. The Man and the Girl.*

"Please call me Walt. I'm not a military man."

No, I can see that. "So, where're you from? You live in Portland?"

"Appleton, Wisconsin actually. I've been out to Portland half a dozen times, I expect. Now, it looks like I'll be spending some time here in Medford." His face flashed a little pink. "But I sure don't want to stay in that Medford Hotel."

"I'm sorry about that…Walt. You can blame me. Since I was sent to pick you up from the airport, I knew you didn't have a car. The hotel was the closest place, if you were going to be on foot awhile."

Hustad rested his clasped hands on George's desk, leaning forward, as if about to divulge a secret. "This morning in the café I noticed there weren't many women staying there. Mostly men, in twos and threes."

"Yeah, well, it does have a reputation, all right. I gotta confess, I forgot about that when I thought it would be a good place, being so close. You married, Walt?"

"Thirty-six years. You?"

"Never got the urge. To stay with the same person every day, in and out. Guess I value my independence too much. *Or no woman would have me.* Kids?"

"Muriel never wanted them. She's always had a pretty busy life, serves on all kinds of boards." He was looking at his feet while he spoke.

I think I'm getting the picture. "Ok, so what can I do for you first? How can I make up for Saturday?"

"Oh, please, don't feel that way. But I would like to line up a car."

George signed out of the office around eleven and, with Walt in tow, headed back out to the airport for a rental car. George wondered, a little more than in passing, whether Jackie might be working. Didn't hurt to keep some kind of contact. Especially after all these years. On their drive, George signaled points of interest, thrusting his hand almost in Walt's face as he indicated restaurants and bars along the way. *What else is there to see? It's not like he's going to need a hardware store or automobile agency. I'll show him a barber shop, too. Very strange. He's not at all what I expected. Like I made up this Colonel Hustad in my mind, argued with him, got a grudge. All of that was just air. A lot of work for nothing. Made it all up. Fantasized hard ass Colonel Hustad and got frail, tired Walt.*

Once he saw Hustad into his Avis Ford Fairlane, and the Colonel had waved him off when he started in about following him back to the Federal building. *Little squirt can spit.* George got as far as the pneumatic doors to the lounge through which he could see Jackie wasn't behind the bar. *Just as well, I suppose. It's not Saturday. Can't be caught drinking on duty, for christsakes. Sometimes I just wonder at myself. The stupidity I'm capable of. Like with this colonel.*

112

Before Walt left the airport, George had procured him a city map and had drawn the route back. "You can park at the end of the row I'm in behind the Post Office. There's four or five slips there marked 'Visitor'. You sure you don't want to follow me? Make it a lot simpler."

"Gotta find my way sometime, don't you think?" Walt was squinting up through the open window, looking a lot, George thought, like an infant bird in the nest, waiting for a worm.

The sun was still climbing the eastern sky, unblocked by the few high cirrus clouds over Ashland, to the south, as George turned off Table Rock Rd. onto Central Ave. *Fausen family up in smoke on Carberry creek. Things're gonna heat up around here real fast, I'm afraid.*

Chapter Seven

Estimates of the size of native populations in North America at Columbus' arrival are notoriously vague. Not the least of reasons being that those making the estimates were the same Europeans who'd come ashore on the east coast of the continent, cashing in on fertile land, sending native peoples fleeing westward, until there was no more west but ocean. Nonetheless, scholarly estimates range from 5 to 18 million inhabitants already being on the land when Europeans arrived—not exactly a pinpoint figure.

By 1800, indigenous populations in the United States totaled just over 600,000. By the next century, that number was down to 248,000, most of whom lived on reservations. One might expect that what we call national expansion—moving westward—would have to be called something else entirely from the perspective of native peoples. From millions of free-ranging, communally based, highly spiritual individuals to fewer than half a million smallpox infested prisoners. By 1900, native populations in North America comprised only 5% of their assumed 1492 numbers. The newcomers called it Progress, while those indigenous peoples still alive called it The Great Dying.

Sasha and Perry were deep in discussion when they heard the sirens winding through the turns of the river road. Since they were inside the cabin whose door opened away from the river, the sound was muted, damped down, not at all threatening.

Perry was getting Sasha to consider why looking for purposes made much more sense than looking for reasons. "Reasons," he drew the word out, "are useless when you're engaged with other humans. We manufacture reasons to fit our needs constantly; it's how we do our business, you might say. Give someone enough reasons for doing what you want, reasons that are supposed to persuade others to think a certain way. You know, we all got reasons and if you don't like those, we'll come up with some more. Reasons are everywhere, all the time. But if you ask someone 'to what purpose' you're supposed to do a certain thing, now you've put them on the spot, asking why anyone might want or be or think this way."

"It's just my job," Sasha sort of blurted out.

Perry look confused. "What's your job?"

"No. I'm saying people would say that they do what they do because it's their job."

"Yes, that's my point. If they paid attention to why they're having to believe X or Y in order to make a living, having to internalize very specific patterns and rituals, they'd see how stiflingly futile most wage labor is in terms of personal enrichment. Not money paid, but lack of opportunities for unfolding, spreading one's wings. Maybe that's what is meant by alienation of labor, that absence of possibilities?"

"Zane would love to hear you saying this. He sees any kind of full time job as enslavement. But we've nonetheless got bills. We can't pay for our electricity with smoked salmon."

Perry seemed drawn back into the fire again, his chin dropped closer to his chest, his long gnarled fingers intertwined, clasped on his stomach. Sasha tried to check her almost automatic defensiveness when it came to talking or thinking about jobs. Her mother, her uncles, they'd each of them lauded work as fulfilling one's purpose in life. Placing great value on stick-to-it-iveness, on being, as she often heard, a "productive" member of society.

Without lifting his head, or turning her way, Perry seemed to read her mind. "To my way of thinking, we keep coming back to questions of competition or cooperation. Western culture trumpets the holiness of competition as the one true way, as the basis of all meaningful human endeavor. The rugged individual struggling, competing always to get ahead of others. To beat everyone else. Common sense says only one person at a time can occupy that position. Talk about rigged systems. It's like we're condemned to play a losing hand again and again, always hopeful that the next time will do the trick."

Sasha was letting Perry's words sink in when Zane and Greg darkened the doorway. Greg dangled three trout from his hand and Zane's eyes were wide as he spoke. "Did you hear em? Cops came by right over our heads almost. Kind of weird. Even J-Ville Frank had his lights and siren goin. I've never seen him outside of town before." Speech coming out in spurts, pushed by amped up anxiety. Police

116

anywhere triggered chills; sirens and lights, though, bordered on paranoia. Zane was consciously shoving down an urgent sense of being violated, of someone rummaging around in his home, looking for incriminating material.

"So what do you think it was all about?" Sasha asked.

"We're gonna try to find out. Greg an I are drivin up to Copper store, see what's goin on."

"Take me home before you go."

After dropping Sasha, Zane and Greg got back on the river road for the trip to Copper. If anyone could still call it that. A name, suggesting a community. But Copper was only the store with two old-time useless gas pumps in front, Gus's apartment in the back. When the dam went in, the whole place would be under fifty feet of water.

Zane made a mental map of the upper river. Accompanied by the loud putt-putting of the Volkswagen's engine, changing tones with gears and gas. From their farmhouse, Lester was immediately downstream, and No-leg Richard lived on a piece of his dad's property right on the other side of Lester's, Richard's dad having built himself an A-frame back in the trees further downstream. Upstream, it was a mile and a half to Perry's claim and Greg's cabin, three more miles to Copper, another two more to the California line. He tapped his left foot to mark each location as he thought of it. Patterns. *Richard's, Lester's, us, Perry, Greg, Copper.* Like a mantra, he mentally repeated the list, jostling his foot. Two sets of three.

Greg was deep into a monologue describing how the Hessians were holding a jamboree of some kind up above Cook and Green, on the California side. He was sure the police activity must have something to do with the biker gang. "California cops can't even get there without driving all the way up I-5 from Yreka to Medford and then out the Applegate just to patrol less than 6 miles of road on the California side before it dead ends at the rock quarry turned into a shooting range. It's like a foolproof place to party. Backs to the wall an everything in front of em."

"So you think J-Ville Frank is goin up there to root em all out?" Zane's derision floated on the surface of his words like a dry fly twitching at the end of a long, light tippet.

"Four cars to take on anywhere from fifty to a hundred bikers? Who are in California anyway? I don't know what you're thinkin. Don't you remember the logger melee at Trail Tavern back in '64, year of the big flood, year I graduated? Two competing loggin crews got into it?" He took his eyes off the road to see if Greg was paying attention, saw him lighting a joint.

"Jesus, Greg. We're goin up to see what's goin on, not to get busted."

"I don't remember Trail Tavern."

"Oh, yeah. Guess two different outfits were in there drinking beer when one thing led to another and they all ended up in the parking lot. Shovels, chains, axes, mauls, you name it. Killed three and maimed a few more, paralyzed one guy from the neck down. You don't remember that?"

Greg was sucking down smoke and couldn't answer.

"Well. You know my mom works for the ambulance service, has for years. She said the driver of the unit told her that when they finally got out to Trail, there were beaten bodies all over the parking lot."

"Geez, Zane. That was a long time ago. I can't...I don't even remember much about high school."

"You weren't there long enough."

"That's why, I guess." Greg turned to look out the passenger side window, down into the canyon, as the bus had climbed the steep grade above the river. "There's the X," he pointed, but they'd already driven over the intersecting white lines on the pavement. "That's where she's gonna be," he inhaled more smoke to stream out his words in a tight falsetto tone, "The mother-fuckin concrete forever log-jammed dam," seeped out through clenched jaws.

Zane wasn't paying any attention to Greg's mounting vindictive on the Army Corp of Engineers. He was still back in '64, reconstructing the free-for-all at the Trail Inn, and for some reason he couldn't identify, he didn't want to let it just lie there. "But anyway, MacGregor, I think she said there was near twenty guys beating each other to death that evening. I remember it was during one of those weeks-long hot dry spells in early September, when the air up the Rogue smells of powdered red dust and dead fish. She said that when the first cops got there they didn't even try to get out of their car. Had radioed for backup and just watched the blood-letting. I'd forgotten about all that."

"Blood-letting," Greg chimed in. "Maybe those cops we saw were out to get themselves some of those cattle mutilators you're always talkin about. Got em corralled up Carberry creek? Maybe the Hessians are the cattle mutilators?"

Zane felt the pot in his temples, it'd taken up residence there, pulsing rhythm like a line of bongo players, tapping, thumping black hands. With eyes in his imagination that said they'd always know more than he ever would about pain and misery, about being made to feel small. He got all that from breathing in the smoke from Greg's joint. *Communal breathin. The family, for christsakes. All the couples an kids an hangers-on. Was all right when we first started, all of us eatin, playin ball, fishin, chillin out at Vince's place on Sunday mornings for Bloody Marys with peyote in the Snap-E Tom. Writin down places to go for the day on little pieces of paper we threw into Vince's sombrero. He'd draw one out an we'd all bundle into vehicles, kennel up the kids and dogs and drive wherever it was. Unless enough people whined about the choice, in which case Vince would just draw another and the process would go on until someone said it was time to fuckin go instead of sittin around inside with bad air conditionin, talkin about goin. Vince always brought the new people in. It was how the family grew. He found Heavy Duty at the Corner Club in Central Point. Must of been three years ago, right after we moved back, Vince draggin poor*

Duty in one Sunday mornin, an he never really left. Don't know how Vince can spot the good ones, might be his Osage blood. Sniffs em out.

Zane saw Greg in quick snatches as he drove the twisting road. Saw him get a drop of saliva on his index finger and use it to snuff out the roach, stashing it back in his crumpled pack of Camels. "I miss how we used to go out to dinner all as a group," Zane intoned. "We went a lot of places until the blow up at Rogue River Lodge. Since then, it seems we can't get everyone on the same page anymore."

Greg spoke solemnly, wagging his head from side to side. "No more steak an' lobster."

"Even worse for you. As I remember you never really had much to throw on the table when settlin up time came. We must of enjoyed your company, though. Never heard anyone complain except Gifford the time you wanted him to buy you cognac in a snifter so you could light it. You always knew how to get him goin, was worth the money just to be there." Zane switched gears back to the police cars. "I thought for a minute that it might be a pot bust, but it's the wrong time of year an I can't see J-Ville Frank bein in on any such operation." He waited a couple of seconds. "Do you notice how weird things have gotten around here in the last few months? Yesterday's baseball was a real downer, the team has unraveled. An there was the Aquarius party, with Brooks an Aurora an mescalin. I still don't know exactly how that all happened. Christ, it's like there's some cosmic system outta whack."

"Lot a people were really blown away by you guys. Pretty ballsy."

"Pretty fuckin stupid, you mean."

"Well, I don't know if somethin weird's goin on or not. But Wade Perkins did show up last week. Like I was tellin ya. I'm thinkin I'll just hole up out here and let the rest of the world commit suicide on its own time."

Zane thought he detected a strand of bitterness in Greg's voice. *Probably cause I brought up how he never paid for dinner. I didn't need to do that. But I do think it was always an issue that he never had anything to pitch in, but ordered big anyway.* "Problem is, Gregor *Lots of twitchin legs* that while they're commitin suicide they're also killin you. Maybe you haven't noticed how Ruch has become californicated, fuckin gentrified? How the Ruch Café's been turned into a bistro and deli? All the prices jacked up? When the dam goes in, all hell's gonna break loose in property values, which also means taxes."

"Doesn't affect me if I'm not involved, man."

"Whadda you mean, not involved? You're breathin and seein aren't you. I mean, it seems like every day I get more convinced that the whole valley's disappearin, converted into asphalt parking lots an trailer houses. An now the cops an forest service seem to be workin for the developers, protectin *their* interests. There's no way you can step outside it unless you're dead or a Buddhist or somethin. A Jesus freak? A 'get high on life' idiot. Shit, Greg, you ain't none of those. You can't just give up."

Greg dug dirt from his nails with a smudged toothpick. "You act like we could somehow get outta the way of the roadgrader." He looked across the seat to Zane, "You've never been way back in."

"Way in where?"

"Pretty much anywhere, but I was thinkin specifically about the woods behind Perry's place."

"What about em?"

"They look so deep, you know. Like you're out in the middle of a real by-God forest."

Zane leaned as he swung the bus through an extremely tight turn. "What are you talkin about? I'm not followin."

Greg lit a cigarette, adding more smoke to the haze they were breathing. "I've walked back in, away from the river an the road, up to the ridge line behind the claim, maybe a mile or so. An there aren't any trees back there. There ain't no forest. Just stumps an slash an downed lodgepole too small to haul. Looks like a fuckin A-bomb went off back there."

"What's that got to do with you givin up?"

"See if you can stay with me on this one, Mr. college man," Greg stabbed at the windshield with his cigarette. "Look around you. See? It looks like a nice postcard, these tree filled hillsides. BLM and Forest Service make sure to keep the trees growin next to highways an roads. Makes things look natural, sort of. But on the other side of these ridges," he waved his hand through a cloud, creating eddies and whirls in the smoke, "there's nothin man, nothin." He lowered his voice, trailing it off as he emphasized his point. "It's all damn sure enough empty out there."

Zane let Greg's response sink as slowly as the twitching grasshoppers earlier in the day. He felt hemmed in by the smoke in the bus, by the staccato flashes of trees and hills and narrow pastures on the corkscrew road. "I dunno. After all this cheap talk about what's bound, what's bought-and-paid-for to come down around here, you're still talkin about just sittin back and watchin the whole thing like it's a situation comedy, for christsakes. 'Leave It To Beaver?' What're you talkin about? This isn't fuckin 'Ozzie and Harriet,' you know."

Greg shifted on the bench seat, pulled his gray felt hat down across his eyebrows. "But what good does it do to fight against the inevitable? I mean, look when the salmon come up an start headin for the banks. You know, those black, hook-nosed, spawned-out bastards no one wants to catch. When I think of that seriously, I just wonder if it all ain't sort a pre-ordained, pre-determined. Like those salmon are dwindlin every year cause of over-fishin in the ocean. Like the log trucks keep rollin, takin trees to turn into plywood or paper. An once the dam goes in, we can kiss the river good bye. An you want to know why I don't want to get all hepped up? Seems crystal clear to me. I didn't read Perry's copy of *The Tibetan Book of the Dead* for nothin."

"No, you got a point," Zane admitted, twisting the steering wheel to the right for the next turn. *A point. Shit! He's got it all down. Not just true, but correct. You know that. Is...has...an will be. He's just tryin to lay something out to you straight an you're too involved in that political science-*

egotistical trip you used to believe worked for you. Why do I always want to get ahold of people and squeeze my reality outta their pores? "But maybe it'd stop happenin if enough people want it to?" He heard his own words as ominously hollow and pleading.

"Aw, Christ, Greg. You know what I mean. Like watchin the farms sellin out to California on the Applegate. Look at what's happened to McKee bridge, all shiny an new an twice as expensive. Jackson park has been asphalted over with yellow lines markin each car slot, everything regulated an ordered an cemented."

Greg widened his eyes in a way that Zane found uncomfortable, the staring. Like he'd shape-shifted into a seer on a mountaintop with hippy leprechaun dancing eyes. "You bet. But I'm sayin that I've already done too much time behind steel bars. Already come head to head with too many of em, an now all I want is to stay invisible."

"Can't be done, McGregor. Flat out can't be done." But Zane knew Greg had some experience of being invisible, back when he owned Black Beauty, a Ford Falcon with faulty muffler. He'd heard the story from Heavy Duty of how he and Greg had decided to go to San Francisco when they were on about a week long runner. They'd gotten on I-5 going north and didn't realize they were headed in the wrong direction until they passed Grants Pass. Eventually, they got to the city only to get pulled over in the Embarcadero by a city cop who stared at the collection of empty beer cans that covered the backseat floor up to the lip of the seat itself. Greg's Oregon license was expired and Heavy Duty didn't have any ID at all. The fairly young cop took in the whole scene and told them to "get the hell out of here. Go back to Oregon." Of course, Zane only had the story from Duty's reciting of the events, so who knew what really transpired? But Greg swore it was all verification of being invisible.

"Slow down, Z-man, we're there."

Zane had already seen the lone Sheriff's car next to the faded and stained white front of the store, but, lost in thoughts, he'd forgotten why he was there, just for a split second or so, enough for him to mark

123

the gap, the milliseconds of not-knowing, like when the world stopped being video and became a still shot, a photo. Greg's terse tone brought him up short, brought him back to the present sunlit spring day where the temperature wouldn't get above 52. Sunny but chilly.

"Who'd a guessed it?" Greg droned, as Zane slid the bus to stop on the loose gravel just past the abandoned gas pumps. "There's a cop here an we're honest-to-God gonna go in on purpose."

Zane killed the engine and took in the random splatter of bugs on the windshield, looked through them to the high peaks of the Siskiyous looming over the narrow valley. Looked at the heavy green mosaic of forest that rose on all sides to dwarf them. Thought of Greg's descriptions of clear-cutting. "Try not to steal anything," he said softly.

Sasha was sipping Lemongrass and Rose hip tea, warming both hands around her chipped blue Lowenbrau mug. She'd turned the FM up high when she got back to the snug heat of the house. It was almost noon and she should have known that the station from Ashland would be spinning out slow blues. Weekday mornings were always ballads and blues and she usually let them caress her with throbbing, rhythmic fingers. But today they pierced her solitude in high-pitched, anxious female voices that echoed of someone else's unfulfilled dreams and splintered self-confidence. Janis Ian and Emmylou.

She wondered how the male disc jockey with the emotionless hypnotist's voice could possibly know she was here, listening. She wondered why today's music choices seemed somehow determined to pry into the kernel of her doubts, piling one wistful melody upon another, when what she really wanted was some soothing instrumental upbeat tune. But she knew she didn't have long to wait.

She looked around the front room, surveying the discards of the night before: empty wine bottles, full ashtrays, a half dozen circular stains on the Indian print. The litter was disgustingly clear in the daylight, with no candles to waver dancing shadows high up the walls, with her left alone again to clean up the mess.

Looking at leftovers swung her thoughts to how much she hated the smudged white poster by the front door. Zane had nailed it up proudly, she remembered. She could still see him twirling his hammer as he'd stood there, smiling, those hundreds of mornings past. He'd had to ask her if it was straight and she'd just nodded in response. He'd never asked her whether she wanted it there, or she wanted it anywhere, for that matter.

He'd appointed himself decorator when they'd finished covering the inside walls with old sun-bleached wood from the abandoned farm on the other side of Perry's claim. She had helped him tear the planks off the sagging, skeletal barn, working her crowbar carefully to keep from splitting the brittle wood. It had taken them a week of afternoons, three years ago, when they'd first moved in. Bright, sunny, sweaty August days. *When we still did things together. He wasn't wearing a shirt and the boards scratched thin red lines on his skin that I wanted to lick. And the second day we stopped to cool off and walked, my god!, walked hand-in-hand. Do you remember? Down to where Squirrel creek turns that lazy corner in the summer, where the birches hung quietly in the dead air, shading the water. And remember? I took off my top and we both slid into the water waist-high in the pool, splashing on each other's back, laughing. I felt connected to him that day, like this farm was going to be our real beginning, away from town, away from always having to be around so many people wedging between us. The sun reflected off the creek around the pool and he took my face between his hands. I could feel the rough calluses, and he said he loved me. Said it slowly and I believed him because I could see it in his eyes, could see that he wasn't lying right then. He kissed the drops off my eyes and nose and ducked his head down to get to my lips while my forehead dripped and I could feel the hair on his chest against my skin. We made love on the grassy bank in the shade of the birch trees and he stayed with me, waited for me. Afterwards, we washed off in the creek again before going back to the boards. But even then, even working, he kept touching me. Like he didn't want to let me out of reach. Like it was me he really wanted.*

Neil Young with Crazy Horse blasted out of the speakers and she realized the morning blues were over. Seated on the sagging couch, her eyes were still fixed on the poster where they'd been while her legs trembled to Zane's touch as she remembered. Disoriented. For an instant, she wasn't sure whether she'd been lost in a past experience or captivated by a present fantasy. Whichever, her body quivered a couple of times in a row. She knew he wasn't there, just then, and that thought solidified around her like the heavy crust of her oat bread. Now she saw the poster full on again and realized how much she disliked it, but didn't exactly know why. It wasn't much, really. Just a black and white line drawing of a pair of manacled hands pulling against a chain which joined them, having pulled with so much force that one of the middle links had broken, sprung apart. "It my wall, too," she said to no one.

She got up from the wooden rocker and walked around behind it toward the kitchen. She pulled out three drawers before finding a hammer. Humming to herself in harmony to the guitar chords from the FM, she pulled four nails and watched the hands fall to the floor, palms down.

When Zane and Greg shuffled through the front door of the Copper store, they almost ran into the Sheriff's deputy who was leaving. He frowned at them and Zane tried to avoid looking at him, worried that they'd be held up, stopped, questioned. "Detained" was the word that fit his fears, and it popped up fully toasted. Zane saw the nameplate, "Weaver," the black belt, gun handle strapped in, but that was all as the officer side-stepped through the door and let them pass without any more notice than what Zane thought was probably a perpetual authoritarian scowl. Greg lifted a hand to Gus Mitchell, who was standing behind the wooden counter, Dickey's shirt and overalls. Gus pushed his steel-rimmed glasses back up to the bridge of his nose with one, crooked index finger.

Zane heard the Sheriff's engine turn over while Greg tried out his best down-home Oregon drawl. Zane knew the voice well; Greg could put it on in a heartbeat. It came from sawmills and logging crews, from Saturday night dances at the Dreamland Ballroom above Mel's Poolroom, next to the Bear Creek bridge on Main street in town.

"Ok, Gus. Fill us in. What's all the fuss out here?" Greg had already gotten to the counter, as Zane watched his back, watched Gus's eyes bouncing between the two of them like a pinball ricocheting off bumpers. Gus pushed his glasses back up again and squinted in what Zane thought was feigned incomprehension. "You mean the cops?"

"What the hell, Gus," Greg swung his head to take in the empty store. "Don't look like nothing's changed in here," he turned back to him. "Of course I mean the cops. A whole goddamned posse of em passed us, three or four to a car. What's shakin?"

Zane was staring at the huge square aerial map that took up most of the left wall and he moved toward it a few steps, noticing that Gus had backed away from his counter as if to keep them both in view, as if they'd suddenly been transformed into street fighters, circling their victim.

"The deputy told me a family's missing up Carberry creek canyon."

"Missin?" Greg echoed incredulously. "You mean someone disappeared?"

"Not just somebody. It was Gary Fausen from J-Ville." Gus hesitated, but Zane didn't look up to see. "And his wife and two kids."

"Jesus!" Greg whistled. "You mean the guy who worked over at J-Ville lumber?" Zane was trying to spot his farm on the map, downriver, but he had to mentally reconstruct the shadings into ridges and pastures. And he had to keep his ears to the conversation.

127

Gus's scene painted itself quickly into Zane's imagination. A family abducted. Couldn't be lost, not with little kids. *I knew that guy. Knew who he was, anyway. Used to see him playin pool at the Jubilee, wearing a black HYSTER cap, had a chin-shadow beard. Never really talked to him, but can hear his voice. Had that "nothing's too fuckin important" edge. I envied him that ease.*

"So what else," Greg pushed. "Who did it? They know?"

Now Zane looked back to see Gus's head shake slowly sideways. "They just got up here awhile ago. No one knows much of anything yet, except that it's very suspicious. That's all I know."

Greg turned to Zane, his face wrenched tight. "Jesus, LaRoux! You hear that?" Zane nodded.

Gus had relaxed enough to sit on the stool beside him, his faded overalls folding over his lap. "So, boys. I'm supposed to keep a lookout for strangers, or for any sign of the family." Gus shook his head again and Zane thought it was all becoming boring already, thought Gus was trying to draw sympathy to himself, as though the missing family were his relatives. Gus sighed heavily, weight of the southwest corner of Jackson county on his back, "You guys want anything?"

"You mean buy somethin?" Greg shrugged to Zane. "Get a beer?"

Zane drew a tangle of bills from his jean's pocket. "Yeah," he said, walking over to toss the crumpled money on the counter. "Make it six. Bud."

Gus drew back the sliding aluminum lid to the dented Coca-Cola cooler he kept behind the counter and came up with a six-pack.

Zane got his change and picked up the beer, started back toward the door. He could see the bus bathed in sunlight. He wanted to be home. He wanted to dump Greg on the side of the road by the swinging bridge. He wanted to be in his own front room listening to Mose Allison singing "If You Live." He took another look around the store before stepping outside, seeing dusty boxes of Chef Boyardee spaghetti dinner, tins of Nalley's chili. Boxes of stick matches. Wasn't really a store, he thought, beer and wine at a handsome markup. That's what kept Gus going, that and cigarettes at $3 a pack.

"Oh, hey!" Gus yelled after them. "If you guys see any suspicious vehicles, make sure you get the license number." Zane didn't know whether it was Gus's voice, or the news about the family, or his last request, but Zane felt threatened. By the missing family. By Gus's manner. By Greg's easy way of getting him to pay. "Come on," he said, peering at the steep hillside across the road with its blackberry vines that coiled and twisted together like barbed wire. "I need to get you back."

As he climbed into the bus's front seat, Zane suddenly thought of Dino Valenti: "I feel like a stranger in the land where I was born." *His real name was Chet Powers, but he went by lots of variations. Like Shirley Jones, Partridge mom, that's a phony name. I wonder about Shirley Ellis...the line broke, the monkey got choked, and they all went to heaven in a little row boat. Someone else was in the back window watchin us. Saw the curtains part an then close back up again. Someone who shouldn't have been there.*

129

Chapter Eight

A little northeast of towering Mt. Shasta, the Lava Beds form intricate labyrinths of caves and ravines in the dusty, flat plateau around Tule Lake. It was to the Lava Beds that the Modoc leader Kientpoos—Captain Jack to the settlers—took his 53 braves with women and children when they left the Klamath reservation—where the government had decided they should live with their ancestral enemies—and fled to what is known now as Captain Jack's Stronghold, a natural lava fortress of interlinking caves and passageways.

From this in-the-ground position, for five months Captain Jack and his men held off a US Army force that eventually grew to ten times their number. The Modoc War, as it was known, required that howitzers be brought in to pummel and pulverize the cave entrances. As the troopers stumbled about in the catacombs of twisted, glass infused rock as sharp as coral, they were picked off with army rifles by braves they never saw. All tolled, the five month siege resulted in the death of 83 soldiers, with another 85 injured. The Modoc lost 14 warriors. Eventually capturing some braves who were attempting to get water at an inopportune time, the army brass gave them a choice of being hanged immediately or helping them capture Jack.

Captain Jack and three others were hanged at Fort Klamath October 3, 1873, while their tribe was forced by armed soldiers to watch.

***

In 1942 the Tule Lake War Relocation Camp was built as one of ten concentration camps in the interior of the US for the holding of Japanese-Americans who had been forcibly relocated from the West Coast. Two-thirds of those incarcerated were United States citizens, as anyone with at least 1/16th Japanese blood had to be rounded up and relocated. The Tule Lake internment area was a maximum security segregation camp, a place where those deemed disloyal were sent. Many of those shipped to Tule Lake were called "No-No's," meaning they'd written "No" on questions number 26 and 27 of the Loyalty Questionnaire. Those two questions asked whether the individual would forsake all allegiances to the Emperor of Japan, and whether the individual would help fight the enemy. A great number of the "No-No's" answered in the negative to those two questions because they believed that answering "yes" to either question would split up their family. Inhabitants of Tule Lake camp lost all their property to confiscation by the government.

When the war was over, each Japanese-American was given a paltry amount of money and a bus ticket to go home, a place which obviously no longer existed.

Five weeks after the Fausen family had vanished from Carberry creek, George Cruikshank awoke on a Friday morning with a hard-on he wasn't remotely in the mood to do anything about. No sweaty thrusting fantasies of wrapping limbs and arching backs. No perfunctory stroking into a Kleenex just to get the job done. No relief, in other words. Instead, he took a hot shower and decided, while toweling off his heat-splotched, beginning to sag skin that he wasn't going to spend the last working day of the week in the damned office. He'd brought the bureau's green pickup home last night, left his Camaro in the Post Office parking lot. He hadn't gotten down and planned it all out, but obviously he'd set the stage for a Friday escape.

Too bad Walt Hustad had flown back to Wisconsin. George realized he'd formed a bit of a bond with the Corp of Engineers colonel, liked their conversations, thought Walt was an essentially decent guy, an ally. *Gone out of my life now, probably forever. Strange how that works.*

He left a message on Heidi's answering machine, telling her he was working in the field, had country sausage and eggs at the Jubilee café and took Old Stage road from Jacksonville to Gold Hill, following the route that skirted the western foothills of the Rogue valley. Headed for the middle section of the Rogue to check on a string of BLM-managed campsites and small parks sprinkled alongside the river from Merlin down to Graves Creek. Being outside on such a sunny late spring day rather than sitting at his cluttered desk felt like a vacation. Alone again on back roads.

Taking old 99 instead of I-5, he'd driven through Grants Pass, steered the staccato of curves on the back way to Robinson Bridge where the Applegate rubbed itself into the wider channel of the Rogue. Sheer rock walls on the far side. Could be lingering, late arriving salmon in the deep, dark slack-water. Stragglers still in the river from the winter run. He'd fished here a few times over the years.

He followed the larger river downstream, stopping frequently to see what shape the bureau's holdings were in, how they'd weathered the winter, what the maintenance crews had already repaired. He made detailed notes about what needed doing at each site, complete with quick, freehand drawings. Mostly, he listed repeated acts of vandalism, evidence of the constant scourge against public property. *Can you vandalize your own place? Damage is evidence of an epidemic of selfishness. Screw everyone else. Or maybe it's just animal basic marking your spot, like putting your scent out for others to smell and know you were here?*

Intermittent breezes down the river canyon pulled clouds of pollen from bankside evergreens, bushes and grass, perfuming the air like those dark green, pine-scent cardboard trees that dangled from so many rearview mirrors. *Fresh-Its?* Something like that. *Except that the pollen dusts everything, leaves a physical trace.*

Around three-thirty, thinking seriously about having a beer, he pulled the department rig up to the payphone outside Galice Lodge to call the office. He waited, phone pressed to his ear while he watched two retirees. But what did he know? They could have been anyone. He was just guessing about the two older guys in regulation woolen plaid, lawn chairs on the dock, plunking.

He waited for Heidi's programmed spiel "Bureau of Land Management. This is Heidi. How may I help you?" before identifying himself.

"It's George. I'm in Galice."

"Oh...Oh, Mr. Cruikshank, I'm so glad you called." She sounded clearly keyed-up, words rushing out, tumbling over one another, syllables slurring. *What now?*

He noticed the phone book had been ripped out of its U-shaped bracket, saw scratched graffiti on every metal surface, felt his spirit sag. *What's she saying?*

"I tried to tell him you were out on site, but he pretty much demanded that Eugene record the claim transfer deed this afternoon. He was very insistent on that."

"Who? Heidi, slow down. Let me catch up. Who demanded what?"

"Captain Brereton, sir." He could hear her swallow, could tell she was now pacing herself. "From downstairs. Came in right after lunch. Said he needed to file a deed transfer for someone who couldn't physically get to the office. Had a handwritten letter—a scribbled note, really—signed by the original claim holder, he said, already notarized. Most irregular."

"So what happened?" George was rubbing the back of his neck with his free hand. Cords beginning to tighten.

"Well, like I said, Eugene tried to tell him the deed couldn't be officially filed until Monday when you'd be back in the office to approve it." She paused, as if what she'd just said should have closed the matter.

"And?"

"And the captain said why doesn't Raymond approve the H7A form since he's in charge when you're gone." She waited again.

"Then what happened?" Like pulling teeth now.

"Then Raymond told Eugene to fill out the form and he'd sign it. And that's what happened. But I thought you should know. Everything was so crazy; the captain kept saying it had to be done before close of work today."

"Where was this claim, do you know?"

"Tanaka Flats, on the Applegate."

George made a noise deep in his throat, a sigh and guttural moan pushed together. "I'll see you on Monday, Heidi," and he'd hung up. *Old man Louvelle's place. Why would he sign off the claim he's worked for forty years? And why's Brereton got his fingers in this pie?*

He knew he shouldn't be surprised. Rumors about Dave Brereton and his partner Wade Perkins had been circulating for years. Childhood friends at Applegate elementary in Ruch, all the way through high school in Medford. People said they'd always seemed to come as a pair. Painfully tall and skinny Dave with his short, squat sidekick Wade. Raymond was in the same year at MHS and had described them as hovering on the fringe in high school, not particularly socially adept. Wade's buck teeth, often inappropriate laugh. Dave's attitude of aloofness, based on no one knew what. Both still lived on the Applegate, having houses about a mile apart on the stretch between Ruch and the Provolt store by where Williams creek ran in.

George had heard stories of how Dave and Wade liked to give solitary hitchhiking hippies a free ride to the county line, along with a rough, unprofessional haircut done with scissors, maybe a few bruises. Not that public opinion would have found any fault. The Medford Moose lodge, after all, had paid for the billboard on Blackwell hill by the freeway: "Beautify America. Get a Haircut!" with a scroungy longhair frowning down on passing traffic.

It was common knowledge around the courthouse that Brereton and Perkins pretty much had the run of the Applegate valley—each had managed to be assigned to his home territory, so to speak. They *were* the State police and Forest Service on the other side of Jacksonville. So what was Brereton up to at Tanaka Flats? George hadn't the slightest, but his interest was up. *Sits above the river, not that far from Carberry creek where the Fausens went missing. Should be lakeside property once the dam's in. Holy shit!*

Zane was amazed by all that had happened in the month or so since the Fausen family's disappearance. Hank Aaron had broken Babe Ruth's all-time home run record despite multiple threats to his life. "Retire or Die" one letter advised him. Another sent him a crudely drawn diagram of how he'd be shot from the stands. Stick figures and a dotted line for the bullet's path. *Cracker avant garde. Saw it in The Oregonian.* Without missing a game, Aaron set the new record against the LA Dodgers in Atlanta.

Patricia Hearst, now known as "Tania," wearing a jauntily slanted beret, awkwardly held an M1 carbine as her compatriots robbed the foggy Sunset branch of Hibernia Bank in San Francisco. Twenty-some days later, a few of those same Symbionese Liberation Army members were killed after a shootout with SWAT teams in sunlit LA. The house they were in burned to the ground. Tania was still on the loose, Zane knew, with seemingly half the country looking for her.

India set off a nuclear test it called "Smiling Buddha" in the Rajasthan Desert which edges up against Pakistan. The detonation was the first on the sub-continent and Indian scientists had the benefit of Soviet technology, enabling the world's second largest population to become the sixth member of the nuclear club. The US civil defense agency responded by increasing the number of early warning tests on television and radio.

Zane hated those high-pitched whines that ominously interrupted radio and TV broadcasts, hated not knowing whether it was for real until afterwards. "This has been a test of the early warning system. If it had been a real emergency..." Hated knowing he lived every moment under the threat of ICBMs raining down. Since the Cuban missile crisis, since the 64 campaign and Johnson's ad with the little girl and the flower that ended with a mushroom cloud boiling. In fact, for his whole conscious life he'd understood he and everyone else lived under a constant blanketing threat of annihilation. Gone in a split-second. *Idiots pushin buttons.* Indiscriminate erasing, as if he'd never existed. Blast survivors wouldn't last for long in the steadily settling radioactive dust. Fewer and fewer windblown-haired boys on *Schwinns* circling suburban neighborhoods. Such were the visions conjured by the frightening alarm tone—futures flatlining. *Barry McGuire. Eve of Destruction.*

Former Vice-President Spiro Agnew was disbarred. Shown to be a thugish crook and bully. Nixon finally handed over a partial transcript of Watergate recordings to the Senate special committee, ending a long period of yank-and-pull politics in which the President maintained he had "executive privilege" to withhold what was on the recordings. Pictures of the transcripts showed large patches of blacked out words that, according to the administration, might contain sensitive national security information. The committee was crying foul.

Meanwhile, the mystery of the Fausen family continued to occupy conversations throughout Oregon, even spreading across the country. In the press, the Fausens took on mythical proportions, representing the perfect American family so tragically gone missing. Parents, two kids, boy and a girl. Stereotypical Levittown. Zane thought descriptions of the increasingly idealized family's disappearance sensationalized it to mini-series proportions. *Rich Man, Poor Man.* Nationally-known psychics pitched in with theories, including that the four of them were being held in a subterranean fallout shelter by Soviet agents, or had relocated to a house trailer near a rural community in the Willamette valley to escape debts, or had been whisked away to a different solar system by some alien mothership. Zane particularly liked the scenario which suggested the family had stepped through a time warp and were living as landed gentry in Renaissance England. *Jesus! Idiots come out of the woodwork. Everyone knows they're dead, just haven't been found yet. Not for lack of tryin.*

He'd seen the school busses full of Boy Scouts passing on the river road. They'd been put to work scouring the steep slopes around Carberry creek, along with the Sheriff's Posse from both Jackson and Josephine counties. For over three weeks, organized and methodical search teams had looked for the Fausens. The likelihood of kidnapping brought in federal help from Portland. Jacksonville sent a squad made up of bar and restaurant employees, along with Gary Fausen's co-workers from the lumber yard; the steeply rugged country around Carberry creek got a severe going-over to no good result.

During the first week after the disappearance Zane often saw flashes of police vehicles through the Scots pine across the river—Sheriffs, State police, crime scene vans—the road stayed busy most of the day. But all that traffic died down to the occasional official car or truck after the first week. Now, after a month, it was as though

137

nothing had happened. No more police. Seemingly no clues. Lester took to keeping his 12 gauge loaded in the pickup window rack, just in case, he said.

Heavy Duty had, for all practical purposes, moved in with them, settling into one of the two empty rooms upstairs. Mattress and sleeping bag on the floor, scattering of books, dripping candle stuck in an empty wine bottle, clothes neatly stacked. Zane still didn't know how it had happened exactly. One day Duty and Richard came by and Duty just stayed.

A couple of days after his arrival, Zane had taken him into Medford, over to Vince's, where Duty grabbed two duffel bags out of his van with blown valves, parked on Modoc street in front of Vince and Soapy's house. Duty intimated that he was expecting a check from the VA, that he could get the van repaired when it came. Seemed a perfectly natural course of events to Zane, as if the vet were a long absent sibling suddenly come home again. *Sit Down Young Stranger.* In fact, Zane was relieved to have him around to keep Sasha company, took some of the heat off, he felt. Not having to keep up every conversation himself. Not being responsible to her ideas of what to do. Duty filled in admirably.

Zane had learned long ago that Duty's given name was Philip Torgesson. Had, at the same time, heard from Duty's cousin who lived in Central Point how he had acquired the name he now used. Before becoming a sniper, he'd carried his rifle squad's M60. Since he was pathologically afraid of running out of ammo, he'd also crisscrossed four hundred rounds over his torso—four bandoliers, this even though everyone else in the squad carried at least a hundred rounds for his gun. *It's like a funnel, if you think about it. Everythin drained toward Duty and his weapon. The whole squad had to feed him. Heavy Duty. A nom de guerre that stuck.*

Zane had never asked how Duty ended up as a sniper. Sometimes it was better not to know everything, not to be too inquisitive. Just as hardly anyone other than Sasha knew much about his own previous

138

life as an organizer—and even she didn't know how much or how often that life was coming back to him, intruding on his daily being—as he remembered crystallized fear and amped-up excitement being perpetually close companions. *Somethin to be said for that, the energy. The doin somethin. Drivin to Seattle in '69 with guns in the trunk, listenin to Miles Davis Saturday Night at the Blackhawk on cassette. Muted but frantically forceful. Had no idea what I was doin. Could of ended up in some federal lock-up on a weapons charge, but of course I just had to play the pirate adventure out. Some guy I halfway know tells me about this other guy who knows someone else who needs someone to drive this Buick with the radio ripped out, bald tires and Washington plates up to Seattle. He'd had to take a Greyhound back...how fuckin stupid could I be? An just cause I didn't get busted at the time doesn't mean they don't have a nice file somewhere, just waitin for me to stick my head up again.*

This overcast and drizzling mid-May Saturday morning, with Sasha and Duty having driven to J-Ville for shopping, Zane was flipping through pages of his memory while Herbie Mann played "Comin' Home Baby" in the background and the living room wood stove ticked with heat. He'd just washed his face with Dr. Bronner's and deeply breathed in the familiar, distinctive smell. *All-One-God-Faith.* He could see that river mist had flooded the pasture, driving the cattle to ground. They were huddled in several small groups, kneeling or lying on the wet mixture of grass, alfalfa and weeds.

Zane had been working in Medford for the last week, painting a house for one of his mother's widowed friends. Getting on the road by 7, only arriving home near dark left Duty and Sasha on the farm with no transportation. Unless Richard came over, they were stuck on the river. If it had been anyone else, Zane would have been jealous as hell, especially given the still filtering emotional debris from the Aquarius Party. But jealousy and Heavy Duty didn't belong in the same thought, and Zane was sure that anyone who knew him would have agreed.

He'd finished the painting job yesterday, gotten paid in cash no less, and had driven straight to The Alibi where he bought a ten-dollar bag of weed from Danny Colbert, who did business from the tavern. Then he'd gone next door to the OK Market for a half gallon of *Hearty Burgundy* and a short case of Oly—stocking up on necessary provisions. He'd given Sasha what he said was the rest of his painting money and felt quite good about himself for doing so.

Herbie Mann's sextet launched into "Summertime" and Zane began humming along to the vibes' resonating tones until his thinking turned south, turned so that the Fausens and death impinged on the inner swirls of his consciousness. He didn't believe in any seed or germ of thought. Not like a plant growing—ideas aren't things, he maintained—not a core of thought which could grow apace, which could be identified and defined and developed according to some natural law of origins and growth. No ferocious thing called an Id, characterized as a Tasmanian devil with pointed teeth. No miniature being that followed its own rules: angel on one shoulder and devil on another, whispering in his ears. And yet, he still fell victim to the sanitizing effect of communal euphemisms, lies really. *We had to put Spot to sleep; laid him to rest. Christ! People say the same thing about someone who's died, like they're still alive, floatin in some ethereal sculpted garden, bein conscious, thinkin about them.*

When he imagined the Fausen family dead, for instance, he saw them prostrate in well-manicured grass. Neat and clean, like they were just resting. Faces averted. *I've been trained in this sterile stupidity. Seventy-eleven angels dancin on the pin head. I've been trained to consider absurdity as sane. Like Marx askin who teaches the teachers? Good question, but no one hardly ever asks it. Or even thinks it's worth askin.*

Herbie's flute was carrying "Summertime" along now, the vibes laying down platforms from which Mann improvised, and Zane latched onto the soaring flute that was building musical structures again and again. Each one a variation, but each rooted in the chord progressions of the song, building a pre-orgasmic-like tension, holding features of the melody in the background while exploring harmonic edges. The way he could shuffle through his own past, zoom in on some moment without losing touch with the present, hang on to a double vision, if only briefly.

Zane lost his thread of thought as the song ended, however, and he automatically began looking for something else to play, acting DJ for his own mood as always. Came up with Jackson Browne, "Before the Deluge." Then, Phil Ochs, "Tape from California" which led him to Joni Mitchell, "For Free." Ended with Jerry Jeff Walker, "Desperados Waiting for a Train." He lifted the tone arm and dropped it for each cut. By the time the four songs finished, his mood had darkened considerably. Nagged by memories of driving past what seemed at least a couple miles of Army vehicles parked in frighteningly straight, unwavering rows just outside Billings, Montana in June of 70, on their way to Minneapolis. Not in mothballs like the Suisun fleet down by San Francisco, but seemingly ready to roll. He remembered how paranoid he'd become.

It had been unseasonably hot for early June and the VW camper had virtually no air currents inside. Driver and passenger door plastic windows were more like prison cell viewing slots than anything else. Not much could get in. Sweating and swearing, Zane watched Highway 90 unroll eastward in front of them. Everything after Butte was flat, windswept high plateau, heading for the badlands, becoming Interstate 94 at Billings.

They'd pulled into Teddy Roosevelt State Park just over the North Dakota border to camp for the night. Erasmus ran up what few trees there were, ears laid back, eyes wild and crazy, tail swishing rapidly. After their standard dinner of soba noodles with stir-fried beef and vegetables done on a hibachi, Zane got out the Road Atlas to study highways of the West. Sitting at the picnic table, under an umbrella of bug-swirling light from the propane lantern, uncomfortably high from hashish, he wanted to know why all that war equipment was lined up in Billings, Montana.

141

If he believed that blood could run cold, he'd have pointed to that night as proof. As he stared at the networks of highways, freeways and roads on the Atlas, a chilling, stultifying pattern emerged clearly. Billings was at the center of an irregular circle that included Seattle, Portland, San Francisco, Denver, Salt Lake City, Omaha and Minneapolis. If the government wanted to deploy to urban disturbances, all those cities could be reached, he figured, in roughly one day's driving.

To his mind, he was looking at the freeway systems that could be used to move armed forces to virtually any big city in the West, or Midwest for that matter. Chicago wouldn't be an insurmountable obstacle, just a few more hours of driving. St. Louis, Milwaukee, Kansas City, Oklahoma City—they all seemed plausible. Billings was a hub of sorts, he decided, and that recognition explained the row after row of armament they'd driven past the day before.

In 1970, such conclusions were hardly the stuff of conspiracy theories, not after the burning cities of '67 and '8, not considering the all-out offensive Nixon's administration waged on the anti-war movement. *I knew, at the time, sweatin in Billings, that I was puttin myself in jeopardy by hangin posters all along the route from Portland to Minneapolis. Crossin many state lines to incite probable riot. Same charge the Chicago Seven got hit with. But that night I came face to face with my own fears, seein the tentacles of military power in waitin, ready to roll, capable of reachin numerous cities at the same time; there were so many combat machines parked in Billings. Tanks on flatbeds. Jeeps with mounted machine guns. Armed personnel carriers. Truck after truck. Remember thinkin at the time lookin at the Atlas that I might be stoned, but I wasn't stupid. Large scale armed resistance was futile. I knew then that if I wanted to fight, it'd have to be in a different way, it'd have to be intellectual, not physical. An up to now I haven't even done that. I've silenced myself. Hidin out here on the river, hating from a distance.*

He stuffed some wood into the stove, poured himself a cup of coffee from the pot that sat there, put B.B. King, "Indianola,

Mississippi Seeds" on the stereo. Using the cover flap from a book of matches that promised to make him a commercial artist from home, he scraped and sifted marijuana on a tilted plate, separating seeds and stems. As he lit the thin joint he'd rolled, he was aware of a general unease, something nicking under the surface. *Of course Sasha wants it this way, wants me far away from any active work. Our politics are the same in terms of understandin the power of ideology, its depth and breadth, but she doesn't want me to get involved, doesn't want me to disappear for chunks of time probably. Can't say I blame her. But that doesn't change the leopard's spots, I've only really felt alive when organizin. I was good at it. Despite havin always been a depressive, despite the panic attacks, I was able to rise to the occasion when it mattered.*

His active work had come crashing to a halt in late August of 70 when the Oregon governor, acting in fear of thousands of young people descending on Portland during the American Legion Convention—the well-advertised "People's Army Jamboree," the event his posters had touted—turned an off the beaten path riverside park into Oregon's own Woodstock, calling it Vortex I. The five day event diverted erstwhile demonstrators down to McIver State Park near Estacada where the State of Oregon paid for the rock bands and the police and National Guard were told to ignore nudity and drug regulations. Estacada businessmen railed against the open disregard for law and order as they used both hands to rake in the money that flowed into town.

Zane had seen it as a masterful political move. Even though detractors labeled the free concert "The Governor's Pot Party," the relative calm in Portland for the American Legion bought considerable wiggle-room for the state administration. In the end, Nixon hadn't come to Portland and Zane hadn't shown up to either site, neither for the sparsely attended marches in defiance of a dirty war still grinding on, nor for the heady hedonism of Vortex I. He'd understood clearly that political activism couldn't compete with sex, drugs and rock n roll. *Like Earth Day sucked the life out of the anti-war*

143

movement. Ecology was so much cleaner and neater than strugglin for power. An when the draft ended last year, the frat boys quit worryin. We'll just drain out the inner city and rural poor. "Need a job, fellas? Need a way out of the shithole you're livin in? Join up." An they will. They do. But "volunteer" sounds a lot like "draftee" when it's the only choice you have.

"If we make it through December, we'll be fine." George Cruikshank wondered how many more times he'd have to hear Merle Haggard warble those words this Saturday. It'd been on the jukebox all morning, and he knew he'd be hearing it through the walls, bass reverberating, until closing time anyway. Unless he medicated himself to sleep with *Sominex*.

Earlier Lloyd had been in rare form, waving his hands wildly as he spun abduction narratives to anyone who would listen. Talking about the Fausen family got him more air time than usual with customers—it was still that hot a topic—and he definitely had theories about what had happened. George noticed that Lloyd's story changed, however, whenever someone who actually knew Gary Fausen was in the bar. Toned down. No clear perp. A shame, was what it was. As Lloyd refrained from his more outlandish claim that it had been "godless hippy satan-worshipers" who'd abducted the family for ritualistic killing.

Since regulars John and Velma had taken the two seats at the short end of the L-shaped bar, George couldn't miss seeing his own red-veined eyes in the back bar mirror. He greatly disliked having to look at himself. That's why he thought of the space at the end of the bar as his own. Everyone knew that's where he normally sat, but John and Velma didn't seem to care this Saturday. Velma liked to keep her eyes on the "Sweet Shawnee" against the wall between the rest room doors. Whenever the two of them got change from their beer, Velma would quickly hop up, pedal-pushers bulging, to dump coins into the machine. George couldn't remember a time she'd actually won anything.

He wondered, trying not to look straight ahead, wondered if there weren't perhaps some deep-seated connection to martyrdom in his personality. Perhaps some ancestral linkage with serfs and slaves that lay hidden in the foldings of the centuries that preceded his appearance. What else could explain why he continually found himself in positions of submission. To John and Velma. To the Bureau. Now to fucking Brereton. Usually to his own worst ideas.

The Fausen family's disappearance had hit George hard. Not that he knew them personally, not that he had any dealings with them. More like how he felt when he first heard about the Manson family and Sharon Tate. An uncomfortable gnawing in the pit of his stomach. A concrete sense of unsettling disruption that took him back to swollen, gas-bloated bodies of twisted men that he'd trudged past in Korea. Cruelty become normal. Seeing kids' bones picked clean by squawking scavenger birds. And now it was all happening in his territory, on the edges of what he'd call home.

Just last week, Cleatus Fausen had put a .22 pistol to his temple and pulled the trigger. He'd left no note.

Family vanishes. Grandad kills himself. How could that not raise suspicions about what was happening out on the river? The Courthouse stayed abuzz with conspiracy theories when, in actual fact, no one knew anything. Workers on the fourth floor had a pool for when the Fausens would be found. Closest one wins. All the early dates had already passed, he thought.

This early afternoon at the Jacksonville Tavern was boisterously sweaty. When the place got crowded, the inside of the windows steamed up, the smell of Lloyd's beer sausages and pickled eggs intertwined with cigarette smoke and spilt beer. Merle Haggard was going again, "Got laid off down at the factory." George knew he could scream with the slightest provocation. *Strutting and posing. That's what all this is, when you boil it down. Putting on faces, acting parts. Can't just*

145

play pool, have to carry on, yell at each other. Toss slurs and bravado. Shuffleboard clanging and banging. Players jumping up and down in excitement; girls grabbing a hold of each other with high pitched voices as their competitor's puck slides off into the ditch. Damn! I've gone off the deep end of negative. Got to change my thinking. Like I did about Walt?

That, at least, was somewhat of a bright spot for him. He'd found, over the last month, that he'd liked Walt Hustad. Instead of his manufactured fears about what it would be like working under the Army Corps' expansive thumb, George realized that the reluctant colonel was all but invisible on the day-to-day. When they did meet, Walt came across as respectful and a bit timid. George chalked it up to home life. From the few clues Walt divulged about his married life, George had formed the picture of a husband very much at the mercy of an unmerciful spouse. He remembered their dinner together across the street at the Jacksonville Inn just four days before Walt left.

The restaurant was half-a-flight down from street level, in the basement of an old, gold rush era bank. Jacksonville had passed city ordinances in the sixties to retain as many original buildings on Main Street as possible. So what used to be reinforced concrete and vaults, was now an upscale dinner house. Even though he lived within a block of the restaurant, George had never set foot in it before. *Issues of class. I'll be paying for the snootiness.* He'd heard people describe the place as "elegant," and he knew he was about as elegant as a pit toilet, so he was on his guard from the beginning.

He made sure he was there early enough to be seated when Walt came in. Something about wanting to make the Army Corp executive—that's how he had come to think of Walt, as an executive instead of a colonel—he wanted to make Walt feel at home. Which he knew was completely ridiculous because he had absolutely no idea how Walt lived at home in Wisconsin. As ridiculous as heart-warming westerns where the whole town is waving goodbye to the hero riding off into the sunset. And if the film had sucked him in, he'd have a

146

tingling nose and slightly damp eyes no matter how much he knew he was being played. Like the popularity of The Browns and their sappy songs. Like the Star Spangled Banner causing gooseflesh. *Jesus!*

Nonetheless, he put on his most fraternal face when he saw Walt peek around the entryway apprehensively. George waved him over, welcomed him. A cocktail waitress with severe eyebrows, in Levis and a periwinkle blouse, pounced on their table before Walt got fully seated. Double Jack on the rocks for George; gin and tonic for Walt, who was craning his neck to scope out the dining room, his eyes darting from side to side. George watched the waitress head to the bar before turning his attention to his guest.

"Thanks for coming, Walt. Haven't seen you much lately. Thought it'd be a good idea to catch up, see how your dam's coming?"

"I certainly wouldn't call it *my* dam." He moved his silverware back and forth on the embroidered napkin. "I just make sure acreage gets cleared."

"I was joking, Walt."

They'd gotten through ordering from their waitress who jingled when she moved from collections of gold and silver bracelets on each wrist. George saw her as exceptionally ballsy, what with the chartreuse mascara and black lipstick. He thought she'd gone out of her way to confront others, in this case customers, and George recognized a subliminal attraction on his part though he could never be as brazen. He and Walt had been engaged in breezy conversation, nothing too serious until Walt complained about pushy and gung-ho coworkers.

"I know exactly what you mean. Fools, hucksters and shysters abound, conniving their way to success. But you're not one of them."

"That's nice of you to say, George, but I'm often left feeling like I've just messed in someone's bed."

"I think you're giving folks around here too much credit for logic. Even though we're in a town—I'm talking about Medford—people still pretty much have a back woods mentality. They like to know

147

which way the wind's blowing, but they also have a fatalistic strain. Like what's going to happen is what was always going to happen regardless. At any rate, it's not you that's crapped up their lives."

Walt patted his comb over self-consciously, and munched on a bread stick from the basket on the table. Its sign guaranteed "natural grain." "Well, you can't tell me the dam is a popular project."

"You'd be surprised. People around here will support most anything that brings money into the valley. The timber industry is suffering and we don't have what you'd call a strong environmental lobby." George smiled at his own joke. "Matter of fact, we barely have any hippies outside of Ashland, if you don't count here." He watched their waitress bending over a neighboring table, paisley skirt billowing.

"But I get the impression that you don't really think the dam's a good thing."

"Good for some. Not so good for others. Same old story. Protecting farmers from flood damage is one thing, Opening up the whole length of the river to commercial development—re-zoning farmland—is quite another." George twisted his rocks glass of Jack Daniels back and forth on its napkin and looked around the restaurant. Low ceilings. Diffused light. Globe candles with red plastic mesh on all the tables. The room two-thirds full, a bubbling of sound blending without losing individual voices. The Jack on low burn in his stomach. Feeling good. "Aw, hell. Whatever reservations I have aren't your fault. All this shit's way bigger than the two of us, right here, having dinner. Dam or no dam, in the blink of an eye we'll be too old to care much either way." He swallowed from his drink. "You close to retirement?"

"Another two years and I'm done."

"And then what, if I may ask?"

Walt's pale, watery eyes watched the bartender running a blender as he talked. "Don't have a frigging idea. How's that? Work your adult life at the same job so you can retire in grace, but then not have

148

any idea who you're going to be, what you're going to do." He turned back to George. "I suppose I sound like a whiney old man, now."

"You sound like me, and I'm looking at twenty more years if I stay with the Bureau." He was interrupted by the arrival of their dinners. Sauteed oysters for George, while Walt smiled hopefully at a small grilled filet. Both had glazed carrots and brown rice.

George wanted to change the subject; he couldn't take much more drivel about growing older—*a dead-end undertaking*, he thought cleverly. Still, he wasn't immune from noticing his steadily thickening torso, his sagging jowls—not like bags, but obvious to him nonetheless. The unavoidable erosion of aging. He swallowed lemon pungent breaded oyster, well chewed.

"So, Walt. Let me tell you about wonderful southern Oregon. Maybe it'll give you a glimpse into what it's like to have grown up here." He leaned back away from his plate. "Have you seen any colored people since you've been here, by the way?"

Walt speared a chunk of carrot, stopped on the way to his mouth. "Now that you point it out...no. I haven't. But Appleton isn't what you'd call integrated either, so I haven't really paid much attention."

"I guarantee you won't see any in Medford. Not unless some African student wanders down by mistake from the college in Ashland. The valley's full of Mexican laborers, but they're kept separate, in shacks behind orchards. You won't find any of them walking down the street. An they're gone right after the pear harvest, off to some other picking job somewhere. I can definitely guarantee you won't see any black people. I grew up in the Rogue valley and never met a real, breathing black man until I joined the Marines. In Eagle Point, when I was young, I saw more confederate flags than old Betsy Ross-es by a long shot. I know Grants Pass and Medford were the same way." He started working on another oyster with his fork. "Hell, Ashland held the last public KKK convention in Oregon in the 1920s. Full regalia, burning crosses and everything."

149

Though chewing, Walt pitched in. "I thought the West was more forward-thinking, for some reason." He swallowed. The chewing ice whine of the bar blender seemed to be going all the time, covering the numerous dinner conversations from neighboring tables.

"Medford, Central Point, White City, Grants Pass, Phoenix, Talent—they all have sundown laws. Still enforced."

"Aren't they unconstitutional?"

George flashed a broad smile. "Nobody cares about that, not the local politicians or the people who elect them. Lots of folks in the valley think that the legislators in Washington are all socialists anyway. The Federal Government is the enemy."

"And what do you think, if I can be so brave?"

"About what? Sundown laws? Embarrassing. I saw blacks, Puerto Ricans, Navahos, Mexicans—you name it—I saw them pretty much all die the same in Korea. After that experience, I just can't summon up white-skinned outrage anymore. Can't listen to the jokes: nigger this and wetback that. I'm not claiming any sanctified nature; I told all those jokes myself when I was a kid. Seemed like everyone did."

"We all talked that way, too, in Wisconsin. Just seemed natural since there weren't very many minorities around. I never thought about it. Never really tried to put myself in their shoes, consider the consequences. The Corp of Engineers is a mostly white group itself. Very white." Walt bent his head down, staring at his dinner plate. To avoid anyone else's eyes, George thought.

He raised his empty glass so their waitress could see. She bustled through the maze of tables. "Another round please," George said when she stopped beside him. She nodded, turned toward the bar and its perpetual blending. *Margueritas. Daquires. Grasshoppers. Never ordered a blended drink in my life.* "So, Walt. Let me tell you a story. In 1964, I was working in the BLM office—this was before my promotion—so essentially I was just another body. Our director was forced to retire rather suddenly due to a heart condition. We were informed by Washington that a new program director had been assigned and was on his way from Virginia."

Their waitress returned with drinks and George waited until she'd finished replacing cocktail napkins, picking up the empties. He took a sip before continuing.

"Getting a new manager, especially one from out of state, created a quite a stir in the office. Folks wondered if policies were going to change, whether their jobs were safe. We knew nothing about our new boss other than that he'd been a project manager in Richmond, Virginia."

"Let me guess," Walt pushed in. "Was he black?"

"Exactly. You're pretty quick tonight, Walt. That's exactly what happened. But the story is how Medford reacted; he brought a wife and two pre-school age kids with him. You'd have to imagine how foreign that was. A carload of black people at the A & W? Unheard of. We had to send our receptionist Heidi to rent them a house because no realty agency was willing to help them. Raymond and I often did their grocery shopping because even the wife and children were targets. "Niggers go home" yelled out of car windows. People talking right in front of them like they weren't there. It was truly hideous. Joe Marsh was his name."

"Was he any good at his job?"

"He was a nice enough guy. Bit standoffish, but I didn't blame him. He couldn't know what he was getting into, or whether he could trust anyone. Fact is, the Bureau yanked them out after only six months. One day they were just gone. I got a phone call from the regional office in Seattle telling me I was 'acting' director. None of us ever heard anything about them again. They just disappeared. No traces."

"Just like with the Fausen family." Walt had added, as he was bent forward, working a steak knife through his meat.

151

Chapter Nine

The first wagon trains of settlers began arriving in Southern Oregon during the 1840s, unleashing massive and deadly biological warfare on native inhabitants. Smallpox and measles were endemic among those pushing westward, and indigenous people had no acquired immunity to counter the sicknesses. From 75% to 90% of Oregon native peoples died in the first generation of homesteaders.

Armed conflicts over who was going to live where finally led to the Rogue River Wars of 1855-1856, in which United States troops and a volunteer militia comprised mostly of unemployed miners and landless settlers waged full-scale warfare against what remained of the many various tribes that made up the Rogue Nation.

At the end of the Rogue wars, over 260 surviving natives—mostly women, children, and old men—were marched north up the Oregon coast more than 200 miles to a reservation at Grand Ronde. A little over 50 of the party finally arrived, as sickness and citizens shooting from behind trees or rocks whittled down their numbers. Only a small handful of them survived longer than two years in Grande Ronde.

George watched rain bounce off the street and sidewalks through the J-Ville Tavern's smudged front windows, feeling mildly sorry for scurrying pedestrians, trying not to let maudlin country lyrics from the jukebox get to him. Lloyd only worked till noon on Saturdays. Now, two-ton Mickey with splotchy skin roamed behind the bar in patched jeans and a yellow Kawasaki sweatshirt. "PUT SOMETHING EXCITING BETWEEN YOUR LEGS" in red letters on the front. *Sweet Jesus!*

He'd been thinking, for no particular reason, about how the companies selling sugared cereal made sure to blanket Saturday morning cartoons with ads so the little tykes would pitch a fit in the breakfast aisle if their mom didn't buy Tony the Tiger or the dancing leprechaun. From there, he glommed onto the idea that when anyone went out of their way to assure him their motives were pure—had nothing to do with personal gain—he could be sure it had everything to do with them getting over on someone. People lied. Those at the top seemed to lie more than most. *Just look at Nixon. Or Spiro Agnew, for christsakes.* When it came to accumulating and protecting money or power, organized deceit seemed to be a built-in factor, like an I-bar in a bridge. Yesterday's news from Heidi—rushing a patented claim transfer through—had everything to do with his attitude. Brereton seemed to be playing fast and loose with procedure. *What's the reason? There has to be a reason.*

Someone played "Waltz Across Texas" by Ernest Tubbs on the jukebox, and the phone by the cash register started ringing.

Next he knew, Mickey was waving the handset back and forth. "It's for you, George." *Who knows to call me here?*

It'd been his father on the phone, clipped and emotionless. Wanting to know if George was coming for Sunday dinner because it'd been a few months. Because no one was getting any younger. George was shamed into agreeing. What else could he do? *My seventy-three year old father phones me at a tavern. Goddamn grim.* "Try to get here by one or so," he'd been told. *Shoots tomorrow all to hell.*

Two slowly nursed beers later, through which he'd sulked and stewed about what was going on at the office, a strikingly attractive, olive-skinned, dark-haired young woman took the stool next to him at the bar. She was accompanied by a massive guy who looked like he could have been a linebacker for the Raiders—muscularly huge, with long curly blond hair and a couple faint scars on his forehead. She was wearing a black sweatshirt with a small pink peace sign and jeans, both a bit baggy, while his gray sweatshirt had a picture of a Royal Coachman with the words: "Bite Me." George noticed that both were suppressing laughter when they came in, as if unwilling to let a recent joke go.

They weren't a couple, he'd surmised pretty quickly. Not enough touching, leaning, catching each other's eyes. Not enough intimate ease. Some restraint apparent. But George could also tell she wasn't available, that she was involved with someone. He trusted his ability to notice, pick up on, tune into the signals women sent, even if he tended to err on the shy side. When in doubt, assume the worst. In this case, he didn't think his interest was sexual; he was old enough to be her father. *Oh, Christ, George. Get real. Of course it's sexual, at least you'd consider it. Don't pretend otherwise. Can't separate all the threads of attraction so easily.* But he was clear something else was going on. As they talked to each other, and George paid particular attention, they'd stirred-up his feelings like a storm at sea churns the bottom. He thought they represented what he'd never had himself: friends who shared, or cared deeply about each other. He sensed himself drawn to these two, felt a gentle tugging at his own loose emotional ends. Wondered if anything could unravel his tightly woven defense mechanisms, his tendency to settle for less, his increasingly thin skin when it came to his own failures.

The young woman's name was Sasha, he'd picked up from eavesdropping, and as far as he could remember her companion was called Dewey, or something like that. He'd been going by what he'd been able to hear from their conversation and he'd had a hard time catching the guy's name amid the clinking of glasses, the jukebox, the chatter and laughter of a nearly full bar on Saturday afternoon. People off work. What he did overhear clearly was the woman talking about Perry, about his system of trolleys and pulleys. *Tanaka Flats claim. That's the Perry she means.*

He'd waited half a minute while Mickey delivered their beers. "Excuse me," he bent forward so he could see them both. "I don't mean to be butting in, but are you talking about Perry Louvelle who has a mining claim up by where the new dam is going in on the Applegate?" *What the fuck am I doing?*

She'd brightened into a broad smile. "You know him? I love talking to Perry. I've learned so much from him. He's a beautiful man." She'd half turned toward her friend, including him. "We live on the Applegate, too."

All at once George was clear he didn't want to admit the truth to them, that he was a member of the elaborate complex bureaucracy that exercised control over so much public land. He could tell they

155

were free spirits while he was part of the establishment. While he was The Man, and in no way felt beautiful. "I've known him for a long time." *You sound like a complete idiot.*

He'd been simmering about Tanaka Flats, the patented claim, and Dave Brereton's connection to it since the phone call yesterday. He wondered, for instance, whether Brereton had waited for him to leave the office before coming in, get him out of the way. But that didn't make any sense because Heidi had stressed the state cop wanted paperwork filed on the spot, before end of day. No one knew he'd be out of the office; it was a snap decision he'd made that morning. So Brereton couldn't have known ahead of time. Nothing was adding up.

Then, these two fresh faces had come in, sat next to him, and immediately started talking about exactly the place he'd been thinking about, talking about Perry. George felt he was at the center of some rapidly spinning cyclone swirling around Tanaka Flats. *Out of nowhere.* He suddenly felt slightly giddy, cut-loose from his moorings, things out of his control. "And you live close to Perry, did you say?"

She'd been sipping from her glass. "We live…"

"On the river," the meaty guy interrupted, smiling as he leaned past Sasha's face to make contact with George, to let him know. Something at the edges of his eyes had said "drop it." George knew the look, knew he'd gone too far. It was a generational thing. Trusting. Besides which, he'd just clicked in on the fellow's stare, knew what it was, had seen it more than he cared to remember. *The long, flat gaze.*

Merle Haggard was whining about making it to December again. Background to the steadily rising pitch of mostly male voices, the too-easy attenuated laughter, the ca-chinging of the cash register that echoed above them all.

By the time Zane saw the VW bus turn off the river road, returning from the trip to Jacksonville, he'd worked himself into quite a state. Had been hitting wine the last couple of hours, draining half the big bottle. He hoped the shoppers had bought more—what was left wasn't going to last long.

The mid-morning mist had evolved into late afternoon sheets of rain that slanted across the pasture from the mountains, wavering with the wind, billowing like sailcloth. Blue-black clouds hovered over the valley, darkening, thickening the air. Riverside birch and alder trees being yanked from side to side as the wind gusted across the river.

Through the front room window, he watched the bus slewing water sideways from the wheel wells as it came off the swayback bridge. Definitely in a mood, he'd been beating himself up all afternoon with past failures. Reliving helter-skelter moments of embarrassment stitched together by a selective memory operating on its own dubious logic. Long-repressed intimate betrayals and secretive slimy deceits blinked back into focus until regret pulsed with his blood, spreading, shaming him to the quick.

Some painful emotional disc had slipped out of line, compressing conflicting feelings—sexual need, phobic fear of abandonment and years of guilt—into a dizzying mass of impressions like swirling mirrored carousels flashing by. A systemic sickness. *Something from Hironymus Bosch, deformed arms and legs sticking out haphazardly. Devils devouring the blank-eyed guilty headfirst.* In these states he often fantasized being murdered, shot without warning from a distance like JFK and Martin. Not up close and immediate like Bobby. *Discrete holes rather than mangled flesh. Like the newspaper photo I saw in Minneapolis of Che's riddled corpse in Bolivia. He was laid out on a table with smiling brown faces squeezing together to get in the picture. So many holes in his body, crusted with black dried blood. So many goddamn holes. Warren Beatty and Faye Dunaway in their car at the end. Sonny Corleone twitchin and staggerin—tommy guns at the toll plaza. Tattooed Attica inmates caught in the same crossfire as their hostages, killed by New York State troopers. Fred Hampton lying in his Chicago Black Panther bed where police bullets stitched patterns through the walls. That many holes. Overkill to demonstrate superiority, havin the hammer. Like realizin that when he finally quit beatin on me, I'd just picked up where he left off. Takin it out on myself. Have been doin it ever since. Even though I know it, am aware, once the mechanism clicks into place, I'm fuckin done for. Because I've always known I deserved it. All the roofs cavin in, tunnels collapsin. My badness squeezes and shoves and squirts its way in, blottin out anything else that might shed a better light. Heavy black sound-deadening shrouds wrapped all around, closin in. Suffocatin me. Seems I don't deserve to ever feel safe.*

He lit a cigarette and blew the smoke out quickly, as if expelling demons. Sucked in more, saw Sasha animated behind the wheel, talking with her hands as she pulled the bus up by the front porch, parking as close to the house as possible to avoid tracking mud inside. She and Heavy Duty were laughing as they came through the door, plastic bags hanging off their hands and arms, water sliding off their clothes, a trace of river smell wafting in with them. Erasmus had been on the front porch, calmly watching the rain. He dashed between the shoppers' legs and started howling for food, following Sasha into the kitchen.

Zane was struck, once again, by how physically imposing his friend was—filled up a lot of space—but today Zane was also aware how much Duty's face reminded him of a small child, wavy blond hair framing a visual impression of brute strength and sensitive vulnerability. He'd never seen Duty in that light before, but watching him now, smiling and laughing with Sasha, unfiltered innocence was the primary hit he got. *An angelic sniper. Watch out!*

Duty spoke over his shoulder as he followed Sasha into the kitchen. "I was ragging her for driving that bus like a jeep. She wheeled that thing." Zane didn't share in the humor; he was out of synch again, outside looking in.

"And," Duty continued, muffled somewhat by the half wall between, "I've never met anyone else who double-clutches. Did you teach her that?" Voice now clear as he came back into the front room.

At first Zane didn't react, pretending to be reading. But just as he lifted his head to say something, Sasha emerged from the kitchen. "I knew it before I met him," she pointed out sharply, as Erasmus yowled for attention at her feet.

"She never told me where she learned," Zane nearly mumbled, mired in the swampy, sucking wilderness of self-doubt. "Some guy taught her, probably."

His words hung in the room like a mid-air collision, raining debris. Worse yet, he didn't know why he'd said it. Another example of the dark side coming out. He'd bought Sasha a Mother's Day card right after the abortion, but had never given it to her. Couldn't bring himself to that ultimately dangerous edge, that "do it and damn the consequences" free fall. But he could convict himself of the most heinous interpersonal crimes just on the strength of having thought about them. That's all it took these days, like when he was seven and prayed his parents would be killed in a car wreck, wanting out from under the denigrating glares, the continual shaming comments.

Sasha was staring at him incredulously, silently mouthing "What's wrong with you?" Zane ignored her, busying himself with stuffing the wood stove. Duty seemed to sense the tension stretched tight and excused himself by saying he had reading to do in his room. "Let me know if you need help cooking." Zane could hear his feet on the stairs, could trace his path across the ceiling.

"What in the world is going on with you, Zane?" Sasha asked plaintively. "Why are you being such a jerk?"

"Did you guys get any more De Blah-Zay?"

"Is that what you've been doing all afternoon? Drinking?"

"That 'n' tryin not to feel sorry for myself."

She laughed tightly, brushing wet hair off her forehead, shaking her head, her breasts swaying visibly inside her green sweatshirt. "Sorry for yourself? Mary, Jesus what for? Look around you for pity sakes. We're living in the lap of luxury compared to most of the world."

"I understand that, but it's not enough. I feel like I'm not doin anything. Hidin out here while the country's on a beeline to fascism."

"You're saying that living with me isn't enough? You're wasting your time?"

"Oh, hell. You know I don't mean it like that."

"I don't know what you mean," her voice honed to an edge.

"I mean," he sagged down onto the couch, small puffs of dust rising. "I don't see the point. What are we doin?"

"I thought we were trying to live together." Sasha moved in front of the couch, towering over Zane's inwardly cringing body. "You know. Be a couple."

"Yeah, but to do what? You wanna go back to Payless, make a career out of it? Climb the corporate ladder?"

"Jesus, Zane. I'm not the enemy here, but you're talking to me like we're at opposite ends, have conflicting goals."

He looked up, eyes flat. "You can always have Brooks, I'm sure."

She stood straight, arched her back. "And you can play around with bubble boobs Aurora."

While he stared at her, her face seemed shaded, unfamiliar somehow. Like the proportions had changed. Familiar made unsymmetrically strange. "Sorry," he said. "You're right. It was a cheap shot you didn't deserve. We've just never dealt with that night."

"I thought we'd both tacitly decided *not* to discuss it. What are we going to resolve by going through it all?" She was frowning. "Uncle Andreas taught me to double-clutch," she added.

Zane was ready to try backing his way out of the topic. "I just want to hear from you that we both fucked up. That however it got started, it was a disastrous mistake."

Sasha didn't answer, but bent down, draping her arms over his shoulders, drawing him in for a sedate perfumed Aunt–like kiss. "We have to agree not to throw Brooks and Aurora in each other's faces. No place to go from there."

He could tell the danger was past. After a very brief stint of ill-timed defiant jealousy, he knew he'd survived. Her facial features back in proper alignment, comfortably familiar once again. Safe at home; the throw was late.

"Bubble boobs?" he asked with his eyes scrunched up.

She laughed. "I don't know what that means. You shouldn't get me going like that."

She was right, of course. He shouldn't get her going; never worked out to his advantage. She exuded an earthy sense of intuition that didn't suffer fools. And that quality attracted him deeply. He found it impossible to stay irritated with her when they were physically sharing the same space. *Bubble boobs, for christsakes. How could I argue with that? But at the end of the day I'm still neutered in a way. Disarmed. Impotent. Just a short step from worthless, playin for a tie. She took down my poster without a word.*

"I feel like that Savoy Brown song, "Troubled by These Days and Times." You know it?"

She shook her head. He could see she'd tightened her lips, her shoulders stretched taut again.

"Well, hold on." He crossed the room and began riffling through albums stacked on edge on the floor. Then, he stood up again, looking puzzled. "I forgot. I lent it to Richard."

"Doesn't matter, Zane. The title says it all. You're back in your black cloud."

"Must be the rain."

By 7 pm, darkness had closed in around the house tightly, opaquely. The incessant rain pelted noisily against the window glass, pounding the roof, competing with the hourly news report from the living room FM. Sasha moved a boiling cast iron pot of potatoes to the front of the kitchen woodstove, straining to hear if there was anything new going on with the presidential hearings. *Looks like we won't have Nixon to kick around much longer.* She opened the oven door to check on

161

the three trout Zane had caught on Thursday, poking each at its thickest with her index finger to measure cooking time.

Zane was reading his much-thumbed, dog-eared hardback copy of Gramsci's *Prison Notebooks* while he slouched on the couch by the front room woodstove, but she knew he'd be paying close attention to the news, would no doubt have plenty to say about the so far week-long Senate investigation. She was once again glad they had no television since the committee meetings were being broadcast on all three national networks and she could easily see him drinking, smoking, staring and swearing at the tube all day.

It's men, she thought with sudden irritation. *The hearings. All about men, ham-handed posturing men exerting authority. Political pissing matches. Marking and defending their territory, worried about looking good and moral in the process.* She couldn't help thinking men were responsible when she passed deer or raccoons, or any number of small mammals dead on the highway. Broke her heart to see the smashed bodies inert on the road while cars and trucks zoomed by, lifting their fur. Women could be driving, of course; she knew that. But the machines themselves she chalked up to men, something essentially masculine in seemingly inconsequential brutality. Like log trucks, one after another carrying the forest to sawmills, hour after hour, day after day. She was sure it was a man or men responsible for taking the Fausens. Men made the war. *So much tearing apart. So much smashing and hurting. In some tribal societies, men dashed female children's brains out against a tree or a rock. Swung them by the feet.*

She carried the potatoes over to the sink to drain, steaming the window which in daylight looked out onto the steep hillside on the west side of the house, but just then only reflected her own foggy, spectral image. *And men seem to have a tough time sharing in their own or anyone else's emotional lives. All the stories they've learned, all the hero crap and rugged, stoic individualism. Gary Cooper and John Wayne. Zane lives a parallel life to me, only able to be truly intimate in brief snatches when he decides. Always his lead, his timing, his need.*

162

She snapped out of herself because, just as she pulled the sizzling pan of fish from the stove with the calico oven mitt Adeline had pressed on her when they'd first moved in, Duty appeared at the top of the narrow, open stairway that climbed the wall directly in front of her. He was standing on the landing, watching her, with Erasmus curled at his feet, eyes closed, absorbing the heat funneling upstairs, his chin resting on lazily crossed front paws. She had to back away from the stove for Duty to make the last step off the stairs when he came down—it was that tight a fit in the kitchen. He made a point of looking admiringly at the cooked trout in her hand. She'd used Swiss chard as a wrap for each fish individually, the green leaves drying crisply brown in the oven. Trout meat had pulled away from translucent bones at the edges where the skin curled up.

"Looks good, milady." He laid a broad hand on her nearest shoulder, squeezing once. She unconsciously flinched at his touch, the eye-twinkling tone of his voice. She tried to utter some witty deflecting rejoinder. *Are you Sir Gawain or the Green Knight? You can't be d'Artagnon cause Zane's already claimed it.* Instead, she was fixed to the floor with her mouth open, nothing coming out. To recover her composure she turned away to set the pan on the counter by the sink, hoping Zane hadn't heard, though she didn't know exactly why she hoped that. Was Duty crossing boundaries, hitting on her? *What's he doing? Should I be paying more attention? Or maybe I'm just too sensitive, over-reacting?*

Duty walked on out into the front room, wiggling a piece of paper he'd brought with him from upstairs. "You guys need to hear this. I just threw the *I Ching* and the answer is too far out, freaking right on."

"What was the question you asked?" Zane still on the couch, crushing out a cigarette.

"I can't tell you," Duty was staring at his paper, holding it almost reverentially with both hands. "That'd invalidate the answer. It's got to be kept secret. That's the rules."

163

Sasha stuck her head through the passageway from the kitchen to announce they needed to get their plates for dinner. The news had ended. They tried to time their eating to the nightly "Dinner Platter" hour on FM, when the DJ played an entire album without interruptions. Tonight, *Blind Faith* weaved through the ginger and curry scented air; she'd sprinkled spices liberally on the kitchen stove. Having both woodstoves burning heated the first floor to a toasty warmth while the cold rain outside continued to rattle down.

"You're fuckin' crazy," Zane was getting up, groaning dramatically with the effort. "I never heard, OR READ any such thing about the *I Ching*. You just made that up."

"Perhaps," Duty smiled, as Zane walked around him to get to the kitchen.

After they finished dinner, with Duty and Zane washing up, they'd all returned to the living room in which they'd lit up a scattered assortment of candles. In Mason jars, on saucers, and one three-foot high, free-standing, octagonal rainbow layered monster that measured ten inches across. They all had red wine since Duty had sprung for a gallon of *Vino Primo* at the IGA in J-Ville. Sasha had re-curried the front wood stove and the FM was playing Saturday night blues. Old time: Bessie Smith, Big Bill Bronzy, Billie Holiday, T-Bone Walker. Duty busied himself rolling up joints as he sat on the couch with Zane, who was staring at his own feet as they tapped in time to the music. Sasha had taken the wooden-armed chair by the window so that she was facing them through flickering light across the deep red, intricately shadow patterned Persian carpet. *Is this symbolic? Me sitting here and my two men there? Is that the dynamic we're now living? I'd never have thought so before. Hated Jefferson Airplane, "Triad," with its flaunting: Why can't we go on as three? Or am I just fantasizing? I'm racing miles ahead. Not like me. I don't know if I could handle such an arrangement, or if I'd even want to. Everything's gotten so damned complicated since the Aquarius party. Like some line's been crossed, some social fabric ripped that*

we can never get in front of again. And Duty was the one who gave us the
mescalin, started the whole thing.

After he'd licked the last Zig-Zag edge, rolled the joint between his lips before lighting it, Duty lifted his piece of scribbled paper, held it in front of him as if he were studying it. "Are you two ready to hear this? I'm telling ya, it's pure, unadulterated wisdom." Sasha thought his eyes were twinkling with impishness, that he dearly loved the put-on. Over the last few years she'd noticed how Duty would invariably attract groups of children around him—was like a magnet for them—a big stuffed animal, warm and fuzzy. But he also seemed to enjoy setting mind-fucks in motion. Just like with the mescalin, he was the distributor, the one who supplied the intoxicant or the deviation from safe normality, though she didn't really think there was such a thing as normality. Not in the sense of some ubiquitous, stable, level, even-handed state of nature. Even if concepts of normal were nothing more than handy fabrications, she knew, Duty loved to instigate drastic turns from the myth or ideal itself. *Guerrilla theater. San Francisco Mime Troupe came to Portland State, put on a sketch in my Urban Sociology class. Threw language at us: "cunt" and "prick." No one said such things in a classroom. I was eerily pleasantly shocked. I remember the textbook for that 1967 course was copyrighted 1939, as though nothing substantial had changed in cities over the intervening 30 years. So much time wasted on nonsense.*

"Ok, kids. Are you ready?" He cleared his throat. "I'll just read you one line at a time. Normally, they wouldn't necessarily seem connected since each one is the result of a separate throw. What's amazing here is how much they all have in common. Like, the message is absolutely coherent." He handed the joint to Zane who took it over to Sasha, waving his hand back and forth to tell her to keep it. She'd taken two deep drags by the time Zane regained his end of the couch.

Sasha was seeing them through her exhaled smoke and the wavering, diffused candlelight from the hatch cover table; they were backed by faded barn wood and Ansel Adams at Yosemite. The worn fabric on the arms of the couch, threadbare in places, seemed perfectly suited to her new high mood. *Use value's what's important, after all. That's been clear to me since we came to the river. Not much point in accumulating stuff for show, for status. Zane's mom does that. Has a house full of things to be looked at. Not Adeline. I could live in her place.* Thoughts were stuttering past as though she were watching a disjointed, badly spliced film. Thinking was somehow strangely and fluidly visual. Ideas had shape and density and played out in front of her, images forming and breaking apart, dissolving, words twisting and swirling like mobiles in the wind. *I love it here, this warm and fragrant place.*

"Absolute coherence is what we're lookin for, all right. You, if anyone, should know that. We keep fightin wars to prove it." Though speaking to Duty, Zane was fixed on her with an odd sideways beseeching stare, as if he'd been caught stealing a look but couldn't let go. She was embarrassed to have seen how vulnerable he'd seemed. The word eviscerated came up in her mind. *Empty and hollowed out.*

Finally he broke contact and grabbed a cigarette, actually looked at Duty. "You gonna read us the damned couplets, or whatever they're called?"

"Sasha? Would you turn down the radio a little?...Thank you," as she obliged.

He held his paper in front of him, wiggled a little like a cat about to pounce, and slowly—emphasizing each word, raising his hand at the end of each line—he delivered.

"Change
When the day is over, there will be confidence.
A foundation for progress.
It is beneficial to persist.
Aversion goes away.
There is a change. It takes some time to adjust,
but then it'll be clear that things have changed for the better.

Just hold on. Initial aversion to it will go away."

"Isn't that amazing? How each line fits in to the same theme?"

"It's certainly something," Zane said to the floor, "but how can we know what it means without knowing what the question was?"

"Typical western response," Duty poured more wine into both his and Zane's glass. He lifted the jug toward Sasha but she shook her head without making eye contact.

"Looking for some identifiable, empirical answer, some simple cause and effect, instead of opening yourself to the experience. Experiencing instead of knowing. Learned that in Nam."

"When you were a sniper?" Now Zane was focused on Duty's averted face. Sasha wanted to hear more about Duty's time in the war, and silently thanked Zane for bringing it up.

"Well, after…"

"Why'd you choose that job?" Zane jumped in when Duty hesitated. "Wasn't it much more dangerous?"

"Than staying in the unit? No. In fact, I did it to improve my survival odds. Ask Richard what happened to his legs. It wasn't him stepping on a mine; it was the guy next to him who wasn't paying enough attention. I decided I wanted to be responsible for what happened to me. Not get wasted because of some stoned-out fool stumbling through the brush, drawing fire. As a sniper, I could disappear by myself into the jungle for days at a time without anyone else caring. I'm sure the CO figured me for dead every time I left and was surprised when I showed back up. Anyway, after a couple of months everyone pretty much left me alone."

Sasha saw that Zane was coming back to life, sitting straighter, not exactly puffing up, but definitely more contained. She watched him plug in to his friend's story, engaging again. "Did you know Richard in Nam, then?"

Duty expelled smoke in a steady narrow stream toward the ceiling. "Nope. But I found out from him that we were both in the first Cav.

In the A Shau in '69. My company was sent out to capture hills—blood, guts and body parts on sixty degree slopes—but his company was deployed on the other side of the valley in a blocking action to keep any NVA from getting in behind us. That's where he got blown. Lotta guys got it in the A Shau."

"So, when you were out in the field by yourself, what'd you do," Zane asked. "Wouldn't shootin someone give away your position?"

Duty looked at him over the edge of his tumbler of wine. "Exactly. Shooting wasn't such a good idea. I usually just dug in and watched from cover. Sometimes there'd be dinks all around me. I'd see them dropping down into tunnels, or in patrols threading through the elephant grass. But once I was on my own, I never shot at anyone." He put his empty glass down. "And if you don't mind, I'd rather not talk about this shit anymore."

Sasha leaned back in her chair and didn't know what to think. She found the very brief glimpse Duty had given them of his Nam experience quite upsetting, far more than she'd have ever predicted ahead of time. She didn't know the source of her queasiness, except for the obvious senseless slaughter. But she had watched the dying, heard the screams of terror escalate on the nightly news for years, so it was more than that—something about Duty's delivery gnawed at her, his sort of canned speech tone, flat and without affect. But that wasn't it, either, she realized. It was that he'd used the word "dink."

Zane, however, seemed to have had some kind of mood transfusion. Instead of slouching, head down, he looked energized. Sitting up. Alert. Wheels turning, gears meshing. Reminded her of how taken she'd been that drizzly Moratorium morning in Portland. *Zane actually believes he has something unique or important to share, believes he can persuade people, change their outlook, organize them. After he told me about his father, I thought we'd draw closer together. I wanted to think we'd be somehow rejuvenated, we'd rediscover each other. That hasn't happened, but when I look at him now, this minute, sitting with his legs*

168

crossed widely, his hand on his propped up ankle, he exudes the graceful passion he's capable of. No one would see that but me.

Duty interrupted her musings. "You could turn up the FM again, Sasha. Storytime's done." She got up and twisted the dial. Before she could get back to the chair, the front door burst open, blowing out half the candles. Duty was on his feet in a millisecond and Zane's mouth was wide as though yelling. A forceful rush of cold, wet air circled the room when Greg stumbled in, drenched and dripping, wild eyed and red-faced frantic.

"What the hell," Zane said sharply, as Duty moved quickly to close the door and turn on the overhead light. "What's wrong? Did you walk here? You don't even have a hat."

Sasha was frozen in front of her chair, immobile, frightened. Stuck to the floor as her mind started a string of *No. No. No. Don't tell me. I don't want to hear.*

Greg gasped out his words, stopping to catch his breath between bursts. "Was in town. Got a ride out tonight. When I got there, Wade Perkins was sitting in his pickup on the highway in front of the bridge. He stopped me, wouldn't let me past. Said Perry had fallen off the bluff down onto the river rocks last night and was dead, that someone had called an ambulance and he'd picked up the news on the ambulance service's CB. Said I couldn't go on the claim anymore, that if he caught me there he'd get Dave Brereton to haul me in. To make sure, he drove me down here to your driveway, told me to get out of his truck, warned me again that if he even saw me on that part of the river, I'd wish he hadn't."

"Perry's dead? Jesus fuckin Christ! How'd it happen?" Zane pushed, but Greg only stared while Duty steered him over to the warmth of the stove.

Sasha's thoughts went blank for a moment, stunned into abject adrenaline rushing emptiness. As she stared at Greg dripping by the stove, his coat steaming, some words finally came, if only to herself. *I just can't bear it.*

Chapter Ten

Andrew Jackson, noted Indian fighter and slaveholder, was the single most powerful voice behind the Indian Relocation Act of 1830 which required native Americans to move west of the Mississippi river, giving up millions of acres on which they'd lived for centuries. As president, Jackson told these original people that "If now they shall refuse to accept the liberal terms offered, they only must be liable for whatever evils & dificulties may arise. I feel conscious of having done my duty to my red children and if any failure of my good intention arises, it will be attributable to their want of duty to themselves, not to me."

Sasha hadn't slept at all through the long, starless, cloud-covered night. Painful stabbing realizations of Perry's death came in convulsive waves, like amplified menstrual cramps, punctuated by violent episodes of noisy, beating rain that didn't diminish until near dawn. Zane had been releasing noxious wine gas as he slept, and his not-knowing put her out more than the olfactory assault itself. *Oblivious yet again. Completely unaware.* She was already irritated with him for not bothering to get close to Perry, as she had. A refrain kept cycling to the forefront: Zane hadn't admired Perry enough. She guessed that was what tugged at her already weakened sense of equilibrium—that Zane hadn't cared properly. An unflattering admission for sure. But there it was.

She'd lain awake, racked with visions of Perry's broken, bloodied body. She saw him lying there, boneless, a leathery sack draped like a coverlet over river rock. As these imaginings took shape, her mind on full speed brought forth one agonizing gut-punch after another. *Mom's cancer. No father. Getting the embryo vacuumed out. Brooks pushing into me. Zane and Aurora. I can't bear to think about the two of them together. Perry.* Like a movie scene being filmed take after take, in her mind's eye she watched Perry lose balance in slow motion, and fall headfirst. No sound. Tumbling over and over. *He took me seriously. Cared about how I thought. Listened. Wasn't out to get anything from me. Called me "young lady." Paid attention.*

171

Coming to grips with the fact that she'd never hear his steady, resonating voice again—admitting the starkness of that—was physically painful. Her throat throbbed, raw from sinus drainage. Her eyes burned from sudden crying jags she couldn't predict, or effectively stop. Her temples were sore to the touch. She pictured herself looking at herself in the mirror of her vanity. *Yes, dear girl, you're quite the mess.*

Her mother's death from cancer had been the inescapable conclusion of a logical process. Certainly not unexpected. Sasha had watched her physically and mentally draw inward, shrink, retract. Bones like a bird. Skin hanging in folds. Eyes vacant, though the Orthodox nuns wrapped head-to-foot in black twill had told her she could hear what they were saying. Sasha found that information particularly hurtful at the time, unduly painful to contemplate. That her mother was listening to the nuns explaining why they weren't hydrating her. "Let the Lord do his work." That her mother was condemned to be aware of such impersonal care right up to the end? Well, that was cruel, though not unusual. The dying being written off as viable beings well before they actually expired.

But Perry had been ripped away violently, as if in the middle of conversation. She'd had no time to prepare, to steel herself or fortify her feelings. When she tried to recreate his face from memory, he was already a past tense jumble of smeared pictures with indistinct edges. His death wasn't just another loss, though it was certainly that. More demoralizing was that she felt as though some beastly hand had reached out into her future and torn out a large chunk of rewarding and enriching possibilities. Leaving her with a shuttering series of isolated moments back-lit in her memory, a scream out loud anguish.

She'd had no idea she'd be reacting like this, as she watched Zane's chest rise and fall with his breathing. *The meaning of quotidian, this unthinking, involuntary suspiration. Breathing until you don't anymore. Happens to everyone.* She found herself brought up short, face to face with mundane and silent finality, by its brutally impervious hardness, its unforgiving inevitability. *Shoving Katmandu and Angor Wat to the back burner is a bad bargain. That much I'm coming to understand. That much I learned from Perry.*

Greg had spent the night on the front room sofa, wrapped in a green wool army blanket Duty had brought down from his room. When Sasha looked in before making coffee—not wanting to wake him—she'd been greeted by the unwelcome sight of a ginger-haired testicle poking its way through a gaping hole in his underwear, quivering with his sleeping breath. His legs were sprawled apart, knees bent, holding the blanket up like a tent so she could see inside. *Great. And a good morning to you, too. Am I living in a barracks now?* Not that she wasn't used to seeing men naked. Hardly anyone wore swimming suits, for instance, down at the river. When they all took Diamond Jim's gutted school bus to the commune at Takilma for softball, the Illinois river there was full of nudity. Everyone just hanging out, swimming, basking in the sun. Even all the little kids. She found that refreshingly natural and never gave a thought to feeling uncomfortable or vulnerable. But Greg's display on the couch was unexpected, unsettling, and in her own damned living room.

She'd never warmed to Greg, despite Zane's assurances that he was actually quite smart "when you get to know him." Sasha hadn't been able to summon any energy for getting to know him, even though Perry obviously had seen something in Eamon, as he always called him. She knew Greg and Zane went all the way back to grade school in Medford and their Roosevelt Roughrider teams; but, as near as she could tell—and she'd had over three years to accumulate evidence—he was a layabout, someone who didn't seem to have any redeeming qualities to make up for his habit of drinking himself into a coma every chance he got. *Soapy said she caught him peeing on their living room philodendron one night. Thought he was outside. Laughed it off the next day.*

173

As she filled the electric percolator with water, she bent forward slightly and craned her neck to see the narrow band of sky through the kitchen window, visible above the towering hillside. Baby blue and clear. Maybe things would dry out? No need to fire up the kitchen stove.

Dumping Yuban into the percolator basket, she snapped the top on and plugged it in. *Now Greg's without a place to live. We still have a spare room upstairs, but I don't think I could take playing den mother to another Oregon pig-boy. Be like living at The Alibi: weed, beer and loud music day and night. What used to be our home is turning into something entirely different. First the Fausens disappear, and clouds of paranoia settle in. Now Perry's gone too. The dam's coming. Happening here on this piece of river. We used to be almost isolated, being so far out, quite peaceful. But now I feel we're in the grasp of some negative force field, some sucking black hole. Zane's withdrawn again, not really present, preoccupied, distracted. And Duty? Mary Jesus, I don't know what's happening with him. Don't even know how I feel about any of it, except that I worry I'm being battered by circumstances and other people's needs. And right now I'm exhausted from no sleep, from grief. Not just for Perry, that's true, but God this one hurts.*

"You makin coffee yet?" Zane was coming down the stairs wearing a pair of draw-string pants Sasha had made from a thrift store tablecloth, his powder blue San Diego Chargers t-shirt stretched tight. She had to admit he cut an intensely magnetic and attractive figure, despite everything.

"Shush. Greg's asleep."

An hour later everyone was up, bumping into each other in the tiny kitchen, getting their coffee before dispersing to the living room. The FM was on low volume, except when the news came on and Zane cranked it up so as not to miss what Nixon was lying about, or who had recently been called to testify. *The noose is tightenin,* Zane thought. *This Watergate stuff is a lot of anti-war disgust comin to a head. Nixon's the one who bombed the shit out of Cambodia and Laos. Well, with Kissinger's*

174

help. Anyone who's read his book on American foreign policy could have predicted it. Dogs should have been on Nixon's ass for that alone. He's losin white house staff by the hands' full. Bout time. After most of a year pretty much twistin in the wind. He took his coffee into the living room, sat down in the chair by the front window. *Sasha's in misery. Perry's death has thrown her for a loop. I can tell from how the little muscles in her lips tighten up when she's hurt or angry.*

The closing bars of The Youngbloods', "Darkness, Darkness" leaked softly into the room, sound flowing like smoke swirling. Zane hummed along under his breath. *Be my blanket. Cover me with your endless night.* Sasha was cleaning up dishes after having fed everyone pancakes. She'd had to make two batches of batter since Duty put away eight himself.

Zane concentrated on Greg, who seemed to be in shock, sitting on the sofa, staring at the floor. His already-wild hair was matted in places, stringy and tangled. He'd put his clothes back on. They'd been hung over chair backs around the wood stove to dry all night.

"How can Wade Fuckin Perkins keep me away from my cabin?" He spewed it out like projectile vomit. Wagging his head back and forth slowly, looking at no one specifically. "He's not even a cop, just a Forest Service flunky."

Zane put his coffee down on the table, shaking out a cigarette and lighting it. "Doesn't make sense. The Forest Service doesn't have a goddamn thing to do with it."

Duty sat down on the living room couch next to Greg and began rolling a joint, licking his fingers for traction. He was wearing fatigue pants and a gray sweatshirt with a leaping salmon on the front. "Sasha and I met a guy who said he worked for BLM yesterday at the J-Ville Tav. Seemed nice enough. Maybe a little nosey. Marine Corp Korea vet."

"You guys went to the tavern?" Zane tried not to sound whiney.

"Relax, Zane." Sasha stood in the kitchen doorway with a pink dishtowel over her left shoulder, her right thumb hooked into a back pocket. "It wasn't a date."

Greg interrupted, picking up his thread as though he'd been the only one talking. "Perkins said Perry fell off the trail and hit the rocks. But Perry built that trail, walked on it every damned day for forty years. Besides, he never went anywhere without his wizard's staff for balance. I don't believe it—that he fell. Didn't start raining until this morning, so everything would have still been dry when it happened."

Duty passed Greg the joint and immediately set about rolling another. Small clouds of smoke hung in the air, mixing with Harvey Mandel's guitar riffs from the FM. "Sure seems fishy," Zane commented. "Who found him? Do you know?..."

"I got no idea," Greg blurted quickly.

"...cause sure as hell no one could have seen him from the road. You'd have to be right down on the river."

Sasha still stood in the kitchen doorway, leaning against one jamb, and Zane could tell she was barely managing to hold things together. Her face was drawn and pale, her eyes red-rimmed. Shoulders a bit hunched. Head tilted down. *She's devastated. I know she thinks I didn't like him enough, didn't share in their connection. But I really wanted to stay out, let her have him to herself. Wish I knew what to say or do, how to help her through it.*

He decided to change the subject. "So, Greg. Sasha tells me you put on a show for her this morning. Exposing yourself for all the world to see."

Greg was hardly listening. "Huh?"

"Private parts poking through your shorts." Zane could see he had him at a severe disadvantage. Poor guy didn't have a clue.

"What are you talkin about?"

"When Sasha came down this morning, your blanket was all hiked up to your waist an your nuts were hangin out."

"Are you kiddin me? Man, I was asleep. How would I know?"

Zane kicked himself for putting Greg on the spot. Why did he want to pile on? Wasn't how he wanted to come off. He tried to see if he could sound magnanimous.

"Don't feel too bad. There's a classic story that the ancient Greek philosopher Diogenes was famous for masturbating in public regularly. Right there in the agora with all the movers and shakers he'd whip it out, get to work. If anyone objected to his behavior, Diogenes said somethin like it was too bad that when he was hungry he couldn't just rub his stomach to feel full."

"Not exactly a philosophical analysis," Duty waved the joint to see if anyone wanted any.

"Like you'd know," Zane smiled. "After that ridiculousness about not tellin anyone what your *I Ching* question was because it wouldn't come true."

Duty pretended not to hear. "Wasn't Diogenes that cat who carried a lantern around looking for an honest man?"

"That's him," Zane said, "the great Cynic. He'd shove his light right up into people's faces, stare at them awhile before rejecting them. Course that's just a story."

"I knew a guy like that in Nam," Duty said, sucking deeply, holding it in, his voice stretched into a wispy falsetto. "At Pleiku. Crazy spade by the name of Duvall." Smoke billowed out and his voice dropped back down to normal. "Had this sly smile, man, really wild eyes like Steppen Fetchit. Drove around in a jitney delivering mail and shit. Talking to himself. Always the same, like a mantra. 'Don't believe the man. No siree. Can't believe the man. He only lies. Can't believe no one, 'cept Duvall. Duvall don't lie.' Rumors said he'd been assigned to base cause no one would go in the bush with him, especially if he was armed. Great scam he had going. He'd figured a foolproof way to make it back home in one piece."

When the conversation died, no one picking it up, Greg reminded them that they promised to take him up to Perry's so he could get his stuff out of the cabin. "I don't have much there, but it's all I got."

"If we can get Duty to go over to Lester's an call Richard, we could all go together. Richard knows everyone, be good insurance."

Duty responded without looking up. "Nice passive aggressive. Get me to do it. But you're right, no one is gonna give Richard any shit when he's staggering around on his aluminum legs and crutches." He had begun another roll-up, while Janis and Big Brother started "Piece of My Heart" quietly in the background. "But why bother Lester? I hardly know the guy. Just give me the bus keys and I'll drive down to Richard's."

"Sasha's got em."

By around one in the afternoon Greg, Duty, Richard and Zane had sufficiently primed themselves for the drive upriver to Perry's, or what used to be Perry's. Duty was on auto-pilot, rolling one joint after another, handing them out, until he finally forgot what he was doing and locked onto watching the cattle out the window. Richard's eyes sparkled, his eyebrows arched as though someone were pulling his skin up toward the hairline, as if he'd suddenly had a bad facelift, one that left him looking perpetually shocked like Phyllis Diller. A sure sign he was stoned out of his gourd, Zane knew. Richard's eyes gave him away.

Sasha and Erasmus had retreated upstairs in the last hour, right after Greg discovered the un-opened half gallon of wine where she'd hidden it under the sink. The volume of the music and the pitch of their voices had been creeping steadily louder as the wine disappeared.

Zane wasn't unaware of Sasha's need to escape; he knew she disliked loudness, especially coming from multiple sources—too much going on at once. She'd said as much and more. The 'more' being that he knew she resented their space being invaded by partying males. He also knew that he was more than merely complicit in fomenting these invasions, that he often organized them. That he would, like Duty today, drive down to Richard's to collect him when

Sasha was obviously angry about something, when he felt skewered, on the spot. Was as likely as not to prolong his nights out by dragging someone back home with him, usually some down and outer. Zane knew he did it for protection, having a shield. Sometimes he'd bring a couple, once a bi-racial pair he'd suave-dogged from *The Jubilee*, though they'd seemed aware they might be in the wrong place. Brought them back with him, waking Sasha to help play host at two in the morning.

He knew she saw through him, saw that his habit of bringing strangers home was, to a great extent, driven by his own guilt from leaving her alone in the house while he was out on the town.

It was their pattern. Or his, at least. Feeling guilty, waiting for her to react to his behavior. He imagined what he thought she'd be feeling or thinking—always something negative—and fabricated responses to these made-up complaints. Bottom line was he knew he was continually stretching her trust to breaking points. *You always hurt the one you love. Clarence "Frogman" Henry.* So that a frown or sharp word from her could send him scurrying for emotional cover which he usually found in alcohol or weed. Easily managed in what he saw as a new counter-culture leisure class where jobs were one thing but careers were tantamount to selling out to the establishment. *Greening of America. Wear headbands and bellbottoms, do macrame, throw the frisbee. Free sex. Outlive the bastards.*

He knew the flaws in thinking all the militant crazies would just fade away, though the knowledge itself rarely helped. Logic, common sense and any lessons he'd learned from his own painful experiences went out the window when he'd watch himself plow headlong into disasters waiting to happen, pushed by a desperately constant need to spit in the face of authority, or anything that represented it. So that, in his mind, settling down, joining the rank and file, was tantamount to suicide. Was giving up to the grinding powers of business as usual. He'd read his economic theory and understood that, at heart, the concept of profit always entailed getting over on someone, tricking them, schmoozing, lying—either to the customer, to employees or both. *So thanks for the analysis Zane. Stephen Dedalus talkin about Lessing in Portrait of the Artist. Ultra fuckin profound. I gotta get us outta the house and on the road if we're gonna go. I'm losin focus.*

Zane weaved his way between Richard's crutches and Duty so he could cut the FM. With that source of noise silenced, Richard and Duty's voices sounded inordinately loud. They seemed to notice that themselves and damped down their argument about whether Leon Redbone was just a scam.

"I mean, listen to him, man," Richard's voice almost squeaked it was so high. "Whatever it is he's doin, it ain't singin."

Greg was captivated by the cover art on the Savoy Brown *Hellbound Train* album; he was leaning against the cold woodstove, the large wine bottle dangling from his free hand, bouncing slowly off his knee. It occurred to Zane that all four of them were lit enough that, if they didn't start soon, the afternoon would ebb into darkness and they'd likely still be in the same places, arguing about immensely important trivialities. And he could envision that all-too-familiar scene too. *Can't do that. Not now, after everything else already.*

He headed for the front door. "In the immortal words of Boon Hogganbeck: Them that's goin, get in the goddamn bus; them that ain't, get outta the goddamn way. Richard gets to sit in front cause his legs won't fit in back. Time to kennel up. Leave the wine, Greg."

"VA says I'm gonna get new legs next year. With knees that work," Richard announced, his eyes still weirdly wide open.

"That's the least they could do." Duty was steering Greg down the porch steps to clear the way for Richard's lurching method of four-point walking. Zane took up the rear, feeling he was herding cattle, it took so long to get everyone moving.

He wondered whether the cloudless skies would hold. Living on the river between high ridges meant that the tiny strip of sky he could see wasn't a reliable indicator of what the weather might be in half an hour. Dark and brooding clouds, purple-gray, could boil up over the mountains in a hurry, and all too often did.

By the time Zane pulled onto the river road, the bus laboring with the weight. Richard and Duty were already deep into an arms-waving, exaggerated facial expressions discussion about whether it mattered how you died. Greg had got them going when he said something to the effect that he hoped Perry hadn't suffered, which ignited Duty's bio-philosophical side to tell Greg it was a stupid thing to say. Perry was dead, so what did it matter what his last moments were like?

"It's not like he's going to remember it," Duty said sarcastically, looking out the windshield from the wooden bench Zane had built for a back seat. "He's dead. Doesn't matter what he was thinking. One second you're conscious, the next you're not there anymore. Come on, Richard, you saw it over and over in-country. Someone's there, then they're not. Not aware of anything, especially not what they were thinking or feeling or doing the second before. They're just fucking gone."

"You're talkin about dudes getting smoked by mortar rounds, artillery or landmines, where there was nuthin left." Richard couldn't turn around to speak directly to Duty since his metal legs were wedged into the tight floor space of the front seat. "I'm talkin about like someone being tortured for a long time. Or being murdered, choked to death. Terrified. How can you say it doesn't matter?"

"Because once they're dead they're not terrified; they don't exist. They could have suffered a lot beforehand, but it's not like they're gonna carry that around with them. For them, everything stops. They stop. Nothing exists anymore. The big void, ya know. Oblivion. Being and then nothingness, man."

"Perry had that book," Greg said, looking at his hands folded on his lap as the bus vibrated and rattled over the rough highway.

The road hugged hillsides—it'd been cut into the slopes like an L— and as they followed the cratered asphalt upstream, the narrow

181

twisting upper Applegate valley lay on their right, a few small pastures for grazing marked off with barbed wire or cyclone fencing. Cattle milling lazily in the sun. Thin strands of smoke rising from farm houses cloaked in shade, tucked in against the opposite hillsides.

Zane realized this was the second time in a month he'd been forced to drive upstream because somebody had died. The Fausens. Of course they were dead. No clues, no sign of them. He didn't subscribe to theories they'd been scooped up by some UFO. Not that he didn't believe in extra-terrestrials. From his perspective, given even our meager understanding of the vastness of the cosmos, to think that only earth supported conscious life was right up there with notions of immortality as convincing evidence of just how moronically egotistical people, as a species, generally were. This was a refrain he couldn't shake. It was infused into every institution he could think of. Waspishness woven dominantly into the social fabric. Heaven above somewhere in fluffy clouds beyond the Van Allen belt—maybe in a different dimension—and hell deep under the planet's crust. Fire lit grottos of burning, screeching sinners. One or the other. Like depending on Nero or Caligula's hesitating teasing thumb, up or down, and eternity waiting in the wings. He didn't buy it for a second.

Richard was still goggle-eyed; not surprising since he was sucking on what was left of a joint mashed between his thumb and index finger. Zane checked the rearview mirror to see Duty staring straight ahead out the windshield but seemingly somewhere else, somewhere distant. Greg contemplated his dirty fingernails, his mouth screwed up on one side like he was displeased with what he saw. Zane flashed on *Should name this bus "Further." Spray it with day-glo swirls. Course then the cops'd be stoppin me all the time. Duty with a camera and microphone. Button-holin the uptight like Kesey's cross-country trip. Electric Kool-Aid. I'd have to skip doin all the acid, though some opium would come in handy. Be feelin again like I'm wrapped in an electric blanket dialed to*

about four. Oriental wisdom flowin. Siddhartha. Krishna. Sun Tzu's Art of
War. Breeze from the East, Cal Tjader.

Without any advanced notice, Richard launched into a story about how he'd totaled his Firebird 400 two years before just this side of J-Ville hill, after closing time at the tavern. Fumbled the hand controls coming off the downgrade and ran into the hillside ditch where he hit a protruding boulder—flipped the Firebird up on its side. The sheriff's deputy who'd showed up at the scene was Bradley Deerdorf, a guy he'd known since middle school in Ruch.

"Bradley...you couldn't call him Brad—he hated that...Bradley said, 'Richard. Let's put your legs on one side of the car and you on the other. Make it look like you've been cut in half.' So he got me to lie on the uphill side. That is, me, my real body pressed against the front wheel, the stumps you know, and then he put my legs with levis and fake shoes stickin out the other side. I was freezin my butt off, squashed down on the wet ground. Took half a dozen pictures with his flash Polaroid. I still got one on my wall. Plus, he wrote it up that I'd had to swerve to avoid a trophy buck that was standin in the road. And, he didn't bother with any breathalyzer, did Bradley. Gave me a ride home before anyone else could arrive, me bein a disabled hero an all. Hell, he even came in and smoked a bowl with me. So's we'd be even-steven. He had somethin on me; I had somethin on him. Leveled things out. The law of the back woods."

Zane could see that neither Duty nor Greg had been paying attention to Richard's story. Mostly under his breath, and clearly fuzzy about any concept of being in key, Duty softly hissed The Marine Hymn, keeping his eyes front and center, though not seemingly focused on anything. Greg was running his fingers through his long, frenetically curled and heavily matted hair, tugging to separate strands. *Probably twigs and bits of leaves buried in that mess.* Zane concentrated on the twisting road, trying to stay in his lane. *Feels like a Firesign Theater skit. "We're all bozos on this bus. Antelope*

183

Freeway, one-sixteenth mile. Roll another bummer and leave it on the side table."

The first thing Zane noticed when they came out of the last turn before Perry's was that the trolley was gone. The swinging bridge still spanned the chasm between high banks, but the red rusted wire cables that had secured the trolley now hung limply against the rock face across the river. When he stopped the bus at the dirt turnout fronting the footbridge, Zane saw that the large pulley wheel that used to be bolted to a tree trunk on this side had been ripped out, leaving deep, sap-leaking wounds, chunks of bark strewn on the dusty ground. Someone had strung an official looking "Keep Out" sign from the rope and wire sides of the swaying bridge to block access or at least discourage it. Zane took it all in at a glance.

He jumped out of the bus as soon as he'd set the brake and hurried to the edge of the cliff where he could look down into the thirty or so feet deep canyon. On the far side river rocks he saw what was left of the trolley, jaggedly splintered sun-bleached boards, bent chicken wire still clinging to some of the pieces. Zane thought it had broken all its bones. Retaining its basic shape, but looking like it had been stepped on by some Bunyan of the woods.

Richard's legs banged against metal as he wrenched himself out of the bus, swearing loudly. Duty helped him gain his balance while Greg joined Zane at the lip of the cliff, hands on hips, staring. "Jesus," he whispered, "it was still here last night." By now, the four of them stood in bright sunlight, their shadows stretched out behind them.

"Makes no sense," Duty still had his arm draped over Richard's shoulders. "Why just tear stuff up? What's the point of that?"

To keep us out. Zane smiled to himself—his lifelong habit of inappropriately responding to bad news. *Mrs. Kevner's nursery school, smellin of sour milk upchuck. Is that a cliché? But it is what I remember. Pudgy little kid said his father had died in the hospital, then asked me why I was smilin. Just like that, put me on the spot. I didn't know, couldn't say, just grinned like an idiot. There's a column of smoke comin from the flats.*

"Hey!" He pointed at the dense doug fir, lodgepole pine and cedar patterned forest and the thin winding stream of smoke across the river. "Somethun's burnin."

Chapter Eleven

From the earliest days of white settlement, native peoples faced organized and over-administrated bureaucratic efforts to separate them from their traditional spiritual life and convert them to Christianity. Natives, especially children, were also discouraged—primarily through corporal punishment—from speaking their ancestral languages and were similarly forced to adopt white clothing and culture. Those who best adapted were taught table etiquette and manners in these religious schools, under the assumption that this knowledge would help them obtain work as domestic servants. Most of the children, however, were destined for stoop labor or unemployment.

For several decades, the U.S. government awarded control of reservations to various denominations of Protestant churches. These churches were thereby provided with captive audiences to educate in their own particular doctrinal ways—with no oversight whatsoever— as long as they continued their work of getting native people to assimilate into white culture as largely unskilled workers at little or no cost to the government. Christianity thus helped create yet another labor underclass of the dispossessed and unwanted.

Tribal lands, millions upon millions of acres, were silently folded into the physical fabric of a steadily expanding United States with silent cruelty reminiscent of The Inquisition.

From their upstairs bedroom window Sasha watched the VW bus lumber down the long driveway, cross the narrow wooden bridge and disappear behind the line of Scots pine and vine maple crowding the bank that separated the highway from the river. Thank God, she thought, softly stroking Erasmus who yawned luxuriously, curled on the bed. Finally, she had the house to herself, if only for a brief while. Quiet and calm. Living out here, she'd come to value the numerous tones of nature: small animal chatter, the whisking of wind through bushes and trees, the continual backdrop rustling of riffles on the river, so she felt assaulted when the house filled up with men. They'd be back soon enough, she knew, and once again the downstairs would be saturated with testosterone, weed and alcohol-fueled maleness.

Increasingly raw voices rising. Music cranked up. Conglomerated, layered, infuriating racket. *Are they all going to stay?*

The instant Greg had barged through their door last night, nearly hysterical and thoroughly soaked—before he'd said a word—she'd felt the plug pulled on her visions of a calm and comfortable farm house in the country. Something crucially pivotal about the moment: the sedating curry/ginger living room warmth pierced violently by a chilling rush of wet, cattle-stenched wind. From that moment on, and through the long night, the reality of Perry's death insinuated itself into her consciousness like a rampant, spreading infection loose in her cells, soaked into every thought. A cloudy film over everything she saw, distorting balance. A violent, shocking, existential loss. Emptying out. Draining away. *Really thrown for a loop. Feel like I'm shrinking, evaporating.*

But losing Perry was only one cause of her emotional chaos. *Zane. Mary Jesus. I asked him how long Greg planned on staying here and he just hung his head, left the room without answering. He disassociates when he feels threatened in even the most trivial ways. Acts like he's under attack. Non-responsive. It's excruciating having to drag out every word. And then, when I put them together, they invariably add up to a convoluted way of saying "I don't know," like he'd just been neutered and couldn't possibly be expected to act like any kind of equal partner. Is my sense of betrayal sticking out? My disenchantment? Learning he was abused by Larry, I've been trying to cut him some slack. More than usual. But if nothing changes, if he can't get outside his neuroses, then childhood trauma or not, sizzling sex or not, compatible politics or not...I wonder if I won't have to save myself. It's a cruelty of nature that he's so persuasive and confident in front of a crowd but goes tongue-tied with me as if I've somehow morphed into the enemy. But he knows I don't like Greg, can't find any of his so-called redeeming qualities. Perry saw something in him, I guess. Let him live in the small cabin. But I don't want him hanging around, god forbid moving in. So I say something about it and Zane feels guilty, like he always does when he brings someone home with him. Becomes the victim. I can't help but think he's not able just to be with me, that he needs others for safety, for a buffer kind of, a shield...from what? From me? Easy to see and even easier to feel that he's more comfortable surrounded by his friends, but even strangers get the royal treatment. Then, when his sheepish guilt kicks in, he goes away, slams the door, locks me out. And I'm by myself. Talking with Perry gave me a sense of connecting with another being. I mean opening up, expanding. Zane once said I was using Perry as a father substitute. Cheap shot, and I told him so. Perry gave himself to me, let me in on conversations that mattered. What Zane used to do. Now all that's in rubble and I'm alone again. I can't remember exactly how his voice sounded; his distinctive tone has disappeared like the final reverberations of a gong wearing off. Won't hear him say "Young Lady" anymore. Never could pin down whether he was having fun with me or being quaintly respectful. Didn't matter. He was talking to the me inside the shell. The me Zane seems to want to avoid these days. I don't think I'm being some kind of clingy, spoiled bimbo. I'm not Charo. I just don't want to be stuck filling a secondary role as Zane's "old lady" in a man-centered universe. With Perry I felt seen as a person with integrity in my own right.* She ran her fingers against the grain through Erasmus' thick fur. He twitched slightly but didn't open his eyes. She smoothed him back down before she went downstairs.

The living room was a mess and, as she surveyed the clutter, she was struck by what a tired cliché she was acting out. Cleaning up after other people, having to flee from the brain-numbing noise without recourse. She wasn't exaggerating. That was just fact. *Duty is pretty easy to have around; he knows how to read people, knows when to fade into the woodwork. But Greg can't even remember to take water for the toilet tank in with him, for heaven's sake. Someone has to hand it in while he's sitting there stinking with his pants around his ankles. He invariably leaves the empty water jug on the floor when he's done. That's the least of his irritating traits. I could count the ways. He trashes the atmosphere, and certainly doesn't bring out the best in Zane. Richard's more interested in staying loaded all the time than anything else. Quite the group we've collected. Not what I envisioned in Portland, when his blunt honesty drew me in. Where'd that go? We're not exactly living in a healthy relationship, whatever that is, whatever it means. Since the abortion. Since the Aquarius party. Mescalin and stupidity. But we're not connecting in ways conducive to growth, emotional enrichment, or expanding horizons. Backing each other up? We used to do that. Used to share that between us—a commitment of support. I admit the sex still almost always takes me to another place. Our parts fit exquisitely. We find rhythms together. Pulse-racing, breath-taking passion. Hot and radiating attraction. But that doesn't happen so much anymore. We don't ball enough. And we don't talk nearly enough.*

She heard squirrels chuddering outside, turned to look out the open front window and saw the top of Lester's pickup lurching between the oleander, creeping ivy and blackberry vines that clung to the fence lines bordering the driveway. She supposed Lester was coming to get a hand with the cattle, though he usually waited until later in the day.

As the truck pulled up by their front porch, she was surprised to see Adeline driving, her head barely visible over the steering wheel. Sasha's first thought was that Lester had gotten hurt in some way and Adeline had come for help. She'd never seen her driving Lester's truck before. Egged on by an apprehensive curiosity, she went out on the porch to see what was up.

Adeline climbed down out of the pickup, holding onto the door until she had her rubber boots safely on the ground still soggy from the heavy rains last night. In this afternoon's sun, the air was muggy. Like invisible steam rising, Sasha thought. Adeline was wearing a red striped t-shirt under splotchy bib overalls, her boots splashed with mud and cow muck. When Sasha looked at her face, she knew something wasn't right. She'd never seen Adeline when she wasn't smiling—it was her natural expression, her face to the world—but today she appeared distraught, twitchy, obviously bothered.

"Can you give us a hand, hon? We got a breech-birth springer and now we gotta pull the dead calf." She hadn't let loose of the truck door and Sasha could tell she wasn't going to. The woman was clearly agitated, nervous. A way Sasha had never seen her. Almost unconsciously, Sasha began walking toward the porch steps, and next she knew she was down on the ground, her tennis shoes squishing, as she rounded the front of the dirty and dented truck to the passenger side like a sleepwalker. That is, she knew she was getting into the pickup, but she hadn't the foggiest idea what a springer was, or why a calf was dead, or what she was supposed to do about it. *Shit just keeps piling up.* Normally, she wouldn't use that word, would have found it offensively crass, a common denominator for common people, like saying fuck and fucking every tenth word. *Like Greg.* But today it seemed sadly appropriate, just popping into her head.

Adeline had regained her place behind the wheel, pulled her door closed. The windows were down and Sasha could smell wet alfalfa, stale tobacco, a hint of slimy river moss. "Don't worry, honey," Adeline said evenly. "All you gotta do is wave your arms and stand there. Nothin to it. You'll see once we get goin. We need to get her to a fence corner so Lester can get a rope on her, tie her down." Adeline drove just like Lester, grinding gears. Red dust puffed out the dashboard air vents as they bounced over the sagging bridge when Sasha finally found her voice.

"I think I know what a breech birth is, but what's a springer?"

Adeline threw her body weight against the steering wheel in order to make the left hand turn onto the highway, forcing Sasha to jam her feet onto the floor and press a hand to the roof of the cab to absorb the bouncing torque. Once on the pavement, Adeline kept her eyes on the road as she spoke. Sasha could swear she was looking through the steering wheel instead of over it. "A springer's a heifer that gets pregnant too soon, too young. Happens sometimes. This one took off trottin around when she started to birth. Seen that before. Usually the calf just slides on out, fore feet first, if the heifer takes off. But this one's a breech, so back legs and butt came out. Then it stopped. So the calf's still in there. Maybe it's already dead—no way to tell—but now we got to pull it. Damndest thing I ever saw."

191

Sasha couldn't help cringing. It came involuntarily, stomach muscles clinching, bile rising. As Adeline leaned her upper body against the steering wheel again for another tight, left-hand turn onto their bridge, Sasha spotted Lester standing in the middle of his big pasture, the one bordered by the river and stretching far back to the timbered hillside. He was a khaki stick-figure at first, but took on form as Adeline slowed the pickup, stopping finally at the gate used for feeding and moving the tractor in and out. Cattle grazed in the sunny half of the pasture closest to the river. Sasha realized, since she hadn't thought about it before, that maintaining this herd as well as the couple of dozen cattle back at their place was more labor than she'd given Lester credit for. She'd seen them all before, of course. Every time she visited Adeline she'd driven right past, and sometimes through them. But somehow she'd never factored them in as work for Lester. *Funny I'm so closed down myself. Maybe it's catching?* Made her think differently about helping him out when Zane wasn't around. Gave her a new slant. *How old is he, I wonder?*

Adeline turned toward her, hands still on the wheel. "Jump out, would ya hon? Make sure you close the gate behind me."

Sasha didn't need to be told what to do. Once on the ground, she carried the gate to one side and waited while the truck rolled through. Standing amongst a handful of cattle, Lester was holding one hand up in the air like he was worried no one could see him. After she secured the gate Sasha followed, heading into the pasture where Adeline had pulled the truck to a stop beside her husband's hunched, shuffling figure. She watched, while she walked, as he pulled two coils of old rope from the pickup bed. She scanned the small, milling group of cattle, looking for the breech-birth heifer to see if what she'd visualized from Adeline's description was accurate, but she couldn't find it.

As soon as she reached them, Lester shoved a furry rope at her. "She's over there." He talked with a sagging home-rolled stuck to his lower lip as usual, jerking his head over his left shoulder. Her eyes followed the movement, looked over the hood of the truck to see a smallish cow staring back at her.

"Walk round behind the truck," Lester almost whispered, "an see if you can get her movin toward the fence. Wave your rope. Go slow so she don't spook. Adeline'll drive an I'll be on this side."

Sasha found herself thrust into actions she didn't fully understand. As she took up position to the right of the now slowly moving pickup, the heifer turned away from them and she saw two legs protruding from the cow's rear end, sticking up like antenna.

"Wave your rope, Missy," Lester urged over the noise from the engine, "Move out farther. Keep her from gettin outside you."

From that moment on, her sense impressions—sun heating her back and neck, pungent odor of cow droppings, her hesitation to get too close—all these sensations moved in midair like paper debris swirling in a wind tunnel, like some lucky housewife in the money booth on *The Price Is Right*, she was trying to grab what she could.

Sasha held up her rope, veering further right, following Lester's command. But she couldn't actually bring herself to wave the rope or her other arm, so she just walked mutely with her arms up. Lester was whistling and clicking his tongue, the pickup crawling forward, as she fixated on—couldn't take her eyes off—the grotesque, upright legs, even as she occasionally stumbled on the uneven ground.

The system seemed to be working because they were gradually nearing the right angle corner of the fence above the river, keeping the heifer in front of them. She could imagine what a strange sight they must have made if anyone could see. That thought only lasted a second, though, because Lester had given Adeline the cut sign, hand drawn across his throat, and she'd stopped moving forward.

What followed next was more like a nightmare than reality, searing itself into her consciousness. Lester slipped a halter over the cow's neck and tied the other end to the corner post of the fence. Sasha watched numbly, frozen to her spot, as Adeline reversed the pickup, turned it around and backed up to within a few feet of the now

193

anchored heifer. Lester took Sasha's rope, tied one end around her right front leg and secured the other end to the closest fence post. He repeated the process with another rope on the left leg. Sasha groaned to herself as Lester dragged out a rusty length of chain from the bed of the truck. She could tell what was coming.

Lester looped the chain around the base of the legs, locked it in by setting the metal hook through a link. Adeline was still behind the wheel of the idling, smoking pickup when he tried to wave away exhaust as he wrapped the other end of the chain around the trailer hitch, tightened it, and told her to drive on. Sasha had been drawn to the heifer's bulging frenzied eyes, frantic with fear, like those of a wildebeest she'd once seen on *Wild Kingdom* being dragged down from the haunches by a clawing cheetah. A terrorized doomed look she'd never forgotten. *Tommy Watson shoved his fingers in me in eighth grade, got me to touch him. Can still remember the anger and shame.*

When the chain pulled straight, the animal let out a sustained unearthly bellowing that seemed to fill all the available air, molecules intermingled, in a scream of painful outrage that echoed off the narrow valley walls, slicing through Sasha's very being, as what appeared to be the lifeless calf thudded to the ground like a dropped garbage bag and Lester yelled for Adeline to stop the smoke-belching truck.

Adeline said she'd drive Sasha back home after Lester had unhooked the chain and waved them away, after it was clear the calf was dead. Sasha felt as though she'd been holding her breath for an uncomfortably long time as they came out onto the highway. Her window down, she sucked in the afternoon air now scented with riverside mint and blooming yellow scotch broom, and watched Lester untying the heifer from the fence. Like an old home movie, she thought, frames stuttering through the trees, Lester in jerky slow motion like dancers under a strobe light. She lost sight of him when they rounded the hill that sloped down to the river between their houses.

"I'm sorry we had to come get you for that, honey." Adeline reached out her right hand to lightly touch Sasha on the shoulder. "But we couldn't've done it without you. I know the whole thing wasn't very pleasant."

"It's ok. I admit I was a bit taken-aback when I first saw the legs sticking up…"

"And well you should be," Adeline nodded with certainty to the steering wheel.

"…but then I felt sorry for the cow. Her eyes were so scared. I just wanted it to be over."

"I 'magine she did too," Adeline said, while making the turn onto the wooden bridge. "She'll be fine now, I think. An' Lester'll probably have that calf butchered by the time I get back."

"You're going to eat it?" Sasha couldn't help herself from blurting it out, emphasis on *eat*.

"It's veal. Can't afford to buy it."

An hour later, Sasha walked halfway down their driveway in the fading afternoon, staring at the still slightly damp dirt underfoot, focusing inward on the sheer magnitude of what she'd experienced this day. Pulling the calf. The muffled thud when it hit the ground. These images bumped up aggressively against her gnawing, relentless sorrow of loss. Not only loss of Perry, but of herself too, in a way that quite frankly scared her, poked another hole in a thinning sense of confidence that she was in control of her life.

As she'd climbed out of the pickup when delivered back home, Sasha was stopped by Adeline. "There's something we've been meaning to ask you two." The smile was back to the older woman's face, though Sasha felt it was a little strained. "Lester an' I been thinking we'd see if you kids wanted to buy this place. Ten acres. Ten thousand dollars. A thousand down, an' a thousand a year. No interest."

Sasha hadn't known, at the time, how to answer. The best she could do on the spot was to stammer out a thanks for thinking of them and that she'd tell Zane when he came back. But in her imagination, zooming forward, visions of a Bierstadt painting with their house nestled up into the notch of the descending hillsides, gauzy smoke, maybe a grazing fawn or two in the foreground. She rejected that idealization quickly, though it tugged a few strings, especially after what she'd just gone through in Lester's pasture, especially given the way she saw their lives falling into well-grooved, separating ruts.

It was becoming a dependable pattern, like driving past the same houses on the highway and knowing their order from either direction. That, after seeing another smashed animal in a ditch or on the road, her reaction was increasingly both cerebral—a clean sureness of anger—and an in-her-bowels pain. Her sensitivities drawn and quartered as strong emotional currents yanked her in every different direction at once. She'd go from the dead cat or raccoon or possum to seeing all human activity as inherently bruising, bottom-line ugly and fetid. Just look around, she'd tell herself. *We—people everywhere, every era—seem unable to outgrow the need to kill each other. Like the chickens in the yard, pecking away at the weakest among them, the sick or injured bird, until it was a mangled carcass in the dirt. Like Beckett kneeling at the altar, carved to pieces by noblemen's swords, or Tokyo bamboo houses exploding from firebombs. Not to mention Dresden and Hamburg, Hiroshima and Nagasaki. The Trail of Tears or Buchenwald ovens. This current rice-paddy war.* The inevitability of it all was what clung to her thoughts, was what stung and sickened her in those moments. Like there was no alternative.

Then, when she reminded herself that she couldn't survive in such bitterness, she'd force herself to draw inward from the global, the historical, to focus on what brought her pleasure in the present, like walking down the driveway in the fading afternoon sun. Taking pleasure in beauty where she could find it was her only reliable coping mechanism, and she supposed it must be that way for others. That she wasn't singular in despairing. That most everyone must do the same thing: pretending the big picture is incomprehensible and only paying attention to what impinges on them or theirs directly. Her problem was that she found it impossible to relax because of so much noise, so much discord in the air, so little honest touching in the midst of death and disappearances.

Chapter Twelve

By October, 1855, native Rogue River peoples had been forced onto a reservation near Table Rock where they were guarded by a small detachment of US soldiers. A handful of Indians called the Butte Creeks left the reservation and returned to their ancestral lands above present day Eagle Point, saying they would not go back to the encampment where they were slowly starving, where they were counted by guards every day, and where no one was allowed to leave without written permission from the Indian agent of southern Oregon who didn't actually live in the district.

Using these Butte Creeks' departure as excuse, at a Sunday church meeting on Oct.7th, 115 men who favored extermination formed themselves into war parties to attack the Table Rock reservation. 106 defenseless men, women and children were slaughtered outright,

A spokesman for the attackers blamed a policy of "Indian philanthropy" for the "necessary, but unfortunate" events.

Zane had long clung to high-flying fantasies of finally being discovered, picked out of the crowd. Becoming an iconic, once-in-a-lifetime star along the lines of James Dean, joining *60 Minutes* as a featured investigative reporter, or rising to the highest levels of social commentary like Marshall McLuhan or Buckminster Fuller. He saw himself as someone people paid attention to. "When Zane LaRoux talks, people listen." *That* level of widespread fame and notoriety. If nothing else, he thought on the grand scale. The demented king moving wooden ships and armies on a paper mache battlefield the size of a ping-pong table.

He theorized, gave vent to complex and intricately woven analyses. Once, after dinner at an organizer's stuffy, crowded, and under police surveillance apartment in Knoxville, he'd made use of a wall map of the world and his pointing finger to explain how the Cold War would end, going on to predict the inevitable disintegration of the modern nation-state. He thought he'd held the stage well, sparking animated discussions that lasted till near dawn. Everyone too exhausted for the usual pairing up.

His junior year at Portland State, he'd persuaded one of his political science professors to let him teach part of the class after the professor had drawn a small circle on the board with lateral left/right arrows labeled 'liberal' and 'conservative,' claiming that the Weathermen and the John Birch Society were, in fact, just liberals and conservatives ranging further out on the same continuum. Zane disputed that configuration, maintaining that neither the Weathermen nor the Birch Society believed in the validity or efficacy of the federal government—neither had any faith in the system at all—and therefore were certainly not merely more radical examples of mainstream left/right politics. A friend of his said the same professor had taught Zane's theory in his night class the next week. Being validated as a mind at work was as close as he got to any identifiable sense of fulfillment, was what gave him confidence in his own abilities.

But in the same moment he could fantasize basking in the sentient world's acclamations, a kernel of cold reality would sting, and he'd secretly squirm with the knowledge that he was an imposter at heart. A fraud like his dad. A salesman, able to fabricate whole cloth technicolor narratives.

While working as an SDS organizer he'd proved he could mobilize people, convince them to stand up, to follow his lead. Despite all that, no amount of success in exhorting crowds, no number of loud, chanting marches or swelling media coverage could ever completely neutralize the acidic core of self-loathing in the pit of his stomach.

As long as he could remember, as a way to explain his father's abuse, he'd figured he must harbor some deep debilitating flaw, some inherent brokenness in his own character, must have been born under a truly bad sign. *Albert King, '67. An then everybody recorded it.* That he'd come out of the womb already grotesquely warped. Not just that his behaviors warranted punishment, but that his very embryonic dividing and multiplying was stained with the mark of Cain from the start. This was the only way he could even begin to find a reason why his father treated him as a target for his rage, that he was marked by the deepest and most hideous sin. Around high school, he'd managed to get out from under the clouds of fire and brimstone, but to this very day he hadn't found a way to reach the bitter seed that he feared formed the center of his personality, his own ground zero feelings about himself.

He supposed it made perfect sense, given the extremes he continually bounced between. Grandiose visions and utterly deplorable character flaws linked together like Tony Curtis and Sidney Poitier in *The Defiant Ones*. In his mind he was either conquering the world or descending into a numbing panic attack. Which was evident in the way he pathologically sabotaged his own best interests or went all in, energized or enraged in a cause. Hardly a unified, single-minded self. Though if given a straight-up choice between what people called normalcy and his own brand of deviance, he knew he'd go with shoving at the margins, howling at the moon. Knew he was just wired that way. No sense fighting it. He could even stitch together scenarios which told him that coming to grips with and accepting his conflicted, contradictory nature was a unique esoteric strain of Buddhism. Emphasis on 'accepting' made it so, he reasoned hopefully.

Like a lightning round of three-dimensional chess played by speed freaks, all these thoughts competed in his mind, jostling with each other as he, Greg, and Heavy Duty walked back down the trail from the ruins of Greg's cabin, where not much was left but smoldering embers. The air in the clearing was quiet, reeking with the acrid, cloying smell of smoke like the lingering after effect of a gunshot in a closed room, or the smell from pounding a roll of caps with a rock he remembered from his Davy Crockett coonskin days. A blackened metal hurricane stove and the skeletal iron frame of a small bed were the only standing remains. Everything else had burned, leaving a foot-deep layer of charred wood, twisted-by-fire tin cans, and steaming coals, with a few blackened logs sticking up at acute angles, still flaming in small spots.

When they'd first emerged from the forest-thicketed uphill trail into the small meadow and could see what had happened, saw where the smoke was coming from, Greg had begun stumbling around in tiny circles like a broken windup toy, almost sobbing. "All my stuff was in there. It's all gone." Neither Duty nor Zane had responded. Nothing they could say, though Duty did try to get an arm around Greg's shoulders to quiet him. Greg shook him off. "Mother-fucking Wade Perkins did this. I KNOW it, that cocksucker!"

For reasons known only to his subconscious filing system, Zane recalled a frozen moment from the month before when he and Greg had gone to the Copper store to see why all the cop cars had screamed past them on the river, the day the Fausens disappeared. When they'd left that afternoon, as he was climbing into the VW bus, he'd seen curtains moving in a window of Gus's apartment at the back of the store, the blurred image of a man watching them. Funny, so much had been going on that he'd completely forgotten. Now he remembered it clearly while Greg screeched about Perkins. *Gus lives alone. Everyone knows that.*

Halfway down the trail Duty finally managed to get an arm around Greg's slumped shoulders and was trying to console him. At least that's the way it looked to Zane, who was following the two of them downhill on the narrow dirt path through the trees and brambles. He couldn't hear what Duty was whispering in his ear but could see Greg's hanging head slowly shaking back and forth, as though fending off the words. *One more night. Can't just push him out. I'll take him to his folk's place tomorrow when I go to Medford. Sasha'll be livid, but it's only for tonight. Those two look like tramps, Duty's long curly hair, Greg's tangled mess, the way their raggedy clothes hang. The three tramps by the railroad tracks behind Daly Plaza. I was a junior in high school. My introduction to the world of politics, though I didn't know it at the time.*

Greg had begun kicking loose rocks down the trail, having broken away from Duty's grasp. Duty turned to make eye contact with Zane, giving him a shoulder shrug and palms-up gesture, as if saying "you try."

By the time they emerged from the forest and he saw Richard waiting next to the bus on the other side of the river, acute angled sunlight bouncing back to them off his aluminum walking crutches, Zane had formulated a plan of sorts. He remembered what he'd said to Greg the night before. That if Perry had fallen off his trail onto the river rocks below, then no one could have seen him from the road. So who had called the ambulance two nights ago? Who'd been down at the river to find Perry's body? Did that someone see him fall? Or...?

The ideas distilling in his mind hinged on the fact his mother worked at Medford Ambulance. He knew the ambulance crews had to file trip slips for every call they responded to, so he might be able to find out who'd called it in. And he really wanted to see what the emergency crew had said about Perry's injuries when they found him, how they'd written their report.

He'd pay her a visit tomorrow and see what he could dig up. The more he thought about it, the more suspicious he became about what had happened to Perry Friday night. *Just doesn't make sense. Doesn't add up.*

Zane knew that prying into the mystery wouldn't do anything for Greg, or for Perry either since he had no family, no one with any interest in finding out how the old man had died. But he could feel his organizer juices beginning to flow again, jacking him up. A fire in his belly re-igniting. Serious questions needed answers.

A family disappears and the husband's father commits suicide within a month. No explanation, no note. That guy in Gus's room at the Copper store watching them through the curtains the same day of the disappearance. Perry ends up dead Friday night and Greg's cabin is torched the very next day. All this happening within a two mile radius of the dam site. *Like a swirlin, bloody flood comin downstream.*

The weakening sun was sinking down to the western ridges as they'd all squeezed themselves back into the VW bus. But not before

Greg had regaled Richard with an expletive-laced description of the scene at what used to be his cabin. He kept it up once they were loaded in. "That fucker Perkins, little Barney Fife; I can see him laughin when he lit it up. How can they just do that, man? Ain't there some law or somethin? Didn't even bother to take my shit out first. Just burned everything. An' then hung that fuckin 'No Trespassing' sign right there," he nodded toward it from the back seat, "ripped up the trolley, for christsakes." Zane started the bus, slowly began backing away from the river.

"Tin soldiers and Nixon's comin," Duty chanted softly, just a hint of a melody at the edges, the scars on his forehead wrinkling slightly as he frowned to no one in particular. "We're finally on our own."

"Who's got a joint?" Richard demanded. "You guys went off and left me high and dry here."

"Not high enough, I guess," Duty zinged. Richard played deaf.

Zane could hear Greg's dramatic moaning sighs as Duty lit and held the Zig-Zag up to the front where Richard snatched it, half-turned, looking Greg over as he inhaled. "Gregor," he said, expelling smoke, "after all these years, you know Wade don't do shit without someone tellin him. He's not smart enough. My dad's known him since grade school in Ruch. Is and always was a flunky, he said, a go-for. So whatever you think he's done, you can be sure the idea didn't burst outta his empty melon. An we all know who's the mastermind. Fuckin Brereton, for the whole Applegate valley, from Cook 'n Green all the way out the lower river to Murphy."

"Mutt n' Jeff," Zane said, craning his head around to finish the three up-and-back, start-and-stop maneuvers required to get the bus headed back downstream. "I keep wonderin why those two would have anything to do with Perry's minin claim. They don't have jurisdiction, don't usually pay attention to such things. It's BLM business."

He meant the question for Richard, who'd given up staring at Greg and was now looking out the front, bumping his metal legs together in a nervous rhythm. The smoke from his joint streamed to the back, where Duty made every effort to suck it in while Greg was holding his head with both hands like the Munch painting. Zane could see them in the mirror. That's all he could see; their heads and shoulders blocked his view out the rear window.

He shifted into third and kept it there while negotiating the series of four tight turns immediately downstream from the torn-down trolley and the swinging bridge. In a tiny crevice of his understanding, he knew, without knowing how he knew, that the foot bridge too would soon be gone.

Zane glanced sideways at Richard, who was smiling broadly out the windshield, probably, he thought, at the intricately textured and fluctuating view of farm, field and forest that kept sliding by as they drove. Stoned again. Or just more so.

"Earth to Richard. I was askin you a question."

"What?"

"What're Brereton and Perkins up to? Do ya know? Hear anything from your old man?"

Richard handed the joint to Duty, who held it under Greg's downturned face to no effect. Duty leaned back and luxuriated with the smoke by himself, holding it daintily between thumb and index, his little finger crooked up in the air like a long time drinker. All this time, Richard was talking to the passenger side of Zane's head.

"Ya gotta remember who lives back in here, the people ya never see. Dad's always said there's a family of KKK's hidden up off every loggin road. Most of 'em inter-related, like tribes..."

"An' he doesn't think that's a bad idea, does he?" Zane interrupted.

"...Naw, ya know he's always nigger-this an nigger-that. All his jokes. I was that way myself before Nam."

"The war gave you a social conscience?" Just a tinge of sarcasm, nowhere near dripping.

"Everything. Had to learn to trust who had my back. And it was black dudes that saved my life. Carried me out to the Medivac. Tied off my stumps so I wouldn't bleed out. They coulda just left me on the ground. I'd a come home in a bag. 'Course I wouldn't know."

Greg suddenly erupted from the back, his voice stretched tight, almost squeaky. "You guys don't give a fuck about what's happened to me. I've been burned out, man. I got nothin now."

Duty instinctively put a hand on the back of Greg's neck, squeezing lightly, massaging. "Come on, Greg. You know that's not true. We're here aren't we? I know you've been screwed on this, but there's not much to be done right now. There really isn't."

Zane was stuck back at Richard saying he wouldn't know when he was dead. Wasn't that the same thing Duty had said on the way out? The not-being, the nothingness? If it's nothingness, then there can't be a 'the.' He couldn't wrap his mind around it. Descartes was right in that respect—not that cogito created existence, but that awareness always assumes there's a self doing the thinking. So he couldn't comprehend any vast, black infinite. No wonder people are self-centered, he thought, everything funnels through your perceptions, locking you into yourself. *No, that's not right; perception isn't a thing. But I can only know what I'm aware of. It's not the Big Sleep then, Mr. Chandler. I won't be dreamin. More like the Big Empty. All of time before and after me. Like Pascal wonderin why now rather than then; why here rather than there? I can't even think about that. No comprende. Nada.*

Duty had Greg in a bear-hug of sorts, jiggling him good naturedly like ruffling his hair, telling him everything would be ok, that he wasn't some isolated, ostracized outcast, that he had friends and family, and that he should count himself lucky for having been able to live in the cabin as long as he had. It'd been free, after all.

"I guess you're right," Greg finally admitted, beginning to look sheepish.

That flare-up extinguished, Zane tried to get back on topic. "So Richard, are you sayin Perkins and Brereton are connected somehow with these backwoods skinhead survivalists?"

"Only makes sense. I'd bet my legs on it."

By the time Zane steered onto his driveway, after dropping Richard off, his mildly altered mind was trying to sort out how he was going to explain to Sasha that Greg was staying another night. He thought perhaps the best avenue was just to throw himself on the mercy of the court. What choices did he have? He wasn't about to drive Greg to his parents in Medford and then come all the way back out the river, just to turn around in the morning and make the same trip again. There's stupid, and then there's beyond the pale. Duty might be willing to carry Greg home, but whether he'd come back tonight was pretty iffy.

He'd have to make nice with Sasha. Not in a negative, manipulative way, he thought, simultaneously knowing it was more true than he cared to admit to himself.

I live in fear of potential attack. Don't trust anyone, not even her. At least at rock bottom. No one. I keep a wary eye peeled all the time. For protection. I know it's irrational with Sasha, but can't just wave away the deep-seated distrust, the knowledge that no one ever stepped in to shield me. That's how I saw it. And so I perpetuate my own guilt by letting her down, even when I don't want to. Because at heart I figure everyone'll betray me eventually, even her. See it as a pattern and figure it's the way most people are when you strip away the pretense. And there she is.

Sasha was standing next to the overgrown fence close to the house as they drove up. Though she had to have heard them coming, she didn't acknowledge their approach, instead staring at the ground where she was rubbing one tennis shoe around in a small circle, her shoulders drawn in. The sun, now beginning to slip behind the western hills and ridges, made her black hair gleam dark blue, Zane noticed, particularly where it hung down the front of her favorite white linen shirt, the one with pastel flowers stitched on the pockets. He supposed she must have a blouse somewhere in her boxes, but he couldn't remember ever seeing her in one except at the Prineville wedding. She mostly wore sweatshirts or work shirts of some kind, men's sizes.

That mental diversion kept him from feeling guilty for a few seconds. *But she is a radiant beauty. And incredibly smart.* He thought of her with an idealized slant, as the steady and perpetually honest one—he knew she was a stand-up person and valued her for that, was quite aware everyone who knew them loved "Sweet Sasha"—while he saw himself as more than a bit oily, mostly because of his lack of trust, the numerous secrets he kept, his sleazy behavior. Those secrets seemed to him a basic character trait, more important than anything he did, whether he'd slept around or kept his word, or poured too much money into nickel pinballs at every tavern he hung out in. It wasn't that he was unaware when he shut her out, went elsewhere, hugged to himself, even saw her as the enemy. So why couldn't he...open up...totally...lay himself bare...be what she needed? He was losing words that fit his failings.

As they drew up to where she was standing, Zane said "We're back" out his open window in a wise-cracking voice. She met his eyes for a millisecond while they slid by, vivid green flash. He could tell she was not amused. He watched out the side mirror as she turned toward the house, began to walk slowly, head back down. I'm fucked, Zane thought.

Within a few minutes of the three of them entering the house, Duty had pulled out the electric skillet and was making grilled cheese sandwiches for himself and Greg with Sasha's homemade wheat bread which filled the small kitchen with a warm yeasty aroma. Zane had declined, feeling he shouldn't be seen enjoying himself while Sasha was obviously upset. He didn't want to be stuffing his face when she came back inside. Little things like that mattered, he habitually reasoned, crazy as the proverbial bedbug.

Erasmus had stationed himself at Duty's feet where little balls of Abundant Food Program processed cheese fell from Duty's hand, one after another, until he finally told the cat he'd had enough.

Zane marveled at Duty's ability to effortlessly slide into their lives. He was already a fixture of sorts, had assumed a quasi-head-of-household position. Not that Zane felt pushed out or that he'd been replaced. More like having a brother, he thought, someone who could be relied on for support. As near as he could tell, Sasha didn't see Duty as any kind of negative in their lives, quite the opposite. But he could imagine someone looking in on them from the outside, wondering about the exact relationships the trio shared, who was sleeping where.

Greg and Duty had taken their sandwiches into the living room, turned on the FM to Quicksilver's "Edward, the Mad Shirt Grinder." They each had bowls of Sasha's homemade applesauce in front of them, heavy on the cinnamon. She still hadn't come back inside, leaving Zane to stew about the cultural messages he'd internalized of what being a man in the US of A meant. It'd been on his mind quite a bit lately, what with Sasha continually pointing out how so many men acted like entitled pricks, so he struggled with understanding how he could get out from under what he knew to be an oppressively paternalistic worldview. Not surprising he'd want out, given the *pater familias* he'd experienced firsthand.

He'd been raised on valorizations of rugged individualism, the strong, silent Fess Parker types. Television shows had formed the staple of his upbringing: *Wanted: Dead or Alive. Have Gun; Will Travel. The Rifleman. Rawhide. Wagon Train. The Lone Ranger. Wyatt Earp. Bat Masterson. Hopalong Cassidy.* Blazing guns and sanitary bullet holes that didn't bleed. He could run the list of such shows as a steady stream through his memory. *Lawman. Gunsmoke. Laramie. Cheyenne. The Virginian. Sundance Kid. Sky King. Sergeant Preston. Texas Ranger Hoby Gilman. Daniel Boone.* And when westerns faded, all the private eyes and cops and marshals and sheriffs were cast as lone heroes. Clear up to *Columbo, Barnaby Jones, Cannon, Rockford,* and whatever drama Dennis Weaver was in. Oh, yeah. *McCloud.* Jesus! The Evil Box constantly at work. He'd watched a lot of television when they were living at his mom's.

He'd read all the Ian Fleming books in high school, James Bond another singular male setting things right. Seeking to emulate 007, he sneaked into Earl's Pipe and Gift to buy Player's non-filter, Navy-cut with the sailor on the box who wore a hat that said 'Hero.' Zane basking in the ethereal ozone of make-believe glory, dreaming of being a hero himself.

And yet. Whenever his LaRoux family gathered, most of them living up around Eugene—the seven L's—he naturally gravitated to the women, liked their conversations, their subdued but welcome support; not quite admiration, but shading that way. The males in the group he found consistently abrasive and crude as they argued, sometimes raising their voices to indoor shouts about whether taking the cut-off road just past Union Creek would get you to the lake in winter. Or whether you could tell a doe from a buck at night by how their eyes reflected light. "One's duller than the other," some republican uncle would be sure to enlighten him. Or what highways to take for the fastest trip to Pendelton, even though none of them were going there.

He remembered those occasions like they were stage plays with actors he recognized but really didn't know. A whole shitload of family gossip about untimely pregnancies, how Lionel killed a 4-point over by Chemult, or why Lois' grandkid wasn't walking yet. He lived through the Cuban Missile Crisis in their company, what he could remember of it. "Europe's gotta quit sittin on the fence," Luella's Irish husband Paddy kept repeating to averted faces and turned heads. No one paid any attention to him for reasons Zane had never heard mentioned. And everyone drank scotch.

Those were the days. *What trite crap, completely meaningless.* He'd scribbled his own lines about the good old days last winter. "The only good thing about the old days," he'd written with a smirk, "was that I didn't know then where I'd be today." *More trite crap, I suppose.*

He remembered clearly when television was one black and white channel—KBES TV—Douglas Edwards and the News on CBS was only fifteen minutes long when he was in the fourth grade. That original station was followed quickly by KMED TV, an NBC affiliate. Neither of those call names existed now, and eventually each of the stations had switched networks. Before too long a third one had emerged to carry the other major network, ABC. All three went to color at the same time, in 1965, the year after he'd graduated. To think it was only that long ago, less than a decade.

But back in his grade school and junior high days, local television was padded with home grown programs like *Ore-Cal Panorama* and its peroxided, braying hostess; *Your Social Security* where a pasty-faced guy wearing a lop-sided, scraggly little moustache and bushy sideburns answered questions mailed in from nervous widows. *The Pappy Colman Show*: "If you're too busy to fish, you're just too busy." Filler shows for otherwise empty air time since network feeds didn't cover all the time slots. Hickville, Oregon at its best.

He'd never get rid of his anger at being forced to watch *The Big Picture*, produced by the US Army and narrated by the same voice that did the lead-in for *Superman*, emphasizing how the Army protected our freedom. His dad forced him to watch, telling Zane he might learn something, repeating each time that going into the military was probably the only way to make a man of him. He also had to sit still for *The Dan Smoot Report*, an unabashed harangue on how the Illuminate were secretly pulling all the world's strings and the radical right was the only hope. Sponsored, he couldn't forget, by Dr. Ross pet food that was "dog-gone good. Woof!"

He despised that part of himself which was forged in the post-war mythology of the solitary man. As much as he personally exemplified the misogyny inherent in seeing women primarily as potential conquests *find em, fuck em, forget em*, he nonetheless understood how impossible it was to sustain a healthy, caring relationship as long as he clung to such notions. A glance to the long line of different coaches he'd been at the mercy of through school was enough to cause an in-the-flesh shudder. Only a couple seemed worth remembering, but unfortunately he could recall them all, and their particular brand of sadism he decided was rampant in the profession. That's the way he saw it. Men being rough and getting away with it.

At the ground floor of his attitudes toward the world he knew he needed Sasha as a partner, knew she was good for him, acted as a corrective, could bring out his better instincts. He just couldn't live up to her, too easily succumbing to all the weaknesses flesh was heir to, to give it an Elizabethan twist. He managed to let her down when he least wanted to.

At least today he was aware of the absurdity of those mantras of individualism, the out-and-out lies perpetrated and perpetuated by his culture. Anything that smacked of the social, the group, was automatically suspect after McCarthy and HUAC had convinced people to look under their beds for commies hiding with the dust bunnies. Socialism was anarchy and atheism according to the national psyche, anathema.

He was reminded of Plato's doctrine that 'the few are always better than the many.' And that ancient bearded guy, in a major distortion of history, was credited with being instrumental in creating democracy, a political system the philosopher who would be king loathed and railed against every chance he got, even though in Greece democracy at the time the only Athenians who could gather in the agora and participate in government were wealthy landowners—the few. Even though the entire city-state economy relied on a massive slave labor force—the many.

Such were the tangled incongruities messing with his mind as he wondered where Sasha was and what she was doing, what she was thinking about. *I always believe she's angry with me. Projectin my own inferiority and guilt. Or worse, that she doesn't think about me at all, that I'm just an irritant below the conscious level, like some miniscule seed stuck in her gums.*

212

Stevie Wonder was singing about life in the city when Sasha came through the back door into the kitchen where Zane had been rattling around, wiping out the electric skillet, lost in his mind games. He was immediately defensive, on alert to monitor her mood. She averted her eyes, not meeting his, kept her head down and went straight up the stairs without speaking. *Fuck me all to hell. I'd best leave her alone for a while.*

Zane slouched into the front room where Duty was giving Greg a lesson in Malthus and mortality. "How much longer can cemeteries exist, do you think?" His forehead was wrinkled like a too-often folded road map, whitish pressure lines crisscrossing into his hair. Despite his frowning, he was keeping his tone smooth and even, no pushing, a leaf floating on a still day. Greg sat beside him on the couch, within reach, and Duty was availing himself of his favorite conversational style, touching, tapping, rubbing Greg's shoulder as he delivered his lines. "When there's too many people for too little habitable land, billions and billions more of us eating and defecating and reproducing—and habitable includes things like having safe water, sewage systems, protection, stopping pollution—then putting dead people in what little land there is, putting 'em there forever. Get that! Forever." He squeezed Greg gently, "planting people in the ground will be against the law, whatever kind of law you have in mind."

Zane doubted Greg had any idea about 'law' in his mind right now that didn't spring from his experience over the last two days, but he didn't appear to have tuned out. Duty was probably keeping him so stoned he could barely blink, another crucial element of his discourse community of one, incapacitating the audience. "So, if we can't somehow harness nuclear power to vaporize dead bodies, cremation will be the only practice allowed. It'll be mandatory. Unless we go Soylent Green, an then whoever's in charge will make sure no corpses go unused. Imagine Asia an Africa an South America. Hell, imagine

California with the population multiplying exponentially. Where'll their food come from? Their water? Where'll they fucking live?"

Zane took to the empty easy chair across from the sofa, couldn't keep himself from piping in. "Duty? How in the world do you manage to keep it together when you're loaded to the gills all the time? How do you even think at all?"

"Not a matter of thinking so much as just going with the flow. If I could do it under fire from Charlie in the goddamned jungle," he poked his head forward a little, staring dead at him. "... then everything else is small potatoes."

Zane watched Greg nodding as if he were taking part in the conversation, tightening his mouth in affirmation. Of what, he had no idea. "Problem is," Zane said, "flows always go downhill. I'd like to aim for higher things."

"Good fucking luck on that," Duty said to the joint he was rolling on the table. Greg was swinging his head like a scythe roughly in time to the music, and Zane knew he needed to break through to Sasha before her feelings hardened and he had no way in.

"Looks like dinner's gonna be catch-as-catch can, boys, so fend for yourselves. I'm goin up."

"Where's the rest of that wine?" Greg asked without a hint of embarrassment.

Sasha had lit half a dozen candles in front of her on the floor as she sat on the day bed under the window, rolling loose yarn into balls. Now a muffled announcer's voice floated up from below, words mostly indistinguishable, though Zane was sure he could make out Nixon, John Mitchell and Senate hearings clearly enough. He was reluctant to sit down on the blanketed mattress with Sasha, didn't want to push himself on her, felt he was on very thin ice. So he stood, candle flames wavering between them, points of warm light against the enclosing dusk outside the window. He was uncomfortable standing but caught betwixt and between as to where to plant himself,

214

off balance to the nth degree like a hat-in-hand petitioner. The room smelled of frangipangi from the incense burner at her feet. He watched the thin ribbon of scented smoke rising as he shifted his weight from leg to leg, waiting for her to react, his pulse pounding his eardrums. Finally, she looked up at him, still mute.

"I know you're bummed about Greg stayin," he said nervously, breaking the taut silence, "but I really had no choice. It's only for tonight."

"Oh, Zane," she said, her body sagging like a deflating balloon. "Greg is the last thing on my mind. I knew he was going to be stuck here." She patted the space beside her, a sign for him to sit. Which he did, carefully avoiding the candles. "I've had the most horrible time since you left."

"Why? What happened?" Tentatively putting an arm around her waist lightly.

"I'm still shaking."

"You're trembling, yeah. I can feel it. What in the world's goin on? Are you all right?" *What a stupid question. I'm an idiot.*

"Adeline came and got me. I didn't know what it was. Couldn't really say no. It was so ghastly."

"Ok," he pulled her to him gently, their sides touching, legs against each other. "Back up a little. Adeline came...? He waited a breath or two.

"She was in Lester's pickup, so I thought maybe something had happened to him. But that wasn't it. She said they needed help, so I went with her back to their place." She swallowed before continuing. "I'm still shaken from the whole experience. We drove out into the pasture where Lester was standing. On the way over, Adeline told me that one of the cows had a breech-birth and the calf was still mostly stuck inside her, that they'd have to pull it out."

"Jesus. What'd they want *you* to do?" Watching her face in profile, he recognized the familiar flooding warmth of passionate attraction, could feel her firm body against him, her breast pressing into his side.

215

Not now. "I had to help them capture the cow. We herded her to the fence. That's what they needed me for, to keep her corralled so Lester could tie her up. It was gruesome, the calf's butt and back legs sticking out. But the heifer's eyes...I've never seen such helpless fright before. Such raw terror. Really got to me." She rested a hand on Zane's closest thigh.

"So how'd they get the calf out?"

"Adeline backed the pickup to where she was tied to the corner of the fence. Lester hooked the calf's back end up with a chain and they just pulled it out. I don't have words to describe it. The calf was dead, being dragged on the ground, its tongue hanging out. Just horrible."

Zane could hear a blues harp through the floor. *Paul Butterfield?* He knew he was in a dangerous spot with Sasha. She was clearly distraught, whacked out, and he wanted to acknowledge that, stay focused, but the candles flickering in the failing light, the smoking incense, her body heat, her hand on his thigh—all combined to stir pheromones. He could feel his blood moving. *Please not now.*

"And on top of all that, Adeline said Lester was going to butcher the calf. They're going to eat it. Can you believe it? Feel like I've been kicked in the stomach, the heifer's eyes, the dead calf." Her voice dropped to a near whisper. "And Perry gone too."

"Sorry I wasn't here to help," he said, knowing it was a feeble line that could fit a number of occasions in their lives together, he'd left her alone so often. "You know, someone burned up Greg's cabin. He's convinced it was Wade Perkins. But that's what we found when we got there, nothin but glowin coals. The trolley's been torn down, the swingin bridge's got a "No Trespassing" sign. Seems it's been a bad day all around. Like the bottom's droppin out from under us and everything's in free fall."

He felt her lean into him, pressing closer. "What we need is some sexual healing, I think," she said, sliding her hand up between his legs. "That's what I want right now." Turning to face her, he saw her eyebrows arched in vulnerability, eyes wide, as her fingers stroked him through his jeans.

He'd brought her to the first shuddering climax with his mouth, her musky juices soaking his moustache. They'd risen and fallen together in crescendoing harmony, nails digging, spasms like cresting breakers, leaving his limbs tingling and weak. A few of the candles had burnt their way out, darkening the room considerably.

Sasha's hair lay sprayed out on the red and white checkerboard cover of the day bed as they were stretched out side by side. Zane had gotten the burgundy wool blanket off their regular bed and she had it pulled up to her chin. "I haven't told you what else Adeline said to me today," her voice mellow, seeming to come from deep in her chest. "She and Lester want to sell us the house and ten acres for ten grand. A thousand a year, no interest. No money down. They want grazing rights for the pasture as long as they need it."

Zane sat up quickly, fumbling in his jeans for cigarettes. He slid a saucer with a burned out candle over to him for an ashtray, lit his cigarette in the flame of another. "Are you kiddin me? What'd you say?"

"I said I'd talk to you about it."

"Holy Christ, Sasha. What's to decide? We could make a thousand a year pickin ferns, or cuttin wood. Paint a couple houses in town. Jesus! Why wouldn't we do it? They're practically givin it to us."

She didn't reply at once, still lying flat, staring at the knotty wood plank ceiling. Zane could hear Duty and Greg talking downstairs but couldn't distinguish the words, filtered as they were through Pink Floyd's "Dark Side of the Moon" which he'd picked up at Ranch Records in Ashland right after it came out a year ago. He hoped they didn't scratch it.

"It's a commitment," she finally said, propping herself up on one elbow to look at him. "We'd have to be willing to stay here, to make a

217

home, not run a boarding house. And I don't want to live hand-to-mouth, always scratching to make ends meet."

Here it comes, he thought, rolling the tip of his cigarette against the edge of the saucer. An immediate involuntary response, keeping himself distracted for protection. *From orgasm to outrage. Feelin good is so fuckin fragile. Why should I be surprised? Should be what I expect. That's the point, isn't it? We expect what's impossible, again and again. Ah fuckin men.*

"So what are you sayin? You wannna just let it go?"

"No," she said firmly, "I want to feel we're both working toward the same ends. I want, for lack of a better term, some sense of security. That we're committed to each other. That I come first with you instead of somewhere down the line. You know that little apartment in Portland was the first place I ever felt was mine. I wasn't sharing space with my cousins. Andreas and Sofia were great to me, but I was always the extra kid, the one that wasn't really theirs. And yeah, I love it here, love being on the river. But I want our relationship to be healthy and to be for us. So far, I haven't noticed that being the case."

"Anything else?" He tried not to be sarcastic, knew that would be the wrong tact to take, but he wasn't sure he'd carried it off. Since she didn't seem to wince or frown, he thought it might have passed unnoticed.

"Yes, actually," she started matter-of-factly. "I'm not willing to eat meat anymore. After today especially, I've got to make this change. Been thinking about it for a long time, but today I'm sure. I have to do it."

"Don't you think you might be over-reactin?" He ground what was left of his cigarette into the saucer, expelled the last lungful of smoke.

"That's insulting, Zane. Poor little dear subject to hysteria? Is that the person you think I am? Don't you know me at all?"

"Yeah, you're right. I'm sorry. Don't know why I said that. Probably 'cause it's so sudden. It'll mean no more venison hangin in the smokehouse. What about fish? Can we still eat fish?"

218

"You can eat whatever you want. I'm not saying you have to follow my orders. Just that I'm committing myself to being vegetarian. I don't know about fish yet. Maybe."

"I don't see how I could keep eatin' meat if you quit. Wouldn't be right. We wouldn't be on the same page. It's not that I'm dead set against quittin; it's just kind'a sudden." He lit up again. New cigarette, shift of position as he unfolded his cramping legs from where he'd been sitting on them. "I know the moral arguments about eatin other animals. I never understood, for instance, how those 4-H girls could raise a steer, name it, care for it, love it. Get a blue ribbon for it at the fair, get their picture in the paper, and then sell it to the local butcher."

"But that's exactly what happens to all kinds of animals. Not the pastoral American Gothic farm with Bessie the milk cow, but industrialized slaughter. Pigs, chickens, turkeys, cattle, sheep—they're born, live and die in the same mechanized corporate factory system. They're *harvested* for fuck's sake."

"I get that. I really do. People buyin meat in styrofoam and cellophane so they don't have to connect their stew meat to anything with feelin."

"But you keep shooting deer."

"I know. But they're wild. I'm not raisin 'em to hunt."

"Then they should matter even more."

"I feel it's like you're askin me to give up part of myself. Are you goin to throw me over for tofu?"

"Oh, Zane. Don't go bad on me now. That's such bullshit. What part of yourself are you giving up? The manliness part? The patriarchal part? Don't tell me you're the provider because you can shoot straight." She laughed and he thought she sounded light and amused, not bitter, not angry.

"Ok, Miss Petrovsky. You win. Just don't tell me I have to quit fish too."

Now she was smiling, a touch of humor at the corners of her mouth. He realized she liked to spar with him this way. Probably because she could wind him up whenever she wanted.

"So what about buyin this place?" he asked, aware he was taking a risk.

"That we'll have to talk about."

Chapter Thirteen

The Native American Party, renamed the American Party in 1855 and commonly known as the Know Nothing movement, was an American nativist organization that spread nationally in the mid-1850s. It emerged to take the place of a defunct Whig party and was rabidly anti-Catholic, xenophobic, and hostile to immigration, starting originally as a secret society. This secret wing of the Party was known as the Order of the Star-Spangled Banner, and Know-Nothings got their name because whenever a member was asked about the party's enrollment, the member claimed to...yes, wait for it...know nothing.

In Southern Oregon, the Know-Nothings gained considerable power, owing to the large number of Chinese laborers who came to placer mine—all men, as the white population wouldn't allow Chinese women for fear of a rapidly multiplying yellow 'horde." Not surprisingly, these Know-Nothings were also at the fore-front in calling for the "total extermination" of all native peoples still living in the Rogue Valley.

Many political scholars see the platform of the Know-Nothings as foundational to the formation of the modern Republican party.

On his way to work Monday, George kicked words around in his head to best describe his Sunday dinner, trying to see if he could find one that vibrated with the same dolorous frequency as his emotional response to another evening at the farm. He'd been to college, for christsakes, wasn't some run of the mill local yokel with bad grammar and a limited vocabulary. He knew how to use words, finally settling on torturous to sum up his experience.

From the insinuating smell of boiled cabbage locked in the fibers of the scruffed and faded kitchen wainscoting, to his father's long pauses before coming out with non-sequitur cliches apropos of absolutely nothing. "Time'll tell, right enough," or "Depends on the man upstairs" or "You gotta take everything as it comes." George dreaded every one of these infrequent visits. His father had missed the two World Wars—too young, too old—so George didn't put any credence into his moralizing. To George's mind, any idea of morality died on the vine when it came to kill or be killed. Something his father could never understand, having never lain in a ditch shaking from the sky—

tearing, shrieking insanity. *I'm the prodigal and only son returning every time I come.*

His second story room across the hall from his parents' had been converted years ago into storage. George knew there weren't still any model airplanes dangling from the ceiling or faded orange Beaver pennants plastered on the walls. Nothing of him left in the room full of boxes. Making him just like any other guest in that way. Which he knew was an absurd comparison since he could count—albeit on his good hand—the number of people who'd ever come to dinner in all the time he'd lived there. No out of town relatives on a visit. No neighbors dropping by. No fellow-believers from the hard shell Baptist church they'd dragged him to until high school.

What sparse information about his parents George had been able to piece together over many years told him they'd both migrated west in their early twenties from somewhere in the humid fundamentalist flatlands of North Carolina. The Piedmont, he'd heard in their conversation, back when they conversed at all. But that was the most he knew, if he didn't toe too hard a line about the meaning of knowing. Asking questions of his parents had mostly been met with shrugs and silent stares, a pattern that only intensified after he'd escaped. *Been off the farm for over twenty years. I'm definitely not the same person, and I don't mean in minor, insubstantial ways. Coming back from the war. Christ. After that orchestrated slaughter, I found I'd lost patience for nitwits, fools and chiselers. Much less for circus tent Oral Roberts types. I remember his low-rent black and white TV show when he'd grab people, latch onto their offending parts. "HEAL," his oily hair loose over his forehead, white shirt with sleeves rolled up, sitting in a folding chair and sweating profusely with righteous zeal. Now he's got his own college and only wears suits. Religious charlatans one and all.*

His father's name was Garland, though few in Eagle Point knew that since he'd always gone by Sam. George didn't call him by any name. Not dad, not Sam, nothing. Emblematic of what little connection he felt to the man who'd sired him. George couldn't

222

remember him ever talking about much that wasn't directly connected to the farm, its animals and machinery, or the weather. His words usually uttered in the form of flat, emotionless commands or statements of what he considered facts, unless he was repeating aphoristic gems from others. "Carl says..."

His mother Phyllis Ann, abnormally thin, gray and aproned, kept her head down most of the time, looking out from under, except when she offered the steaming platter of pot roast and potatoes, or when her liver-spotted hands ladled buttered vegetables from pale chipped translucent bowls, nervously biting her upper lip, silently serving. He'd noticed, at an early age, that when she was motivated to speak beyond answering a question, when she dared to try to contribute her own ideas, she always began with "Oh, Ah..." A silent gap afterward. Clearing the deck before broaching her subject, nervous about attracting attention to herself. And she'd have her eyes closed.

George couldn't say he'd ever been drawn to her for comfort—she wasn't one for displaying physical affection—no tender touching. She used to lightly bop him on the head as she walked by as a sign of affection. That stopped about the time he'd learned to masturbate up in his room. *National Geographic topless natives I got from Alden down the road. Whenever I had free time I'd pedal like hell to his house. Get away.* So he had no comforting memories to call forth in darker hours when his grasp on just what the hell his life was supposed to be about grew weak. His dad was mostly unapproachable, busy always with matters of importance, it seemed. His mother also fended him off as far as empathetic understanding went. George couldn't imagine her with a daughter, someone she'd have to teach, show the ropes. He'd sensed growing up that his mother didn't have the highest opinion of men as a sub-specie. He had to admit he was thankful for her stolid distance in some respects; she'd never gone on about why he wasn't married yet, hadn't bombarded him with complaints about not having grandchildren. No meddling into his privacy. In their smallest of family units, so much remained unstated, unspoken, not meant to be gotten into. *Part of that is generational. You don't discuss un-pleasantries; you silently bear up. She'd put on a sour face when displeased, wear it around for a day or so. But that was it.*

He'd once seen her brushing her hair in front of her dressing table—he must have been eight or nine. In her not quite see through peach nightgown. Chiffon. She'd been smiling at her image in the mirror as she pulled the brush gently, smoothly, through her auburn hair. Only instance he could point to where she seemed feminine. At least enough so that he felt strangely guilty for having observed her when she thought she was alone.

One thing was sure; he could hardly expect her to be supportively warm and fuzzy like sit-com moms when he knew how much work she did. Every. Single. Day. Without breaks, vacations, or time off. Who peopled her thoughts before sleep in her twin bed while her husband snored and snuffled? He hadn't the faintest idea, except a lingering sense there was another, different personality buried deep, one she'd covered and hidden all these years, or more likely given up on.

On her dresser was a framed photograph of her family posed on rickety wooden chairs arranged on a leafy rural front porch. Pinched, dour-faced, gray-hair pulled back women in black, neck to ground. Men in Sunday suits, vests, ties. Special occasion black. No one was smiling. Young George had studied the photograph for glimpses into his chromosomal heritage whenever he knew she was busy elsewhere and wouldn't catch him at it. Long ago, when he was in grade school, she'd pointed out different relatives, saying their names wistfully, but that was all. No connections. No idea how he might be related. When he'd asked, she said she was nineteen at the time. In the picture she's sitting on her husband's knee. He wore a starched, upright, Victorian collar that touched his jaw as he stared resolutely off into the distance like there was some other world out beyond that needed to be conquered, a wilderness writhing to be tamed. And they were so young.

Her eyes in the photo, staring right down the camera lens, danced and flashed with what he, George, as a teenager, could only describe as wantonness, highly sexual and in your face wantonness. Sharp vixen eyes told him she was aware her looks could snare. She'd also been smirking, taunting the camera. What a thing to think about your mother. He wondered how long it had taken to extinguish her spirit, drive her into a grinding servitude. *World without end. So many conscious beings, and all the psychology I had to read in college telling us we don't even know ourselves how or why we think what we do. It's a crap shoot.*

Dinner at the farm was for eating not for talking, as he'd learned from years of simple, rudimentary repetition. Slurps, fork edges scraping plates and sounds of chewing predominated, along with the occasional request to pass something. A cough at the table had always seemed fraught with tension, like it was some shorthand way of expressing displeasure. So silence had been just fine with George yesterday evening because lurking behind every thought, distorting and elongating all his minutes and movements like a guilty conscience was Dave Brereton. *Mr. String Bean with a badge*, tainting the air around him with a pervasive, pungent uneasiness. That and Heidi's voice from Friday had been running through his head in a recycling loop. Another brain worm eating away at his confidence, his tenuous managerial sense of self. *Already notarized...What's that all about?...Had to be recorded before the end of day...Tanaka flats...Most irregular...Raymond gave the go ahead.*

George had come away from Eagle Point last night firmly convinced of at least one thing: when his parents were gone or relocated into some care facility, he'd put the farm up for sale. Used to be he'd thought about moving back, retiring as a landowner. Having a couple goats and a few chickens. Selling off all the other livestock, sharecropping out the pasture for some local to grow alfalfa. But yesterday evening he'd again come to grips with how gut-raw he'd hated living there, a viciously narrow life. Slop the animals. Muck out the stalls. Don't get kicked. Every mind-numbing chore had to follow

225

the same schedule, day after day. He couldn't help it; all those embedded memories were triggered by simply looking at the place. Even if he could live there without any work whatsoever when he retired, just the thought of being on that same piece of land, in that same house, was enough to curdle the gastric juices in his stomach, bring on a chilling sweat. *The beginning of death, I guess it would be for me if I came back. Retiring on these same 20 acres to pretend I'd accomplished something? Is that what this living has been about? That's what it all adds up to? Am I having a mid-life crisis that's snuck up on me? Mostly I just feel hollow, wondering what disaster waits just around the corner, wondering what I can do about it. Hell, I even miss Walt to talk to. Is this all there is? Peggy Lee sang that. Am I just staring into a time tunnel winding down? Waiting for my words to slur cause I'm too feeble to get them out clearly? Worry about falling? Lose control over my body—what's worse, my bodily functions—drool and pee and shit myself? Lose my memory and not know who I am? Or be completely aware that I was on the edge of slipping into eternity? That idea alone terrorizes. All my memories of Korea. And who would care? Don't have friends, really. I know scads of people for bullshit banter, jokes at the tavern, but no heart to heart comrades. Who would remember me? If I died tomorrow a few degenerate alkies at the J-Ville tav would mention my name for a couple days. Lloyd would fabricate stories to make himself look good. Raymond would buck for my job. And then? Like the billions upon billions whose star has winked out, it'd be like I was never here. When my insignificant little performance folds up for good, is that all? Katie bar the door? Don't know why I came up with that. Doesn't fit. Not by half, but I love the sound of it. Shoot, Luke. The air's full of pigeons.*

After dinner, while his mother cleared the table and began washing dishes, he'd followed his injury gnarled father to the living room. Sat in an old chair with stuffing compressed and hardened like fiberboard while his dad put Homer and Jethro on the hi-fi. Farm humor, the closest his father ever got to overt laughter.

Felt like the goddamn bottom of the barrel to me. The dumbing down. Wasn't for the GI bill, I'd still be slogging away in the barnyard. It's their

226

life, their reason for being. And when I was in high school and wanted to play football or basketball...forget it. Farm sucked up damned near every waking minute, was all there was. Get up in the dark to find the sow had rolled over half her piglets. My job to dispose of the cloudy-eyed, squashed little things. Cruel daily life. Should have prepared me for the war. Didn't. Couldn't.

When he turned into the federal employee parking lot behind the post office, his heartbeat had quickened as he'd been shuffling through his dinner experience again. Felt the pumping through his body, noticeably throbbing at his temples when he checked in the rear view. Could see veins on his temples pulsating. His face flushed, splotched red. And he hadn't even gotten to the office yet.

By the time George had climbed the wide granite staircase to the fourth floor, he'd calmed down considerably. If he stormed in angry, he'd decided, he'd be working against his own best interests of unraveling what was going on at Tanaka flats, and what Dave Brereton had to do with it. That was the part that really puzzled him, how Brereton was mixed up in whatever the hell had happened. But, as agitated as he was, he knew if he sounded accusatory, they'd probably clam up, stare at their feet, act guilty. *Like chastised children.* So he purposely restrained himself *You're the boss; you'll be responsible if it all goes belly up*, took a couple deep breaths at the top of the stairs before walking down the hall, pushing through the double glass doors, trying to act casually normal.

George had been sent to Parris Island, South Carolina for training before he'd been deployed to Korea; he'd seen how cockroaches scattered when someone turned on a light, especially in a kitchen or bathroom—any place with drains. The same edge-of-vision sensations rippled when he entered the office. Whatever everyone had been talking about, huddled together just prior to his appearance they'd all separated quickly and returned to their desks in a flash. Heidi was running her hands over her ample rump, smoothing her skirt as she regained her seat behind the counter, blushing up to the dark roots of her newly bleached straw-colored hair, a cosmetic alteration she'd made over the weekend, streaks of tacky blaring blonde. Throwing George a bit. Pissing him off actually, like she should have asked his permission first. A sudden inner anger that came and went quickly, leaving him feeling cheap for his own thoughts, a short but savage wrenching of his confidence. *Couldn't she bleach all of it at the same time? Is she trying to look like a skunk? I've known her for so long, since she was seventeen. Hard not to feel I have a responsibility to her, like an uncle or something.*

Eugene and Jeffrey kept their heads down, lazily shifting pieces of paper on their desktops quietly, partners in crime listening intently. George now stood behind Heidi so he couldn't see her face, but Raymond's eyes were expectantly wide, like a restrained puppy waiting for release.

"Heidi, Raymond," George announced without emotion, as though he were simply too tired. "In my office with everything you've got on Tanaka flats, whatever the hell happened last Friday. Walk me through it." He went straight into his glass-walled sanctuary. Leaving the door open, he sat down in his wooden swivel chair, picked up a pencil and nervously began tapping its point on his desk blotter, purposely not looking up until both were seated opposite him, neither making eye contact. *Twiddle Dee and Twiddle Dumb...but that's not fair. They're not adversaries. Raymond's petrified.*

George cleared his throat, swallowed the phlegm he'd brought up. "Show me the paperwork. I wanna see what Dave Brereton just had to have processed last Friday."

Raymond looked to Heidi, silently begging for help. None was forthcoming, however, as she kept her eyes down. A clear sign Raymond had to go it alone. "Um...we don't have all the originals. The captain took some with him. We did make copies, if you want to see em."

"Of course I want to see them, Ray. But why...how did you let him walk off with our paperwork?"

Raymond scurried to Heidi's workspace behind the front counter, grabbed a couple papers clipped together and returned, handing them to George's waiting, outstretched hand. Raymond either had not heard the question, or he'd decided to ignore it as he stood next to the desk, watching George. Heidi's face was drained of color, George noticed, regretting his unvoiced disapproval of her streaked hair. *My expression must've given me away.* So many slippery variables in office politics. He'd had to get used to stuffing his feelings in crucial moments, *but this crap with Brereton is too much.* He began reading from the top of the first sheet. *So what've we got here?*

Zane awoke Monday morning on the fringes of a panic attack. He wasn't sure whether he'd suffered a nightmare he couldn't remember, or whether he was sliding into another trough of churning anxiety. He lay still for a few moments, breathing slowly and deeply, trying to get a fix on his feelings. *Helluva way to start the day.* He smelled fresh coffee perking, could faintly hear a fire snapping and popping from the kitchen woodstove. As usual, Sasha was up before him. Another of his failings, sleeping in while she was already busy. Story of their lives; he was constantly working from a deficit. *I gotta make some changes.* Just admitting that smoothed him out enough that he could congratulate himself on not making a federal case out of Sasha wanting to quit meat. He was looking for positives to grab hold of.

Getting out of bed and pulling on the clothes he'd dumped on the floor last night, he replayed asking her, just before he dropped off to sleep, about the BLM guy she and Duty had met at the J-Ville tavern. *White hair. Missing fingers. Name's George. Semper Fi tattoo on his forearm. Shouldn't be hard to find.*

Zane and Greg didn't start for Medford until after noon. A weak sunny day on the river, pale light fractured through trees, little noticeable warmth. The weather report on the morning radio news predicted rain clouds by afternoon so before they'd left Zane and

229

Duty had restocked the wood bin by the front room stove with thick slabs of bark they'd gathered from down fir on the back hillside.

Zane asked if he should pick up anything while in town. Duty suggested a gallon of *Vino Primo*. Sasha came in from the kitchen to say she was making a quiche and would be using up all the eggs, would he get another dozen. He guessed this marked the beginning of their vegetarian life.

"I'll need some cash," Zane said defensively, force of habit. Duty dug in his front pocket and came out with a wadded up twenty.

"Spend it all," Duty grinned magnanimously, "found it rat-holed in my van when Sasha and I went by Vince and Soapy's on Saturday."

"I thought you guys only went to J-Ville?"

"Naw. We took the grand tour," Duty beamed. "I needed to see if my VA check had come in. I'm using their address, you know."

"Anyone want anything else?"

Duty held up an index finger. "Yeah. See if you can find one of those sprinkler heads, the big round ones with lots of holes—looks like a big sunflower—and I'll make us a shower outside. Hook it up to the hose. These sponge baths are getting old, and summer's coming." Zane winced. *Sounds like he's gonna be here forever. Is this what Sasha means? I thought she liked havin Duty around.*

He tried to visualize where he'd seen a lawn and garden store in town. *Behind Payless across from Hawthorne Park.* He liked to plan his trips, put stops in order to minimize time stuck in downtown traffic. He hated Medford proper, a provincially redneck working-class place flat on the valley floor except for the surrounding hills, the high ground occupied by anyone who could afford it. Particularly in the eastside hills where the country club attracted wealthier, tree-lined neighborhoods around it like the skirting under a Christmas tree.

The nub of downtown was framed by parallel one-way north-south avenues, gridded by four busy east-west streets. Penney's, Woolworth's, Newberry's. Purucker's Music where you could sit in a booth with the head phones on and listen to any record in the place.

Where Harry Lightfoot spun stories about famous musicians who'd played in town. The Craterian Theater, and the Holly. All of them boxed-in to the kernel of downtown, a five minute slow walk to everywhere. But then the Medford Shopping Center was built on land across from the park, bordered by I-5, with the open sewer of Bear Creek sludging slowly beneath the overpasses. Before the shopping center, he'd played war in the accessible parts of those acres of dense undergrowth: blackberry vines, thistles and waist-high dogwood. He and his grade-school rangers with cap guns, sticks-for-rifles and pinecone grenades often found used rubbers, cigarette butts or empty bottles scattered in smoothed out patches that otherwise looked like deer beds, hidden from easy sight. But it all got developed, graded and cemented over before he went to jr. high.

Until the fourth grade, when they'd moved to the two-story house up the hill on Eastwood, he and his parents were squeezed into a claustrophobic brick duplex on a dirt side street a short distance from Hawthorne park. Greg lived a block over, his folks still did. Zane knew from previous trips that taking his old friend home would be like returning to the site of his own worst punishment, but it was the price he had to pay to get Greg out of their hair.

"You ready, Greg? We oughta get goin." He went into the kitchen to remind Sasha he probably wouldn't be back until 7 or so, that he was stopping at the J-Ville tavern after 5 to see if he could run down the BLM guy she and Duty had met. He wanted to know why Perry's place was suddenly off-limits, why the trolley had been ripped out and Greg's cabin torched. Last night Zane had asked what she thought about that George they'd met. Did he seem like someone who might talk to him about what was going on? She and Duty had gotten good hits from him on Saturday, she'd said, but that was all she knew. "He put out friendly vibes."

When Zane watched Greg slink out to the bus, he thought he might as well be headed for the gallows going by his dramatic body language, his droopy eyes and beaten-dog expression. Plus, he'd been in the same clothes at least three days, most likely many more. Face it. He was a mess. Was probably put-out that he wouldn't be around when the wine got back. Still, he thought, the poor guy had just been burned out and now had to go hang out with his parents. *Has to be a downer all around.*

Greg's dad Jack managed McLoughlin Candy Company over by the high school in the crisscrossed maze of streets named after bushes or trees: Fir, Grape, Holly, Ivy, Orange, Peach. The warehouse cozied up to a siding of railroad tracks that ran through the edges of the commercial district, straight through to the packing plants at the south end of town where the valley's pear production was boxed up and sent out in freight cars to a world market. Zane knew Greg could get a job through his dad at the candy company anytime he wanted, but also knew Greg's attitude about punching a time clock came straight from Alfred E. Newman and Maynard G. Krebs: "What Me Work?" Not far from his own feelings. He didn't think he could ever have anything like a career if he wasn't an organizer. He'd had enough of being micro-managed, bossed around. Organizing was a whole other world in which he usually worked alone, far from anything resembling an office. No superiors to check in with every day. Of course, it didn't pay either. That was a bitch.

They drove the Applegate highway in uncharacteristic silence until Zane slowed down the hill to the junction at Ruch and off-handedly asked Greg if he got along with his parents.

"Whadda ya mean?"

At the stop sign, he turned right toward Jacksonville, after craning his neck to make sure the road was clear. "I mean, do you like them; do they like you?"

"Sure. They're my parents, man. Of course they like me. They get pissed at me sometimes, but I can hardly blame them, the things I get up to."

Zane lit a cigarette with a stick match. He kept a small handful in his pocket. He offered Greg the pack, passed on a match. Soon the air up front was layered with smoke. Zane cracked his plexiglass window and returned to his questions.

"An do you trust them? Like do you think they have your best interests at heart?"

Greg squinted. "I trust em, yeah, it's just weird bein there. I know I'm puttin em out, but they don't say anything about it. Why are you askin all these questions?" Now his eyes were wide and round, looking genuinely puzzled.

"Just tryin to get a handle on what it must be like," Zane said, "to not hate your old man, or to have a father who didn't hate you."

Greg stared, stupefied. "Whadda ya mean? Larry? He always seemed like such a nice guy."

Zane downshifted into third to take the backside of J-Ville hill. "The operative word there is 'seemed.' Everything was on the sly so no one would notice. Hell, he used to call me a snivelin shit behind someone's back, just mouthin the words, not sayin 'em out loud, only I knew. He'd send me vile hateful looks, glarin and frownin when no one else could see." *Lived with a rage I had no place to vent. No safe harbor. Ended up turnin that anger back on myself. Repeated the same character attacks to myself. Once those patterns are grooved in, how the hell do you get out from under?*

"All the time you lived on Stark street when we were kids? I never knew, man."

"That's the worst part...havin to keep it secret for my own protection."

"What about your mom, couldn't you tell her?"

"Tried once, about the 6th or 7th grade. Told her I didn't like bein alone with him. She slapped me in the face, sayin I oughta be ashamed. Who did I think I was? I know she told him 'cause he was twice as bad for a few days. I never brought it up again."

233

The sun disappeared once they'd crested J-Vill hill. The Rogue valley socked in with low clouds and hazy ground fog. Zane quit talking to weave through a long series of tight turns at the bottom of the hill just before the road became Jacksonville's main street. What Zane didn't say was that, in those moments of emotional and physical stress, he coped by seeing himself as tragic hero, the open cockpit flying ace with silk scarf streaming, glazed eyes and a sardonic smile, diving into the certain death of enemy fire. *Jesus! Walter Mitty. Could you be any more ridiculous? Maybe that's been your problem all along? Where'd you learn it...from Snoopy, for christsakes?* Charity North, his European Lit professor at PSU had once taken him to task for an essay he'd turned in on *Confessions of Felix Krull: Confidence Man* in which he bemoaned his own split personality, citing lots of examples, playing the 'what ifs.' In her voluminous scribbled comments she'd pointed out that successful people relied on discipline, dedication and direction. "Three D's which you clearly lack," she'd written at the bottom of the last page. Still stung when he thought of it.

Greg crushed out his cigarette in the miniscule ashtray sunken in the bus's dash. He tried to leave the butt in but it jiggled out immediately and fell to the floor where he put a raggedy Chuck Converse on it. "I remember something Perry told me over an over. I figured I was s'posed to learn some lesson from it. I don't know if I learned anything special but I remember his words exactly: 'if you don't heal what hurt you, you'll bleed on those who didn't cut you.' Told me that I don't know how many times."

"Sounds like somethin Duty would say. All his chakras an mantras an quatrains. Tell it to me again."

Greg obliged, taking it more slowly this time, looking over expectantly to Zane as he finished.

"Damn," Zane spit out, "doesn't tell you how to get well, but sure as hell makes sense what happens if you don't. I kept all the shit with dad to myself for years. Like livin under a heavy smelly oppressive guilt quilt. I only told Sasha after I knew he was planted in the

234

ground, an she was the first person since the time with my mother. Now, you're the second, Ea-mon." *This is the guy Sasha knows nothin about, an I can't seem to explain him to her. He still looks a fright, his hair sticking up all around like an afro. An he could seriously use a shower, but every now and then there really is someone home.*

Neither of them spoke as they passed the steamy front windows of the Jacksonville Tavern and just down the street the fog-fuzzed neon Jubilee Club sign that burned day and night, dancing figures in boots and cowboy hats, swinging at arm's length. He didn't know if he was just blatantly projecting, but Zane sensed that Greg ardently wished they'd stop for a drink. He felt the subconscious tugging, but wasn't having any of it. Three more blocks and they'd run out of downtown, were surrounded by old homes and small farms, heading out Stage road to Medford.

A half hour later, Zane dropped Greg off at his parents' house on Sherman street and got out of the neighborhood without triggering traumatic memories, although he did avoid driving past his old residence just to be safe. Since he was already in the area, he swung by Thompson's Lawn n' Garden in the parking lot behind Payless and easily found the sprinkler head Duty had ordered. $3.49, not bad at all.

Having built in some time for The Alibi in his route planning, he took Riverside north to the tavern, parking around back by habit. It was always a good idea not to advertise you were inside drinking by leaving your car where everyone could see how long it'd been sitting there. Besides, the back porch was for smoking dope, for sharing space with the dented green stale-beer dumpster. Regulars coming in through the back was a common occurrence, even though they had to thread through a storeroom and emerged behind the bar when they finally made it in. *Always wondered whether Doors' Backdoor Man was about anal sex. How 'bout Momma's got a squeeze-box an Daddy never sleeps at night.*

235

Fat Jack was pouring Blitz into a frosted mug when Zane appeared beside him. "Z-man, what's up?" Jack was wearing a sweatshirt with Evel Knievel soaring high over the fountain at Ceasar's Palace in '67. Everyone knew how that one ended, like the ski jumper on the lead-in to *Wide World of Sports* every week, a horrifying, sickening crash. Evel broke over forty bones trying to land, but on Jack's shirt he was flying high, looking good.

"Just killin time," Zane tossed over his shoulder as he lifted the hinged piece of bar so he could get through.

Once on the other side, he tapped a quarter on the wooden counter and Jack set a mug down. No jukebox in the tavern so Jack kept the TV on the wall tuned into game shows every afternoon. Allen Ludden was hosting *Password* with celebrity players Buddy Hackett and Joanne Whorley.

Zane took the closest bar stool, quickly scanning the room to see who was there in the middle of the day. A handful of men, most staring sullenly into their beers. He knew them all by sight if not by name. In fact, today he only knew Enema Bob's name, so-called because of his penchant for striking up conversations about dietary practices. How no one should cook fish at higher than two hundred and twenty-five degrees because heat destroys the cell membranes, kills important enzymes. But he earned his nickname for promoting, sometimes to total strangers, the benefits of high enemas for cleaning out toxicity. He could walk them through their inner workings in graphic detail, his heavily pockmarked face and long black ringlets leaning in while he poked a finger into their abdomen to differentiate organs.

Zane knew he wasn't in the mood. He twisted on his stool to face the game show, turning his back to everyone else, a physical statement that he wasn't interested in conversation. *Bar culture. Every place has its own protocols, accepted standards of behavior. An you never know who might be a narc.*

236

Four beers later, after having watched the $10,000 Pyramid and Match Game, Zane, now mildly buzzed, bought two half gallons of Gallo burgundy and a dozen eggs at OK market next door to the bar. He'd stared longingly at some Almaden Mountain Claret but decided to go with volume over quality, a well-worn choice.

He drove across town to the newly completed Ambulance Service headquarters on West Main and Peach. A powder blue cinder block building that took up half a block, with two ambulance bays and an office up front, employee apartments on the second floor. Quite the operation. He remembered when his mom worked in an old wooden, lap-sided house with one ambulance under a metal canopy. Being the office manager, accountant and general do-everything, she had been instrumental in obtaining the small business administration loan that paid for the new building and a second rig.

For years now, Zane had harbored the sneaky feeling she had something going on with the owner, Dwayne Walterson. The way they'd interacted in the office was vastly different from how she'd behaved towards his father. Teasing innuendos, an intimate familiarity he'd never seen her display at home. Not that he blamed her. Particularly after he'd enrolled at Portland State and found any excuse he could not to come home. On those occasions when he hitchhiked down to Medford for a holiday he couldn't avoid, Dwayne and the Ambulance Service was all she talked about. Gushing, her admiring preoccupation obvious. After the old man moved out, what was there to stop her? *An now the fucker's dead, so enjoy yourself. I gotta believe you deserve it. Too bad you swapped one rabid military asshole for another.*

The ambulance service served double duty as a medical supply store. Except for two small offices, its main space was filled with oxygen canisters, wheelchairs, even a couple hospital beds shoved into a corner. Walkers, canes, hoses, bedpans, blood pressure monitors—Zane saw it as a miniature warehouse of evidence to the frailties of age. Lots of small metal boxes with tangles of wiring and luminous dials. Scared him every time he came. *I'm only a block from Medford Mortuary. Aunt Luella and Paddy lived in an apartment on the third floor with an elevator in the living room. When Paddy worked there. Used to stay with them sometimes when Mom and Dad went out of town, usually up to Eugene. Listened to The Lone Ranger on the radio, Bishop Fulton Sheen on the tv explaining the satanic sharing nature of communism. Something about how if your neighbor's house burned down they'd have to come and live with you and there was nothing you could do about it. Jesus! Those Catholics. Paddy told me the dead people were in the basement floating in a big vat of chloroform, not to ever get in the freight elevator or I would end up down there. Aversion training. Had me convinced.*

He saw his mother bent over the desk in her front office, working with a pencil on papers spread in front of her. She'd gotten her black hair cut fashionably short since the last time he'd seen her. Joan Armatrading, he thought. *But you're not a lesbian. At least not that I know of.* She smiled when she looked up to see him approaching. "Hi, Honey. Fancy seeing you today. Everything ok? Sasha's alright?"

Zane stole a quick glance to see if Dwayne was in the other office, but thankfully it was empty. He wouldn't have to make nice with her boss. The ex-marine had a drawing of a peace symbol hanging on his wall with the caption, "Sign of the American Chicken." Not exactly Zane's kind of guy.

"Yeah," he said, "we're fine."

"So what's brought you in? Just had to see your ol' mom?" She rocked back in her swivel chair, gave him a once-over.

"I'm lookin for information. Our neighbor Perry died Friday night and I understand your guys picked him up on the river." He took a quick breath—this was the moment that mattered. "Any chance I could take a look at the trip slip?" He waited all of two seconds. "I'm just curious to see what they said."

"Oh, I don't know. Those reports are really just for our records. We don't make them public in any way."

238

"Yeah, I understand. But he was like a mentor to Sasha. She's completely devastated and I promised her I'd do what I could to find out what happened to him. Somethin's not right, Mom." *This might get her, she loves Sasha.*

Shirley shook her head as she sat upright, pushing papers, infinitesimally touching each as though she needed to make contact with them. She spoke without looking up. "You're lucky Dwayne's not here today." Then, shoving away from her desk, she stood up, put a hand on his shoulder, fixed his eyes. "Not one word to anyone. If this comes back on me, there'll be hell to pay. Friday night you said? What was his name?"

"Perry Louvelle. It has to be the only call out the Applegate, isn't it?"

She didn't answer, brushing past him to the counter inside the front door. He watched her thumbing through a stack of memo size papers until she found what she was looking for. Handing it to him, she told him he couldn't take it with him.

"I'll just make notes," he said, "can I use the counter?"

"Remember, Zane. I don't want to be reading any of this in the *Mail Tribune*."

"Don't worry. I only want to know what to tell Sasha," he lied, focusing on who had placed the call. *Just what I thought. Goddamn Wade Perkins.* He started to read the EMT's written description of Perry's injuries *Holy fuckin Christ!* before cold claws gripped his intestines and twisted savagely.

Chapter Fourteen

The old concept that man [sic] is conscious of and conceptualizes reality through language is basically correct. It is true that no distinct or clear consciousness of the world is possible outside of the word. Language and its forms play an essential role in the process of the consciousness's refraction of existence. However, an important point must be added to this principle. The consciousness and cognition of reality is not achieved through language and its forms understood in the precise linguistic sense. **It is the forms of the utterance, not the forms of language, that play the most important role in consciousness and the comprehension of reality.** *To say that we think in words, that the process of experiencing, seeing, and comprehending is carried along in a stream of inner speech, is to fail to clearly realize what this means. For we do not think in words and sentences, and the stream of inner speech which flows within us is not a string of words and sentences.*

We think and conceptualize in utterances, complexes complete in themselves....These integral, materially expressed inner acts of man's orientation to reality and the forms of these acts are very important. **One might say that human consciousness possesses a series of inner genres for seeing and conceptualizing reality. A given consciousness is richer or poorer in genres, depending on its ideological environment** *[my emphasis].* (133) *Bakhtin M.M./P.N. Medvedev. The Formal Method in Literary Scholarship. Trans. Albert J. Wehrle. Cambridge & London:Harvard UP, 1978.*

Zane left his mother's office knowing full well he was bent on complicating his life. He still needed to talk with the ambulance techs to fill in some blank spots, but what he'd learned from their report painted a ghastly picture, one that amped up his anger, rekindled his fires. Back on a mission, he felt. Outraged. Ready to fight. The condition of Perry's body, as described by the emergency crew that transported him, told a far different story from that of an old man accidentally falling twelve feet onto a rocky river bank.

According to their write-up, both of Perry's kneecaps were broken, a clear indication the impact came from the front. His left shoulder dislocated, out of the socket, twisted backwards. Again, a frontal injury, as was his fractured nose. Numerous visible contusions and abrasions on his face, neck and hands—areas not covered by clothing. Zane could see how all those injuries might be consistent with a fall.

What wasn't consistent, however, what couldn't be explained by falling was that the EMT noted the back of Perry's head was caved-in, his skull crushed. Zane argued it out with himself. *You can't have drastic impact injuries on both front and back at the same time. Ok, then, let's say he bounced, flipped over. Fine. But, in that case, the second set of injuries would be much less serious, just bruises. There's nothin from the trail edge down to the river except ferns an weeds. No rocks to hit on the way down. Did he fall twice?*

Zane was on Stage Road again, headed back to Jacksonville, reversing his earlier route. Aware that much had changed in the time between drives. It wasn't five yet; he'd probably be too early for the BLM guy named George, but he could wait in the tavern as well as anywhere else. Have a beer. Try to sort out the bombshells from his freelance investigative visit to the ambulance office. Because there was more than what he'd learned about Perry's injuries. After he'd jotted down all the pertinent information he gleaned from the trip slip, his mother matter-of-factly told him his dad had a life insurance policy and that he would be getting half of the payout—twenty-five thousand dollars. "We both know what you went through," she said. "I'm splitting the money with you. Should get it next month."

To say he was taken aback by her out-of-nowhere admission didn't begin to plumb the depths of the violation he felt. *All these years she knew, an kept quiet? Never said a thing? She does this right after I've realized Perry was most likely killed by someone with a baseball bat, or a chunk of wood, or a shovel blade? She lays this other stuff on me right when I'm leavin. Like it's about as important as saying goodbye. We can use the money to buy the farm—that part's great—but I can't help feelin it's mostly a way for her to wash herself clean without ever havin to discuss it. Pay the money; close the books. Pay me off. If we buy the place I'll always know I owe it directly to him. Like we'll be livin in a house and on land that's a constant physical testament to his malignancy. Somehow I'll have to come to grips with that. I can imagine folks sayin that I'm just bein difficult. Your mom dumps twenty-five grand on you an you're complainin. Ungrateful. Ingrate, he spit at me. As I say every time, like I'm genuflectin to his altar, it's not even a fuckin word.*

Before he'd left The Alibi, Fat Jack had laid three wheatstraw Zig-Zags on him. Said they'd been soaked in hash oil. Sticky and black. Jack couldn't help giving his stash away, part of his charm. Some phobic need to share what he had with whoever was around. *In 3rd grade, Melvin Minks came to school with a five-dollar bill he offered to anyone who'd agree to be his friend. Everyone knew they lived down in the gulley behind Sacred Heart hospital. Shacks, really. 'Melvin Minks Stinks,' we used to chant on the playground.* Zane trusted Jack enough that he didn't have to worry about whether the hash oil would turn out to be PCP or some kind of speed, so as soon as he'd escaped his mother he'd rolled a joint in the bus. Smoked half of it before he hit Stage Road, after taking back streets through newer residential neighborhoods with house after house of T-111 siding painted in Golden Eagle or Saratoga Brown or Lexington Tan, earth tones. *Did four or five houses those colors last year. Real popular. Dutch Boy called it the Colonial Line, for fuck's sake. Imperialism forever.*

He parked behind Jacksonville Lumber with the employees' cars and trucks, where there was usually a spot, and walked the block and a half to the tavern through the damp, clinging air. Pushing through the steamed-up glass front door, he entered the familiarly humid country-n'-western ambiance of twangy jukebox, a few straw cowboy hats sprinkled amongst the battalion of baseball caps advertising farm machinery, firearms and fishing equipment. Lots of faded, worn or stained denim. *Way stoned again. Hash oil was for real. Find a stool an get outta the way.*

J-Ville tavern was normally safe territory despite the distinctive cowboy nature of the place. His appearance didn't raise an eyebrow here, no disgusted glares or under-breath mutterings about his long hair. But some of the most rabid racists and war-mongers his own age looked like they'd just stepped out of Haight/Ashbury: beards, tie-dye

243

and ponytails aplenty. Until they talked, you just didn't know. Vicissitudes of southern Oregon.

He took an empty seat farthest from the door, smelling the greasy beer sausage from the bubbling crockpot on the back bar, the lingering floating scent of popcorn mixing with clouds of cigarette smoke. He'd felt the hash oil kicking in hard just as the door closed behind him, as if on cue. Like coming on to acid in a crowd. An adrenaline rush that left him nervously unsure of himself, worried how he'd make it through the crowd stacked up by the bar. Obstacles he threaded his way around carefully without making eye contact.

As he waited for the bartender in the polyester Hawaiian shirt— Floyd or Boyd, something like that—who was busy yukking it up with a couple of beehive beauties with plunging necklines, he flashed on the redneck restaurant scene from *Easy Rider*. Saw it in his sharpened mind's eye.

He and Sasha had experienced their own version on the way to Minneapolis in '70 at a diner a dozen miles off I-94 just east of Bismarck, North Dakota. It was the day after Zane's propane lit conspiracy with the road atlas that explained those miles of armament lined-up in Billings.

He'd been in a near-belligerent, reckless mood that next morning, imagining columns of tanks and armored personnel carriers surging into Seattle or Portland, ready to suppress civil disorder. Put him in a dark, feisty place. That, and breaking his own transcontinental safety rule of never leaving sight of the freeway. They'd driven twenty minutes into the undulating, treeless, clichéd heartland to find a place to eat. Had to have been a Sunday. He remembered dressed-up, freshly scrubbed and combed families squeezed into shiny red vinyl booths, kids twisting their bodies and craning their necks to check them out, table conversations suddenly subdued.

As soon as they slid into their booth Zane had started flipping the metal pages of the jukebox unit mounted on the wall at their table. Three plays for a quarter. He'd punched in the code for "Okie from

Muskogee" three separate times. Sasha shook her head and clucked some, mostly pretending, he'd thought.

The fresh young waitress without makeup, in pressed jeans and a red-checkerboard shirt, had taken their order as if under duress. She'd seemed scared to be talking to them, looking up furtively as she wrote. Brought the bill before they were even halfway through their breakfast, laying it face down on the table with a sigh. "We don't get people like you in here," she'd said apologetically.

While Johnny Paycheck growled "Take This Job and Shove It" behind the raised voices and strained laughter of the J-Ville Tavern, Zane thumbed the edges of that bizarre mid-western morning, folding it over with Jack Nicholson's mugging face in the leather football helmet from the movie, mingling memories.

In the bar mirror, he could see the flashing lights of a pinball machine in the far corner, against the foggy front windows. Not one of those flipper and bumper machines you gyrate, wiggle and jam trying for the high score. This was a gambling pinball that he could feed rolls of nickels to jack up the odds, activate sliding screens for easier shots if he was lucky. Had a large "For Amusement Only" banner on the top, but locals knew the Liquor Commission usually just turned a blind eye. If the bartender recognized him, had seen him around before, they'd pay off, sliding winnings across the bar in a ludicrous song-and-dance that didn't fool anyone who was paying attention. He still had five dollars and change from Duty's twenty, felt the rising, tugging urge to pour nickels into the machine. Quite clearly his addictive tendencies coming to screw with his life some more.

He needed to keep a dollar and a half for gas. It was up to 49.9 a gallon after the OPEC embargo last year, when people could only fill up on days the last number of their license plate matched the date, odd or even. He did some figuring. A draft Lucky Lager was only a quarter, but he'd run out of smokes, too. Had forgotten to get them at OK Market, so the pinball was a no-go. Besides, as if sweeping away cobwebs with his hand, he reminded himself he was there to talk to the white-haired BLM ex-marine. When the bartender finally quit with the women and made it down to his end, he ordered a draft and a pack of Pall Mall reds, put the five down in front of him. *We can actually own the farm. Cash on the barrel head.*

After he took a deep swallow of beer and got a cigarette going, he relaxed. His high had mellowed a bit with time; he didn't feel stretched tight like a timpani anymore, had recovered his composure. And with that came his THC-inspired theorizing. As if he'd stepped through a dimensional wormhole that deadened the bar noise and gave him clear focus. He could identify complex layers of interlocking connections, could see whole narrative outlines laid out plainly. Of course he thought of himself as a mastermind. He knew that. He was stoned, for christsakes. But nonetheless the pictures clung together like metal to a magnet; he could see crucial events linked in watertight causal imperatives.

Perry wouldn't get an autopsy, this story told him. Since he'd had no family, no community contacts, no bank account, he'd be treated like any vagrant found by the tracks. There wouldn't be an investigation into his death, either, because it was already classified as an accident by the Sheriff's deputy at the site, based on Wade's account. He'd learned that, too, from the ambulance trip slip. Old man slips, falls onto the rocks. *I wonder how Wade explained bein there?* And they'd never have to justify their decisions to anyone. The county would bury him in cheap ground and pay a reduced rate for the ambulance. Whatever Zane thought he knew was beside the point. Case was already closed.

That was one of movies he was watching. Two were running at once, going in opposite directions like double helix strands in a DNA molecule, electrons whirling, bonding pairs together. The second full-blown, fitting-together story sprouted from his mother admitting she'd been aware of what was going on with his father. At least at some point she'd known, but done nothing, said nothing. This story, this alternative version of his life—who knew what and when?—

246

knocked his previous narrative askew, shattered the cemented foundations of how he'd thought about himself, of thinking he was isolated, that he had to keep the secret. If she knew, did anyone else? As soon as that question surfaced, he saw, as if skyrockets were showering him with vivid booming colors, what he'd never put together before. Lee. His uncle. His dad's brother who had been so overtly kind to him, taking him fishing most every evening at the lake. Taught him how to run the boat, tie all the knots, drift flies, pee in the coffee can. *He knew, too, didn't he? That's why he went out of his way for me, treated me like his own. He knew what his brother was capable of, probably imagined what was goin on. Kept me from bein alone. So the story I fabricated about myself an carried around all this time wasn't quite real. I did have someone on my side, someone who knew. Jesus! All those lessons he taught me. Of course, I don't actually know for sure, beyond any doubt. But stranger things have been known to happen. Look at Agnew, for christsakes. Who'da thought Mr. Law an Order could get indicted for conspiracy, bribery, extortion an tax fraud while in office? Took kickbacks all the way to the end. Must'a stepped on the wrong toes. That smug sanctimonious asshole is gone. Nolo Contendere. Change is possible. Maybe even for me?*

George shed his office clothes, pulled on some jeans and a comfortable green and blue Pendelton that had gone thin at the elbows. What a colossal cluster-fuck of a day, he thought, lacing up his boots. After having a burr in his butt all weekend from not knowing what the hell was happening out at Tanaka Flats, he'd finally seen the paperwork and still wasn't sure what to think, except that Dave Brereton was involved up to his scrawny neck.

If that had been his only problem, he'd have considered it trouble enough. But Mondays were habitually busy, the mail bag usually stuffed with government traffic, enough business to keep the office occupied for the week. One of the logging contracts Walt had approved raised hackles in the Denver regional office and it took hours working through all the details before he'd found errors in one small set of survey computations. The BLM cabin at Whiskey Creek had been broken into again. That happened almost weekly; he just had to phone a field agent. Most of the rest of his day was spent allocating and assigning specific jobs for his staff, explaining what needed to be done and when. Whenever he let up for a moment, however, the weird transfer of claim for Tanaka Flats pushed back into his thinking. *Why would ol' man Louvelle sell his claim? For one dollar? Haven't been out there to see him in four or five years, but when I was in the field I stopped by often. Never struck me as the kind who wanted to be anywhere else. Always knee-deep in work on the place.*

Raymond had filled out the H7A transfer form on Friday. As near as George could see, nothing was amiss there, other than that the new claimant's address was in Redding. That puzzled him. How a virtual hermit would get mixed up with some Californian. And why Brereton was doing the footwork, using his influence. The fact that he'd walked off with the original of the scrawled, hand-written bill of sale set George itching like he was breaking out in hives. *But the signatures on the copy were notarized by that realtor in Ruch, so, as far as that goes, it's all kosher. Not that I can really see Perry getting to Ruch on his own. Someone had to drive him. But why? Why would he leave everything he'd worked thirty years or more to build? And for one goddamn dollar? Gave it away. Doesn't make sense. What was so frigging important it all had to be done last Friday?*

Ever since the Fausens had vanished off Carberry Creek over a month ago, George thought the Applegate valley was under some malevolent hex or spell. More like a curse, actually. He didn't know why; it was just a feeling. Reports of Hessians loose in the woods kept cropping up at the tavern, how they cruised in packs on logging roads, looking for hapless victims. Conventional wisdom floating through town—and when wasn't that dead on?—spreading gossip that Schumann and Sons was taking more out in gold from the sluice pond than the construction contract paid set lots of folks on edge. Nearness to fortune, but lifetimes away from sharing in it. Didn't matter if it was true or not. Once the idea caught hold, people started choosing up sides, staking claims. Whose land was it anyway? That settling pond was lit at night like a football stadium, guards all over the property, fitted-out pickups patrolling the roads. And now this Tanaka Flats mess.

On that depressing note, George left his apartment and took the five step walk to the tavern's back door. Time to recalibrate his thinking, though he suspected it would take more than Lloyd's banter and Lucky on tap to do any real good in that department. It was busier than usual. The boisterous after-work crowd obviously didn't want to go home yet, groups of drinkers revved up like a weekend. He decided he'd just mind his manners at the end of the bar until the energy level ebbed a little. He didn't come in for excitement. The tavern was his family room, where he spent most of his time when he was home. He liked it best at a low key, when he could carry on a conversation without shouting, more civilized. Ray Stevens' "The Streak" blared through the wall speakers to a smattering of giggles, as he tried to navigate through the knot of people mingling around the pool tables. *Just as mindlessly stupid as Walter Brennan and "Ol' Rivers" or Bobby Boris Pickett and the Crypt-Kicker Five. Sheb Wooley, "Purple People Eater." What some people laugh at. The old man and his Homer and Jethro. Gawd A'mighty.* He saw two empty stools at the end of the bar, close to the toilets, as far away from the action as he could get. The same place he parked himself most nights. As he settled on the last stool, he noticed the half glass of beer, change and pack of Pall-Malls in front of the other empty seat and realized his luck was even better than he'd thought. *What's that say about me, though? The one place no one wants is my favorite. Like those tribes in desert cliff dwellings. Always figured that's why they lived there, that no settlers would come to push them out. Unless they found minerals or oil, I suppose.*

Lloyd made another trip down the bar, picking up empties, dumping ashtrays, swiping his damp towel half-heartedly while he exchanged barbs with regulars. Ever the garrulous host. "Mr. Land

Management," he said in mock seriousness. "How's our Federal government going today?"

"Fine, Lloyd. Be much better with a beer, though."

As he waited, George felt rather than actually saw someone behind him, and shifted to his left a bit to make room as a lean and lanky figure sat down next to him. The kid in his mid-twenties—young man wasn't in his lexicon—lit a cigarette and drained his glass, pushing the empty forward with a quarter. Lloyd picked up both, nodding, after he set George's beer down. Charlie Rich began "Behind Closed Doors," as George took in what he could of his new neighbor. Slightly faded Levis, a blue work shirt frayed at the cuffs, black hair down to his shoulders and a Joe Namath moustache.

Standard look for his age, George thought, now aware that the kid's face was turned toward him with an expression bordering on shock or surprise.

"Excuse me," he said, "are you George by any chance?"

"By every chance, yeah. Do I know you?"

"No, I...well," he swallowed, "my old lady said she met you on Saturday, when she an our friend came in for a beer. Said you knew Perry Louvelle." He waited a second for a response, but George just nodded. "We live out the Applegate just downstream from him a few miles. Lester an Adeline Crawford's place."

George knew the lay of the land the kid was talking about. Knew Lester and Adeline, though they'd never particularly been friends. Nothing wrong with them, as far as that went, but he hadn't struck up any kind of relationship with them. They'd never been on his visit list. He did remember talking to the stunningly beautiful young woman with the linebacker, though; she'd said she saw Perry all the time.

"I'm Zane, by the way," sticking out his hand which George gripped for a millisecond. "Sasha—that's my wife—told me you worked for BLM."

George nodded again, very quickly, as if he didn't want to admit it too overtly. He was trying to get a fix on what this Zane was up to.

He's got some kind of agenda going. This all wasn't just a lucky happenstance. I get the feeling he was looking for me. Wants something. Lloyd appeared with Zane's beer, casting a side glance at George as if questioning his choice of conversational partners. George ignored Lloyd's slightly mocking smile, but was aware of Zane staring fixedly for a few seconds at his missing fingers. Neither of them was speaking now, and he wasn't sure how to proceed. So he waited, taking the opportunity to contemplate his beer before taking a sip. He hated being observed, the object of attention.

"Well," Zane finally broke in. "I was lookin to see if you could tell me why the Forest Service burned down my friend Greg's cabin on Perry's claim."

"What? Burned down? When?"

"You didn't know? It was the day after Perry died an…"

"Wait!" George blurted, cutting the kid off, feeling a seismic shift coming on. "Perry died? *I can't believe this.* What happened to him?"

"Yeah. Friday night. Wade Perkins said he found him down on the river rocks, said he must'a fallen. Leastways that's his version."

"Friday night you say?" *Same day all the claim transfer shit happened. Perry fell?* Questions bumped into each other in his mind, piling up in an onslaught, smashing into each other until he couldn't form a coherent thought. Stunned and suddenly angry that this was all news to him. He felt side-swiped. T-boned by a runaway semi.

For the moment, no music flooded the room. Above the layered noise of voices blending into a muffled background, Lloyd's antique cash register sang the real national anthem and George realized, with a sinking sense of finality, that some major gyroscopic wobble was shaking the Applegate like a death rattle, a force more fibrous and steady than the quick jolts of dynamite blasting out the new lake bottom.

251

Chapter Fifteen

Human beings do not live in the objective world alone, nor alone in the world of social activity as ordinarily understood, but are very much at the mercy of the particular language which has become the medium of expression for their society. It is quite an illusion to imagine that one adjusts to reality essentially without the use of language and that language is merely an incidental means of solving specific problems of communication or reflection. **The fact of the matter is that the "real world" is to a large extent unconsciously built up on the language habits of the group. [...] We see and hear and otherwise experience very largely as we do because the language habits of our community predispose certain choices of interpretation.** *[my emphasis]. (26) Lee, Penny.* Studies in the History of the Language Sciences. *Vol. 81. The Whorf Theory Complex. Philadelphia: John Benjamins Publishing Co., 1984.*

Sasha and Heavy Duty spent much of Monday afternoon making a cheese, olive and onion quiche. Using an old copy of *The Joy of Cooking*, fresh parsley and basil from her herb garden on the sun side of the house. What sun there was, since high clouds had closed a lid over the valley a little after three. She'd enlisted Duty into making the pie crust. Of course, she had to put the instructions in front of him, and he managed to end up wearing a good deal of the flour. She said he looked like a flocked Christmas tree.

Once the quiche was in the kitchen woodstove oven, they'd moved to the living room where Sasha put *Harvest* on the stereo, sat in the window chair, Erasmus on her lap. Duty was sifting through some pot, using the cover of a book of matches on an inclined plate to separate seeds and bits of stem. She watched him work, and basked in the warmth and ease she felt being around him. Not a hint of harbored resentments. No subterranean stream of unvoiced invectives straining to be unleashed, the way she visualized what she thought was often going on in Zane's head. Like a plastic tub of eels she'd seen once, a writhing mass. Being around Duty, she didn't worry she was entering a mine field whenever she tried to get close. And that meant a lot. The way it'd been with Zane that drizzling Moratorium day in Portland, and still was occasionally, though now with some degree of fear attached that he'd seal himself off, be unable to reciprocate. She was aware how desperately she craved a steady connectedness, a caressing feeling like soft, warm light penetrating a dark room. The way it had been when Zane managed to be a reliable source of passionate strength despite his secrets and the emotional scars she didn't know about at the time. Now, however, Duty seemed to fill the bill as confidant, someone she could trust to have her back.

Until a week ago, she hadn't been quite sure what to make of his habit of touching her when walking by or if they were sitting together talking. Her shoulder, her forearm, the back of her neck, he sometimes squeezed gently while resting his hand on her. He did it whether Zane was around or not, which confused her, tangled up the signals she thought he was sending.

Last Wednesday afternoon, when just the two of them were home, she and Duty had been drinking wine, taking turns picking albums to play. After she put on side two of *Rubber Soul*, she came right out with it. "Are you hitting on me, Duty? I can't decide, so you'll just have to tell me."

He laughed, face ablaze with what looked to her like pure impish delight. "Oh, Honey Child. I've always been on the other team, knew it from an early age. You're perfectly safe with me." He throttled down the mirth. "I love you whole-heartedly, but not in that way. I'm sorry."

"Please. Don't be sorry. I'm the one who feels like a fool." As indeed she did. Relieved she wouldn't have to rebuff him; if, in fact, that's what she would have done. Embarrassed to have thought he was after her. Though she had spun out a few mind movies of the two of them together somewhere exotic, as a couple. They'd been escape fictions, she knew, pretending to a more exciting future. Nothing seriously worked out. Not real. She'd never been attracted to him as a lover.

Duty had sworn her to secrecy on the spot. "I'd rather keep it between us. You know how fragile male alliances are, and Medford isn't exactly San Francisco." She'd understood his reticence to come out. *How would people treat him, people from the family? I'm assuming no problems, but what do I know? We're all white, presumably hetero, and still male-centric from what I can tell. It's the men who talk about 'sex, drugs and rock-n-roll?' Emphasis on sex first and foremost. Another male fantasy playing out in our otherwise counter-culture world.*

Erasmus jumped down, lazily twitching and stretching his way towards the kitchen and his Friskies. Neil Young was singing about needles and despair when Duty spoke up from the couch.

"What I love about Neil Young," he said, licking the roll-up he'd just made, "is that he…it's like he doesn't actually sing specific notes, more like his voice is a container for lots of sounds. That each note is really a collection of semi-harmonic tones." He looked at her helplessly. "I know. That doesn't make any sense." He put a match to the joint. "But it's so encompassing…I'm no musician, so I can't explain it…Guess I just hear it…feel it."

"It's a haunting voice," she said. "Sticks with you."

They were silent for the final songs on that side. Sasha getting up once to take a couple hits, handing the number back to him and returning to her chair. In a laser-focused memory that was suddenly "there," occupying all the space, she hummed the tune to "If you wanna be happy for the rest of your life, don't make a pretty woman your wife," while simultaneously hearing the words. Queer it would pop up out of nowhere. Except she didn't believe in sheer chance for a moment, reasons could always be found. One of Perry's favorite lines. Her subconscious reasons must be hidden in the basement of her psyche. Some dark cobwebbed room that housed her fears and phobias.

"I heard on the news this morning that a 14 year-old girl was trampled to death yesterday at a David Cassidy concert in London.

Eight hundred others injured." Duty's voice yanked her back into the room.

"What?"

"David Cassidy concert. The bubblegumers and teenyboppers freaked."

"Are you serious?" Sasha had regained her normal place on the space/time continuum. "David Cassidy?"

"I know, not exactly Altamont and the Hell's Angels. Next time it'll probably be the White House Easter Egg Roll. Toddlers squished by aggressive parents. Maybe that would finally bring Nixon down? Folks don't like seeing the social fabric rip open, reminds them that godless disaster is always bubbling behind the curtains." He took a long toke and puffed out smoke rings to the ceiling.

An unexpected aftershock realization of Perry's death sent stinging icy flashes through her body. Not again—waves of dread, the bottom dropping out everywhere at once—frighteningly physically vivid. No warning. No alarm signals. They'd started even before Greg had blubbered out the news the night before last. When he'd stumbled through the door, before he said anything, she'd suffered a sudden lower abdominal seizure, pain telling her that some major dislocating change was occurring.

"What do you think happened to the Fausens?" she asked him, following her line of thought.

"Oh, they're dead as a wedge," he said. "Imagine they've been dead since the day they disappeared. Can't really see any other explanation."

"And then Perry, too. Zane doesn't believe that was an accident. Creeps me out, not knowing who's behind it all."

"You never really know what your neighbors are capable of, what's going on with them. You see how Lester drives around in his pickup all the time, checking on his fences? Richard told me he started his herd by picking up other people's calves, stealing strays. So Richard says Lester figures all the other people with cattle are doing the same

256

thing. He's always on the look-out. The way liars assume everyone else lies. It's like their Ego, in a Freudian sense, just reproduces Idic needs instead of mediating them. Their world view is it's them against everyone else." He'd walked to the stereo while talking, had put on the John Mayall's "Turning Point" and lowered the volume.

"But what if it's true?" he asked, regaining the couch, leaning back while muted blues harp provided a background. "Not that all the farmers are rustlers, but what if the us-against-them mentality is rampant? What if, back in the woods, there's armed survivalists committed to staying isolated? Who see the dam as a clear invasion of their territory. Remember, the Fausens were camping at the very edge of the one-lane dirt road forests that go back for miles. They weren't more than half a mile from Applegate highway, for cryin' out loud. Absolutely no sign of any kind of struggle. They didn't walk off. Someone had to get them into a vehicle. They didn't just leave on their own."

"Zane says the same thing about Perry. That someone must have helped him over the edge. I think Greg convinced him that Perry wouldn't have put himself in a position to fall. He was too careful. Knew his limits."

"We were on that trail yesterday. It doesn't get any closer than three feet or so to the edge. He'd have to have a running start. At ninety plus years old? Come on."

She was choking up, fighting back tears, her voice becoming raspy. "I keep coming back to knowing I'll never sit with him again...never hear his voice...such a loss." John Mayall filled the living room air for about thirty seconds.

"How much longer does that quiche take?" Duty smiled as he said it. She knew he was purposely trying to change the subject, calling attention to himself with a goofy expression of manufactured bewildered innocence like Frankie Fontaine playing Crazy Guggenheim on Jackie Gleason, her uncle's favorite show. Duty's round, slightly pudgy face looked so ridiculous she couldn't help herself from lightening up.

"Probably ten more minutes, but I'll go check. I can tell you're anxious to get at it."

"We're not waiting for Zane?"

She hadn't quite made it to the kitchen, was standing in the arched doorway with her hands on her hips, in jeans and a yellow sweatshirt. "Duty," she waited for effect. "Zane's going to the J-Ville tavern after five to find our friend George from Saturday. *Just the day before yesterday?* Plus he'll have whatever's left from the twenty you gave him. Considering those facts, what kind of bet would you make about when he might show up?"

"Far out. I'm hungry."

When Zane turned off the Applegate highway into his driveway, he focused on the pertinent pronoun. His. *Twenty-five grand. We'll be owners. Lots of river frontage. Have to do something about this bridge.* He'd left behind the low hanging clouds and sticky ground fog of the Rogue valley when he cleared J-Ville Hill, so his drive out had been partly clear, billions of galaxies pinpointed in the night sky.

Once again, as happened with regularity, he struggled with understanding how the universe could be constantly expanding, speeding up in fact. To where? Space that was already there, empty, just waiting for the universe to fill it? *Enough already. There's plenty'a other fish to fry, long as Sasha doesn't ban em...Christ on a crutch. Should'a left that hash roach in the ashtray. I gotta get all this in some kind'a order. Like what do I say first? "We got the money for the farm?" or "you wouldn't believe what that George told me?*

He'd been going back and forth since he left the tavern, trying to figure out how to explain what he'd learned. If he started with Shirley and the life insurance payout, Sasha might think he didn't care so much about Perry. If, instead, he tried to get all the pieces of the Tanaka Flats story in line, the way George had spilled it, there was a

258

good chance, wasted and troubled as he was, that he'd start raving about corruption and cover-ups, like everyday's news on the national stage, except this was right here on the river. He knew where his righteous anger could take him, recounting how state controlled organized crime always played out the same way. Not with a sanctioned killing here and authoritarian frame-up there, disconnected and singular. More like well-grooved systems perfected from centuries of practice, built on straight-faced lies and litanies about death struggles between haloed gods and horned devils. *Sartre. No Exit. I get it now.*

He parked the bus, grabbed a half gallon of wine in each hand, eggs tucked under his arm. Stepping up on the lightless porch to stand in front of the door, he kicked it a couple times before Duty opened. "Gang way," he said louder than was necessary. "I'm not Greek, but I am bearin gifts. It's been a helluva day."

Duty took the wine and Zane delivered the eggs to the refrigerator. Sasha saw him staring at what was left of the quiche on the counter. "Go. I'll bring some in for you." He'd barely had time to sit down on the couch and empty his pockets on the hatch cover before she set a plate in front of him. A wedge of custard pie, a bunch of ladyfinger grapes and a chunk of cheddar. *Our new diet.*

Duty brought three Mason jars from the kitchen, half-filled them with burgundy, and took the other end of the couch while Sasha sat in her window chair with the wide flat wooden arms that served as TV trays. Minus the TV. Zane had tried more than once to adjust the aerial on the roof—they had a small black and white set—but couldn't pick up any of the three signals from Medford because of the high ridges and narrow valley. And cable hadn't even made it to Jacksonville yet, so they'd become wedded to the FM from Ashland for what news they got on NPR. It was after eight, Monday night reggae. Peter Tosh, Desmond Dekker, Jimmy Cliff, the Melodians, Bob Marley. All of them low enough that he couldn't make out words.

259

Erasmus had crawled onto his lap and was tentatively stretching a paw towards the cheese. Zane pinched off a corner for him, put it on the rug. When he looked up, he caught two sets of eyes zeroed in expectantly. Erasmus let it be known he was in the market for all he could get, yowling and digging his claws into Zane's leg until Duty came to the rescue by scooping the cat up and disappearing into the kitchen. "Gave him his own bowl," he said, returning to his seat to finger one of the black stained Zig-Zags on the table.

"Yeah," Zane managed around his chewing. "Fat Jack gave those to me. Hash oil. We're gonna need em, everything I gotta tell ya." He popped some grapes into his mouth. "I like the quiche, Sasha." He knew it was probably the last good thing he could say for a while, and he dreaded the pain he was going to inflict through the telling. As for the other news, he'd wait until they were alone. "Lemme finish eatin, an I'll tell ya what I learned."

He watched Sasha tense up in her chair, her hands gripping the arms. She was staring at the floor, eyes already glazing over. Preparing herself, he knew from experience. Like those late nights in Portland when he'd spun stories about where he'd been and what he was doing. More residual effects of his secrets, her stiffening in self-defense. *My fault she reacts this way. I set the goddamned pattern.*

Zane took his plate into the kitchen, lit a cigarette when he returned. "Ok," he blew out smoke. "I got a hold of the ambulance report on Perry. As I suspected, Wade Perkins called it in. Must'a used his CB to contact Forest Service headquarters an had them send the ambulance. So far as I know, he's the only person who was there before it arrived." Duty rolled one of Jack's papers around the shake he'd cleaned earlier. Sasha hadn't raised her eyes from the carpet yet. Zane kept checking in while speaking.

"Then I read how the techs described his injuries." He didn't rush, purposely flattened his voice. "It was pretty graphic, I have to say. He was busted up quite a bit." *There!* She finally looked at him. He was talking directly to her now. "No way he could've done it in a fall...major frontal injuries *and* the back of his head was crushed...couldn't happen at the same time. Someone hit him from behind, I think, sendin him down on the rocks."

"Mary Jesus," Sasha cried out. "You mean he was murdered." It wasn't a question. "Somebody murdered him."

"My money's on Perkins," Duty said, getting the joint going.

"Me, too," Zane nodded professorially, assuredly, with solid authority.

"But why? Why kill him?" She looked from Zane to Duty and back again, as if searching for a place to roost. "What was the point?"

"Well, now's when the stuff I got from your buddy George is important. I didn't even have to look for him. I came out of the head and 'bang' he's sitting right there. The person I'm looking for finds me, for christsakes. Anyway, first of all, he didn't know anything about Perry's death, didn't know he'd even died. I told him what the ambulance report said, described the injuries in detail. That got him, I could tell. He became real serious, real fast. I asked him why Greg's cabin was burned down, an he didn't know that'd happened either. I could tell the man was shocked, what I'd said really bothered him." He took the joint from Duty's fingers for a hit, handed it back. "Then he told me that Perry'd sold his minin claim for a dollar, if you can believe that. Said the claim transfer was filed last Friday.

"Who'd he sell it to?" Duty asked, hand-delivering to Sasha in her chair. "What?...I don't know. George didn't say, an I was too stupid to ask. I'm goin back to talk to him again, so I'll see if I can find out."

"Could be important," Duty said, as he resettled on the couch. "Especially since whoever it was filed the new claim on the same day Perry was killed. That's gotta be more than just coincidence. Sounds more like a conspiracy. Somethun else George told me was that Tanaka Flats—where the minin claim is—would most likely end up bein lakefront property after the dam goes in."

"Good ol' American capitalism," Duty said in a put-on voice like some platitudinous politician making a 4th of July speech. "Kick out the natives and bring in the trailer hook-ups. Manifest destiny and cement'll make us all rich."

Zane was watching Sasha, running mental fingertips over the contours of her body, remembering. But she was rigid, and he was harshly reminded of watching a tape of Nixon's Checkers broadcast in a political theory class. He was horrified to think that, right now, she looked like Pat Nixon during that speech. The second lady at the time posed on a divan with no affect whatsoever. Sitting absolutely still, transfixed as though staring at nothing, unblinkingly gazing into the bottomless abyss of history.

He'd felt tugs of sympathy for Pat, or what he thought was just the shell of her, the pancake-and-rouged, plaster-cast figurine he'd watched on the film. Dad's telling lies to the camera while Mom presents her painted smile to the world, he'd thought at the time. And now Sasha seemed the same, without the smile.

"If Perry was murdered," she finally said in a faint, wavering, anguished voice, "then can't the cops figure it out, piece it together?"

"Won't happen, I'm afraid. No witnesses. And the official cause of death was listed as accidental. Copy of coroner's statement was stapled to the ambulance report. Mom told me it was the same thing that happened often with deaths of old people found way out in the sticks. Even though he was dead, they took him to the hospital where the coroner was called to sign off on the death certificate. Guess it's pretty much standard practice."

Duty got up to stoke the living room stove. As if a spell had been broken, Zane recognized they all needed a rest. Sasha sank into her chair like she'd been holding her breath. He lit another cigarette and fumbled with stick matches on the table, the fading refrain of "Get up/Stand up" seeping into the room. *Seventh inning stretch. Funny how we all seem to know we needed a break. Maybe it's the collective unconscious? Don't tell me Jung was right? Thousands of different languages but everyone shares the same preconscious thoughts? How can anything preconscious even be thought, that's the point, it's also pre-*

language. It'd have to be some divinely implanted non-linguistic idea, common to every human at birth. But that's ridiculous. I don't know what the fuck I'm talkin about.

Reggae hour was over and the FM announcer with the slithering molasses voice began the top-of-the-hour news. "Since you're already up, Duty, would you crank the radio a little louder? Please?"

"Aye, Aye, Captain. Your wish is my command."

"Shush, now. I wanna hear." He wondered what it was that tied him in knots when he knew Sasha needed some strokes, if only a hug. She was devastated, deeply hurt, while he acted like a defiant kid, unable to offer her any explanation, unaware why he was frozen to the spot. And he hadn't said anything about the money yet. So far, it'd all been bad news.

Speaking of which, both the US and Britain had set off nuclear explosions at the Nevada test site over the last few days, though the announcer was quick to report that the USSR had conducted over four hundred tests of their own at their site in Kazakhstan.

The DJ was reading the news as though the fate of the world depended on the gravitas of his delivery. "Gerald Ford, who took over as Vice President when Spiro Agnew resigned last year, delivered a speech to the Federation of Teachers conference in San Antonio on Saturday in which he called for a national commitment to K-12 education with a focus on the inner city. Ford intimated that plans were underway to introduce appropriate legislation.

"In Watergate news, *The Chicago Tribune* published an editorial calling for President Nixon to resign. The presidency must (quote) be separated from the man who now holds it. We must return to the day when people can shiver with pride instead of shudder with embarrassment when they see the flag or hear Hail to the Chief (endquote)."

The announcer waited a few seconds before continuing in even more measured tones. "Josephine County Sheriffs are investigating the weekend shotgun slayings of two men at the Takilma commune, a spokesman affirmed today. No further details are available at this time, but the Sheriff's department said it would schedule a press conference in the next few days."

Zane heard Sasha gasp. He felt Duty put a hand on his shoulder. "Remember that slogan 'Bringing the War Back Home'?" Duty asked. "It looks like it's already here."

Chapter Sixteen

Learning and memory are conditioned, at every level, by social and historical agencies. Information is neither in substance nor conceptually value-free. Ideology, economic and class circumstance, the historical moment do much to define the content, the relative hierarchies, the sheer visibility of knowledge as knowledge, of information or experience as worth recording. These categories are not permanent. Different societies, different epochs expose the central nervous system to different fields of stimulation. (241)
    George Steiner. After Babel. 3rd Ed. Oxford UP

Diamond Jim Anders bought a ten-year-old, 62 passenger Blue Bird school bus. All but the driver's seat had already been removed, so Jim said he was immediately attracted to the bus's potential as "the family's" road machine. Friends contributed old rugs, two threadbare upholstered chairs and a sofa with sagging springs. Bean bags, a mattress and piles of blankets provided the rest of the seating. Brooks Gervais donated his artistic talents, painting forest landscapes on both outside panels with "The Chicago Bears" in red, white and black arching over snowy mountain peaks.

Diamond Jim had admitted to Zane that he'd purchased the bus primarily for the summer trips to play softball against the commune in Takilma, "The Takilma Ticks." Vince wired a radio and cassette deck sound system to the batteries, saying he sure as hell wasn't riding anywhere he had to listen to out of tune, badly played guitars and *Hootenanny* folk songs. "If I have to hear House of the Risin Sun one more time," Vince complained, but didn't finish the sentence. Jim boasted that all they needed was a 50-gallon plastic garbage can to put a keg and ice in, and 'presto,' a rolling party, a proud moving violation. And so it was. On game days, Jim drove the bus to the Medford High parking lot to collect folks. Everyone knew he'd leave at 10 am on the dot. Be there or be square.

Adopting the Pranksters' classic line from *Electric Kool-Aid Acid Test*, he'd yell "You're either on the bus, or you're off the bus," and fire up the engine. Family, friends, kids and dogs would kennel-up inside, find a place, spread their stuff around. The kids loved when Richard took off his legs and, using his fists against the floor, scuttled around after them like a chimpanzee, wrestling with them until they'd knocked into too many people. Most everyone else just kicked back for the hour-and-a-half ride, arguing relatively good naturedly about what cassette to play, trying to relax amongst the competing fragrances of strawberry, jasmine, patchouli, dope, tobacco and sweaty, gassy dogs.

The Chicago Bears vs Takilma Ticks get-togethers were anything but contests. Usually, nothing got going on the pasture ball field until late afternoon, when the sun had dipped toward the western hills. The hottest hours were spent on the Illinois river where clothes were considered so optional that few had any on, unless they were headed to the Takilma store down the road which did a steady stream of business in wine, candy, chips and cigarettes—fresh money from the townies.

By the time play began, campfires would be burning along the third base line where several topless young women in hippy cloth skirts thumped conga drums and swayed in unison to their own tuneless melodies. Ron Johnson, who had won the state high-hurdles in 1958, was official custodian of the bottles of Boone's Farm Apple, each laced with hits of mescalin, though he was known to share with commune residents, especially later in the day after he'd sampled each bottle. Every game, by the fourth inning, each side-up lasting as long as " In-A-Gadda-Da-Vida," it was impossible to say for sure what the score was. Ballpark figures.

Rosters became increasingly fluid as players switched sides, mostly trying to put moves on someone. Because although the festivities began with all-male teams taking infield, flexing, jawing—they became co-ed quickly. Hit balls bounced past players who were either busy conversing, gloves tucked under an arm, or who just hadn't noticed. By the draggling end, only kids, dogs and a few souls having

266

religious experiences were still out in the field. America's pastime with a definite drug-induced twist, Zane remembered fondly. Halcyon days, he thought, though he'd never use that word in public, thinking it more appropriate for long dead British poets. But he knew the meaning, and that's what he was after. The bright, joyous days before now.

They'd first heard about the commune killings on Monday night, same broadcast they'd learned that Duke Ellington had died. But no concrete details had emerged on the airwaves until today. Friday morning, the last day in May, to be exact. All this week, the three of them collectively worried whether any of their Takilma friends were part of the story. Duty had even driven down to Richard's to call Vince the day before, wanting to know whether his VA check had come. It had. He'd also asked Vince if he knew who'd been shot at the commune. He didn't.

They were all in the living room, ready for the 10 am news, when informed that Israel and Syria had signed an agreement to quit shooting at one another over the Golan Heights, that the USSR had set off another nuclear test in Eastern Kazakhstan, and that famed nutritionist Adelle Davis had died at age 70. The savage punch came shortly thereafter when they learned the two men killed at Takilma last Sunday night had been identified as Emilio Perez and Richard Longstreet.

Sasha caught her breath with an audible 'oh' before putting her face in her hands, her upper body shaking. "Not Emilio," she sobbed through her fingers, "Oh, my God. When will it end? I can't take anymore. I really can't." Meanwhile, the announcer continued the gruesome, step-by-step account of how the two men had each been hit in the chest from a shotgun blast. Had then been decapitated with an axe, their heads dumped in the East fork of the Illinois where a steelhead fisherman netted them about a half mile downstream. Then, for reasons none of the authorities could explain, their headless bodies had been hung from a tree and gutted. "Like a deer in the smokehouse," Zane thought, "but I knew em alive and laughin."

The announcer concluded, with no obvious reaction to what he was reading, by saying no motives had been determined and the investigation, of course, was still ongoing.

"Jesus," Duty exhaled. "Didn't even hear anything like that in country. Skinned maybe, but not all this. Old Emilio and Rainbow Rick. Can't think of less likely victims, really nice guys. Both of 'em at the same time? Fuckin' Christ."

Zane turned down the FM after the news. Sasha left the room with her head down, her hair hanging loose, swaying with her walk. Erasmus followed her closely. He heard her footsteps upstairs and assumed she needed some space. *First Perry and now Emilio. Two old men she'd loved bein around.*

He replayed scenes from their numerous Takilma trips. The first time he'd seen Emilio he'd thought the heavily wrinkled, bronze-skinned, jovial old man wearing nothing but a colorfully embroidered breech cloth looked like someone conjured up by Carlos Castenada. Long grey hair and beard, sparkling brown eyes, a wide smile revealing a few missing teeth. The very epitome of an earth spirit, someone you could tell had been around the block more than a few times. He'd been astride his brown mare named Frida Kahlo. In fact, Zane had never seen him off the horse, giving kids rides around the pasture, one or two at a time until every small child who wanted had gotten their turn. Ron Johnson made sure to hand up a bottle of Boone's Farm for the old man to take long pulls. Between rides, Emilio sat on Frida cross-legged and repeated news about the goings on at the commune, sort of a town crier for a community that wasn't officially a town. Eventually, he'd ride off into the woods by himself, waving a hand without looking back.

"Rainbow Rick gone, too," Duty said, as though he'd been thinking along the same lines as Zane. "He was the only real athlete they had.

A great first-baseman." He looked at Zane. "Whadda you figure? Some drug deal gone bad?"

"Have to be someone completely enraged, don't you think?"

"Who knows? I'm never surprised by what people can get up to. How little it takes sometimes. But this wasn't any professional hit, you're right. It has all the earmarks of pure vengeance. Now *that* I saw a lot of." He hesitated a few seconds before getting up from the couch, nodding to himself. "I'm gonna walk over to Lester's, see if I can talk him out of a couple trout from his pond."

"Take the VW. We're not goin anywhere."

"Naw, I need to walk some stuff off." He got to the door, was halfway through before stopping, looking back at Zane with tired eyes. "You ever there when Lester feeds those fish? Water flat-out boils with 'em."

He smiled at Duty's ability to wipe the slate clean, switch topics and moods on a dime without losing a beat. *Got that from the war, I'll bet. Not fallin apart in the middle of the bloodbath. Keepin his head.*

Zane had skipped his college graduation in '68. Instead of standing in line for hours, listening to milk toast philosophical exhortations about being the best he could be. He detested these vile, medieval, pomp and circumstances ceremonies. Instead, he'd taken what ended-up being a four-day series of Greyhounds from Portland to LA...LA to Pensacola...Pensacola to Ft. Myers. The last leg from Ft. Myers to Immokalee, less than an hour away, was a regional south Florida carrier crammed with latino families.

Some exceptionally dreary stories to tell about that tiring trip from Oregon. Smuggling pints of vodka on board, *Thunderbird* or *Ripple* in liquor-control states, scrunching down in the seats to drink. Listening to the sad case male alkies he managed to attract like lint, and a few others who were interested in him for obviously fawning reasons.

Early in the journey, he'd fantasized meeting exotic, alluring women who could be the basis for a steamy *Penthouse Forum* story no one would believe. Or imagined sitting next to a mildly well-known writer who was trying to find the real "heart" of the country. But all he managed was to feel big because he was the one paying for the bottles. Gave him a cheap and flimsy sense of superiority.

He lived in Immokalee from the end of June to the middle of November, all of hurricane season. Torrential rains that year, but no hunkering down in a bathtub waiting for the roof to come off. Working for Migrants United, which was housed in a gray cinder block building across the road from Collier County Cannery, he took care of public relations, such as they were.

Mostly, he fed stories about labor abuse practices to *The Miami Herald, St. Pete Times* and *Tallahassee Democrat,* after having spent his first month making media connections, dropping names of publicized activists he knew, or said he did. Establishing relationships so they'd recognize his name when he called. He was lucky enough, one evening when he was alone in the building, to take a call from National Public Radio who wanted to interview someone about *coyotes* and how they did business. Zane, of course, offered himself. That broadcast aired a couple weeks later and gave him some stature, at least among the small group of hardcore migrant advocates in— from his Oregonian perspective—the oppressively slimy, humid, heat soaked, insect riddled south Florida flatlands.

When the State Department of Labor wanted to conduct meetings of the subcommittee on Migrant Affairs—a group formed of state legislators and growers, all appointed—they'd try to find the most out of the way obscure venue for what were supposedly public hearings. But Zane could call someone at the media center next to the state capitol in Tallahassee to find out where and when the subcommittee would conduct its bi-monthly, legislatively mandated meeting. He'd then get in touch with his contacts at Channel Two Eyewitness News out of Miami and they could be depended on to send camera crews to a remote, one room church miles down a corrugated dirt road somewhere no one ever visited.

Zane enjoyed watching how committee members literally changed their tunes when being interviewed. Drawls tightened up, slang disappeared, bureaucratic double speak began to flow again from their starched smiling faces. The "old white men secretly making decisions in back rooms" atmosphere evaporated as they wedged and elbowed their way in front of the cameras for their turn at free publicity. Mouthing all the usual vapid, patronizing inanities dressed up as serious thought, reaffirming with feigned religious zeal how their only concern was for the "people of Florida."

Zane loved it. Even his limited time watching the gut-of-Florida politically powerful was enough for him to know that the growers' representatives were light years more dangerous than any elected official. No comparison. They spun narratives of how they represented mom-'n-pop farmers all over the state, painting linguistic pastoral landscapes, church-and-fried-chicken-on-Sunday pictures, fending off with the toe of their shoe any notions that corporate chemical agriculture was keeping their kids in college or paying for the club memberships.

He kept vodka in his daypack. *Dark Eyes* with a sketched Cossack on the label. Appropriately named, he'd learned soon enough since he couldn't help looking at himself wherever he was reflected. Between trips outside for quick slugs from the bottle, he would drop hints to the TV people about whose face to stick their mikes in front of. Give them any incriminating info he might have, alert to the tics and twitches of those inexperienced with being in the camera's gaze.

As much as he'd detested Florida with its unbelievable variety of creepy crawlers, biters and stingers keeping him on edge, the multiple pronged racism embedded in every aspect of living, he'd thrived on the work. Only twenty-two at the time, he nonetheless realized he had a knack for political organizing, could get all kinds of folks to talk to him, and in the process learned which dark recesses to shine a light on. He'd come to rely on his instincts when filtering through the stakeholders' yapping, trying to decide whom to trust. By the time

271

he'd left Immokalee to work for SDS he'd internalized an experiential understanding that, despite his alcohol consumption and occasional anxiety attacks, he was a quick study who could do work that mattered.

After Duty left, Zane climbed back into his squeaky mental squirrel wheel, running fast but going nowhere, unsure whether he really wanted to seriously dig into the meshed layers of what was happening on the Applegate, wondering if Sasha would go along if he tried. Perry's death and the Fausens disappearance seemed connected, though he couldn't put his finger on the exact nexus point. Certainly the new dam was a prism of sorts, focusing energy and attention on the upper reaches of the river, but he was still in the dark as to how it all fit together. He needed more time with George because Wade Perkins and Brereton kept popping up on his radar. He wanted to clarify their involvement and motives. They were at least peripherally implicated, he was sure. Feds and state law enforcement to take on, and he understood implicitly how much he *didn't* know. So the odds weren't good from the get go. At heart, he wasn't clear whether he was willing to put everything at risk by threatening authority, *or German-speakin survivalists, for all I know?*

He still hadn't told her about the insurance money. Couldn't say why, exactly. Thrashed it around all week while he and Duty built a chutes and ladders irrigation system for the fenced garden. Water troughs and wooden gates. Yesterday, while Duty mangled Canned Heat's "Goin Up The Country" lyrics in a low droning repeating chant, Zane carried on both sides of a yes/no conversation with himself as to why he couldn't just tell her. Wasn't it good news, after all? And yet he held back. Each passing day deepened his dread. What would she think when she realized he'd kept it to himself this long? Was he going through an anal retentive phase, holding onto information, refusing to let it out? Seemed so. Seemed he'd been doing it all his life. Secreting, keeping his withered inner kernel from prying eyes. Made absolutely no sense. But it was wired in.

Perhaps he was frozen by a fear of finality, of assuming the responsibilities of ownership? Knowing that once the deed was done, he'd have committed himself to standing still, becoming rooted, isolated from the political whirlwinds that always beckoned. Not to mention the financial ties they'd assume by buying the property. Upkeep. Taxes. Putting in a proper bathroom and shower, which meant they needed a hot water heater. Made him dizzy. On top of which, nudging into his thoughts since Duty left, he was seeing himself again in south Florida. A rare success story he'd never forgotten, one reminding him that, like Duty shifting gears seamlessly in the doorway, he was capable of juggling variables while in motion, adjusting on the move, changing tack in midstream. This particular series of events replayed like a home movie in color that he could rewind to watch again and again, one in which he figured in a minor but important role. An antidotal prescription for the brutality of recent weeks, the ennui he'd languished in for at least the last year, since Planned Parenthood.

He remembered the day he met Betty Estes so well because of what had happened that same morning, when he'd walked into his closet-sized office at Migrants United and found a loaded .45 in his only desk drawer. Tony Ojeda and his gang of four organizers from Texas had hit town two days before and were conducting teach-ins in economic theory to bewildered looking farm workers in a side room. Everything in Spanish, which Zane had been glacially slow to pick up. He had taken the gun outside, ejected the full clip, checked the chamber and put it back in his drawer empty, stashing the clip in the bathroom medicine cabinet on the shelf with his bristle-shedding toothbrush and a can of *Pepsodent* tooth powder. When Tony made it in that morning, Zane let him know where he could find the .45 clip and told him he didn't appreciate being set-up by so-called allies. "If you gotta have a fuckin' gun, then keep it with your own shit, instead'a makin it look like it belongs to me, for fuck's sake. I gotta live here an you guys're just passin through." Tony had sputtered apologies, which is to say he blamed his lieutenant Jesus, and agreed it was way out of line, wouldn't happen again.

That was how Zane's day had begun, and he was still fuming when a diminutive, shriveled and wrinkled black woman appeared in his office doorway. She looked barely five feet tall including her wide-brimmed straw hat, and he was sure she couldn't weigh a hundred pounds. What he'd call a wisp of a woman, but he could tell from the seriousness of her face, the sharpness of her eyes, that he'd be well advised not to do so. "I need help," she said, fixing him with her stare. "They tells me to come here."

He gave her his wooden straight back chair and excused himself to drag in a folding chair from one of the other rooms. Once situated, he took a second to compose himself, taking in her flat canvas shoes, knee-high white stockings—assuming he could see her knees, which he definitely couldn't—a worn but pressed blue skirt over a slightly frayed white blouse. She meant business, he could tell, her hair shot with grey and pulled back primly. She crossed her thin, veined hands palms down in her lap.

Zane finally plugged back in to why he was there. "What can I do for you?"

"It's the gator pond," she said with a strong, confident voice. "Behind the little ones' school. Some chillen sure 'nuf gonna drown in there."

He'd asked her whether she'd done anything with the county, had she put in any formal requests or complaints to the commissioners' office. "Oh, yes, indeed," she seemed to perk up as if he'd questioned her energy level. "Phoned there five different times. Wrote three letters to Mr. LeRoy Jennigan, our commissioner. Yes, indeed. I let 'em know. Been lettin 'em know the best of a year now."

"And nothing?" Zane didn't drop his g's this time. Was trying to sound measured and thoughtful.

"Nuthin'," she'd looked down at her hands, fingers rubbing each other slowly. "No sir. Not a thing."

Zane knew the name Jennigan, it would have been hard not to with all the "Jennigan Farms" signs lining the tomato and cucumber fields south of town. The idea of poking a finger into the eye of a farm grower county commissioner appealed to him immediately. He saw it as a chance to wax eloquent on the safety of children, put the commission on the spot, and enhance his standing in the organizing community if he played his cards right. Things were looking up considerably, he'd thought. So he made the necessary calls to get on the committee's docket, using Migrants United as sponsoring agency.

Naples, Florida had a reputation as one of the richest per capita cities in the country, so it was no surprise to Zane that the county offices reeked of opulence. The commission met in a luxuriously carpeted, air-conditioned boardroom, with leather swivel chairs and microphones for each commissioner. Quite the contrast to Immokalee's littered streets and deserted buildings, farm worker families living in cars.

With Betty at his side—he'd thought of her as a necessary prop, evidence for the case he planned to make—he scanned the room. The commissioners, all fleshy white men, sat on a raised dais behind a curved, continuous mahogany desktop, engraved name plates for each. He disliked the lot of them on principle, felt his adversarial pulse quicken. The gallery was full of padded folding chairs for the audience, the first few rows filled with reporters from newspapers, radio and TV. Note pads on knees, video cameras focused and ready. Zane had alerted his contacts that it might be worth their while to attend. He'd also carefully rehearsed the spiel he planned to deliver, seeing the meeting as a chance to perform, to be in the lights. He'd as much as guaranteed to the others at Migrants United that the story would get airtime across south Florida, raising their visibility.

When the secretary eventually called him for his slot on the schedule, however, instead of walking up himself, he'd gently helped Betty to the standing microphone, lowering it to her level, whispering in her ear to "just tell them what you've told me." He stood behind her until she'd introduced herself, and then taken his seat as her voice echoed through the sound system.

Zane didn't have the first idea why he'd changed plans. Wasn't a conscious, point A to point B, reasoned decision. Wasn't a decision at all, in fact. Just happened. Like knowing a trout waited behind a current-splitting rock, or breaking on a line drive at the sound off the bat.

As Betty described the situation with the gator pond behind the school, commissioner Jennigan interrupted her in patronizing tones. "This isn't a matter to take up right here," he said with a jaw-clenching artificial smile. "Why don't you just contact my office and I'm sure we can get to the bottom of things?"

"I done that," she said calmly, not to be foisted off. "Five times I done that. An' nuthin' happened. No sir." Zane watched as the press corps elbowed each other, sensing blood in the water, video cameras capturing the interaction.

It had been a moment to savor, one which he'd returned to often in the intervening years. How much more forcefully the tiny grandmother had made the case than he could ever have done with all his planning and practice. He pulled out this memory whenever he doubted his ability to operate intuitively, to get out of the way when necessary. Betty Estes appeared on both Miami and Fort Myers TV news. *The Miami Herald* featured her in a two-column photo with accompanying article. Within a week after the story aired, county crews erected a five-foot high cyclone fence around the sinkhole pond. Observable consequences, which he'd seldom experienced when trying to storm the ramparts of power.

He supposed it was the rarity of anything resembling success when facing the forces of authority that was hanging him up now. What he knew about Perry's death itched like crazy, but he was clear there was no straight line way to hold anyone accountable, to redress such a grievous act. At the moment he was stymied, feeling wholly inadequate on the surface, yet still wanting to believe in what, for lack of a better word, he thought of as justice. *Just another star-spangled phrase...and justice for all. When was that ever the reality when crooks are in charge, treatin the country like a piñata filled with cash? Bebe Rebozzo. John Mitchell an' his sloshin' wife. Everything's about money. Duh. The dam comin in is nothin more than a modern day land grab. Like a row of standin dominos, every piece of property from here to Ruch'll fall when push comes to shove. The whole fuckin' valley'll be officially re-zoned for profit. So who's makin all the money here? Knowin that could point me in a direction. Still. Not sure I wanna put us at risk, now that we could stay here, that it'd be our property. 'Course we'd get re-zoned just like everybody else. Maybe not tomorrow or next month, but it's inevitable. Maybe that's why they wanna sell it to us? Their taxes are goin up? This is all too much. I gotta tell her.*

Chapter Seventeen

"...in actual fact there is no fundamental dividing line between the content of the individual psyche and formulated ideology....An experience of which an individual is conscious, is already ideological and, therefore, from a scientific point of view, can in no way be a primary and irreducible datum; rather, it is an entity that has already undergone ideological processing of some specific kind." (87)
V.N. Voloshinov. Freudianism. Indianapolis: Indiana UP, 1976.

Sasha and Erasmus were on the bed, her still-trembling hand stroking him softly while he purred, his crystalline blue eyes open just a slit. *At least you're not channeling that vision of my mother in the waiting to die place. "When will this be over?" the emaciated woman yelled out of nowhere, her face blank as the wall. None of the women in mismatched chairs lining the room batted an eye. Especially not the minders, who didn't even flinch. Like the outburst was perfectly normal, just another day at the end of the road, the last stop.* She didn't have to ask herself why she'd dredged up that scene once more, even without Erasmus' telepathic help; it was as obvious as breathing.

After the news, she'd felt the walls closing in, Zane and Duty's faces suddenly too big for the space. She'd had to get out, escape from a barrage of words as ineffective in treating her despair as a handful of sand flung at the wind. She'd found herself—she didn't think her way there—making mental lists, laying down opposing realities, differing experiences, deciding what went where. Plusses and minuses. Joys and disasters.

Chased upstairs by the horror story of Emilio and Rainbow Rick, while not yet having fully come to grips with the loss of Perry *no place to grieve* or the fate of the vanished family. All this so harshly pressed in her face, so close to home, like a belligerent neighbor. She was clear she had many more disasters than joys to work with. *The dead calf last week, the abortion last year, the Aquarius party at Aurora and Brooks'.* And a hundred minor bruises and slights that left her feeling invisible for long stretches. Loud men's voices talking over and around her. Not that anyone attacked her, or got in her face in any way she was silenced by constantly being outnumbered. What did any of them know about what she wanted? Even Zane, sometimes especially him? She wasn't putting her years of study to any good use that she could see. Who was she, after all, in these relationships? Used to be that she and Zane would talk, even read the same things so they could compare notes, disagree without hurting. A Marxist analysis of *Pride and Prejudice*, or Buckminster Fuller's newest article about Spaceship Earth, or something they'd seen in *Rolling Stone*. In those times, the idea of creating their own healthy lives in the country was attractive and seemed possible. Her Bierstadt fantasy with curling chimney smoke, warm yellow windows and a doe grazing in the foreground. A shared pastoral home. She'd never seen why her feminism meant she had to be anti-men, even though gender roles seemed to be at the root of so many aggressively oppressive social realities. In some ways, she saw men as equally trapped in historical patterns; she didn't reject maleness as such, just the cultural pig-headedness that defended entrenched and bone-headed patriarchy. Simone had her Sartre, after all. Hannah had her Heidegger. *That's a mouthful. But there's no reason I can't understand male privilege and still see Zane as worth the effort. I know what strength he's capable of. I keep thinking he'll get a vision and realize he can rely on me as more than handy sex and a housekeeper to boot, that I really am on his side. His inability to trust keeps getting in the way.*

Especially lately, she wasn't discovering new avenues to fulfillment, wasn't even looking—which said a lot, which said everything. She didn't feel seen as a complete person, except sometimes with Duty. Now she was doubly worried Zane was going to immerse himself in another consuming fight with bad odds. She *had* wanted to know about Perry—no question—but she was afraid and intuitively sure he wouldn't stop there. Not this time.

She'd kept her eyes closed the last time they made love. Not to fantasize someone else...Well, not in that way. She preferred the dark because if she looked she'd see the him of today. When she wanted the him from working on the house together when they'd first moved in, living in a tent on the porch until they'd cleaned out the downstairs. The him who'd paid attention, who'd reached out, who'd cared how she felt. Not that he'd ever entirely quit going to Medford to hang out with his buddies at The Alibi, often not showing up until the next day with some feeble excuse. *The battery went dead.* It didn't happen all that often, usually only after a shouting, sarcastic, up and down the stairs, slamming the door argument about making ends meet. Money matters. Guaranteed to send him flying into town on a runner, leaving her on the river with no transportation. Alone until he'd dragged himself back, acting like it was no big deal. Lingering a moment on those nights with no idea where he was, what he was doing, she saw for the first time that his ritual of burying the phone in the pasture wasn't so much about declaring independence from the grid, as it was to give him built-in immunity. He couldn't very well call her if they had no phone. *Mary, Jesus! I'm so stupid sometimes.* So when she heard him on the stairs, she felt her space invaded yet again. *What'll he be this time? The unsure little boy seeking redemption, or the brash man wanting his way? Or maybe he'll just be real? Like he says...it's always a toss of the dice. You never really know.*

When he came into the room, she'd been watching cattle milling in the pasture ground fog of a gray morning. "I've got somethin to tell you," he said halfway across the floor. She turned, bracing herself for more bad news, another stabbing wound. *God. I'm posturing.*

We can buy this place," he said, sitting down on the edge of the bed, reaching out to stroke Erasmus who shifted his body in response. "I mean, we'll have the money."

She pushed up to a sitting position, tilting her head so black hair hung down in front of her shoulders. "How so?"

"Seems Dad did somethin useful in his life. Had life insurance, an Mom's givin me half. Twenty-Five grand with no strings."

She couldn't meet his eyes, throwing her hair back with a shake, looking at the blanket, then out the window again. *He said given to "me," not to "us."*

"I think we need to talk about it. Not just rush into anything." She ventured a glance at his face which had broken into a broad smile.

"Why? You gonna throw me over, Miss Petrovsky?"

"You always go for the extremes, Zane. Like, it's either just fine, or a total disaster. What if we buy this place only to have the dam bring the suburbs out here? What will we do for money on a continuing basis? What if we get rezoned; you were talking about that the other day. I don't think these are minor things to at least consider." She had no idea what she'd just said, except that it wasn't at all what she meant. It was parallel to what she meant, perhaps, like a euphemistic metaphor.

He kept petting Erasmus, seemed transfixed. Had gone mute again. She saw his smile frozen. Tightened lines under his eyes. *He wants to walk out right now.* Recalling what Perry had said about Zane early in their friendship. "He's a fiery guy, all right. I can see that. He wants Technicolor." He'd also told her that, if she wanted her dreams and desires to flower, she'd have to stake out her territory—physically, emotionally and politically all at the same time. That was the trick, striving to see everything as intertwined, blending not compartmentalizing. She'd need to be willing to stand still in the storms, and forge ahead when she could, when the universe opened new avenues. "On thing's for sure," Perry had mused in front of the fireplace, his fingers steepled on his chest. "There's never a shortage of people lined up to tell you how to think, what should be important, how you should live your incredibly short time."

Watching the cattle outside in the fog, she spoke to the shape of her image in the glass. "When did you find this out?"

"Monday. When I went to the ambulance service. Mom told me then."

"And today's Friday. So you knew all this week, but didn't tell me? What were you thinking...that you'd maybe just keep it all to yourself?"

"Of course not." Still stroking the cat, not looking at her.

"What then? What stopped you from telling me?"

"I dunno. Didn't find the right time."

In that split-second she felt like slapping him as fast as a dangerous dame from Film Noir. "That's such crap, Zane," she said instead, leaning back against the wall by the window, gaining some space. "I'm insulted you don't think I deserve better. This is our problem, right here, the way you're acting.

His head snapped up at that, eyes narrowing as if there was too much light in the room, words spit out. "I don't know why I didn't say anything, alright."

"Well, you see, that's the difficulty, isn't it? I can imagine you telling Richard or Greg or Vince or even Fat Jack before you'd let me in on it....Don't pout, Zane. It's terribly unbecoming....All this hooks back into how you see yourself in relation to me. How you see me. Those times when you go out of your way to take my desires into account are the exception, not the rule. I'm not saying we haven't had wonderfully tender, intimate moments where I look in your eyes and see myself reflected back. And you know you can most always turn me on, that part doesn't take much. I love you. But there's all the rest of it...I can't put it into words, exactly the way I feel. But it's like I have to constantly chase after you. Left to yourself, you'd just as soon carry on your separate life only having to relate to me on your terms, when you want some sex, or when you're in a good mood. Which I have to tell you, is not that often." She stopped. She'd said enough.

Fuck me runnin again. I don't know what she wants. He jammed the gears into third, downshifting to take an uphill turn, hugging what was left of the yellow center line at 10 mph faster than the last sign advised. *Quit meat didn't I? Just like that. Went to find out about Perry,*

*didn't I? She wanted me to do that. So where'd everything go off the rails?
Not tellin her about the money, I know. But it's not like I already had the
payout an didn't say.* Which, in point of fact, was exactly how he'd
squirreled away fifty dollars from the last paint job, hiding it in his
copy of *Containment and Change*. The twenty crimped in his pocket
was all that was left from his secret stash of beer money.

He was headed to Ruch, to the *Sunnyside* market for a half-case of
longneck Buds to drown his sorry ass. *Nothin's simple. I thought she'd be
all-in on the farm. Thought settlin down was what she wanted? Four of those
ten acres are in timber. We could sell off a couple trees now an again. It's not
like we'd be penniless. I can always paint houses in town, pour beer for Jack
at The Alibi even.* He knew he was fishing without a hook. No way in
hell would he ever again submit to sloshing suds and making
conversation with Alibi regulars, friends or not.

He'd filled in as bartender a few times when living at Shirley's, and
they'd been the most stultifying string of hours he'd experienced
outside Florida. The finale was a 4 to 1 am shift he'd covered for
Loraine, who'd dropped acid for lunch that day. No one noticed
anything wrong when she came in. But then she poured her first beer
into the drain trough, set the still empty mug in front of a stunned
customer, and couldn't make change for a dollar because she said the
cash drawer was talking to her in Latin, which she didn't understand.

So Zane had reluctantly stepped in. Jack gave him keys to lock up,
told him to bring them back the next day, reminded him to run a mop
over the bathroom floors before leaving. By nine o'clock, the bar had
thinned out considerably, three or four loners left on the stools and a
late-twenties couple who'd gotten married at the courthouse that
afternoon and were celebrating the occasion playing pool, drinking
beer, and eating fried pork rinds from greasy plastic bags. The
certainly-not-blushing bride wore tight black stretch pants that
emphasized her broad beam and a lavender sweatshirt with the NRA
logo above a pistol aiming out. Her straw hair was bunched on the top
of her head with a rubber band, looking to Zane like a shock of wheat

284

waving in the wind. Her new husband, decked out in camo *Did he get married in those?* with an unrestrained bushy red beard and Harley-Davidson baseball cap, was continually spitting tobacco juice into an empty mug. *No way in hell I'm cleanin that.*

As the night lengthened, the newlyweds' behavior changed from pelvic grinding, whispering smooches between shots to bumping unsteadily around the table without speaking to line up their next miss. By midnight, after running off everyone but Zane, who was trying to watch Humphrey Bogart and Lee J. Cobb in The *Left Hand of God* on cable, they were hurling loud, less-than-kind comments to one another, each ending with "you fuckin' sleaze" or "you limp prick," or words to those effects.

At 12:30, Zane announced he was closing early, sending the complaining honeymoon couple on their way with two 6-packs of Blitz to go. *One'a the grimmest goddamn nights I ever spent,* he remembered, *except for that jail in Saskatchewan.* Sasha and Erasmus had loaded back into the camper in Minneapolis on the last day of the National Student Association convention, after the headliners, featured speakers and big-name organizers had already left town.

Rather than driving straight back to Oregon the way they'd come, Zane wanted to visit an English professor friend who'd been denied tenure at PSU two years before and eventually found a job at Wisconsin—Stevens Point.

"We're already in Minnesota, Wisconsin's the next state over. After we visit Allan an Judy, we can drive up into Canada, go over to Winnipeg, hit Trans-Canada One goin west, an end up in British Columbia. Be a great trip. Banff. Lake Louise. I've planned out the route. When else're you gonna get a chance to do this," he'd asked with his best Robert Redford shading into Burt Reynolds smile, openly warm but a tad pugnacious. As if she had a choice; he was driving.

Allan and Judy Elder, and their three kids—two in grade school, one in diapers—had rented a ramshackle paint-peeling farmhouse nestled in a stand of oak on the fringes of Stevens Point. For two days, he and Sasha relaxed in the late June, heavy Midwestern warmth. Erasmus was a great hit, letting the kids maul him for long periods until he'd finally have enough and escape up a tree to wait until their attention turned elsewhere. Judy played the perfect hostess, bringing iced tea and, more importantly, corralling the kids so he, Sasha and Allan could engage in animated, wide-brush political conversations sandwiched in-between listening to early, pre- "Jeremiah was a bullfrog," Three Dog Night. Or Jeff Airplane "Volunteers." The Chambers Brothers. CSNY "Deju vu." He and Allan had kept the living room filled with a constant haze of pot, cigarette smoke and Blue Nile incense.

When they were ready to leave, Allan gave them a three pound Folger's can of bright green home grown, telling them that going through Superior and Duluth would get them to International Falls the quickest. "I felt sorry for Judy," Sasha had said, as they pulled out the driveway. "Spends all her time busy in the kitchen or with the kids. Doesn't seem to me like a very progressive family, actually." Zane remembered admitting that Allan had his faults, for sure, one of them his proclivity for attracting young coeds. Sasha had responded quickly with a string of words that included "typical," but the rest were now lost in the numerous folds of time.

After camping outside Winnipeg, the next morning they'd just crossed over from Manitoba to Saskatchewan on the Trans-Canada when Zane saw flashing lights behind them and had no choice but to pull over. The Mountie walked up to his open window and asked for his ID, but then spotted the roaches they'd left in a small glass ashtray on the ledge behind the front seat. After that, everything fell into a slow, following procedure, official crawl.

He and Sasha had to sit on the roadside—she had Erasmus on her lap—while a second Mountie who'd just arrived began going through the bus. Zane remembered how calm he'd been because he'd known, from the moment the cop reached in for the ashtray, the jig was definitely and decidedly up. No sense in panicking, wouldn't do them any good. "Act like a tourist," he'd whispered to Sasha as they sat on the ground. He'd had no idea what that meant, but he'd felt he ought to say something helpful and it was the best he could come up with, given the circumstances.

After fifteen or twenty minutes, a Saskatchewan provincial policeman delivered two more local officers to the scene. The woman took custody of Sasha into the backseat of the car she'd come in, while the man not much older than Zane told him to follow in the camper and got in the passenger side. Erasmus was now back in the bus, lounging on the bed, licking his feet like he didn't have a care in the world.

The three car caravan wound through rural streets until they came to the Moosomin police station which was a converted ranch-style home with two cement cells and an open floor plan. On the drive over, the deputy riding with Zane told him not to worry too much, that since they were US citizens most likely they'd only get a fine when they went to territorial court in Regina the next day. Zane had begun to get an itchy sense that they'd been caught in a money trap. Feelings which were confirmed by the way they were treated. Allowed to wander around the station unrestrained, helping themselves to coffee from the electric urn; convivial conversations for the most part, as the deputies filled out paperwork for them to sign while Zane read *Germinal*, and Sasha stroked Erasmus when he wasn't sniffing into corners or sitting on an unoccupied desk.

For dinner, they were each handed a styrofoam tray with a dry hamburger patty, a boiled potato and some canned peas. All of which they tried to eat with a plastic spoon. Their hosts did, however, give Erasmus hamburger too, so he was quite contented when Zane and Sasha—with cat under her arm—were finally locked into their respective cells at 10 pm.

Next morning, after a mostly sleepless night, and jacked up with coffee and sweet rolls, Zane was again informed he'd be driving the

287

bus while Sasha rode in the police car with the matron. Two and half hours to Regina's territorial court house with Zane listening to a different deputy's running monologue about how much Canadians resented American tourists who broke the laws. "How do you think we feel," he lamented, "when you're sending us all your draft dodgers and druggies?" Either situational tact wasn't part of the deputy's repertoire, or he wanted to purposely be irritating.

Their court appearance was a dizzying flurry of activity. White wigs and black robes. Legalese up the wazoo. Prosecutor calling them a "normal case" when speaking to the judge. They were the first case heard, and it was over inside of ten minutes, after he and Sasha had pleaded guilty as they'd been urged to do by the deputies from Moosomin. "It's standard procedure in cases like this," Zane was told. The judge accepted their plea with a bang of his gavel and they were shuffled quickly out of court and into a side office. "One hundred dollars each," the judge had intoned. "Pay the clerk of the court."

Sasha handed over $200 of American Express checks and received $22 Canadian back based on the rate of exchange. Zane was positively frothing by the time the court clerk handed their payment to the deputies who'd accompanied them. The grouchy, grey-haired guy who'd complained the whole drive told him they had to leave the country by the shortest route, though didn't offer any information as to which highway that might be. But he did confide to Zane, talking behind his raised hand for secrecy, that they should come back into Canada further west and continue their vacation. Fat chance. Zane swore about "fuckin fascist money grubbers" as they drove south, while Sasha lay back on the bed because she was nauseous.

Twelve miles from the US border, the road he'd chosen disappeared into gravel, so they'd bumped and rattled the final stretch. At least, Zane had thought, they didn't have to worry much about getting through some outpost custom's check since the Moosomin crew had kept Allan's homegrown. They'd been amazed at how green it was and had hauled out all the other baggies of weed they'd confiscated so Zane could see what they meant. It was all a show, he'd realized. No moral outrage. No cop attitudes of disgust in the station. Just a blatantly obvious financial arrangement. A weed trap, he'd thought, momentarily pleased with himself. They probably pulled over every freak longhair they saw, on the off chance of easy money. Luckily for the two of them, though the cops had nabbed the homegrown and ashtray of roaches, they didn't find their stash hidden in Erasmus's scented cat litter bag. Otherwise, it would have been an even more ill-tempered trip as they limped back to Portland, having missed Banff and Lake Louise, and beginning to seriously wonder if they had enough money to make it home, being two hundred bucks poorer than they'd planned.

We have that history between us, at least. We've been through heavier things than whether to buy the farm. By a long shot. Brooks an... He couldn't say Aurora, saw that train of thought as a sticky emotional Tar Baby. With no Br'er Fox handy he could flim-flam into throwing him in the thicket for an easy escape.

He'd already been to The Sunnyside. Once inside on the smoothly worn wood floors that smelled of lemon oil and a hint of *Pinesol*, he'd decided he'd better get three 6-packs, which left him with just enough for two packs of Pall-Malls. Laurel, who with his partner Willis lived in the small clapboard house behind the store, gave him three church keys and a handful of book matches. Everyone on the river knew about the two old men living together; they'd been in Ruch over thirty years. Regular customers also knew that if you wanted to run a tab until payday, or were short of cash at the moment, you could work something out with Laurel. Willis, on the other hand, was one class-A, habitually staring over his glasses sourpuss. Rarely, as in never, in a good mood; always with a sharp eye out for shoplifters at the candy rack. Classic case of opposites attracting, those two.

As Zane sped by the upper Applegate Grange, which reminded him of Florida since it was built with cinder block, he theorized that he'd probably dredged up the depressing memories of working at The

Alibi and getting busted in Canada because of the way they'd left the question of buying the farm. Unsettled. Nothing resolved. *What else can I find to beat myself up about? Seems to be my pattern. Couldn't get outta the bedroom fast enough, especially after she let me have it for bein such a lousy partner, such a total fuck-up. No wonder she's so hesitant about the farm, she's probably not sure she wants to stay with me. That'd explain everything.*

He considered the possibilities of his last thought being true with a suddenly cold, abstracted and totally feigned disinterest. *I'd probably buy the place regardless, if it came to that. If for no other reason than it'd be a good investment. I might be a Marxist philosophically, but I'm not an idiot. An' I don't even see any contradiction. Ever since people decided to take tokens, shells, beads or money in payment for their labor, once that system took over, we've had no way to act differently than obeying the laws of the cash nexus. So, yeah, I could put profit to good use, as much as I hate the concept. It's ridiculous to think otherwise....Maybe I can convince her of that, the investment angle? Maybe that'll work?...I gotta not be an asshole when I get back.*

Sasha and Duty were talking in the living room when Zane came in the door, a 6-pack in each hand, another under an arm. He set one down on the hatch cover and disappeared into the kitchen to put the others in the refrigerator. Coming back with an opener, he noticed Sasha and Duty weren't speaking, and she wasn't looking at him, so he blurted out the only thing that came to mind, asking Duty if he'd gotten any fish from Lester's.

"Damn straight, Kemosabe. Three fat ones."

"Lester must'a been in a good mood."

"Adeline, my man. She's the one who showed me how to do it. Said Lester was hibernating in his shack across the creek, and what he didn't know wouldn't hurt him. When we got to the pond, she gave me a long-handled net and threw food pellets out in front of me. The surface boiled in a feeding frenzy. I just stood there, watching fish churn. Quite a spectacle. You know how Adeline is, she gave me some grief, wanting to know if I expected her to net em for me too. When she threw out another handful, I just dipped into the middle and got three."

Zane popped the cap off a beer, holding it up in Sasha's direction. Surprising him, she smiled and nodded. Eyes soft, face smooth. "So," he said, walking the bottle over to her in the window chair, "are we havin em for dinner?"

"Yes, dear," she said with what he thought was an amiable smirk. *Dear?*

He had trouble putting his finger on why Sasha seemed in such a good mood. He'd expected, after he'd left her upstairs on the bed and driven off to Ruch without a word, that she'd be pissed and probably justifiably distant. Instead, everything seemed to be...What?...How could he describe it? AOK? Hunky Dory? It's all Gravy? Or, god forbid, Everything's Copacetic? Easy, empty, overused phrases like those sucked him straight into visions of sloppily dressed, morbidly obese people—men or women, didn't matter—with missing teeth, tattoos and very bad grammar. Made him shiver. He knew he was being piggish. Casting aspersions based on class, fabricating stereotypes like Orwell's proles. Knowing didn't help; his gut reactions often raced ahead of his political aim for tolerance.

But for the first time since Greg had burst through the door with the news about Perry, they'd enjoyed a shared dinner without a dark pall of pain and anger hanging in the room, tainting the air like rotten food in the fridge. This was like being in an alternate universe, he thought, steeled as he'd been to expect Sasha's restrained displeasure. Fires were going in both stoves, ginger and curry fumes sweetening the air. The FM low enough not to drown out conversation. Light-hearted banter. Even laughter, as Duty launched into a monologue wondering how native peoples had learned, through trial and error, what was safe to eat.

"So, let me get this right," he said, his arms stretched out, shoulders back. "Somebody figured out that they had to boil plant

291

roots three times in fresh water before they'd be edible. How did that happen? Someone boils 'em once and poisons themselves. Then, someone else thinks 'maybe we need to boil 'em twice?' and they get poisoned, too. Someone had to have watched that whole process and, after the first and second poisonings, they still came up with the brilliant idea to say, 'Hey! I know it killed a few folks, but trust me, one more boil an' it'll be just fine?' How does that work?"

Zane was tempted to ruin the mood by pointing out that Duty's natives were probably starving. He kept it to himself, though, opting not to insert his own blackened theory of history into the disarming relaxed atmosphere. Sasha touched him on the shoulder as she passed on the way to the kitchen, or the toilet. Full hand pressing, not a fingertip tap. Went out of her way to make contact, he thought. *What's happened? Her touch speaks volumes, doesn't it? Like a jump/shift in Bridge—switch suits AND raise the bid at the same time. Completely changes the game. Well, that hand at least. A paradigm shift. Is that it? Why? Did somethin happen after I left?*

Sasha returned, squeezing herself onto the couch between Zane and the over-stuffed arm, forcing him to shift closer to Duty. While she'd been gone, Duty had lit up a joint which Zane handed her, refusing to take it back until she'd had an extra hit.

"So here's the question," Duty pontificated. "What's worse, the Mike Douglas Show, Elvis paintings on black velvet, or those big-eyed Keane kids?"

"Mike Douglas. Hands down," Zane said, passing back to Duty. "Because his whole shtick is dumbin down anything he touches. Doesn't matter what the subject is, he'll find a way to infantilize it, yuck it up for the camera. Makin faces. Spreadin inanity if any conversation veers even slightly to the controversial. An he's a mediocre singer, at best." He felt validated, one whole side of Sasha pressed against him. He could feel her pulse in his ribs and wondered why his confidence ebbed and swelled so drastically. Was he really that fragile? That tenuous?

292

"Yeah," Duty drawled. "I know what you mean. Silliness as entertainment. But those Keane kids freak me. Saw too many in the flesh, vacant eyed waifs and orphans. Don't need any reminders." He sucked deeply, expelling smoke with his words. "Speaking of reminders, Next time you go to town, I need a ride to Vince's. Gonna get my VA check and see if I can't get the van running again. Might be gone a few days."

"I'm goin to J-Ville tomorrow 'round noon. I can take you."

Sasha leaned into his side, her mouth inches from his face, marijuana breath warm and familiar. "What're you going to do?"

"Go to the tavern. I need to ask that George some more questions. Still not clear how Perry's claim got sold, or why. That story's not straight."

"I guess I'm going with you then," she almost purred, putting a hand on his thigh, squeezing, breathing in his ear, inflating more than just his hopes for the night.

Chapter Eighteen

Once **manual labour** became deeply associated with **loss of liberty**, there was no free social rationale for invention. The stifling effects of slavery on technique were not a simple function of the low average productivity of slave-labour itself, or even of the volume of its use: they subtly affected all forms of labour.[...] The structural constraint of slavery on technology thus lay not so much in a direct intra-economic causality, although this was important in its own right, as in the **mediate social ideology** which enveloped the totality of manual work in the classical world, contaminating hired and even independent labour with **the stigma of debasement.**[...] The divorce of material work from the sphere of liberty was so rigorous that the Greeks had no word in their language even to express the concept of labour, either as a social function or as personal conduct. Both agricultural and artisanal work were essentially deemed "adaptations" to nature, not transformations of it: **they were forms of service** [emphasis added]. (26)

Perry Anderson. *Passages from Antiquity to Feudalism. London: Verso*

George watched Lloyd rub his back against the corner of the beer cooler, his fluorescent orange and green Hawaiian shirt inching up, revealing a hairy roll of jiggling fat above his belt. Great way to start a Saturday, George cringed, but at least the goddamn jukebox wasn't blaring Tammy Wynette or George Jones so loud he couldn't think. Lloyd was talking to Bill Simonsen, known to the bar crowd as Silly Billy, a lapdog kind of guy who liked positioning himself opposite the cash register so he could maintain sketchy banter with the bartender, have someone to talk to, since no one who knew him would sit anywhere close if they could avoid it. His thin, scratchy, wheedling voice and forced cackling laugh set George on edge, even if he couldn't hear the words clearly. Thank God for small favors.

Lloyd had an unsettling habit of talking to one person while looking at someone else. And George was a regular recipient of Lloyd's "watch me put this guy in his place" leers, squints and winks. *He's onstage early today, playing to a pretty sparse crowd. Of which I'm one. Glad the NBA finals're finally over, or the place'd be crowded and steamy, filled with elbowing loud-mouths.*

He'd watched the games peripherally, not particularly interested in the outcomes. Which was at odds with the general atmosphere in the bar. Whites against blacks. Celtics and Bucks. Lloyd had tried to stoke everyone up with his running monologue of how "five jigaboos" didn't have a chance against Cowens, Havlicek, Nelson and Westphal—white boys all—even if the Bucks did have that tall Black Muslim Jabbar. When the Celtics took game seven, the tavern rejoiced as one and Lloyd had set up the bar for only the second time George could remember. The first being Nixon's landslide in '72, well before all this Watergate stuff muddied up the waters.

The popcorn machine by the front windows sent stale buttery fumes down the bar with muffled snapping sounds as a log truck downshifted outside on the street and a grey-haired couple cupped their hands around their faces to stare through the window. Not their kind of place, he could tell from their expressions, like they'd both suddenly become aware of the sour smell. George knew the feeling, draining what was left of his first beer of the day.

Fact was he'd awoken this morning scared of death, sharply aware that it'd be a singular event, as in not affecting a single soul but him, assuming his folks would already be gone. But that wasn't a sure thing, either. He could blow a gasket without ever seeing it coming, burst a vessel and hit the floor. Movie star dead at fifty-eight—in the prime of life—that kind of thing. Happened all the time, always men of course. No one ever talked about some woman having a heart attack or stroke. George caught himself in these thoughts a lot lately, and he didn't know exactly why, though he'd cornered a few good ideas. Main among them was that he was tired of being alone.

As for this new, sudden and episodic fear of death, he recognized its source in the mundane march of time. Not much of a mental leap, he knew. His body thickening, slowing. Veins protruding, lumps and bumps forming under steadily wrinkling skin. He'd recently tossed out bundles of photos he'd kept forever in a closet, swearing for years that they constituted his memory, even though he'd only gone through them two or three times reminiscing. He'd thrown away his history, in a sense, because so much of it had become meaningless.

Forgotten relationships, faded friendship, faces long dead—his own place in the past more like a fleeting after-scent than a firm feeling. Mostly, a case that no one else would know or care about who the photos had captured. He hadn't returned from Korea clutching souvenirs or rolls of film. And today he missed talking to Walt more than any loss he could conjure from old pictures, if he was honest with himself. Perhaps admitting that summed up his increasing spates of despair? The Army Corp colonel had touched a nerve, brought out feelings George had always associated with having a brother. Shared connections. A biological and genetic affinity.

He'd lived with sudden death in the war, of course, often splattered with it, breathed it. But that had been out of his hands. Either happened or it didn't. Never knew from one moment to the next. His current fixation seemed more well-defined. What he'd for years seen as independence, no one yanking his chain except the Bureau during a crisis, he now felt as an isolating estrangement. Being on his own didn't ring with the same defiant clarity he'd relished for decades. Wasn't such a positive position to be in anymore, he'd come to realize. Although still basically confident in his abilities to navigate the day-to-day, he'd begun to lament living without someone to care about, someone who cared about him. Often he wondered if he was capable of a relationship, as people these days liked to call it. Had he kept to himself so long that he'd grooved-in habits he couldn't break? He wasn't sure, but he did know that stewing in his own juices was a pointless exercise. He hated to think in terms of some overly jawed-about mid-life crisis, but his recent struggles with mortality—the sodden inevitability of it—made him wonder. What he did know with certainty was that these fears weren't something that had mysteriously come to him; they came from him, were part of his being. Saturating the way he thought, and saw, and felt. Leaving him to wonder what pieces of himself he'd left at the frozen Chosin reservoir, other than parts of two fingers on his left hand and his once brown hair.

Yesterday afternoon he'd taken another half-day in the field, signed out of the office and driven to Ruch to see what he could learn about the notarized scrap of paper transferring the Tanaka Flats claim that Dave Brereton had submitted with Perry Louvelle's signature. He wasn't exactly sure what he was looking for, just that he was uneasy with a copy rather than the original. Plus, he found it completely out of character for Perry to have gone to Ruch. He'd known for years that Perry's longtime pal August, who lived in Jacksonville, usually did all the shopping for his friend, bringing whatever few supplies were needed to the river. Bags of flour, rice or beans. So, if Perry had traveled to Ruch, how did he get there? Before driving out yesterday, George had swung by August's two-room house tucked into a hollow at the end of a dirt driveway behind Jacksonville cemetery, the old one that hadn't been used since the twenties.

August, who claimed Nez Perce heritage and looked the part with leathery bronze skin and still jet black hair, was wearing his ever-present blue bandana, the paisley inspired neckerchief George saw on hippies and more often on their dogs. August's "Can't Bust 'Em" overalls, one strap unhooked and dangling, mostly covered the ragged thermal underwear top he had on whenever George ran into him. "I'm being unfair," he thought, correcting himself, "maybe it's not the same one every time, but it's sure his style of choice."

August shut the door behind him and came outside to talk, which was fine with George; he'd been inside the cobwebbed, cluttered space several years back and didn't need to repeat the experience. August's age was a mystery, anywhere from sixty to eighty, impossible to guess. But he did know that he and Perry had been friends for decades. As far as George could tell, August was Perry's only contact off the river.

"I'm wondering," George asked after the "how you doin's" were over, "did you happen to give Perry a ride down to Ruch lately, like in the last three weeks?"

"Naw, hell, haven't been out there in a month-a-Sundays. What's he up to? Did he send you because he needed me to bring something?"

"You haven't heard?"

"Heard?"

George swallowed, hating himself for having come. "Perry's dead. Happened Friday before last. They say—the ones who found him—that he must've fallen down onto the river rocks somehow."

August screwed up his face and George worried he was going to burst into tears, or perhaps fly into a rage. "My oldest friend," August finally said, looking up to the overcast sky, his shoulders slumped noticeably, eyes watering. "I should'a kept closer track. An' now it's too late."

"Sorry to be the one bringing you this. Wasn't my intention. Thought you would'a heard….Don't know why I thought that….But as far as I can tell, you couldn't'a done anything. Happened at night. Officially listed as an accident." He stared at his shoes, unable to meet the old man's eyes, wishing he'd never bothered him.

"Fucking hell," he'd sworn to himself as he slammed his door to the BLM pickup. Backing up and turning around, he saw that August was still standing where he'd left him, rooted to the ground, head hanging. Pulling the rig out onto pavement, he was hit with a more clinical thought. "If August didn't give him a ride to Ruch, who did?" Threading the back streets of Jacksonville, dingy houses whose yards were littered with bikes, trikes, toys, tools, scattered refuse and the occasional pickup or car body on blocks, George got stuck on an idea that would have been inconceivable before all the Tanaka Flats craziness began. "What if Perry didn't really go to the realtor's office at all? He's conveniently not around to ask." Thus spurred by a mounting and itching desire to nail down details, facts, specifics, he'd steered onto 238, the Applegate highway that led to the small community of Ruch, eight twisting, up and down miles away.

The realty office of Rodney J. Pence was in a three-unit strip mall across from the Y-junction stop sign, sharing space with *Glenda's Beauty Salon* and *Ruch Gold & Silver*. None of them seemed to be bustling with business as George pulled into an empty parking lot.

"Mr. Pence," George extended his hand to the short, skinny, balding man in his fifties with a prominent Adam's apple who'd stood as George entered. He was wearing wrinkled cords, a short-sleeve white shirt and horn-rimmed glasses.

"Rod, please." He'd gestured to the wooden chair in front of his paper strewn desk.

After introducing himself, George explained he was trying to run down some loose ends concerning a bill-of-sale the realtor had notarized two weeks or so before. "It was a claim transfer from Perry Louvelle to someone named Jason Reeves. Do you remember that transaction?"

"Let's check the ledger," Pence replied, dragging a black binder from the desk drawer. "Let me see," he flipped the cover open and turned a page. "Yes," pointing a finger, "here it is." When he glanced up, George decided he looked like a beagle. "what was it you wanted to know?"

"I'm just wondering what Mr. Louvelle showed you for identification. How'd he verify who he was? I know with some certainty that he didn't have a driver's license, a social security card or a birth certificate."

"Well...Yes, the thing was, I didn't actually see him. Dave—that is Captain Brereton—he said Mr. Louvelle was incapacitated and couldn't be moved." He squeezed the bridge of his nose with a thumb and forefinger, like he'd suddenly developed a headache. "Now normally that would have been all there was to it, but...Aw hell, Dave's my neighbor. I've known him all my life." He began talking a bit faster, anxiously. "When he asked me for a favor, especially since it wasn't an affidavit or a will...I mean, it seemed like a such a small matter...and he told me he was just helping out an old friend who couldn't get around so well, who needed this in a hurry...I guess I....Well, he's a state policeman, after all," he looked at George imploringly, obviously seeking a nod, a smile, some sort of assurance. Receiving none, he tried a different tact. "He is an officer of the law. I really kind'a felt it was my duty to comply, if you know what I mean."

George stood while Pence stayed in his chair looking spent, demoralized. "Thanks, Rod. That's all I wanted to know." He turned toward the door as the realtor spoke in trembling tones.

"Am I in any trouble here?" His voice trailed off. "I was only trying to be helpful."

George stopped, cast a quick glance over his shoulder. "Relax, Mr. Pence. I'm not here on official business." On his way out the door: "You have a nice day now, you hear."

As he drove back to Jacksonville, George realized, in a swirl of generally abstract but nonetheless piercing anger, that he was tired of being inundated with bullshit from every direction. Brereton and Perkins, working for themselves, it seemed. He was sure now that they'd orchestrated the claim business. No doubts any longer. Then, as he steered his way up and over J-Ville hill, he thought of all the impeachment talk in Washington with grandstanding legislators seeking spotlights. Not that he thought Nixon was innocent, Tricky Dick and all. Not that he'd ever clung to notions that those seeking public power were motivated by their kind crusading hearts, committed in their core to improving the lives of others. He wasn't suddenly disenchanted, or shocked to learn the world had always run on varying degrees of inhumanity and savagery. He'd learned those lessons long ago.

All he'd ever had to do was look around the Rogue valley, didn't need to expand horizons any further. Pear-picking Mexican farm workers living in leaking shacks hidden from roadside view, working for pennies, as long as they never showed their faces in town. Been going on since World War II when homegrown workers were scarce.

301

He also knew even piddling little city contracts were habitually granted depending on who was kissing whose ass, that getting ahead has nearly always meant stepping on someone else. But George wondered whether significant planets had recently come into an unholy alignment, screwing people up, pulling brain fluids out of balance so that repeated lies from those in power were swallowed whole by half the country. Reminding him that jungle law was only a paper-thin distance away from the most devout, give-us-this-day Sunday prayer service. He knew all that like he knew he had marrow in his bones.

Lloyd brought down another beer, pulling him back to the present. He realized that having his most pessimistic explanation of Perry's claim notarization confirmed in Ruch hadn't surprised him. Somehow it all fell in line with the Fausen family's disappearance and what he'd read in the *Mail Tribune* or seen on the news about the killings at Takilma last week. He'd said it before, a tangible strain of butchery and mayhem was running through southern Oregon, providing splashy headlines while any news about land grabs through eminent domain related to the dam was relegated to the back pages, buried with reports of soldiers coming home with heroin habits, or Oregon State Extension press releases about a new strain of Elm disease. A goddamn shame was what it was. All of it. Lump the national crises in with recent happenings up the Applegate or out on the Illinois, he thought, we're all affected one way or another by a radiating cycle of deceit and violence.

As coverage of the Watergate hearings had intensified, taken over day-time TV, George began considering hitherto unlikely ideas, like letting his hair grow out. Maybe he'd stop shaving, start listening to psychedelic rock or actually vote instead of sitting elections out. He felt he needed to do something to demonstrate he wasn't just gobbling down all the shit being shoveled in Washington.

Watching corruption unveiled at the highest levels was tantamount to seeing movie stars he'd envied in his youth grown old and wrinkled, bent and shriveled, wearing big round Jesse Helms coke bottle glasses, pink scalp showing through sparse hair, or worse still, their bodies blimped out, stretched beyond any recognizable shape. Even the most beautiful people went to seed. Exactly how he thought about career politicians. Finding themselves in orbits of power made liars and cheats of so many, like marrying into the mob.

He was not an optimist by any means, of that he was sure. How could he be? He was forty-three for christsakes and lived alone with his hemorrhoids in the back of a redneck tavern.

Zane and Sasha had dropped Duty at Vince and Soapy's house, an old, rough wood sided two story at the back of a narrow lot up by the country club in Medford's eastern hills, Duty's white Ford van parked on the street out front. Sasha had decided the day before to come along, after a heart-to-heart with Duty. Zane had already left in a huff before Duty returned with his fish from Lester's pond. She'd realized, at the time, that he probably noticed how upset she was—her face must have been lit up like neon—because he'd hurriedly disposed of the trout in the kitchen and come to sit beside her on the couch. He'd arched his eyebrows at her two quick times in succession without speaking, another of his loveable quirky habits. She'd known what he was asking.

"What?" she'd pretended.

"What's going on? That's what. You look like you could use a friend. Where's Zane off to? I saw the bus headed downstream when I was walking back."

"No idea," she'd said, trying not to look as emptied out as she felt. "I had the nerve to suggest buying this place wasn't something to rush into, that we needed to think about it seriously. What it meant, the responsibility it entailed."

"Entailed...nice word girl. I love being around educated people. Makes life so much more interesting." He'd squeezed her shoulder. "So lemme guess, he balked at the responsibility stuff and then split?"

"Yep." Nothing else she could have added. Duty knew him too. Had been witness to his erratic outbursts more than a few times.

"So? What's your plan?"

"Plan?" She'd thrown it out with a bitter breathy laugh. "Jesus, Duty, I don't have a plan. I'm at my wit's end here. Truly I am." She'd shaken her head. "I love this place. I love Zane. So why do I feel so trapped, on edge and off balance?"

"Maybe you need to go all in?" He'd caught her eyes, held them momentarily. She'd felt he was trying to convince her of his seriousness, but she'd been at a loss for words. Her face must have shown it because he'd kept going. "He's an organizer. That's his bottom line, his base personality. I don't think he sees himself as being built for the long haul....That's just a guess....but I wonder if he doesn't feel he's always alone, him against the world. A pirate adventure. You know he's not stupid; he's aware he keeps shit to himself, hides his motives if he worries about criticism or backlash. His brain's always working to figure out leverage, I think. So maybe putting yourself into his movie, letting him see you're together with him...maybe that'd get him to see how much he needs you. And he does need you, girl. As an outside observer I can tell you that."

Duty's words yesterday had hit home. She knew she couldn't change Zane with an act of willpower, or by continually pointing out what she thought of as his faults. Those roads led nowhere. As she thought about it today, watching him concentrate on driving Medford's increasingly busy downtown streets, she thanked Duty for his advice. She was willing to give it a try, to get more involved in Zane's...she didn't know what to call it. His investigation into Perry's death? That's what they were doing today, at least. She'd convinced herself, tentatively, she was going to have to go with the flow. Nothing else had worked, and last night's steamy, prolonged passion had been a pleasant change from him turning away without a word.

"So, Sasha?" They were stopped at a light. "What happened yesterday? I expected you to still be pissed when I came back from

Sunnyside. Sorry I walked out like that. I know how much you hate it." The light changed and he concentrated again on driving, swearing in low key to himself, shifting up and down in the space of a block when someone cut in ahead and everyone else slammed their brakes As soon as the traffic righted itself, they got into a steady speed which let them hit signals on green. "I apologize for takin off. It's like an out-of-body reflex reaction. I know, when it's happenin, that I'm headed for trouble, but I disassociate. Like I'm watchin myself from above at the same time I'm aware of what I'm doin. Freaky as hell. Violates the conservation of consciousness law that no two thoughts can occur simultaneously in the same person. Look! It's a buttermilk sky."

Sasha looked up where he pointed. He was right about the clouds, but she'd been considering what he'd just said about himself, like why he couldn't admit he had a choice to act differently, that he wasn't helpless, wasn't being carried along by some magic carpet he couldn't control. Given her decision to follow Duty's advice by trying to be supportive, she swallowed those thoughts. *See Zane? Just like that. I can do it, switch off the negative voices, become circumspect. I've seen you do that without a hitch when you're trying to convince someone, that's really your strength. You forget I was with you in Minneapolis, saw you in action. I don't understand how, when it comes to looking at yourself, you seem to go blind. I don't get it. But I'm not going to dwell.* "In answer to your question, I decided you were probably inflicting enough damage on yourself. You didn't need more from me. I wanted you to know I was still on your side. To not let things build into bitterness and silence."

"Thanks." He was smiling, and not one of those sly or sarcastic ones that drove her up the wall. This smile more toothy, less self-conscious. "You've always been the level-headed one," he added, "I can count on that. But why'd you wanna come today? You keepin tabs on me?"

She ignored the jab. "I want to find out about Perry, too. I owe him that."

"Sure, but this is quite a change, you gotta admit. You've always made a point to stay away from...what shall I say?...my political stuff."

"Nothing wrong with changing, is there? I would have thought you'd be pleased that I'm taking an interest."

"And last night? Was that just bein kind, too?"

"I think you know better than that." She said, pinching his closest ear.

Chapter Nineteen

...Can be bring ourselves to realize how much of our "Reality" could not exist for us, were it not for our profound and inveterate involvement in symbol systems. Our presence in a room is immediate, but the room's relation to our country as a nation, and beyond that, to international relations and cosmic relations, dissolves into a web of ideas and images that reach through our senses only insofar as the symbol systems that report on them are heard or seen. To mistake this vast tangle of ideas for immediate experience is much more fallacious than to accept a dream as an immediate experience. For a dream really is an immediate experience, but the information that we receive about today's events throughout the world most decidedly is not. (118)
Kenneth Burke. Language as Symbolic Action. U. of California Press, 1956.

George was daydreaming about drifting a Stonefly close to the bottom of the long, deep channel on the Rogue at Whiskey Creek when he saw them come in, both in blue, jeans and work shirts. The stunningly beautiful olive-skinned woman with shiny black hair hanging below her waist, legs up to there as they say, and the guy with that Joe Namath moustache. He'd known from the second he spied them that they were looking for him. *They want more about Perry. Not sure what I can tell 'em, or should. Then again, who's in charge of the shoulds anymore? Whole story needs to come out somehow, just not from me. I've gotta protect myself. Does that make me a...?* Before he could finish, they were next to him, smiling uncomfortably while shuffling their feet. He forgot what he was going to say about himself, but was sure it was negative.

Zane and Sasha, he at least got their names right. Second time he'd seen them; first time together. In their initial meeting, when she was accompanied by the linebacker with long curly hair, Sasha had made quite the impression on him. For that matter, so did Zane when he came in alone. The kid had seemed fairly straight-ahead, was obviously twisted up about Perry, and he sensed, after their first conversation, that he could probably handle himself in a mental wrestling match. Physically, he was one of those wiry, stringy types

George knew could be surprisingly strong for all their lankiness. Sasha, however, was something else entirely. He wasn't picturing any sexual fantasies yet, but only because he hadn't seen her enough. Off the top he'd have to admit he was struck by the way she carried herself, how she moved. A liquid motion, as graceful as a swimmer gliding, while Zane was more angular, exuding a restrained intensity. Quite the couple, even if they dressed like twins.

They took two empty stools, Zane sitting next to him. He could see Sasha's face when she leaned forward, which she seemed intent on doing, while Zane was the one talking. "I hope we're not botherin you," he said, extracting a cigarette from the pack he'd plopped on the bar. "But I was wonderin if you could tell us who bought Perry's claim? Is that somethin you're allowed to disclose?" He'd turned full-face.

"It's public information," George said flatly, as Zane lit his cigarette, blowing the smoke straight up. George appreciated not getting it in his face. *Why am I edgy? Because right out of the gate he's pushing? Because he's young? Because he has her to sleep with? My antenna's up because I don't wanna get sucked into someone else's problems. Still, I'm attracted. They're the only ones who've bothered to care about Perry. What's their angle? Don't see it. Except on principle, and that's a risky place to live.*

"And you said it was only for a dollar. What's with that? Perry gives his place away and immediately gets killed? An we're supposed to believe it's all a coincidence?"

"Yeah, I agree, a little too convenient. But as far as the Bureau's concerned, whether he sold it for a dollar or a million is none of our business. We've nothing to do with that. Legal title transfer is all that matters." *Jesus, I sound stuffy.*

"I imagine price matters quite a bit to whoever got it for a buck," Zane verbally smirked.

Touche. A number of seconds elapsed before he managed to respond. "Jason Reeves. That's the guy who bought it. Listed an address in Redding." Alarms were screeching in George's head. He was getting involved. Hell, he already was involved, ready to cough up anything she wanted. He saw himself beginning to slide helplessly down a loose slope with no handholds in sight, completely at the mercy of gravity. Since Dave Brereton had pulled a fast one with Perry's claim, since before that when the Fausen saga began and construction on the dam had picked up, he'd been aware of a growing inner burning. Not the kind that *Tums* could solve, more like in his nervous system. It was attitudinal and he was going through changes he couldn't pin down. But part of his edginess came from how often he caught himself thinking that some anti-war types made sense, were more right than not when they railed against the corruption of the establishment, or how legal systems ran on money. He was tantalized by desires to enjoy his life for a change. Shrugging off constraints, exploring hitherto unknown emotional territories. Women who...well, all that free love. So he didn't automatically flinch at the prospects of helping. It'd be an alluring alternative to parking his butt on a bar stool listening to Lloyd. But investigating authority brought its own obvious problems, not least that he was entangled in the tentacles of power himself. He made his living from a government job, had that to lose.

"Do you know him..." Sasha leaned in closer, so George saw both their faces as if suspended in the air like balloons. "...this Jason?"

"Never heard of him. Which is telling in its own right. Perry was pretty much a hermit out there. How would he know someone from Redding? And why would he sign off his life's work like that? I watched him putting in improvements year after year. That land was his love. He used to tell me it was his seventeen acres of heaven." Sasha was nodding, her jaw set. Green eyes beseeching. He could have fallen in. *Dial it back a notch there, bucko. She's no fool. You're just gonna end up embarrassing yourself.* A sharp recognition nonetheless clicked into place, became clear to him in that instant. He watched someone moving in slow motion, walking in water, except it was him, knowing he was going to spill everything about the claim transfer. *Why not? Why'd I tell 'em anything in the first place if I wasn't gonna follow it through? The old man deserved a lot better than what he got, and these two are willing.*

George looked around quickly to see if anyone was listening, lowering his voice to a conspiratorial half-whisper, drawing them closer. "I went out to Ruch yesterday. Wanted to talk to the realtor who notarized the bill of sale." He looked up and around, checking before he ducked back to them. "Turns out he didn't see Perry at all. Put his seal on the paper as a favor for a friend." He was primed to say more, but saw Lloyd ambling toward them, primping in the bar mirror, slicking back his hair.

"What'll it be," Lloyd took a cursory swipe with his towel as he eyed Sasha's breasts. George caught him, but the bartender winked like they were in it together, partners in lechery.

"Three beers." Zane didn't even look up. George knew the attitude. The word petulant came to mind. A single-mindedness driven by the arrogant fervor of youth. He'd been that way himself, though in his case it'd been dreaming about escaping the farm, seeing himself on screen in Technicolor, a leading man in sanitized, bloodless adventures of guns and glory, backlit by sunny auras and stirring strains from the Marine Corp Band.

Korea had knocked those fantasies on their ass the first day. Out for the count. The only harmonic vibrations he remembered were whistles and whines of artillery coming in, tearing the sky.

Lloyd's intrusion struck the three of them mute for the moment, disrupting the flow and stifling conversation. In the lull, George wondered if they were stoned, spaced-out on something. Sasha seemed transfixed, open, unblinking eyes, while Zane frowned as he laid out a dollar and rolled the tip of his cigarette around in the flimsy aluminum ashtray. George decided they were just taking a break until the beer arrived, keeping confidences. Fine by him. The less Lloyd poked his nose in, the better. *He's a kibitzing magpie, squawking for attention.*

As they waited, the jukebox came to life with the opening chords of Charlie Pride's "All His Children." George loved the song. It'd been the theme for a Paul Newman film about logging he'd seen last year. *Shot it up the coast around Newport and on the Siletz.* The lyrics reached in to stir the compressed sediment of his memory. He disregarded the religious overtones, concentrating instead on specific lines. "No matter where you're goin', or where you've been...you're part of the fam-lee of man." *Tony from Boca Raton. Nellie from Missoula. Buck from Las Cruces. What about all the Chinks we killed? Them too? Riddled with jagged, crusted, maggot-infested wounds in the summer. A boy with half a head, like a sliced pomegranate, one cloudy eye open to eternity. A lotta shit I got buried. Some sins still haunt. Maybe these two will be good for me? They're fresh, but not naïve. And they're on a mission. I'm ready for a change, for doing more than just oiling the gears. Only one life to live, after all. Isn't that a soap opera, for christsakes? She's got a body to die for.*

Lloyd delivered their beers with a crooked decoupaged smile, his eyes sweeping them like a *Rainbird* spraying a cornfield. With an exaggerated flamboyant flourish, he swept up the dollar and snapped the quarter change onto the scratched and scarred bar top, hesitating as if waiting for applause. Reality as farce, George thought, doesn't get any better than Lloyd in full feather.

As soon as the bartender moved away, Zane turned to him. "That song's from *Sometimes a Great Notion.*"

"I know," George hurried to say. "You saw it?"

"Yeah, wasn't much like Kesey's book, but that's Hollywood for ya." George let it die there for a beat or two before Zane picked up the investigative thread. "So, who's this friend who got the favor? Did the realtor tell you that? Do you know who's pullin the strings?"

George reached for his beer, buying time, swallowing with a series of tiny sips. He glanced over the rim of his glass. Sasha's face got to him more than Zane's questions. "Dave Brereton," he admitted, setting his glass back down, "in uniform no less." He hoped, in some back channel of his now busy brain, that he wasn't plunging into the biggest screw-up of his life. He felt guilty for as long as it took to flush the idea. He didn't owe the state cop anything, or Perkins either. Besides, he knew he was right: those two were clearly fiddling the dog.

"Holy shit." Zane breathed out in a cloud of smoke as he stubbed his cigarette. "Perkins takes care of Perry, an Brereton runs a scam on the claim. They're workin together."

"And there's nothing we can do?" Sasha asked, her forehead wrinkled. "There must be something."

"'Fraid not. That ship has sailed." George couldn't meet her eyes.

"But how can that be?" She was pleading now, her fingers curled around Zane's wrist, both hands for support as she leaned in closer. He could feel her warm breath. "You mean they can just get away with it?"

"Case is closed. No one is gonna question it. Yesterday's news. The ambulance crew certainly won't bring it up. They would've automatically deferred to Perkins anyway. He was the authority on site, the one who called it in. Coroner signed off. Who's gonna second-guess themselves after the fact?"

Zane butted in. "That means we're the only ones who know what happened." He waved his hand back and forth quickly, drawing invisible lines, connecting them. "Except for Mutt n Jeff, we're it."

"As far as we know," George added, a bit anxious at being included in the 'we.' He hadn't made them promises, or agreed to anything yet. But he knew the die was cast; he'd given them names. He could have smiled and said nothing. He could have flat out refused to cooperate. But it was too late. The kid had told him what the ambulance report revealed about Perry's injuries, told him about the burned cabin – information George wouldn't have otherwise. In response, he'd revealed the crucial details of Brereton's behind the scenes conniving. Identifying Jason Reeves should be public information, but would probably have taken six months or so to officially show up, given the way George knew things went. All important cards were on the table, impossible to ignore. The real question, from George's perspective, was so what? What could they do about it now? Not much, he feared.

Sasha wasn't ready to let go. She tucked loose hair behind her ear and sounded more hopeful. "Maybe we could get some reporter interested? Get the story out?" Zane's quick nod was practically imperceptible. Dottie West's "Country Sunshine" came over the sound system, but George tuned it out, hunching closer to them for emphasis.

"There's no proof of anything here. Perry's already in the ground. The claim transfer's officially approved and filed. It's a done deal. Might be nice to find out who Jason Reeves is, how he fits in, but even then there's no legal recourse. No one involved is gonna be willing to dig into it. They're not gonna investigate themselves to see if they screwed up. And don't forget, you're not talking about some member of the public; you'd be taking on the county, the Forest Service and the State Police. Again, with no evidence to point to. All the realtor has to do is deny what he told me. There's no paper trail except the one with all the appropriate boxes checked. Approved by my office, I'm sorry to say. But that's the way it is. And we're not sure if what happened to Perry is in any way connected to the Fausens." He reached quickly for his beer glass. His mouth gone dry as sawdust.

"You think so?" Zane asked.

"Don't know," he mumbled between swallows. "But a lot of strange stuff's going on up there. You should know. You live there."

George could hear, from the metallic clinks and rising voices behind him, that a shuffleboard game had begun. Dottie's peppy voice echoed through the rafters, which resembled upside-down picket fences. Other conversations came through as incoherent background rumblings. Sasha appeared shocked, staring into space, her fingers kneading Zane's arm. Seeing that, her touching, George filled in the picture quickly. She was never going to be closer to him than she was right then. As sure as he'd known she wasn't involved with that hippy Nam vet. He just knew.

Like he knew footings for the dam were being poured as they spoke. While they slept, in fact.

He'd heard construction crews were running three shifts a day, every day, so he'd driven out late Wednesday night to see for himself. Since Zane had told him they lived on Lester and Adeline's property, he'd made a note of their swayback bridge as he passed, thought of Sasha moving about the house. At the site, he pulled off the road at a wide spot where he could see cement mixers with bellies churning lined up in two parallel rows, inching forward as one after another emptied their loads and headed to the water tanks for rinsing. A grindingly slow process illuminated by vapor lights, drivers smoking, talking on their CBs as they waited. The scope of the project—all those trucks coming and going—reminded him that everything in front of him meant new money flooding into the valley, filtering through several hundred different businesses.

He'd already noticed the tavern crowd in a better mood lately, in just the last couple weeks. Maybe not more people, but the ones who did show up were more spirited than usual, moods lifting. Good-natured laughter instead of dejected, head-hanging complaints. He wasn't hearing "If We Make It Through December" nearly as often. What happened to the Fausens wasn't the main topic at the bar. When the economy cranked into high gear, he knew, folks spent with pleasure, relishing their improved conditions, spreading it around. After over a decade watching the timber industry shrink, mill after mill laying off whole shifts. Bars were filled with unhappy people. But the current jovial joshing and friendly back-slapping told George the dam was pumping cash downstream like fresh Spring runoff. Another Jacksonville gold rush, he thought, wondering who'd be the Chinamen at the bottom of the pile this time around.

The Applegate lay under a blanket of dark purple clouds as they cleared the summit of J-Ville hill around four o'clock and wound down to Ruch, taking the left fork to head home past the newly planted vineyard whose wired and staked rows gridded the bottom end of a valley once filled with peach orchards and fields of alfalfa. Zane swore the air smelled distinctly different since the crops changed, and not for the better.

Sasha had been quiet since soon after they'd left the tavern. Whether she was irritated with him—and he couldn't put his finger on anything he'd done today—or was upset from what George had said, he wasn't sure. She'd kept her face turned, appearing, at least, to be staring out the window. Fixed, like a camera lens. Watching whatever passed by.

He'd caught himself counting his heart beats, losing track somewhere around forty and starting the count over. Eventually mixing up numbers and going back to one in a repeating pattern of constant counting. Until another rhythm butted in, and he'd be tapping a foot for each guard rail post, or for every cement truck or earthmover they met on the road, even for patterns he could control like blinking or breathing. It was the counting or tapping or touching tips of fingers together in sequence that mattered. Once he was in the grips of the behavior, he never knew how long it'd last, how long he'd be held hostage to the manic, in-every-fiber-of-his-being need to keep order. The irony wasn't lost on him. *It's a dis-order.*

He knew some coping skills if he could catch himself early enough. Focus on a film clip of memory, recreate past moments scene by scene, like laying color transparencies over a map, one at a time. Re-telling the emergent story to himself. *To keep from spinnin out. Gettin the whirlies, cold sweats and nausea.* To defend himself he went back to his short stint as a prison guard in the sticky air of south Florida. Working for a less-than-subsistence monthly salary from *La Raza* had sent him searching for income. He'd learned about the job from Catfish John— Zane's name for him because he ran the aqua-farm project at Hendry

315

County prison, raising catfish and bream in a half-acre murky pond just outside the concertina wire topped fences.

He'd met John at Migrants United in Immokalee months before the Texas crew left the .45 in his drawer. Tall and thin with pasty white skin and brillo-like sienna red hair, John began dropping by the office to share gossip, commiserate about the country being run by Republicans. He and Zane became fast friends, even after John revealed he was bi-sexual and terribly attracted to him. Zane turned down John's "don't knock it till you've tried it" argument, but otherwise didn't treat him any differently. That was it, subject never came up again. They shared political postures, three-dollar soul food lunches at "Black Gal's House of Peace and Love," and quarts of Schlitz Malt Liquor to lubricate wide-ranging discussions while playing Risk with Juan and Leslie in the cinder block house where Zane rented a room. Catfish told him to apply at the prison because it paid three-fifty an hour.

After taking a fill-in-the-bubble test on prison policies which Zane passed with simple logic and common sense, he'd been bounced in a jeep to the firing range to qualify with a handgun and a twelve-gauge shotgun. From fifteen yards away, being attacked by dive-bombing mosquitoes, he missed his first two pistol shots at the target which was a solid black male shape, a fitting representation of the inmate population. The weapons officer, with military tattoos up both arms, took the .38 from him, saying "You'll never pass that way," and pumped a cluster of five into the black chest. *An then I blew the poor guy's head off with the shotgun. So I started workin swing, armed an dangerous in a pickup rotatin around the outer fence every two hours, checkin in on the walkie-talkie every half-hour. Smuggled pints of vodka in my pants. Nothin to it until they put me in a cell block cause someone was sick. Couldn't go back out to get my vodka from the car. Was startin to go through withdrawls when I got detailed to the solitary cells to deliver dinners in Styrofoam trays. Found Jimmy Dideaux hangin from a rope tied to the iron cage protecting the ceiling light. Bug-eyed, swollen blue tongue out, closed-in stench from his fouled pants. Supervisor said Jimmy'd been placed in solitary for his own protection. He'd been tellin everyone he was a woman trapped in a man's body. Wanted to be called "Ramona." Like a majority of the inmates, Jimmy was in on a drug charge, doin five to seven for possession of a few joints in West Palm. In the break room, asshole Chuck Lucas, who'd always lived in Immokalee, gloated. "One less fag nigger. Now that's my idea of affirmative action." He'd fuckin winked at us as he said it. An then he added that whoever supplied the rope should get a raise...or a pardon. Could barely see by the time my shift ended, was so far out on the shakes. Sick for three days, lost the job. When I went back to collect my pay I saw they had someone else's social security number on my check. They had no idea who I was. Could'a been an escaped felon, for all they knew.*

He'd succeeded in quelling the counting. But it'd come back if he gave it space, so he hurried to make nice with Sasha, praising her suggestion of contacting a reporter. "I still think it's a good idea. We ought'a think about it."

"Didn't you hear George? We can't jeopardize his career. Besides, he warned us to be careful, to stay under the radar."

"It's just you seem so depressed." At least she was looking straight ahead now, which was worth something.

"I'm sad and I'm angry." She was biting off the words. "No one cares what happened to Perry. And then I learn about all this other crap going on with his claim, and then I don't know what. You and I care. George cares. Greg should care. Who else?"

"Caring without action is a meaningless gesture," Zane said, immediately wishing he hadn't. *Fuck I'm stupid.*

She responded sharply. "Oh, that's good, Zane. Is that one of those sayings you wrote in your little book, saving it till now to spring on me? Like that Mother's Day card you got?" She paused. Dead air while he cringed. "Yeah, that's right, I saw it. You didn't give it to me, but I saw it."

317

"Jesus, Sasha. I'm sorry. I thought better of it later, you know." Adrenalin shockwaves hit like a dose of Niacin. *Was sure I'd kept it hidden till I tossed it in the burnin wood stove.*

"I'd never seen that person before. How could you be so unspeakably cruel?"

She's been keepin this in for a long time. "It's certainly not somethin I'm proud of."

"No, I wouldn't imagine." She turned back to looking out her side window, and he knew this was serious, would be a tough one to heal. One step forward, two steps back. Story of his recent life. He feared he was seeing his hopes of convincing her to buy the farm evaporate. *I've screwed myself yet again. Every time I try to turn around I'm stumblin over my own feet.*

They drove in a silence so tense that clearing his throat seemed a major statement, disturbingly loud and pregnant with meaning. He lit a cigarette to occupy himself, looking for a way to cut through the tension. Two more miles. Three. But he couldn't stay mute, cadences lurked in the stochastic murmuring of road noise, threatening to show up as music. He didn't know how all the mechanisms worked, but when he was in a bad spell all he had to do was think of a song and the lyrics would start their numbing loop. God forbid it was an instrumental like "Third Man Theme," or "Zorba the Greek." Zither music. Could go on for hours.

"I need to stop by Richard's. Get him to come over. See if he's picked up any news from his old man." Another thirty second empty stretch before she said anything.

"Fine, Zane. Have Richard come. Stay up all night. Do what you want. But could we please just give it a rest right now? I'm completely burned out."

Nothing for him to say. He was so far off base with her at the moment that any center fielder with a mediocre arm could throw him out easily. Morphing that metaphor into other genres for the next five miles kept him occupied until he turned in to Richard's driveway.

When the door opened to his knocking, he had to look down. Richard was on his plywood board with swivel wheels, half-a-person whose upturned face framed with hair gone wild made him resemble a newly hatched bird in the nest. Zane was aware, as he was doing it, that he'd bent at the waist and was talking louder than necessary, as if Richard were blind or spoke a different language.

Back in the VW, Zane put out feelers to gauge Sasha's temperature. "He's comin in a while. What've we got for dinner?"

"Whatever you decide to cook, I suppose," she said, this time giving him a full on, defiantly rimmed glare. *So that's the way it is now? Back to our respective corners? If Duty was here he could smooth her out.*

"Brown rice an cheese enchiladas, then. Won't have to fire up the stove. Rice is already made. I can do it all in the electric skillet."

Neither of them had uttered another word over the short distance from Richard's to their house. On her way in, Sasha picked Erasmus up off the front porch. By the time he got to the kitchen, she and the cat were already disappearing upstairs. *This back 'n' forth is killin me. Course it's my fuckin' fault. As usual.*

Zane folded cheese, bell pepper and onion into corn tortillas and arranged them in the electric fry pan, pouring *La Victoria* enchilada sauce liberally over the top. With the lid on and temperature set at 250 degrees, the skillet functioned as a perfect steamer. All he had to do was put the rice in to heat when the enchiladas were soft, and presto!, dinner was served. Used to be, when they'd have a deer hanging in the smokehouse, he'd fill the bottom of the pan with onions, lay in venison steaks and cover them with sliced oranges. Took out all the gaminess. But that was before they'd gone meatless.

Jesse Colin Young's *Song for Juli* played on the stereo. He'd hunted through stacks of records for it, looking for a way to mellow out from the day's fireworks, find a soothing state of mind which this album always brought him, especially the song just beginning. "Ridgetop," with its long, exquisitely layered sax riffs – soprano, alto and tenor all bobbing and weaving, testing and teasing together—pushed by a seductive juke-joint conjugal beat he couldn't resist moving to, his body swaying and dipping to the music as he danced by himself. Caught in the webbed symmetry of notes, rhythm, voice and lyrics that dovetailed like simultaneous orgasms. Ok, so he might be high at the moment, but this song truly got him every time, whether he was stoned or not. He wished it worked the same on Sasha.

That admission brought his dancing up short, completely smothering his brief respite from Mother's Day cards, mining claims, violent death and unsolved disappearances. Deflating his attempt at levity as though every sleazy move he'd ever made clamored to be heard or seen again. *Still crazy after all these years. Christ I'm grandious. Make myself sick.* "Ridgetop" ended with a cascade of notes falling through octaves, quickly fading out.

Chapter Twenty

It is the bones and ash of the Nazi death-camps, the pyramids of skulls in Cambodia or the foul burial ditches uncovered in Bosnia and Kosovo, that are the emblem, the icons of recent history. Millions among these hideous deaths remain anonymous. The names were wiped out as well as the human beings. Acres of unmarked crosses stand voiceless in the war-cemeteries of north-east France and Flanders. Where are the starved, tortured inmates of the Gulag, of the Kolyma mines and ice-forests buried? "Known only to God": a presumption made less and less plausible, less and less comforting, to modern rationalism. (323)
George Steiner. Grammars of Creation. New Haven & London: Yale UP, 2002

When the A-side of Jesse Colin Young's album was over, Zane switched to FM, catching the five o'clock news. Nixon was refusing to give the House Judiciary Committee the so-called White House tapes. Was quoted as saying he'd done enough already and wouldn't be releasing anything else to the investigation. Reporters called it stonewalling. *From a noun, to a verb. Kinda shaky epistemological grounds.* As much as he loathed the president and his gang of scrofulous bagmen, especially Kissinger with the Dr. Zorba hair and barely decipherable English *An the bombin of Cambodia, don't forget*, Zane was mostly taken up with worrying about Sasha's mood, and bloody murder much closer to home. *Think Globally, Act Fuckin Locally. I may be impotent against the military-industrial complex runnin wild round the world, but I live here. "Time to string my bow and cease my senseless runnin." Elton John, Madman Across the Water. When that came out seems like everybody we knew was playin it. Tiny Dancer. Levon. Became a social event, like Sergeant Pepper's or Beggars Banquet. Cheap Thrills. Gettin together to play Disraeli Gears when it was new or Derek and the Dominos. Goin to someone's place for Firesign Theater night, memorizin all the lines, gettin the schticks down. "Shoes for Industry; Shoes for Defense." Like folks who quoted Vonnegut day an night in runnin inside jokes about Kilgore Trout. Little cults sprinkled around Portland. Books you just had to read. Armies of the Night. The Politics of Experience. Future Shock. People who*

321

made you listen to Grand Funk Railroad if you came to dinner. Long before Sasha. Other women, plural. Several plurals. I get years all mixed up. See myself not in frozen linear moments, but as snippets of video tapes replayin a jumbled chronology, Time as a blurry moebius loop.

Sasha had come down for a plate of enchiladas and rice, taking it back upstairs where Erasmus and her yarns awaited. But that was just a guess; he didn't have any other hypotheses about what she'd be doing. Strange he'd never seen her actually knitting, just sorting her yarns. But she could be up there reading or resting, for all he knew. No way he was climbing the stairs to find out. In the living room he'd heard a newsbreak that a 23-year-old man from Selma had been arrested by Josephine county Sheriff's dept and Oregon State Police for the murders at Takilma. No name released yet. That's when he'd heard her on the stairs and felt himself shrink, afraid she might want to have another go. But she stayed in the kitchen and no words passed between them. Luckily, he thought. Feelings too raw. *An the day started so well. Again and again I think she doesn't want to get tied-down to me. Isn't sure she's gonna stay. Same reason she got the abortion, I always thought. Didn't wanna get stuck.*

Setting the electric pan on warm, Zane waited on the couch for Richard to show. *Takes him for-fuckin-ever with those aluminum stilts. Can't imagine how it feels not to be able to get around. He doesn't complain. Makes fun of himself. Just gettin in an outta the car is a struggle, clangin and bangin. Looks painful. I can't imagine.* He'd come out of his hyper, warp-speed manic attack fairly cleanly this time. Wasn't wrung out since he'd focused his thoughts elsewhere soon enough, before compulsion could get comfortable in the driver's seat.

As he looked through the front window at late afternoon sunlight lighting the rising hills across the river, Lester's little speech about how if you want to live on the land, you've got to *be* on the land took a couple spins in his squirrel cage. His landlord's finger wagging about not running off to town at the drop of a hat flapped in the face of trying to chase down a mystery, of thinking he was going to unravel

322

some tightly cinched conspiracy that would explain what happened to the Fausens, why Perry had to go. Obviously it was about money. What wasn't. He simmered with outrage at the insulting audacity of these public servants. *Who believed that anymore? They're slick salesmen, that's all. An not a few are liars, cheats and thieves* who he figured were using the dam as a quick way to make a killing. He didn't know how any of this connected to the Fausens, but he was jaded enough to think it did. So he was torn between chasing down leads, battling the power structure. Did he think he was performing some kind of cleansing penance? Or was he keeping his mouth shut and head down so he could live at the farm without hassle. Another push-pull quandary. *Can't measure velocity and location simultaneously. Heisenberg's Uncertainty Principle, or Xeno's Law."What's the difference between dialogue and dialectic," weasel-faced Dr. Rausch asked us in his pinched pedant voice. "Dialectic forces synthesis," says me, jumpin at the chance to take the bait, "while dialogue is not similarly forged, is not compelled to any necessary outcome or consequence. At the same time, dialectic is, by its nature, generative, active, while dialogue can and often does go nowhere." Really felt I had my which-isms an what-isms together that day, livin in the broad brush strokes of the theoretical. What I'm best at.*

Zane was pulled from this iteration of his greatest hits when he saw Richard's Mustang bouncing down the driveway, a bush of red hair lifting and falling behind the wheel. Several minutes later, when he heard scraping on the front porch, he opened the door so Richard could lurch through sideways, his stiff legs working like calipers, the way you walk a heavy piece of furniture across the floor, point to point. Small gusts of alfalfa and manure-laced air squeezed past until the door closed behind him.

"Z-man. How about grabbing my board from the backseat? My stumps're screaming today."

Zane brought in the roller board and a half gallon of Italian Swiss Colony Burgundy he'd also found in the back seat. "This was just sittin there."

"Couldn't carry it," Richard said, inching himself around in a semi-circle in front of the couch where he eventually collapsed clumsily in a barely controlled fall. A normal maneuver, but one Zane still marveled at – how just sitting required Richard to let go of stability and trust he'd land approximately where he wanted. "You know what we need out here?" he said, digging in his pocket to extract a small, tinfoil ball that he set on the hatch cover table. "Single puss. I'd even take a goat roper if she didn't mind my legs." Zane let that line pass without comment, though numerous responses lingered in the weeds. Instead, he went into the kitchen to dish up dinner, bringing full plates, forks, pint Mason jars and hot sauce to the living room. Took him two trips.

"Where's Sasha," Richard asked while chewing. "Isn't she eating?"

"Already did." Zane poured wine into the jars.

"You on the outs?"

"Could say that. We took Duty to Vince's an then stopped at the J-Ville Tav to see our BLM friend George. Kind of a downer. He laid out a whole lotta reasons why there was nothin we could do about Perry. Especially since he also told us who finagled Perry's claim transfer. George said the notary in Ruch put his seal on the document as a favor to Brereton, that Perry hadn't been there at all. Who knows who signed his name, but I have some guesses. Notaries are supposed to verify identity. You have to prove who you are. But Perry didn't have any kinda ID they could bring in, claimin he was unfit to travel—he lived completely off the grid—so either they faked somethin or went ahead without it."

When they'd finished eating, Zane carted everything into the kitchen and came back to see Richard had unfolded his foil ball on the table. Which prompted him to ask a question he'd been carrying around since his father's funeral, didn't know why he hadn't asked before. "You seem to have a lot of hash lately? Where're you gettin it?"

But Richard was busy unhooking the leather harness to his aluminum legs—one starting just above where his right knee would have been, the other beginning about four inches from his groin—and trying to wiggle out of his tight Levis. Like pants on stovepipes, Zane thought. After a thrashing series of gyrations and swearing, jeans and legs dropped to the floor. Richard sighed from exertion. "Free at last," he smiled, stripped down to his boxers, exposing his pinkish stumps crisscrossed with scars. "What about hash?"

"Where're you gettin it?"

"Guy I know from Valley Forge."

"Valley Forge?" Zane rejoined Richard on the couch.

"That's where most traumatic amputees were sent. The Army hospital." Propping himself with one arm on the table, he reached for his Levis, tugging on the legs-in-jeans until he extracted a small wooden pipe from a front pocket. "They got me outta country fast once the Medivac landed in Da Nang, I guess. That's what I was told. Don't know myself, they had me so loaded. Woke up with no legs, just these stumps wrapped with bloody gauze, in a ward full of other gimps.

"From the second Al stepped on the mine and blew into pieces, I was unconscious. Flew me half way around the world. Even when I got to the hospital, I was only awake long enough to see I was hooked to a morphine drip. Can't remember being conscious for the first couple weeks. Had two surgeries I didn't know about until afterwards. Figure I'm lucky it's all a blank. Lotta guys woke up screaming. Not nightmares about getting wounded, but about having other limbs cut off."

Richard placed a BB of hash in the pipe bowl, sucked in his cheeks to get it going and passed it over. "Not exactly my fondest memories. Month after month on my back, feeling sorry for myself. But I did make a few friends, other guys missing parts."

"Someone sends you hash? What? In the mail?" Zane returned the pipe, trailing a sliver of smoke.

"Chico. Lives in San Diego."

"Sends it in the mail?"

"Packs it in chili spices. Which, by the way, I have more than I need, so if you want some…" Zane nodded.

They each took another toke without speaking, the FM nearly inaudible in the background. Zane reminded himself that he was coming into money. Soon.

After half a minute, he came out with it in a weak voice he didn't recognize. "Can you get some for me?" *Could you sound more whiney?*

"Probably. I'll have to see. Lemme get back to you." He looked away for several seconds. "So, did this George tell you anything else?"

Ok. I get it. "Yeah, well, he said the guy who got Perry's claim was from Redding, if you can believe that. Name's Jason Reeves."

"Reeves? You sure?"

"Why?"

Richard was still holding the pipe in mid-air like a statue. "Jay Reeves is Brereton's brother-in-law. Married his sister Patty like ten years ago. Big to-do at Lower Applegate Grange."

"And he was from Redding?"

"Naw, hell, his family has a place on Messinger road, just past Provolt store. Don't know if it's a Century Farm or not, but it's close. They've been there forever. Jay's dad and my old man worked on the same logging crew at one time up above Williams. Round about when I was in grade school. He's dead now, the father. Jay and Patty moved to California right after the wedding as I recall. Heard he was some kind'a developer down there, but that's been four of five years ago. Don't know if he's still doing that or not. My old man probably knows. He's in with…oh, I guess you could say the more connected rural folks."

"You mean survivalists?"

"Ok. That'd work too."

Zane had been staring at his open palm, trying to remember which was the life line. Not that he wasn't tracking Richard's gush of information. More like he was suddenly barraged with sounds of handcuffs clicking shut, doors slamming, locks latching. He didn't know what to do with finality—the infinite starkness of "it's over"—one of the reasons he'd stayed under a tree when they were burying his dad. Even though he talked tough about how glad he was to see him in the ground, the first whiff of never-again endings scared him shaky. Mortality's leering reptilian face. Learning that Brereton and Reeves were related sealed the deal with respect to Perry, exposing a daisy chain of officials with their hands in each other's pants. Thinly disguised corruption running wild amongst those who enforced authority. *How high does it go? From the banks of the Applegate to the White House it's just the same tired story as always. An what am I doin? Pissin Sasha off, drinkin wine and smokin hash. Hedonism up close. Fritterin my fuckin life away.*

He knew his past, for all his eloquence about fighting the deadening forces of institutional strangulation, was mostly a loose smattering of brief periods when he was politically effective. He'd crammed a series of two-months-here and three-months-there into just three years. From a distance, given his variety of experiences and willingness to talk expansively about them, he could paint a fairly decent picture of competence. For sure he'd been an on-the-road organizer, in short spurts. He'd taken Betty Estes to Naples for the commissioners' meeting—that actually happened. Tony Ojeda's crew had left a gun in his drawer. He'd worked at the prison...for three nights.

Once in Immokalee he'd filled two quart 7-Up bottles with gas, stuck a rag in one for a fuse. His idea was to toss the first bottle through the high open window at Florida Farmgrower's Association, spreading gas, and then throw the lit one. He'd gotten as far as standing under the window in the dark with his gas bombs when a sharp realization cut through his alcohol buzz. He was almost directly across the road from the Sheriff's office and garage. Lots of low-hanging trees in the way, but still, he couldn't have picked a more

327

dangerous place to firebomb. The planning had been done under the influence, of course, huddled over a Risk board on the yellow formica kitchen table with Catfish, Leslie and Juan, talking about how Florida Farmgrowers was the sanitized public face of a vicious stoop labor economy, the well-scrubbed facade turned to the world. Pumped him up with zealous disgust because he knew how teenage girls could earn more in the backseat of the crew boss's hauler than they'd ever see from working in the fields and it wasn't always their choice. Same as when he'd seen the scabs on the back of workers who'd been sprayed with DDT while picking tomatoes, or when he was alerted to another migrant disappearance. *Easier to kill them than pay them.* Black, thicketed, pesticide-sheened canals attracted carrion eaters of every sort, made efficiently hidden dumping grounds. But despite his cynical, sweaty anger, as he stood under the massive Avocado and Live Oaks with the Sheriff's compound lit up across the road, light fraying through the humid, foggy air, he saw himself behind the walls of the same prison he'd worked in, remembered the claustrophobic disinfectant smells of the place. So he chickened out. Like an idiot, he'd left the gas bottles on the ground under the window as a warning, left his fingerprints all over the bottles. He trusted, at the time, that either Immokalee Sheriff's deputies wouldn't think of looking or they wouldn't want to stir up more work for themselves. Getting over on the Bubbas and Bobby Rays in the soggy Florida flatlands. Some legacy.

He'd always known that each stint of frenetic organizing was destined to be short-lived... because he never finished anything. That was his nature, the source of his blanket sense of failure which was as constant as breathing, as interwoven into his body as sinews, ligaments and tendons. He attributed his self-loathing to his father's continual messaging. The constant negativity, harping and criticizing, shaming and belittling. Those cassettes in his mind on automatic replay ate away at him, whispering he was worthless, more damaging than physical abuse. Vignettes of violence, he'd call them in his more poetic moods. But forever in the wings, lurking and looming. He was perpetually at war with himself, a hangover from years of his father's loving attention. A childhood of ducking and flinching he needed to get past somehow. And those old tapes that keep playing? They all said the same thing, regardless of the context or details. Every day was a disheartening attempt to limit the damage. Forget about "things" working out. Chromosomal heredity of a bad seed. That was his first challenge—to rewire, reprogram, erase the messages that kept him on the slippery cusp of the void. He thought he understood how it worked. Being called a worthless, sniveling coward several times a day eventually soaked in, became what he saw when he looked in the mirror, what he said when he talked to himself. Wearing his shame constantly, he thought, like having colored skin.

Coming to grips with all those years meant he'd need to accept his own complicity. What was his payoff? What did he get out of persecuting himself, repeating his father's lazy slurs? That's where he had to start, if he honestly *Let's not get too fuzzy here* wanted to change. And he told himself he did. At least today. Hadn't he managed to cut out hard liquor? Hardly ever touched it unless at a party, and even then he kept his wits about him. Except for the Aquarius party anyway.

Richard sat chemically comatose beside him, absently holding the pipe as if quick-frozen in stop action. *Looks like those bodies in Pompeii caught in mid-stride or human shadows burned into the earth from the vaporizin flash at Hiroshima. Think I'm gonna buy this place anyway. Get ready for the storm. I gotta commit to the long haul for once. Duty would say I gotta change my aura.*

Feeling armed with a new resolve, Zane waved a hand in front of Richard's face, deliberately intruding in his space to bring him back from wherever he'd gone.

"Was just remembering my old man saying they used to call Brereton and Perkins 'the Noodle and the Spark Plug' back in the day," He finally put the pipe down, reached for his wine. "Dad's a few years older, known 'em forever. Said they'd been joined at the hip since grade school. You gotta take into account that everybody from J-Ville hill and half way to Murphy on the lower river went to school in Ruch. Plus all the kids on upper river farms clear to the California border. So everyone knew everyone else."

"Familiarity breeds contempt," Zane added for no reason he could put his finger on as Richard leaned down to shove his disconnected legs out of the way. He gestured to Zane to push his board up against the couch. Richard lowered himself onto it and, using his hands on the floor, rolled into the kitchen where he hooked one arm over the lip of the sink and pulled himself up level, running water into a glass with the other. "Jesus, Richard. I would'a got that for you."

"No need," Zane saw half of Richard's face from the side, splotched scarlet. "I need the exercise." His board was painted gloss black with an orange, buck-toothed beaver decal of "Benny," Oregon State's mascot. After returning to the couch, Richard hauled himself up. "How'd you get connected to this BLM guy?" he asked when he'd gotten himself situated.

"Sasha an Duty met him at the J-Ville tavern a few Saturdays ago. Seems like longer, the way things've been goin."

"You trust him? He's some kind'a bigwig right? A government flunky for corporate logging."

"I don't think that's what he does." Zane wasn't clear why he felt personally attacked by Richard's comment. He'd said the same things about BLM himself. *What do I know? Except that George seems willin. For what I'm not sure. Was genuinely shocked that day I told him. Seems more of a settled anger now.* "He'd been a friend of Perry's since the fifties, when he worked this district. An he knows all about Brereton an Perkins, said he'd been watchin their antics for years."

"What's his angle, then? Has to have one."

"I trust him. He went on about what sleazy flakes Frank Carver and Sheriff Lyle Willets were. I mean, all I had to do was see Willets' billboard in the Armory parking lot last election. Waxed handlebar moustache, pearl button shirts an string ties? Wasn't up more than a couple weeks before juvees or democrats blackened a few of his teeth. Then it was gone for good, pasted over by a Big "O" Tires ad. Only way I know what he looks like. But I've caught his radio pep rallies where he does a rah-rah number about how hard they're all workin to find the Fausens. Comes across as an "aw shucks" snake oil salesman. George calls him a low-rent shyster. Well, actually those are my words, George was more polite. But I know what he meant."

"The old man knows Willits. I overheard him talking on the phone one day. Luckily, he didn't know I was there. The impression I got was he thought our Sheriff was front man for somebody else's money, a pawn."

"Only a p..a..w..n in their game," Zane sang off key on purpose. Richard flashed him an arched eyebrow stare. "What? You don't like early Dylan?" *Or late Dylan? In a New York bar, eighteen straight sent Dylan Thomas home by freight. Can't help it.* "You don't know what you're missin. *Highway 61? 'Desolation Row'? Times They Are A' Changin? Blonde on Blonde* for christsakes."

"Never listened to anything but country till I went to Basic. The old man wouldn't allow anything else, in the house or truck. I used to think that was why Mom left."

"How old were you?"

"Nine. She kissed me goodbye and wished me luck the day she split. Actually said that. Good Luck. Like what the fuck does that even mean when you're nine? What was I s'posed to do with that?"

"What'd your dad do? When she left?"

"Nothing different from just being Ed. Steady Eddie, the old farts call him. No, he didn't change in any way I could see. Didn't seem to react at all. Just went about his business on the farm. He's still the same today. Like nothing gets in except what he already knows or thinks. But overall he's pretty tight-lipped, not much of a talker. And he hangs out with the same guys he always did, most of 'em from back in the woods between here and Wilderville, some from around

Merlin and Galice on the Rogue. He even knows that family who barricaded off I-5 at Wolf Creek last year, saying the Feds had stolen their land. Remember that? An armed stand-off for a couple hours. Jammed the freeway both directions from Grants Pass damn near to Rice Hill. Finally surrendered and were hauled away to Roseburg. Dad drove up for a legal defense fund rally at the time, but they're out now."

"What's he say happened to the Fausens? He must'a picked up somethin, all these folks he knows." He could hear Sasha coming down the stairs; they creaked and groaned under foot. He keenly felt an onset of worrying about how she'd be, but put it behind waiting for Richard to answer. Which took so long that she was rattling drawers in the kitchen—aggressively, he thought—by the time Richard finally got anything out.

"Yeah," with a pause. "Well, I don't know what he thinks. He doesn't talk about it more than to say it's a sad story. No. I don't have idea one about what he thinks."

"Who doesn't talk about what?" Sasha was facing them, framed in the kitchen doorway, sunlight from the window above the sink outlining her body. Zane tightened, all his muscles cramping simultaneously. An abject, out-of-body fear of losing her kicking in. Sudden jolt of adrenaline flushing through. Queasy iciness in the pit of his stomach.

"Hey, Sasha," Richard beamed.

"So, who doesn't talk about what?" she repeated, her voice emphasizing this was the second time through and she didn't plan to be put off.

"I asked him what his dad had to say about the Fausens," Zane said, reaching for his wine, knowing it was a tell even as he did it. He couldn't meet her eyes, pretended to be occupied elsewhere. A well-worn dodge, like so many of his placating survival traits.

Richard piped in. "I was just saying the old man keeps his thoughts to himself, for the most part. Unless you get him going on race. That's his whats-ya-ma-call-it heel."

"Achilles," Zane offered.

"Yeah, his Achilles' heel. Can't help himself once he starts."

"But what about the Fausens?" Sasha interrupted. "What's he think happened to them?"

"I dunno. It's not like we sit around shooting the breeze. Never have. I mean, I know he's pretty rightwing. Thinks Nixon never should'a gone to China. But other than that, he's mostly about chores that need doing, or bitching about taxes—that kind of stuff. I know he knew the father, Cleatus, but he didn't say anything when he shot himself. But like I say, since I got my house built I don't really spend much time hanging around him. And it's not like he misses my company, or ever put a foot inside my place."

"You're kiddin me. He's never been in the roller rink?" Zane latched onto the change of subject. He thought Sasha was pushing, displaying an unpleasantly abrupt edge. Especially when she walked right up to them, stood in front of Richard with a furrowed brow, went back to the Fausens.

"He must've said something when they first disappeared, didn't he? Everyone was talking. He couldn't have missed it." Her expression brooked no messing around.

Richard shook his head back and forth before she'd even finished. "He was gone a few days. I know for sure he wasn't home when they disappeared. Even when he was back I didn't talk to him until I had to. Maybe a week later."

"Where'd he go? Did he tell you?"

"Jesus, Sasha. Sounds like you're accusin him of somethin."

"No, Zane. I just don't know what to think. Too many unanswered questions. About all the things happening around us here. And no one seems to be making any headway in finding out."

"I didn't ask," Richard squeezed in when he could in answer to her question. Then the room went still except for the barely audible FM playing Sonny Terry and Brownie McGhee, "Midnight Special."

Zane couldn't help wishing Duty was around to soften the mood.

Chapter Twenty One

Belonging to a society involves a paradoxical point at which each of us is ordered freely to embrace and make [...] our own choice what is, in any case, imposed on us. We all must love our country or our parents. This paradox of willing or choosing freely what is in any case obligatory, of maintaining the appearance that there is a free choice when there isn't one, is strictly codependent with the notion of an empty symbolic gesture, a gesture — an offer — which is meant to be rejected. (161)
  Slavoj Zizek. Violence. New York: Picador, 2008.

Sasha slipped her way around a tangle of blackberry vines, threading through waist high brush and bushes as she began climbing the hill behind the house on the other side of the creek. What had been a frothing, boiling rush in the Spring had thinned and slowed to a step-across trickle already this summer, with three days still left in June. No measureable rainfall since the last week of May. The river itself had shrunken noticeably, exposing cans, bottles and candy wrappers, fishing gear and other assorted garbage, like debris lines on a beach at low tide. Zane had said they were already limiting river flow at the construction site, getting ready to start filling the clear cut basin.

She flicked sweat off her forehead, tugged at what she laughingly called her "do-rag," an extra large blue Indian-print neckerchief she'd bought at North Country. Medford's first and so far only head shop selling tie-dye, psychedelic posters, incense, macramé American flag belts, clothes with lots of sheer billowing fabric and fringe, flavored rolling papers, back issues of *Zap!* comics. Richard claimed vehemently that the place was a magnet for narcs, out-of-town ones nobody knew. Said he wouldn't be surprised if undercover cops were staking it out, taking down license plates, keeping track. She thought he was probably right. He also made a point that, if the inter-agency narcotic squad was really interested in illegal drugs, they ought to give pee tests to everyone working in the mills. "Those places run on Dexadrine. Whites. Cross-tops," he said. She knew he was right about that.

It was late afternoon, so this side of the ridge, the east-facing one she was climbing, lay in a surreal filtered shade like a gloaming, blurring edges, kind of a visual rounding things off, she thought. Or it could only be the sweat in her eyes. Stagnant air smelled of dust, pine needles and pitch. Lack of rain had begun scorching hillsides brown and brittle, singeing the leaves of small plants she didn't know the names of. An embarrassing failing she didn't like to admit. She regretted she couldn't identify many of the plants and animals, birds and insects she lived in relation to. Something Perry had impressed on her. One in a long string of moments she treasured, his sage and sane advice that wasn't couched in condescension, didn't seem motivated by secret ambitions. She still hadn't fully come to grips with his loss, at least not in terms of missed opportunities. Of conversations they wouldn't have. Of projecting herself without him into a nebulous and uncertain future.

Even though out of the sun, heat pressed in like she was wrapped in a quilt. She was headed up the ravine to her favorite private sanctuary. The small clearing naturally terraced into the slope, where three intricately woven beaver dams made yard deep pools and no one had ever disturbed her. She looked down through the trees before losing sight of the back of their house below, just making out the cold water shower Duty had built with black visqueen against the outside wall of the narrow, sagging back porch. But then she came to the creek again and followed it against the flow until she reached her grassy glade which bent around to the right, taking her behind stands of evergreen where the ground was carpeted with moss, ferns and dandelions and a downed tree trunk formed a natural chaise lounge open to the sky.

As she leaned back against the warm and bleached white wood, she fixated for a few moments on the sunlight cresting the ridge above her to throw itself against the hillsides on the other side of the river. Like sunlight was a thing. A material object with defining edges. Such thinking drew her into a debate with herself, a series of questions really that had plagued her since she'd felt the bottom of their lives falling out about the time construction began on the dam and the river road became clogged with heavy equipment. Diesel exhausts belching sooty clouds that hung in the heated, stagnant air. Lines of log trucks, trunk to tail like a parade of elephants, streaming to the few actual sawmills around Medford that had escaped conversion to plywood.

The hitherto sleepy upper Applegate valley had become rife with traffic, day and night. Rattling metal and the rat-atat-atat-atat of cut-out mufflers, trucks coming down the hill a mile and a half upstream. All of it drifting into the house now, providing new background music to their lives.

Ok, she thought, in answer to herself. Given that the Fausens still hadn't been found, that Perry's murder and theft of his claim would never be investigated officially, that Zane was suddenly uber-obsessed with owning property, an attitude he'd derided for as long as she'd known him—throw in Emilio and Rainbow Rick shot and beheaded at Takilma. Taking it all together, she felt under siege. Constrained by shape-shifting circumstances. Her garden paradise on a seldom used river road that dead-ended as a dirt turnaround across the California line seemed more like a vortex of negative energy now that they were living in the toxic fallout of violence unleashed all around them. Debating with herself was the best she could summon at the moment, however. She wasn't at wit's end yet, but as she looked around the postage stamp meadow where she'd always found peace, she wondered for the first time how many more visits were in store. Which told her a lot.

She'd come up the hillside to weigh her options without interruption. Try to wrestle with her deepest feelings, if, in fact, she could even identify them, as convoluted as they were with competing storylines. She ran her hands over her warm Levi-ed thighs, her eyes

337

closed as she fantasized Zane's touch. He could still do that, spark her hunger. In that mood, she shuffled through their time on the farm, looking for a stand-alone moment to linger over.

Their first winter, when they still slept on a mattress in the living room, before they'd begun any substantial work upstairs, Lester came by one morning to get Zane. It'd been a particularly wet few weeks with snow in the mountains, coming low enough to dust J-Ville hill, and day after day of heavy rain in the valley. Creek, stream and river flows had consequently risen steadily, pasture low spots filled with water to form scattered pools. Lester said there was a log jam piled against his footbridge across Lobster creek to his hideaway cabin, and he needed help before the bridge washed out.

In a cold, misty drizzle they drove over to Lester's, following his pickup as it headed across the empty back pasture and pulled up next to the creek. She could see the jumble of uprooted trees well before they got there, a maze of limbs, trunks and still leafy branches that stuck up about six feet above the footbridge. Lester had backed his pickup close to the creek, and was hauling a thick rope out of the bed. Zane told her to stay in the bus, that there was no need for her to get soaked.

She watched through the streaking windshield as Lester walked back and forth on the mushy bank while the tangled mass bobbed in the pulsing current. Finally, he stood next to Zane and pointed to the protruding, jagged butt-end of a specific tree in the dripping mess. They were talking, their breath fogging, but she couldn't hear. Lester handed him one end of the rope and Zane began climbing into the pile, testing each foot and handhold before moving or shifting his weight. Lester had tied the rope around the back bumper and then stood on the bank shouting instructions as Zane clawed and crawled the last few feet to his target. Sasha caught herself holding her breath until forced to gasp air in, seriously considering getting out to help, though she knew there was nothing she could do. She didn't feel right sitting safely out of the rain while he was in obvious danger scrambling over wet, icy, slippery logs and branches. But she didn't move, afraid to take her eyes off him, transfixed helplessly as Zane tied the rope where Lester told him and then ever-so-carefully picked his way down off the vibrating log jam, slipping twice but holding on. The whole process, from start to finish, had taken maybe ten minutes, but she'd felt time elongated, slowed and stretched by fear.

Then she was out of the bus, touching the back of his shoulder tentatively, as if to see he was really there as a solid being. Stupid, she knew, but had done it anyway. "You're freezing," she said. "And soaked."

"You two get back now," Lester yelled as he started the pickup. They moved away from the creek as he back-and-forthed the truck in short, gear-grinding spurts to get lined-up. Once set, he drove slowly but steadily at an angle, pulling the linchpin log out almost sideways. She was awestruck in that moment, watching the intertwined mass rise up, quiver as if in midair, and then swoosh under the bridge like it was being sucked downstream, disappearing in scattered bits and pieces in the surging water. Orgasmic, Zane had called it later that night as they lay spent and sweaty on their bed next to the wood stove. Strong smell of toasted ginger. Erasmus refusing to move off the foot of the bed, despite their fevered arching and thrusting, tender touching and desperate clutching.

That one went in the plus column, without a doubt. In the same breath, she heard twigs snapping and looked to the creek to see a young deer, small forked horns with fur still on, staring at her. Their eyes locked and she flushed suddenly, felt pleasantly captured in the gaze. As though they were magnetically connected, she thought. Like whole worlds were melding together in the cross-currents of their eyes. *My God. It seems we're on the same wavelength. Animals both of us, connected to each other.* The deer hadn't blinked and she tried her damnedest to keep from doing so herself. *We're at Eliot's "still point in a turning world."* After time she couldn't possibly measure in her hypnotized-like state of communing, pain forced her eyes closed involuntarily. She kept them shut until the burning stopped. When she looked again, the deer was grazing, yanking mouthfuls of grass from the creek bank, its lower jaw working back and forth, chewing intently. *There's a word for that...ruminating. Also means thinking. I can see how that happened.* Connection broken, but it was a warm, intensely exhilarating experience, one that left her realizing just how long simple joy had been missing, had been repressed, stuffed beneath all the day to day baggage of unruly lines at gas stations, of the steadily growing lists of dead, maimed and missing in the grimy war despite Vietnamization, of the Nixon administration scrambling to cover its collective ass with lie after lie, of all hell breaking loose in southern Oregon while the dam kept rising steadily. Zane distancing himself again lately, preoccupied with elaborately intricate pipe dreams for projects on the farm, as though buying it was a done deal as far as he was concerned. Either that, or he was reiterating how he and George weren't going to quit until they got to the bottom of things, even if it meant digging further into Richard's dad's possible connections to the Fausens. Suppositions about which had been the result of her pushing Richard for information, she had to acknowledge the part she played. Still, Zane was the one running with it. *None of this feels like we're living in the light right now.*

The deer ambled further uphill without looking at her again, fading quickly into the trees. Left alone, she leaned back and closed her eyes, letting imaginary scenes flow through. Seeing herself spinning prayer wheels outside a temple in Nepal. Eye-level clouds and smiling people in bright clothing. Clear, bubbling glacial streams and clean, crisp air. Fantasy, of course, but reality right now was pinching tight with a claustrophobic pressure like oppressive humidity. *Always wanted to see Thessalonia, where I supposedly come from. Uncle Andreas and Kostas used to talk about relatives they'd left, about someday going back to find them. Maybe I could do that? Uncover my roots. But not alone, and I can't see Zane going anywhere. Linda Ronstadt, "Different Drum," that's what it feels like. For all his mental acuity, sometimes I think he's been so badly damaged that he can't understand trust. I hate Larry for digging those ditches in his psyche. He short-circuits himself, I think, because he's genuinely afraid of more betrayal. He can't believe it'll ever be different. Don't know what I could have done. Tried everything I could come up with, every self-help-for-others piece of advice I thought pertained. To think of him as a bruised and battered child under constant onslaught from Larry rips a hole in my spirit. Zane is incredibly empathetic. He observes and remembers. He can weave complexities in motion into seemingly simple tapestries. Makes his inabilities that much more stark by contrast. He told me that when his dad would start in on him he'd remind himself that he wouldn't be killed. And if he wasn't killed then he'd eventually get over it. That's what he told himself to cope. But he hasn't gotten over it. Kept everything locked inside until recently. I just don't know if I can devote myself for the duration. Don't know if I have the strength, or the desire, if I'm honest.*

"You know, last week we signed a big military deal with Saudi Arabia. Go figure that. They treat women like cattle and still like to hack people's heads off with swords in the town square for religious reasons. Now we're gonna ship 'em jets so they can fuck with their neighbors." Duty upended his iced sassafrass, draining his jar of the dark red tea Sasha had brewed a gallon of the day before and put in the refrigerator. He and Zane were deep in smoke and conspiracy. Zane had been explaining what Richard had revealed about his father's connection to survivalists and what they were up to, wondering whether those same people had any hand in the Fausen mystery. And why?

"I'm havin trouble figurin out how the Fausens could've run afoul of backwoods vigilantes," Zane said from Sasha's chair by the window, ignoring Saudi Arabia. "Or semi-military white separatists. Whatever their organizin principles are, ya know, this family was one of their own, pretty much." He had to raise his voice at the end

341

because Duty had gone to the kitchen for more tea. Zane could hear the pouring and waited.

"Maybe they're Minutemen?" Duty suggested as he sat back down on the couch, puffs of dust signaling his arrival. "Those cats are bat shit crazy. Colorado's full of 'em. Very organized."

"Even so. Why this family? Let's assume the wife and kids are collateral, just in the way. That means Gary Fausen was the real target. I'm sure the authorities have already thought of that, but I can't see how takin out the whole bunch makes any sense at all. Unless it was some random crazy bent on bloodshed. An I am assumin they didn't just dematerialize."

Duty leaned back, his hands clasped behind his head, biceps bulging, a Dallas Cowboy jersey stretched tight, number 80 in satiny blue. Zane was glad he'd finally returned after getting his van fixed. It was only supposed to take a few days, but Duty told him the mechanic had started it after replacing a valve, only to blow the engine again because he'd left a piece of metal inside that tore it up. "I hitched to Seattle since I had time to kill," he'd said. "Visited my folks. It'd been over three years. Hung with a few friends. Got to see *Chinatown*. A great flic."

Duty had shown up on Wednesday. Zane's mood had immediately lifted when he saw the familiar white Ford van rise over their swayback bridge. Sasha had run in from the garden; she, too, was overjoyed, rubbing Duty's shoulder, a duet of fluttering back pats when they'd hugged. Zane thought it was telling—of exactly what he wasn't sure—that both he and Sasha seemed to experience relief at Duty's return. *It was just the two of us tryin not to get in each other's way. I could feel her irritation, could see it on her face. She can't hide it, the tightenin of lines around her mouth. Dead giveaway. But his bein back works for everyone.*

Today, after Sasha announced she was going up the hill and left out the back, Duty spilled that he was eager to know if there'd been any new wrinkles in the Fausen story, or about Perry. Zane filled him in on Brereton and his brother-in-law stealing the claim. He already knew about Wade Perkins' role that night. As to the Fausens, Zane admitted he hadn't heard anything more than what Duty and everyone else already knew except what Richard had told them weeks ago. He did say he was looking forward to seeing George in the morning. That they'd been getting together on Saturdays. But more importantly, he told Duty, was that last week George confided he planned to look into county property records to see who owned what around the dam site, put names to who was hiding in the woods. Said he wanted to figure out who stood to gain if the dam and new lake behind it sparked re-zoning, automatically jacking up land values.

. "We're both glad you're back." Zane filled empty air, except for Emmylou Harris from the FM on low volume. *Queen of the Silver Dollar*. He felt like a lout, mouthing standby lines and thinking he was getting away with it. One look at Duty's face told him otherwise, so he just gave up, decided to shift gears.

"What's your answer to my question, then? What motive explains them vanishin? I'm not talkin about aliens or satan worshippers." He waited a few seconds.

"Ever think about fraggin anybody over there?"

"Jesus, Zane. You're on a tear. What's wound you up?" Duty fumbled with a joint before getting it lit. "Yeah, I thought about it," expelling smoke and words. Zane felt he was being purposely dramatic. "But by the end I wasn't crazy about killin Charlie, so how could I dust a captain? Even if the ignorant fuckwad deserved it for getting people wasted who didn't need to be. He was consummately stupid, like someone serving bacon and rump roast at a Bar Mitzvah, then wondering what went wrong. But what's your point? That I thought about it? You can be sure I wasn't alone. Making it home, and helping your buddies make it home, was rule number one. And none of the other rules mattered unless they affected number one."

343

"Mostly, I'm wonderin what flips the switch so a person can go from the thinkin to the doin. Assumin the family is dead, who could actually carry out that kind'a thing? Talk about cold-blooded."

"Don't ask me. I flipped the other way." Clouds of smoke hung around his head. He waved away a swath in front of his face. "Besides, you're talking about a deliberate execution. Little kids, for God's sake. I'm not saying that didn't happen over there, but it was a war. Once you unleash vestigial brutality—we're predators, after all— it's tough to go back to empathy." He was shaking his head, blond curls swaying. "But little kids."

"And Perry, don't forget," Zane gushed, adding to the smoke in the air, returning the joint.

"You know they're connected for sure?" He seemed to be frowning, eye's narrowed, his forehead scars standing out as three shaky white lines.

"I think so. I don't know yet."

"But that would mean Brereton and Perkins...

Zane stepped on Duty's words. "An maybe Richard's dad Ed."

"...Jesus," He dipped his head, voice close to a groan. "You're saying they're all in it together?"

"Maybe. That's only three people, not a big 'all'. But if we're talkin about locals, who knows how many relatives or friends're in on it, or know about it, or know someone who knows someone. Eventually, people talk. Homo Loquax."

"So you and George think you can figure this out when the cops, with all their Dick Tracy kit resources, can't?"

"Brereton's a state cop, isn't he? One of the first authorities on the scene at Carberry Creek. An we already know he orchestrated the claim theft for his brother-in-law. Or maybe for himself in a roundabout way?"

"Jesus."

Later that evening, after Duty had driven to the Copper store for a half-case of Bud longnecks when the iced tea ran out, and after Sasha had come off the hillside to reheat peppers stuffed with rice, black beans and cheese for dinner, the three of them sat sweating in shorts and t-shirts with the windows and front door wide open. Encroaching darkness wasn't bringing any cooler air, the house filled with competing, mingling scents of manure, river moss, incense and pot. The near-constant FM as backdrop, tonight's concept album *A Question of Balance*, Moody Blues. Dynamic organ chords and harmonizing British accents weaving the multi-song story, though Zane wasn't listening closely. He'd adjusted the volume, trying to compete with the noise from the flow of trucks on the river road that came in through all the openings.

A candle burned on the kitchen counter next to the sink to attract swirling insects since they had no screens to keep them out. In the living room, they were sitting in a gauzy grayness that thickened and darkened by the minute. Sasha in her flat, wooden armed chair by the window, Zane and Duty sharing the couch. Sasha was explaining why she'd shut Erasmus up in their bedroom.

"He killed a bird this afternoon, out by the smokehouse. I told him his behavior was unacceptable, that he never has to worry about food."

"What kind'a bird was it?" Duty asked.

"Don't know. There wasn't much left, feathers and feet."

"So you gave him a time out? He's being punished for being a cat?"

Sasha shifted in her chair. Zane could barely see her across the room. "I know it sounds stupid," she laughed. "But I had to do something."

"She has a spiritual relationship with him," Zane said in a quasi-drawl, walking over to the door where he switched on the front porch light that immediately threw his shadow against the wall behind him, sent shafts of illumination into the room, bringing form to objects. "They had a séance together in Minnesota."

"It wasn't a séance, Zane." She turned toward Duty. "I was meditating in this field on a full moon and Erasmus got up in my lap. I started having visions, vivid scenes from my past. They stopped when he got down."

"Ah," Duty nodded. "So he's a medium, then."

"Medium Cool," Zane just tossed it out.

Duty grabbed. "Haskell Wexler, man. What a movie. They filmed right in the crowd during the convention riots in Chicago. That guy who plays the dentist on Bob Newhart was in it. Got hassled by some spades, I remember. That was like the film version of new journalism. Ya know, where the reporter is a character, not just an observer. Set a new trend, I think."

"Too bad the main characters had to die at the end," Zane said, his sarcasm showing. "Which valorizes martyrdom. The whole storyline argues against the counter-culture bein successful. Fight corruption, breathe the heady air of standin up to the flak catchers an cops, have your mass media millisecond in the sun, and then die without achievin a thing. That's a deal I'd take all day if I'm the powers that be. So, as a movement film, I think it rings a bit hollow. I mean, I'm asked to care about these two in their struggles against injustice. But then they're killed in a car wreck, an accident. Nonsensical. Or maybe not accidental at all? Maybe it was all plotted by The Man? Works out the same either way. They're dead. Story's over. What kind'a inspiration can I take from that?"

Sasha piped in, leaning forward, arms folded like she was hugging herself. "At least it was clear to see who the villains were. No question. There's something to be said for that, don't you think?"

"My argument," Zane emphasized, trying not to sound strident, "is that the ruling class—an don't be fooled there isn't one—has a strangle hold, not just economically, but more importantly on social agencies and structures. Laws, ordinances, zonings, programs and policies designed to work to their advantage, enforcing systems. Whole civil, economic and judicial machineries that function to keep them in power like the divine rights of kings. To me, that's the corruptness, the rot at the heart of the social compact. It's a circle jerk."

Duty gave him a puzzled look. "But that's been true since cave-dwelling, I imagine. Big dog always steps on the necks of those below. I mean, isn't that what you're saying? Well, like it ain't nothing novel. You're not tellin us anything new here, Roscoe."

"I understand. That's my point: all these millennia an it's still the same story? But that doesn't mean we can't change. Isn't it the myth we've suckled on from birth, been taught from day one? That our vaunted, not to say God-given powers of reason can overcome any obstacles if we just put our minds to it? We're rational animals with free will? Isn't that the load of goods we've been sold? That human rationality is, by its very existence, moral. Left over from German idealism. Cold, divine, objective reason is the model for ethical behavior? Well, we know that's crap, but we can still create possibilities for change, I think. We can always say 'No' to business-as-usual. You know, since the draft ended last year, people've pretty much quit talkin about the war that's still goin. No more body counts at dinner time. People just blot it all out unless they have someone still over there. But as a country, it's obvious we just want to get it behind us. Meanwhile, the systems that feed off defense spendin, armin half the world, an trainin SWAT teams for the ghetto and barrio just keep crankin along. It's those structures of power, the structuring of power that has to change. Anything less will only yield cosmetic results."

Sasha had stood while he was finishing his mini-lecture. "I'm going up to parole Erasmus and do some reading. I'm leaving you two to solve the world's problems. Please dispose of your trash."

"Yes'm," Zane pressed his lips together as she disappeared into the kitchen. Duty was sucking the soggy end of a roach, trying, without success, to keep it lit. As he heard Sasha's steps on the stairs, Zane relaunched.

"I don't know what we fuckin expect when everything of any importance has to be reduced to an over-simplified binary of right and wrong. Complex problems winnowed down to a choice between a donkey and an elephant...doesn't matter what disaster waits around the corner. We've been taught and trained to see the world as a contest, good versus bad. Black and white in a very real racial way. Satan and sanctity. Metaphysical dualism. Mind/body split. Man the measure of the universe. We're too stupid to survive."

"So, you want another beer?" Duty asked, already halfway to the kitchen, his moving shadow stretched up the wall and angled onto the bare planked ceiling.

In a remarkable moment of cosmic alignment, Zane heard the Moody Blues finishing *A Question of Balance.* "He learned love," a breathy Brit voice assured a vast world of completely unknown audiences. "Then, he was answered."

Not likely, Zane thought.

Upstairs, Sasha stroked Erasmus, peering into his powder blue, Himalayan eyes. After her mind expanding interaction with the young deer this afternoon, she was more firmly convinced she and Erasmus shared psychic glimpses into a numinous cross-species life force. Something like that. Some vital, telepathic, emotional touching of...she couldn't say 'souls,' a concept that, in Perry Mason language, assumed facts not in evidence. So no immortality, but certainly something akin to understanding. She didn't talk to him like he was a child, or use soppy, cringe-worthy endearments. He deserved autonomy and kindness, same as all beings, she deeply believed. As to what Erasmus was communicating to her, she couldn't begin to find words to explain, couldn't manufacture representations, paste labels on. And while she didn't pretend to faith in any supernatural sense, she did cleave to notions of creative force, the power of open and unconditional giving.

Instead of dwelling in the warmth of those thoughts, however, as she heard Zane's muffled voice seep through the floor, she remembered coming back from Medford with him a couple weeks before, after catching a matinee showing of *Blazing Saddles*.

They were on west Main street, already passing Sherm's Thunderbird market and Blackbird sporting goods, two huge warehouse stores that Zane said used to mark the edge of city limits, but were now commercial islands in an expanding sea of circular drives and cul-de-sacs jammed with single-story, slab foundation ranch houses. "This used to be pear orchards," he waved to his left, "all through here, clear to Jacksonville. When I was fifteen, Medford merchants ran a little bus back and forth between towns to entice shoppers. I used to take it to visit my girlfriend at the time, whose step-father was Frank Carver, trusty J-Ville police chief. He's been there forever. Once, we were neckin on the couch when he came in, gun on his hip an everything. Scared me limp in a hurry."

She recoiled from the idea of leaving Erasmus behind if she ultimately had to make a break. Just thinking about it was a punch in the gut. But she knew she couldn't take him with her. Not where she was planning to go.

Chapter Twenty Two

Men make their own history, but they do not make it as they please; they do not make it under self-selected circumstances, but under circumstances existing already, given and transmitted from the past. The tradition of all dead generations weighs like a nightmare on the brains of the living.

And just as they seem to be occupied with revolutionizing themselves and things, creating something that did not exist before, precisely in such epochs of revolutionary crisis they anxiously conjure up the spirits of the past to their service, borrowing from them names, battle slogans, and costume in order to present this new scene in world history in time-honored disguise and borrowed language. (1)

Karl Marx. *The Eighteenth Brumaire of Louis Bonaparte*

George hadn't felt this good in as long as he could remember. For a pleasant change, he wasn't thinking of himself as threadbare clothing, some cast-off oddball has-been who spent his life after work perched on a bar stool in a dingy, redneck tavern. He didn't feel that way today, anyway, in his present state of giddy tingling from a mostly sleepless night becoming intimately, inch-by-inch reacquainted with Jackie. Sated. That was the word that fit his marvelously tired muscles warmly glowing from the inside. Satyr. A grinning, sly-eyed, sexually obsessed centaur-like character in early Playboy cartoons. His mind on associative free-spool, ideas crackling with tastefully carnal possibilities. That's how good he felt. *Saturday, the kid's coming in from the river again.*

Following the corkscrew road down off Medford's Manor hill, where Jackie's split-level sat amongst black oaks, with a view across the valley to the high western hills, George marveled at how quickly his life *My life? Did I just think that? There's no 'my life.' There's just one step to the next, if you're lucky* had burst its seams in the space of a day.

He'd taken yesterday afternoon out of the office so he could burrow into county tax records in the courthouse basement, where they were stored in wooden library card files that lined the dank cement walls. Generations of property owners cataloged according to legal coordinates and plat maps. He already knew his way around down there, having foraged through the files on numerous occasions to back check claims. So, armed with a mimeographed directory supplied by Maxine with the goiter on her neck, who pretty much ran the County Clerk's office as she'd been there since high school, George quickly located the drawers containing records for Carberry creek area properties.

Forty minutes later he stuffed his bite size memo pad into a back pocket, his head spinning from what he'd found. He hadn't just looked for who owned what piece of land; he also checked when the latest sales had taken place. Three family names predominated the listings, accounting for more than half of them. None of the names rang any bells, which surprised him. All those years of bouncing along dirt roads. He thought he knew who was who. But the fact that so many separate sites shared ownership wasn't nearly as startling as learning that most of those sales occurred after 1969, within the last five years. No wonder he didn't recognize them.

He'd written down some other names on the chance they might be shirttail related to his big three. Odds were good. Especially since a clear pattern was coalescing, one that told him a handful of people stood to make a lot of money once the lake filled and docks and boat ramps began popping up along the shore. *Trailer parks and asphalt. Maybe a gas station? Boat rentals. Lakeside cabins.* He'd seen it all before when the Army Corps put in the dams for Howard Prairie and Hyatt reservoirs, up Dead Indian highway out of Ashland. *Jesus! Someone's been busy getting ready to make a killing. Why'd I say that, use that word? After all that's happened? Freudian slip? Or my gut feeling the upper Applegate is way out of joint? Too many threads leading back to that Carberry campsite. The more I look, the tighter the knot seems cinched. Of course, I don't have proof of anything yet.*

When he'd left the courthouse yesterday afternoon, he was vibrating from anxious energy with no place to put it. He knew Zane wasn't coming in again until the next morning and was too revved-up to just go back to the tavern for the rest of the day, hang out at the end of the bar till he disappeared out the back door headed for inane Friday night TV and an empty unmade bed. Too many unanswered questions. Hunting through county records, what he'd found had set his juices boiling, his temples throbbing. *Seventeen different places owned by the same three families. That puts me on edge. Tells me a lot, actually, but it'll take some serious digging to get to the bottom of.*

He'd found himself lost in a flurry of thoughts, driving north on Riverside without remembering the turns he'd taken to get there, and without any clear destination. But in the time it took to realize that, he was already aware how ineptly he was pretending to play dumb to himself. He knew exactly where he was going. Started simply as a feeling, that first sexual twitch while digging through tax records in the basement, sensing hidden conspiracies. *Are they mixed up with Brereton and Wade Perkins? Do they have something to do with the Fausens or Perry? Who are the 'they'?*

When he'd parked at the airport, and as he was walking to the terminal, George gave himself a serious pep talk about not wilting if she was there. To play it softly, seem stable, appear confident, though he feared his present agitation would show as trembling fingers, flitting eyes unable to land, or that he'd stammer some nonsense too fast to be comprehensible. *I lived through the worst Korea could throw at me, but I'm scared of rejection from stem to stern.* Because the same burst of mental energy and imagining he'd felt from investigating Applegate land sales—a building torrent of nervous achievement— had rebounded and reappeared somewhere between the pit of his stomach and his prostate. *This is crazy. Maybe I should just forget it?* while he pushed through the glass doors.

And as it turned out, George's self-doubt seemed childishly beside the point, because Jackie had done all the heavy lifting, had smiled broadly when she'd seen him coming, as if she'd been expecting him, like they'd agreed to a date ahead of time. This despite not having seen each other since the Saturday months ago when Walt Hustad's plane was late. He'd probably never to able to explain, to any degree of certainty, how playing the detective had led him back to her, how the tingling in his spine set-off by what he'd learned in the basement had suddenly morphed or blended into libidinous longing. Could have been the silent workings of fate, but George didn't put any stock in suppositional fantasies, of being moved by invisible disembodied forces. Ideas yes, he could understand that, had seen plenty of evidence of people espousing causes, beliefs and dogmas, of becoming narrowed and short-sighted. From his experience, that was the norm. But in the war he'd seen up close that violent death didn't discriminate, took the wise and stupid, the kind and vicious without preference. No, he didn't believe in fate any more than he bought in to fuzzy notions of immortality or celestial choirs on high.

Jackie had been in the *Red Baron*, as the airport lounge was cleverly named, but she wasn't working. She'd been sitting on the customer side, chatting with a slightly heavyset blonde woman who was tending bar. Celeste, he'd learned. After hellos and introductions, Jackie had moved them to a corner table, off by themselves under a balsa wood mock-up of a WWI Spad with five foot wing span that hung from the ceiling. She wanted to know where he'd been, why he hadn't come back again after he knew where to find her. George tried to pawn her off by claiming work and…

She'd put her hand over his on the table, looked him straight on. "Come on, George. It's me, Jackie." He tried to look away, but she gently yet firmly turned his chin back toward her, forcing him to see her. "We've shared bodily fluids, you sap. I thought when you came in that day…I thought I'd be seeing you again. I mean take-you-home-with-me seeing. But you disappeared. Just like the first time when I thought we were fine and you suddenly…you vanished." She let go of his chin and, in spite of his congenital sense of inferiority, he stayed focused.

354

"I'm getting this out of my system right now," she continued, "'cause I don't want anything left over from four years ago, when I thought we were beginning to be a couple and one day you just faded away…it hurt, as if I wasn't worth any explanation, any consideration. Felt like being used and discarded. Oh, I know, you didn't lie or make promises. I didn't expect…" She paused, running an index finger around the rim of her rocks glass. "But I thought we had something together, enjoyed each other. As it was, I found myself left holding a plastic bag with your change of underwear." She laughed with enthusiasm from deep in her throat, not guttural but husky, her teeth brilliantly white, her soft brown eyes never leaving his. "Nice image, huh?" He cringed at the thought.

"I can't tell you what happened," he said, looking out the window behind her at a United flight taking off. "Why I dropped out of sight that first time. But I know it's been my pattern. Not letting anyone get too close." Now, he was flushing with shame, embarrassment, regret. He could take his pick, they all fit. "I've been thinking about that a lot lately, my fear of intimacy, why I run at the first sign of permanence. Lived my whole life that way, fancying myself the Neil Diamond solitary man who stayed above the fray. And it's been just lately I've come to the conclusion that I'm cheating myself out of what people call most important about being above ground. Caring for someone else. Being needed. Having friends who matter. I guess I've finally realized that all this," he waved his hand to indicate everything, "is a one-way trip. I don't want to find myself bitter and alone when I need help clipping my toenails. Be like a cat in the window, staring all day at whatever's happening outside."

"How romantic, George. Can't imagine any woman wouldn't jump at a chance to share that." He felt snugly pinned by her glistening eyes, her soothing good humor. He wondered if she'd always been like this and he'd just been too stupid to recognize a stand-up woman when he saw one. She was even more attractive than he remembered. Perfectly proportioned in jeans and a mauve blouse. She'd let her hair grow so it now hung well past her shoulders. Stunning, even. A quick current of longing ran through as he recalled her thick but soft V-patch of dark curled hair, how she'd arch to meet him, how well he fit. Maybe, he'd thought, blood rushing to his lower forty. He'd pulled his office shirt out of his pants for cover.

"You know," he said, staring at her hand on his, "last time I was here I left thinking you'd crossed me off. I know you had good reason. I toyed with coming in a few times, but I seem to be deathly afraid of rejection."

"Yet you're here now. Only a couple months since I last saw you. What changed?"

"I dunno. I was doing some digging in courthouse records, and when I got done I found myself driving here, like I was on auto-pilot. Just happened."

"Do you remember where I live?" He swore she smirked.

"Unless you've moved."

"Why don't you go home. Take a shower. Get out of those suit pants. Then come take me out for a burger basket at Cubby's. I'm playing hard to get."

"You sure?"

"No, George. I usually proposition men without knowing why."

After they'd finished their drinks, he started for the glass doors. Jackie saying she needed to speak to Celeste. Before he got too far, she called him back. "You might as well bring a change of clothes," she said in a normal voice, "the boys'll be with their dad in Ashland for the weekend. Jim junior is in high school now."

He'd done exactly what she'd asked, arriving at her house freshly scrubbed in comfortable clothes. She'd pulled him through the front door and melted in his arms immediately. They never made it to Cubby's, ordering a pizza delivery instead as they couldn't seem to let go of each other for longer than it took to use the bathroom.

George couldn't believe how drastically her home had changed from what he remembered. Used to be the interior looked like something out of *Sunset* magazine, with well-arranged, expensive furniture, each piece in its tastefully organized place. He'd never been able to completely relax except in her bed, like being on an island. The rest of the time, he'd worried about breaking or ruining something, being the clumsy one in the proverbial china shop. But she'd redone her space, covered the smooth beige walls with cedar wainscoting, wood-framed paintings of mountains, forests and rivers. She'd replaced her showroom couch and chairs with easy living, overstuffed models. The clear glass coffee table was gone, a wood and stone one in its place. What had really jumped out was the working loom in one corner of the living room, surrounded by piles of colored wool. He'd thought, for a self-absorbed moment, that she'd done it all for him, had purposely created this environment so suited to his tastes.

"You've really gone native, Jackie," he'd told her after they'd untangled from their initial fevered bout on the carpet in front of the unlit fireplace. Their clothes dropped haphazardly. Carole King's *Tapestry* just finishing on the stereo. "I'd never have imagined. I mean, you have to admit this is all quite different from what I remember. Even the music is different. Good, but different. What's happened?"

"It's been four years, George. People change," she'd said, drawing up her knees and folding her arms around them. Bob Lind's *Elusive Butterfly* album dropped on the turntable, providing a gentle, musically poetic background for them to rediscover and explore the depths of their attraction.

When George left Manor hill, he'd avoided Medford proper on Stewart avenue and then took South Stage road to Jacksonville, the road that supposedly followed...Well, it was in the name, wasn't it? As if actually talking to someone. He parked his El Camino behind the tavern, came in through the back door. Still exhilarated from Jackie's caresses, her refreshing, remarkable frankness, willingness to tease and please, her strong enveloping arms. Simultaneously troubled by what he'd learned yesterday in the courthouse basement. He couldn't shake the looming questions he'd uncovered, leaving him trying to navigate between righteous indignation at the goings-on upriver and steamy wishes for more of last night's mostly horizontal exercise. What he was certain of was that it was high time to get his house in order. How much more of his goddamn life was he going to fritter away impersonating the self-contained district manager, signing forms and shuffling documents, trying to keep his staff on track? It wasn't him sitting in the office, but some hollowed-out, puffed-up caricature of a model public employee with blind allegiance to a mostly masturbatory bureaucracy. And then he'd reverse roles in the tavern and become the sullen fixture at the bottom end of the bar, radiating a palpable desire to be left alone. He knew he had to change, or inevitably risk joining the handful of pasty scarecrows who crowded the door at seven am, waiting for the first drink of the day, their lives reduced to coughing, shaking and mumbling regrets.

He knew it wasn't fair to Jackie, but he was already imagining she might well be his way out, could be his salvation, the woman he'd assumed he'd never find. This was more than a morning-after, full speed ahead leap of irrational fantasies. He was remembering snippets of when they'd first been together. Not just sex. Fluid moments of simply talking, of quietly watching other people in public, occasionally leaning in to share witty asides of what animal they looked like. Night catfishing at Medco ponds, bundled in sweaters and coats, a lantern on the bank's edge casting probing fingers of light across the black water, foggy breath, Jack Daniels for warmth. Laughing together. Quite a history together for seven months before he'd characteristically whipped himself into a claustrophobic fit and had to get away, save himself. That's what he'd believed, or at least told himself he believed. Painted the picture of. His certainty that being in a relationship was a zero-sum game where he'd have to eradicate significant features of his personality to make it work, where he'd need to be available to someone else on their timetable. He'd habitually shied away from what he feared would be an irreparable loss of self. But what the hell? His life was probably half over anyway. Better late than never.

While George was sorting all that out, Zane walked into the tavern right on time at eleven. Mickey had just set his beer down when he ordered another. "Might as well make it two, please Mick," he added hastily. As he watched the kid come down the bar, he slid Jackie to the back burner, put her on hold so he could attend to the implications of the scribbled list of names he pulled from his shirt pocket. Time to switch gears, get serious. Though that was likely to be a familiar refrain from now on, if his newfound confidence held.

Zane looked like he'd barely made it through a hard night, his long hair hanging in clinging strands, dark stubble shading his face. He pulled a bent cigarette from a crumpled red pack, his hands shaking as he lit up with a Bic. "George," he said, dipping his head slightly in recognition.

"Tough night?" George moved his legs back under the bar to make room.

Zane gushed air. Not a sigh, something with much more force. Elongated. "Duty an I were up late. Talkin politics. The war. Watergate an stuff, ya know."

Mickey put down two beers. George gave her a dollar and she turned to get change. "You got any Snappy Tom?" Zane asked.

"Thirty-five cents."

"Take it outta that," George said, lifting his chin with a jerk. "In fact," he handed her another bill, "keep the change." If Mickey was shocked by his sudden generosity, she hid it well behind her placid, doe-like expression.

Zane thanked him and asked how he'd been.

"Busy." He hoped that was a closing-off, not an invitation to delve into his personal life.

Zane didn't pick it up from there, seemed distracted and preoccupied as he smoked, so for a minute George heard Jack Buck announcing baseball on TV. Zane finished his cigarette, breaking it in the lightweight tin ashtray before drinking off half his beer and refilling it from the *Snap-E-Tom* Mickey had just delivered. Back to her usual sour face, George noticed. *What's it take to get a smile in the world these days?*

"So, whadda ya know?" Zane finally asked, after gulping much of his red beer, shivering in response. "You come up with anything at the county? Or maybe you weren't able to do that?"

George ran a hand over his list, trying to smooth it flat against the bar for easy reading. "I got some names from the tax rolls. Pretty interesting." Zane was looking at him now, their eyes catching for a brief second before George bent down to the paper. "Thirty-one properties in private hands in the immediate vicinity of where the lake will be. Of those, seventeen are listed under just three names." He held up a hand for emphasis. "I had to guess-timate quite a bit as to where the shoreline will be. But most of that area is BLM land, so I only had to focus, as I said, on private pieces."

"So there's thirty-one separate places? That's a lot of people livin out there."

"Not necessarily. I was checking to see who owned, who paid the taxes. Doesn't mean anyone is actually living there. We'd have to follow up on that. Go there and see."

"Got it. An what'd you say about the seventeen?"

"That they're divided up among three last names." George drained his first glass, reached for the full one. "In one case with different first names, but obviously still the same people."

Zane looked to be watching the baseball game in the long bar mirror. Didn't move when he spoke. "You know any of em?"

"That's the thing. After the years I spent on dirt roads from the California line all the way around Ruch, clear out to Murphy, I figured I'd recognize at least a few. But I also checked most recent dates of sale, and almost all of the seventeen were either '69 or '70. So there's been a wholesale turnover out there in the last few years."

"Who're the big owners now?"

360

George moved his list between them for easier reading, which prodded Zane to leave off watching the game and pay attention. "Ed Scott owns eight separate properties of from five to twenty acres. He's the top of the list."

Zane grabbed the paper, held it in front of his face. "Fuck me. Are you kiddin, George? That's No-leg Richard's dad. Ed Scott. Jesus!"

"No-leg Richard?"

"My neighbor. Lost em in Nam. It's his dad. Holy Christ! Richard an I were talkin about the Fausens an he said his old man wasn't home when they went missin. Hadn't been there for like two days."

Alarms started ringing. Like ChiCom bugles echoing off the snow before another attack. All he could compare it to. Same brand of fear from being in the line of fire, if not nearly the same stakes. But George felt suddenly on the edge of dangerous ground, enemy territory laced with landmines. "How well do you know them?"

"Ed I don't know at all. Only seen him twice, an both times all I got was his back walkin away. Never even seen his face. Richard comes over all the time. He's not what you'd call tight with his dad. From what I can tell, they're not rollin in dough. So I don't know how he could own so much land. Jesus fuck, George. This is gettin freaky."

My thoughts exactly. "Ever since Cleatus Fausen shot himself I've thought the same thing, that the real stuff was behind the scenes. That we'd probably never learn what really happened. Everything's hidden in the woods. Maybe this Scott is working for someone else, buying up land for people who want to stay outta sight?"

"Well, we know that Brereton and Perkins, if not outright killin Perry, certainly stole his claim. So they're in it up to their necks…"

George interrupted. "But we can't connect either of them to the Fausens. And I can't help thinking it's all stitched up together somehow. That's what we need next, to figure out what the story is with all that Carberry creek land. Might show us how things line up."

Zane was examining George's list again. "So you've got five places owned by different people named Zander, an four more belongin to," he tilted the sheet, "an Otto Heimland. An' if you don't know who they are, I guess we should try to find out. See if that tells us anything."

By the time he left George at the bar, Zane had decided on convincing Duty to help him scour all the individual properties when the time came. He wasn't about to do it by himself, and Duty's size alone could intimidate most anyone, if it came to that. He'd be substantial insurance. George had said he'd put together a map they could use because some weren't on any roads. Not public, at least. He said he'd have it ready by next Saturday's meet-up.

Zane couldn't get past Richard's dad being legal owner of so many chunks of property. Mind boggling. And simultaneously suspicious as hell. Richard had never mentioned his father being such a heavyweight landowner. Zane figured he didn't know, because otherwise he'd have spilled it, even bragged about it. Weed and alcohol turned Richard's spigot, and once he got going...well, how many times had Zane staggered up to bed, leaving Richard to his own devices? Usually he'd be gone the next morning, only occasionally crashing on the couch. Zane had no idea what he did downstairs alone in a stupor, but assumed the hassle of putting on his legs was just too much some nights. *How's he do it? All day, every day. For the rest of his life. An what about sex? Never talks about that. Duty doesn't either, now I think about it. All these months. Guess I don't have a clue what goes on in the back rooms of their lives. But I gotta get with Richard, do some proddin, see what falls out.*

Before leaving the tavern, he'd troubled Mickey for pen and paper and copied George's list, so he had a place to start. Like with Ray Zander, Margaret Zander, and Philip Zander, all three of them owners. *Why am I thinkin of the Partridge family? Zander GanderGoosePartridge. Ok. Take that, Herr Sigmund in a pear tree. Tie a yellow ribbon. How did Tony Orlando an Dawn get their own show? Bubblegummers in grown-up bodies. Big eyes, slapstick an schmooze. I'm*

362

completely losin it. An I'm not fearless, can admit that all day long and twice on Sundays. The future on the river, what the place will even look like, is a quiverin mirage. Can see it out there, hangin in the air, but I never get any closer. Wait till Sasha an Duty hear about Richard's dad. They're gonna fuckin freak.

He crested the half-mile grade after Ruch and coasted down to the elbow of the river where he'd seen the wading pitchfork fishermen that rainy day in April coming home from his dad's funeral. What crowded into his thinking this time, bullied its way in, was that he should have recognized the salmon slaughter as an omen of what was to come. *Should'a could'a would'a. Always easy after the fact.*

He knew his first concern ought to be how he planned to approach Richard. What story would justify all the questions he knew he'd be asking? Should he set Richard straight on his old man's holdings? Pretty risky. If he alienated Richard he'd be cut off from finding linkages—who had their fingers hooked into whose back pocket—so this shaped up as a real fix. But he'd agreed to do it, felt responsible. George said he'd take care of the Otto guy if Zane worked on Ed Scott and the Zanders, whoever they were. Meant he'd be driving back and forth to town for awhile. George had a job to keep, so Zane volunteered for the legwork. Though he knew Sasha wouldn't be pleased. *Wouldn't be pleased? She'll be pissed. Another stone in her shoe to go with me wantin to buy the place. Me out huntin down shady dealings is not gonna fly far. I'll have to soft pedal this. I owe her, an I don't acknowledge it enough. I think it, but don't say anything. I'm always surprised when she goes off on me. Tellin me I don't care about her dreams or hopes. But I think about her constantly, just don't say so. When does self-contained become self-absorbed? I think that's my problem, not knowin the line I'm crossin in the moment. Also think I'm afraid to let her know how much I depend on her. My hard-headed woman. Whatever degree I'm able to keep panic attacks at bay, I chalk up to her strength.*

Over the next several miles, he replayed a series of events at PSU in '67 that became national news for a week or so. Called "the Black Bag" controversy, it began when someone wearing a heavy black cotton shroud, probably a dyed sheet, started attending an intro Psych class. Dropped off and picked up by different cars, the Bag would sit motionless and silent in the back row of the lecture hall. The professor ignored the extra student, conducting class as if nothing were amiss. Which led most folks on campus to conclude he'd been the one who cooked the whole thing up. Another pinhead Psych experiment. But after a few days people started taking sides. "Ban the Bag" signs appeared on walls, stapled to wood laths stuck in flower beds next to sidewalks and buildings. It became the talk of the town. Local news outlets swarmed campus, microphones shoved in willing faces, video cameras whirring. Tensions rose. Some frat boys conspired to abduct the Bag, now seen as a symbol of defiance to authority, but were dissuaded by the university president's threat of immediate expulsion for anyone resorting to violence.

The Young Republicans organized petitions calling for the school administration to step in. "It's interfering with my education," some said. "Making a mockery of us all." On camera. "It's just plain Un-American."

CBS News sent its West coast reporter Richard Threlkeld up from LA. Portland State was on the nightly news nationwide. Other networks played catch-up, giving the story wide airing. Oregon state legislators raised alarms about public trust in education, and even the governor had something to add, though in his case it was a tepid call for calm. Before long, fellow students began to provide protection, accompanying the fabric draped anomaly on campus, to and from its car which no one succeeded in following for long through busy downtown streets. Those who tried claimed to see a heavily camouflaged male jump into a car going in the opposite direction at an intersection. Student watering holes were abuzz, with raised voices about the Bag replacing arguments about the war, the draft or who the Trailblazers should pick in the NBA draft.

Zane rode those memories all the way to the turn-off for their driveway, including what happened when the Black Bag simply vanished one day, never to be seen or heard from again. The professor, lecturer actually, was quietly sent packing to a private liberal arts school in New Hampshire when the academic year finished. End of story. A minor blip on PSU's radar. Quickly forgotten on campus as skirmishes between police in riot gear and antiwar activists became increasingly common in the Park blocks, often sweeping up some of the vagrants who congregated there and automatically sided against the cops. *Those were the days. Mary Hopkin. 1968.*

Halfway down the driveway, Zane noticed Duty's van was gone.

Chapter Twenty Three

We may suggest that...ideology is not something which informs or invests symbolic
production; rather, the aesthetic act is itself ideological, and the production of aesthetic or
narrative form is to be seen as an ideological act in its own right, with the function of
inventing imaginary or formal "solutions" to unresolvable social contradictions. (79)
Fredric Jameson. The Political Unconscious. New York: Cornell UP, 1981.

Since he didn't see the white Ford van parked next to the house,
Zane thought maybe Duty had taken a quick trip to the Copper Store
for beer. Pulling up to the porch, though, he became fixed on the deep,
calcified, empty ruts along the side of the building where the van had
been parked. He immediately thought of salmon skeletons picked
clean, translucent rib bones waving in an undulating eddy next to the
bank. How many times had he watched their leprous flesh fall off in
chunks while they still swam around, their open eyes all pupil, blank.
Horrifyingly grim. "Given the salmon rotting at the river's edge, how
does hope ever have a chance?" One of his sayings, jotted down in a
solipsistic spurt after seeing blackened spawners clamped onto each
other in the no-name creek, toothless mouth to tail, circling slowly like
senile ballroom dancers trying to waltz. After that bank-side vigil,
those truly hideous visions, he'd suffered recurrent dreams of
decaying fish who spoke of regret in gravely male voices. The scenes
on auto-playback in his sleep.

Getting out of the bus, he heard Erasmus yowling, saw him milling
around the front door, stretching and clawing, wanting in.
"Somethin's not right," he thought. Before the words were fully
formed, a hot flash hit without warning, immediately followed by
chilling waves, stinging bile rising into the back of his throat. Thought
and sensation intermingled so he couldn't tell which caused which.
He was suddenly hyper alert and scared. *Sasha would'a heard him.*

He opened the door for Erasmus to rush in and make a beeline for his bowl in the kitchen. Inside was quiet, no FM, no sounds of movement except Erasmus's claws clicking on the kitchen floor. Then he saw that the hatch cover table had been meticulously wiped clean except for a paperback copy of *Journey to the East* with ZANE in black marker on a folded sheet of paper sticking out like a masthead. The book centered on the otherwise bare table so as not to be missed, silently screaming Look Here First. The longer he stared at his shaded-in name, the more sure he was of what it all meant, until the letters began to shimmer like a lava lamp and he felt himself going numb. *Fuck me. She's left me a message. Ok. Ok. This is what I'm seein. She's gone. An' Duty took her.*

Erasmus's howls let him know there wasn't any food in his bowl. Mechanically, without connected thought, he found the Friskies, poured some in, left the bag on the counter. He felt he was moving in slow motion, trying to walk through deep, dark, sucking water. Time itself was hiccupping, skipping with his now irregular heartbeat. Pulse pounding. His diaphragm in his throat, shallow breaths like panting. Flashes of Sasha smiling, green eyes sparkling, her face swelling, ballooning, filling all the space, taking air out of the room like a black hole sucking up galaxies. His left foot began tapping out a syncopated rhythm, but he forced himself not to count. Guilt and shame began seeping through his cell walls *It's called active transport. Look it up. Professor Hysop Zoology 101* because he knew without doubt that it was his fault she wasn't there anymore.

Initially, he didn't want to touch the book. Definitely didn't want to read the note. Didn't need another litany of his failings, purposely left behind, positioned for maximum effect. "Look what you've made me do" was the familiar refrain of his childhood after he'd caught a backhand to the temple or his arm had been wrenched back. The message was always clear. Whatever pain he suffered was because of his own weakness. Always the guilty one, he didn't need to be reminded he'd let her down too many times, and he sure didn't want to read it in black and white.

Standing next to the table, he tried four times to light a cigarette, even though using a lighter. His fingers weren't working, frozen from adrenalin rush. The house was clearly empty, no sounds other than Erasmus cracking and crunching niblets in the kitchen, his own breathing like a wind tunnel in his ears. He was alone, no question.

In a sudden impulsive movement, he yanked the note out of book, unfolded it to read.

Duty promises to take me to the top of the world. I can't refuse.
Buy the farm, Zane. I know how important it is to you.
Take good care of Erasmus, my love, and be well.
xxx

That's fuckin it? After five years this is all I get? Duty lives with us for free like one'a the family an next I know he takes off with her? Can't believe he's her type even. Can't picture them together. Makes me sick to think it. I can't. Should'a paid more attention to what was goin on behind my back. Were they gettin it on every time I left the house? They must'a talked about leavin, planned it all out. Never got a hint from Duty. "My love," she says, like Aunt Minnie. That really hurts. Jesus, I'm such a fool.

He sank heavily on the couch because the steady trembling working in from his extremities had intensified, had quickened into a spinal shiver, one he unfortunately recognized. He'd experienced this degree of nauseous, painful cramping only once before, when he was twelve. When, on a Sunday morning in late October, he was shaken awake by his mother with tears running down her face. She pushed the front page of the *Mail Tribune* towards him as he lay in bed. "Double Murder/Suicide" splashed the banner headline. "It's Denny," she said. "He shot Dave and Amy, then himself, while Sue was working nights at Sacred Heart." The Walters had lived across the street for five years before moving that September to a custom-built in a development just north. From second grade to Junior High, he and

369

Denny had been inseparable, running around the neighborhood joined at the hip. Just the Saturday before, in fact, Zane had stayed overnight in the new house, riding bikes, reading *Mad* magazines, sneaking looks at the *Playboy* Denny had stolen from the Grandview Market just up Crater Lake avenue.

"Did you notice anything strange about him last weekend?" his mother had asked that morning in a pleading, insinuating tone, as if Zane was either too stupid to have identified the would-be killer, or he'd been aware but hadn't said anything. In either case, he'd felt suddenly responsible as he pictured pools of blood leaking from bodies curled in like they were doing crunches.

He'd tried to ignore his mother's tearful lamentations about "poor Sue" and "how will she ever get over this?" Still reclining against his pillows, he'd imagined he was freezing from the inside out. That is – he knew the room hadn't changed, knew that beyond doubt, but at the same time, rough cold fingers were grabbing at his insides, and squeezing. He started shivering uncontrollably, deluged with close-enough-to-touch memories of the dead when they were still living. Though he understood they were gone, in the swirl of images, pictures and relived scenes careening in his skull, he saw them all tangibly alive. Smiling. Like old sixteen-millimeter movies shown on holidays when the LaRoux clan still met with some regularity. It was too much to take. Too many faces coming in on him. He wanted to go away, so he'd pulled the blankets up and tried not to think of anything while his body shook and shuddered.

That had been the only other time he'd experienced sudden loss as solid physical pain. Not like his panic attacks, which were on a level with unpleasant acid flashback snippets, all mental. But this freezing inside, he told himself, was what it must feel like to inject dry ice. The idea of lobotomy, at least in the abstract, seemed attractive as the walls moved in and out with his breathing. He wanted to suspend thought, stop it all. Flush the systems. Detox memory.

Erasmus, full and soon to be sleepy, wedged against the arm of the couch, licking his tail. Sunlight slashed into the room from the windows. Zane stared without differentiating. He didn't have the energy to finish his cigarette, just laid it on the table to burn out. He should get the abalone ashtray, he thought, but knew he couldn't stand up just yet. Besides, who was going to mind? He was by himself now. The caring ones had left.

When the last daylight began folding over the western ridges behind the house, Zane shook himself into awareness. He hadn't exactly been asleep, but he hadn't been consciously awake, either. In a colorless daze. Stunned into chromatic numbness. Unable to string thoughts. The door was wide open, insects drifting through, buzzing on the ceiling. He must have left it that way, but he didn't remember. Journey to the East lay upside down on the table, Sasha's note wrinkled on top of the book after he'd crunched it into a ball only to quickly flatten it back out to read again, as if it would somehow miraculously be different. His discarded cigarette had burned a black, non-filter groove into the wood. He knew he needed to do something, take action, pick up the pieces. Or some such nonsense. It was all he could summon at the moment, but it got him off the couch.

Closing the door, he then switched on the FM for company, tune into some noises in his head other than his own meek inner voice echoing thinly in an empty barn. The Denis Coffey Detroit Guitar Band finished "Scorpio," and then a new John Lee Hooker release. He didn't catch its name. After he'd retrieved the ashtray from the kitchen, he lit another cigarette and stood completely unhinged, seeing Sasha's note as a thing, all of a piece with her helping Duty pack the van and them heading out the driveway. A vision he'd constructed and couldn't shake. Were they laughing as they left, sharing private confidences, eyes only for each other? Touching and stroking? Nuzzling as they walked, sides pressing? Arm around her, his hand cupping her breast? He realized he was full-tilt running downhill, heading for an inevitable crash.

After his cigarette was dead, he'd remained in front of the couch, beside the table, in a darkening living room, haplessly watching flies mount staccato assaults against the ceiling. Until the eight o'clock news butted-in.

Lead story was that the Supreme Court had unanimously upheld the Special Prosecutor's subpoena and ordered the Nixon administration to turn over the so-called Watergate tapes for the trials of his former subordinates. That news helped sharpen his focus, put him on track. Empty but conscious. *I'm tired'a Nixon. All the hearings. Like pullin out a dirty lint filter from the dryer. Same after every load. The underhanded crap never ends. Can't. It's part'a the system itself, the "matter of national security" lies, the rivers of cash flowin into back rooms. Beginnin'a the end for the tricky one, I predict. Even Republicans see he's caught with both grubby hands in the till. Gotta get that war criminal Kissinger, too. Napalm an Agent Orange, for christsakes. Bubbled skin and boilin blood.* His legs were beginning to wobble so he slumped back on the couch.

The soothing-voiced announcer, who Zane was sure must have forked out good money so a broadcasting academy could file off the edges of his natural accent, soon turned to local news. "The homicide trial of Thomas David Skagget, 23, of Selma, who stands accused of two brutal murders at the Takilma commune, is scheduled to begin Monday in Medford, after a change of venue decree moved the proceedings from Josephine to Jackson county. The trial is expected to last two or three days, according to county prosecutors. Local interest in the case has heightened recently owing to uncorroborated rumors that state police are investigating possible connections between the Takilma deaths and the still unsolved mystery of the Fausen family's disappearance from the upper Applegate last April. Both the police and the prosecutors office have declined comment." *Brereton an friends. They're gonna pin it all on a drug-crazed hippie who didn't have a car? Fausens an Perry? Them too? Richard's dad is right in the middle of it somehow. Sasha thinks the same way.* He realized that line of thought was a dangerous trap, on-ramp to an overpass that stopped in mid-air, so he'd retreated to the Takilma killer, but underneath or inside the realizing, he'd accepted as fact that she was gone. In a crystalline flash of the future as reliable as mortality. He'd have to adjust…so many things. *News reports say it was probably a drug deal gone bad between Skagget and Rainbow Rick. Emilio was just collateral damage, they say, wrong place an all that. Easiest way to solve cases, chalk it up to drugs. They won't even look at other options. Maybe Rick was undercover, every branch had 'em, huntin draft dodgers and deserters. Could happen.*

He knew he was disassociating, sealing himself off into the mostly controllable confines of singularity, a place where he knew his way around. Tamping down emotions, seeing human behaviors as chess moves. Sasha already a fetish without form. Existential loss as an idea. Abstraction quickly replacing any tug of the real. Of course it was crazy. *That's the point. No one gets out alive. The Family's fallen apart these days. Diamond Jim sold the school bus so he could get an Audi, but no one's gonna want'a go back to the commune anymore anyway. Not after this.*

The next morning, Zane came to consciousness in his sleeping bag on the couch with Erasmus draped over this feet. He didn't know when he'd finally gone to sleep, no dreams he could remember. He'd found some burgundy under the sink and then, around 9 pm, debated with himself about driving to town, going to the 10th Street Junction. Crowds on the make and loud music. Maybe get lucky? That thought struck him as cravenly inappropriate for the circumstances, but he wasn't surprised it had popped up. All a desperate fantasy anyway. He couldn't have gotten off the couch by then.

He'd left the FM on all night, so it was probably the high, tight, strained tones of The Celtic Hour that had jarred him awake. *Yeats. Easter 1916. Parnell an the wearin of the green.* "So this is it," he said to no one, pulling his feet from under the cat. "The first day of my new

373

life bein alone." *Ok, then. Shiver me timbers. All hands to the plow. Full speed ahead.*

Erasmus interrupted by hooking his claws into Zane's forearm. "Ok. I get it," he said, venting exasperation as he pulled on his khaki shorts, and headed for the kitchen. *He doesn't care what's goin on as long as he gets his food.* "It's just us now, buddy. So you better not be puttin on airs." He felt a scintilla better, setting Erasmus right. Now, though, he needed coffee. As he set up the percolator his stomach told him he hadn't eaten since breakfast yesterday, so once the coffee was plugged in he surveyed the refrigerator to see what he had to work with. Not much. Eggs and cheese. Leftover black beans with peppers and onions. Butter and a few jars of condiments. *Slim pickings. Ridin the A-bomb like a buckin bronco in Dr. Strangelove. I'm gonna have'ta go to Abundant Food this month. Sasha used to take care of that. Ok. I admit it. I could'a done lots'a things better. Understatement of the fuckin century.*

After a cheese and black bean omelet he made in the electric fry pan and a good half of the coffee, Zane sat in the living room to assess his options, Celtic music replaced by Sunday morning PBS shows of experts predicting the president's downfall. He'd dropped the volume, the better to concentrate. Launching forward to the coming winter, he recalibrated what his daily life was going to look like. Running both wood stoves day and night. Doing the cooking. Cleaning. Shopping. Keeping the place together. Fences would need mending. Cattle might knock the pvc gravity-flow water line out of the rain barrel up the hillside and he'd have to ford the creek at high water. Roof or windows could leak. Brick foundation settle, tilting floors. Plus, he'd still be at Lester's beck and call. All in a day's work, he thought superiorly, egging himself on as he fabricated a solitary future, becoming his own kibitzer for another spin in the squirrel's cage. *Might as well do somethin instead'a sittin around feelin sorry for myself. Visit Richard. See what I can find out. Anything's better'n this. Maybe I ought'a start a collective? That's an idea I hadn't considered. Well, why would I with Sasha an Duty here? I really gotta get my shit together.*

374

Pull in all the tentacles. Stay detached. Protect myself. Figure out where the fence lines are. He put water and more food on the kitchen counter for Erasmus, left a window open enough for him to get through, just in case he went into town.

Driving downstream, bright sunlight glinting off the river's surface, he fumbled through a short list of items that needed attending to. Top of the list he was enroute to now—Richard's. Since it was Sunday, he'd also been fingering the idea of visiting his mother to see when he'd get the insurance money, though it meant driving to Medford. Answer to the money question would dictate when he'd talk to Lester and Adeline, when he'd move from renter to owner, which loomed large on his immediate emotional horizon. Something to finalize, to finish. Something other than losing Sasha to Duty in the blink of an eye. *I'm livin in a new, sharp-edged, surreally boisterous, bad grammar world. That's the battlefield. An I have no money. Twenty bucks maybe if I scrounge, cash bottles in.*

Swinging the bus off the highway and onto Richard's drive, he shoved the rest of his list into a mental back pocket. He'd get to them later. *Greek rhetoricians taught putting ideas into different imagined rooms, like a big filing system. Go into a room and find related arguments. So if I just stay away from those rooms? Like when I had a bad haircut an told myself not to stare in mirrors or windows, just not to look at it. Worked well when I managed to do it. Hair grew back like nothin happened. Except I remember the shaming and shameful first moments like I'm watchin a video of myself, usually in slo-mo, starin at the camera, lookin stupid. There's Richard's Mustang so he's home. Get your wits together. Signify, as the black guys say. That'd really freak the rednecks, get a brother to move in. Or even better, a sister with a wild afro an neon bright dashikis. Power to the fuckin people. Right on.*

He parked next to the black Mustang. Richard, a torso perched on his roller board, opened his door before Zane had a chance to knock. "Whazzup?" Richard asked, lifting his chin as if in defiance.

"Nuthin," Zane lied. He'd work his way into it. Richard looked like he'd given himself a squiggy, his red hair twisted into a sort of coil pointing up from his skull. "Been up long?"

"Since four. My stumps were killin me. Couldn't sleep." He rolled over to the collapsible wheelchair by the leather-brown naugahyde couch, hoisted himself into its seat, released the brakes. "Want some coffee...or a beer?"

"It's afternoon back east, so I guess I can have a beer." He waited while Richard pushed over to his miniature kitchen with short, two-burner stove, half-size refrigerator and equipped sink with counters built low enough to fit him. The living area was largely open space with a modified bathroom built in a corner, Richard's unmade twin bed against the west wall between windows. Water and food bowls for three basically feral cats that Zane had nursed back to health what seemed a lifetime ago. They roamed the river banks and pastures, occasionally coming in to eat and sleep. By winter, they'd be mostly untouchable house cats unless the weather was good. Posters of Formula One cars in stop action hung on every wall, like a constant race circling the room. A portable tv by itself on a wooden chest in the middle of the room, plugged into a power receptacle on the floor, antenna wire going straight up through the ceiling.

Zane had been inside dozens of times, never getting over how drab and empty it seemed, especially since Richard kept burlap curtains over the windows, giving the open room a sepia, caramel tone when the sun was out. And no music playing, ever. Zane sat on the slippery-like-vinyl, faux leather couch and lit a cigarette, as Richard wheeled up with two cans in his lap, setting one on the wire spool table in front of him. *Hamm's. From the land of sky-blue waters. Tom-toms an a dancin bear. How could I forget he has a phone?*

"So?" Richard ran both hands through his reddish hair, pulling tangles loose between his fingers. "What're you doing? On your way to town?"

"I was gonna maybe see my mom, but that's 'cause I spaced-out you had a phone. If I call her, I won't have to drive into town."

"You gotta be kidding. It's long distance from here." Richard kept a straight face, though his eyes danced impishly. Not exactly matching Zane's mood.

"You're pretty cocky this mornin. Thought you'd had a bad night?"

"Better livin through chemistry, my man. Just 'cause I'm awake doesn't mean I gotta be in pain."

"Can I have one."

"What?"

"Whatever you're takin."

Richard spun his chair, rolled over to a squat chest of drawers. "I'll give you five," he said over his shoulder. "I'm due for a refill next week."

Zane suddenly felt like a leech, so he decided on the fly to blurt everything out, cast himself as victim. "Sasha an Duty took off together yesterday when I was in J-Ville. She left me a note. They're gone. Left me Erasmus."

"What? She split with no warning? With Duty?" Richard was shaking his head slowly as he rolled back to the table, set the white tablets down, one landing on edge. "You been sleazin' around?"

"Fuck no," he popped a pill immediately, crunching it between incisors. "What are these?"

"Morphine sulfate. Don't double 'em up."

"She said he was takin her to the top of the world."

"Damn. That's cold," Richard said, smirking at his own joke barely enough to be noticeable. Though Zane marked it.

"I'm buyin the house an ten acres from Lester an Adeline with money from my dad's life insurance. She didn't want anything to do with it. Didn't want to be tied down. Same reason she got the abortion." As he said this, Zane felt his limbs freeze, his stomach drop through the floor. Aftershocks.

"I didn't know she'd done that. Or that you were buying the place, either."

"Adeline offered a deal to Sasha. Ten grand for ten acres. Thousand down, thousand a year, no interest." He crushed his cigarette, pulled the pop-top open with shaky fingers, swallowed in large gulps. Wondered how long it'd take for the morphine to kick in.

"Nothing wrong with that deal. You sure they'll still do it if she's gone?"

"I'm tellin 'em she's visitin relatives back east for a few months. By then, won't matter. So you think a thousand an acre is a good price? Plus the house, of course."

Richard nodded, opened a wooden box on the spool table, pulled a rolled joint out, got it going. "Didn't ever know she was pregnant, either," he said in a cloud.

"I didn't know myself until just before she got the kid yanked." He desperately wanted to change the subject. "What'd you pay an acre here?" The joint was going back and forth between them.

"Didn't. Ol' man owns the property. Built me this place 'cause I came home a gimp. Felt sorry for me. But mostly ashamed I'd come back damaged, I think."

Zane let the last part of that lay still. Didn't want to touch it. But he saw his opening, what he'd come for. "Jesus, Richard. I didn't know he was a land baron. How many other places does he own?"

"None that I know of. It's not like he confides in me, though. I don't even know what the taxes here are. He pays 'em. Always has been a secretive s.o.b."

Gotcha. Either you're lyin or you don't know. An I don't see you coverin for him. Zane decided to push, see if he could take care of another item on his list. Kill two birds. "I got another question. You know any folks around here named Zander?"

"Yeah, why?"

"BLM George mentioned 'em yesterday when I met him at the tav."

"What'd he say about 'em?"

"Only wondered if I knew any. Thought I'd ask since you've been here forever."

Richard leaned back in the wheelchair, stumps aiming forward. Seemed to be considering how to answer, weighing options. Zane couldn't help thinking his friend was tilting toward the imperious, adopting a superior tone from being the one in the know. But Richard proved him wrong. "There's a whole passel of the fuckers strung out all the way to Wilderville," he said, disgust evident. "Can't stand 'em myself. Ray Zander has been tight with my dad since they were kids growing up together around Ruch. Enlisted on the buddy system, served together in artillery behind the front in France during the war. He's always been a cranky old bastard far as I'm concerned. Bitching about commies running the government or too many niggers on TV. Shit like that. A real piece a'work. An' the rest of his brood're cut from the same mold." He stopped and stared, waited. Zane assumed he was supposed to jump back in, but didn't know where to go without showing his hand. "Why the sudden interest?" Richard finally asked.

Zane's mental gears weren't meshing too well. *Beer, pot an morphine. But I gotta tell him sometime don't I?* "I wasn't gonna say anything about what George told me. Right up to this minute I was gonna keep it to myself, but..." He didn't know where to go next, hadn't planned a scheme to break the news.

"But what?" Richard pushed, eyeing him sideways.

"According to George, who went through county tax records, Ed Scott is listed as owning eight different properties off Carberry creek, all of 'em around what'll be Applegate Lake when it fills." *There. Can't take it back. Hope it doesn't blow up.*

He waited tentatively for Richard to react. Swear, shout, argue, deny. But nothing. In the vastness of his universe of expectations, though severely dented by Sasha's sneaking off when he wasn't home, he couldn't explain Richard slowly sipping his beer like an aged spinster with a hot cup of tea. Staring straight at him, no facial expression for a dozen seconds before he said anything. "And Ray Zander?"

"Yeah. He an a Margaret an Philip have like five chunks'a land. Also, some guy named Otto…"

"Christ on a fucking crutch," Richard breathed out like a groan.

"What?"

"Otto Heimland. Another'a dad's army buddies, moved here years ago from Minnesota. Brought some family with him. Son, daughter and a couple cousins, I think. They came as a bunch."

"So you already knew this Otto was buyin on Carberry?"

"Not up there, no. They got places at the dead end of Messenger road by Provolt." Richard sighed. "Man," he spit, pushing himself up for emphasis. "I'm fucking tired of being outside looking in on my own goddamn life. Ever since Al blew into pieces and I went flying I've been treated like a little kid. Go there. Don't do that. Watch out for this. Like losing my legs meant I had to go back to grade school, for fuck's sake. Whadda ya think I do for sex? No woman's gonna sidle up to me at closing time looking for a roll in the hay. Unless they're one'a those freaks who get off on cripples and geeks." Exasperated, he sank back into the wheelchair, like a balloon losing air. "Sorry. I went bad there for a second." Pausing to breathe deeply. "I'm blown away by what you're telling me. Eight different pieces of land? In addition to his place and here? He's gotta be doing it for someone else. He's never had that kind of money, leastways not that I knew."

Zane noticed warmth spreading from his stomach, the morphine starting to work. *Is it my gut or my brain? Feelin or thinkin? Can't tell the difference, not that it matters. Gimme another half hour an nothin much is really gonna matter. Beauty of modern medicine. Should go home, listen to Desmond an Brubeck. Jazz at Oberlin. Put back my hands poster Sasha took down. Move the furniture around, if I want. Think about gettin a deer for the smoke house. No reason not to now. Venison steamed with oranges and onions. Meal fit for a king.* But the idea of eating meat again seemed like a betrayal. Ludicrous, given the circumstances, but he felt that way nonetheless.

Richard brought him back into the room by saying something about Duty.

"Huh? I didn't track."

"I said I don't see Duty and Sasha as a couple the way you think."

"What's that mean?"

"That I don't think they're together for the reasons you're saying, is all. Duty's a teddy bear. Can't see 'em, you know, physically connected."

Zane let out a quick, bitter laugh. "Great euphemism. So, you're sayin they're not doin the in-an-out? Not ballin?"

"Don't think so. Not in their character. They're friends, is all I ever picked up on. Duty's probably just doing her a favor. Didn't have anything else going on here, did he?"

Zane swallowed, warmed fully now from the morphine spreading through his system, and seriously considering Richard might well be right. That would explain a lot, he reasoned. Would put a whole different spin on things. *Need to call Mom before I forget. While I'm at it, think I'll check with Greg at his folks. See if he wants to move into Duty's old room.*

Chapter Twenty Four

Where is the end of them, the fishermen sailing
Into the wind's tail, where the fog cowers?
One cannot think of a time that is oceanless
Or of an ocean not littered with wastage
Or of a future which is not liable
Like the past, to have no destination.
    T.S. Eliot. *"The Dry Salvages."* Four Quartets.

Sasha had been gone close to three weeks when Nixon finally resigned, marking the end of a long, sleazy, embarrassing downward spiral with first-hand witness accounts of heavy drinking, sporadic crying jags and spontaneous profanity-laced outbursts in the final days. "Sayonara asshole," was the best Zane could come up with at the time. Richard had invited him to watch the resignation speech, but he'd declined on principle, saying he had better things to do than watch Milhous sweat under the lights. What those better things were still remained unclear to him, but who gave a fuck?

That had been a month ago. Last night, Sunday, new President Ford granted Nixon a full pardon for any and all crimes committed while in office. Wipe the slate clean for the good of the country, Ford pleaded, calling on God every other sentence it seemed to Zane, who'd caught it on the radio. Meanwhile, the stock market was tanking because of bloating inflation, and otherwise normal citizens were attacking each other in long gas lines since OPEC had ratcheted supplies tight again, as was their collective wont.

Quite the dismal spectacle in the world, Zane thought, lighting his first cigarette of the day, standing in the open front doorway in the brittle sunshine of a clear, early fall morning, while Erasmus crunched hard food loudly in the kitchen. Changing faces at the White House didn't affect him in the slightest, nor Zane either. Not with the proverbial worms turning all around him. Everywhere he looked, his immediate terrain was in flux. Forced changes. So much so that buying the farm turned out to be his easiest adjustment. Once and done. He gave Adeline a thousand and signed some papers that, frankly, he hadn't really looked at before putting them in the kitchen junk drawer. He knew where they were, if needs be. He'd offered to pay all ten grand and get the place outright, but Adeline told him they wanted a guaranteed sum every year, something to count on. She said he should just act like it was all paid off, to do what he wanted.

When he'd opened a bank account with the check from his mother, he'd kept another thousand in cash that he stashed in a dented tackle box under a stack of books upstairs. Finding himself in the totally unfamiliar position of having money for a change, he'd gone on a bit of a runner two weeks ago, spending freely at The Blue Max for a weekend, dinners and lots of scotch Vince poured heavy, crashing with him, Soapy and the girls. But staying in town wore off quickly. Too many friends asking about Sasha. Finally feeling guilty about leaving Erasmus, he'd escaped town relatively unharmed. He'd stocked up with two cartons of Pall-Mall non-filters, six cases of long-neck Buds, four half-gallons of Gallo and a thirty pound bag of Friskies while in town, though, so he felt amply supplied in essentials for the immediate future. And just the day before yesterday he'd plunked down close to two hundred on food and housewares at Sherm's Thunderbird, filling cupboards and cabinets with bags, boxes and cans, giving him an observable sense of permanence, perfidious as it was. Plenty of tuna, but no meat as yet.

Sasha's absence still caved in on him with sudden waves of sharp, aching, nearly intolerable pressure. Coming unexpectedly in the middle of some chore, or if he heard a song he knew she liked. Lacerating whatever composure he'd pretended. He knew his inability to get outside himself came across as purposely cruel indifference, *Talk about a fatal flaw* and that he'd sure enough chased "Sweet Sasha" away. Deserved every tormenting flashing moment of remembering her hot breath against his shoulder, the Dr. Bronner's peppermint smell of her coal-black hair, how she tightened around him once he was inside her, or her body shuddering in orgasmic release, the bottomless green of her eyes afterwards. Fantasies now in a recurrent nightmare crowded with snapshot cameos of good times gone. Because he'd caused it, and karma was a bitch. In these moments, he knew to his marrow that he'd never regret anything else in his life as much as losing her.

He couldn't sleep in their room, couldn't get comfortable enough there to even try lying down on the same blankets they'd shared. So he slept on the couch, and only entered the bedroom to change clothes, get money from the tackle box or dig out a book, feeling like a thief or intruder every time. Consequently, he lived almost entirely downstairs, though he was sure Erasmus could be found on the bed most afternoons.

Last Wednesday, Adeline arrived with a wringer washing machine that she'd said had been collecting garbage in their barn. The two of them had rolled it out of Lester's pickup on some planks and onto the back porch, plugged it in to an outdoor socket where it rattled to life, wringer squeaking. "Best be watchin your fingers, and never have long sleeves on," she'd warned, before asking him when Sasha was expected back. He'd muttered something about waiting for a letter and she'd nodded, smiling slightly. Something about her tone of voice in asking and her expression afterwards, an over-the-shoulder, spearing glance, told him she'd already seen through his flimsy story and it didn't matter. She'd brought the washer anyway.

The 24/7 FM on low featured Dave Van Ronk this morning as Zane leaned against the porch railing, catching glimpses, between riverside trees across the recently mowed pasture, of some ducks winging upstream, only a few feet above the summer-slowed Applegate's surface. *Mate for life, those ducks. Or it is only geese? Have to ask Richard.*

Their friendship had gelled into stronger new forms in the month and a half Zane had been alone. After he'd clued Richard into his dad's mysterious land holdings, his friend had launched himself on a mission to uncover whatever skeletons his father was hiding, or perhaps helped cause. Certainly no love lost there.

The first two Saturdays after "the leaving," as Zane termed it, Richard had accompanied him to meet with George, the three of them working as a team since, though they hadn't met recently because George had said he'd be unavailable for a little while. There were moments when Zane simply sipped his beer as Richard and George shared stories about people Richard had grown up with but George knew only peripherally, if at all. Between the two of them, they'd been trying to put together a convincing picture of what was brewing in the woods around Carberry. So far they'd agreed the common denominator among those they knew was a fierce devotion to white Anglo-Saxon tradition—"our heritage" the faithful called it—and a snarling hatred of the federal government. Armed isolationists who had friends in law enforcement. Sheriff Lyle Willets, for one, according to George. Who'd added that for years he'd heard rumors about weapons and explosives stocked-up in those far-flung compounds, but nothing had ever been confirmed, as far as he knew.

Richard volunteered that he'd begun frequenting the four-stool bar at McKee Bridge store, a hangout normally filled with back woods locals smoking on folding chairs around card tables full of empties. Recently, however, Richard said business had boomed since it was the closest watering hole to the dam construction, only two miles below Copper. All those dusty, thirsty workers streaming back to the valley. The reason he'd never previously bothered with the place was the same as his reason for going there now, he'd carefully explained. "They've got 'Love it or Leave it' bumper stickers everywhere, an' someone'd added 'Absolutely No Hippies' to the 'No Shirt, No Shoes, No Service' sign on the door. It's like a fucking Sons of Liberty meeting." Richard claimed if they wanted any scuttlebutt at all he'd best rub up against some childhood classmates, if not friends. "Like goin undercover," he'd told them, with a wink and a toothy smile. "I just make a big deal out of taking my legs off, showing 'em some stump. Makes 'em feel a little guilty, I think. 'Course I pretend to be the same head-up-my-ass racist prick I used to be."

Richard's fact-finding crusade, Zane understood, was mostly aimed at his dad. But that didn't, for a second, diminish his dramatic transformation from languid apathy to inspired, even radical, firebrand. From Zane's perspective, it was as if, when Richard was flown out of the jungle and eventually released from a series of hospitals, he'd fallen too easily into the role of disabled recluse with no discernable purpose, a mostly morose victim of his times. Trips to the commune being the high points of his predominantly shut-in existence sitting on the couch in his bare-floored room, in differing degrees of self-medication, watching fuzzy TV. Or cruising river roads at night in his hand-control Mustang while seriously impaired.

After recognizing his father's shady connections to white supremacists, however—a conclusion he and George had pieced further together since, linking names to families—he'd shown the focused zeal of a recently proselytized convert. Claimed he'd finally seen the light, finally understood why he was condemned to live the rest of his life on wheels or crutches, and why until he died he'd be at the mercy of the closest VA. He said he'd distilled all the reasons down to the fact that government power was tethered to fat cats, and did fuck-all for everyone else. Zane thought lending him *The Wretched of the Earth* right after Sasha split might have sparked that analysis, but it was hard to dismiss being a war casualty as a main motivating factor. In any case, Richard now showered anyone within reach with spit-flying tirades about how rigged the system was. Fleshy white guys in suits sending whole generations to war or prison because they could. He'd become fully politicized. "I'm not saying I sacrificed my legs for US Steel," he'd said the other day. "That'd be an insult to everyone who didn't make it. But I sure as shit lost 'em for a pack 'a lies and a big bag 'a nothing."

Not seeing any more ducks and dying for coffee, Zane went back inside, leaving the door open. Such an Indian summer day.

Cascading hues of reds, browns and yellows. Cottonwood, oak, madrone, alder and maple splayed amongst the evergreen on every hillside. Wood smoke in the air, blowing up from downriver. Flat light filtering pleasantly through spiky tree tops. Stark contrast to knowing he'd never felt more alone, even as a cringing child under assault from his father. This loss was for keeps, grown-up, life-changing.

He'd debated with himself for several weeks about getting Greg to move in, finally deciding his bad habits were worth putting up with to have someone else in the house. So many jobs needed an extra pair of hands. As fall arrived, helping Lester with the cattle was going to become a daily chore again, so having Greg around might make good sense. But when, after visiting Pacific Gas and Electric in town to switch the house account, he stopped by the parent's house, Greg's mother said he was working as a day cook for Witham's Truck Stop at the Crater Lake/I-5 junction. Reminding Zane of his second grade teacher, Mrs. Gray—tight pin curls and a faint moustache—Greg's mother was clearly in a good mood, explaining with beaming pride that Greg had shaved his beard, cut his hair and planned to get an apartment soon. Zane felt blindsided again, someone else doing a one-eighty all of a sudden. So much for dreaming, he'd sighed. *Ian and Sylvia, 1965*. And couldn't get to The Alibi fast enough to drink bleach flavored Blitz.

Pretending to listen to Fat Jack deliver a meticulous, blow by blow account of his latest parachute jump, a story he imagined had been going on a loop all day, Zane picked up a copy of the *Mail Tribune* off the bar to see headlines that the trial scheduled for the Takilma killings had been called off. In exchange for taking the death penalty off the table, Thomas Skagget had pleaded guilty to the murders, the report said, and would get two life sentences without possibility of parole. When asked by the judge why he'd beheaded, gutted and hung the bodies after he'd already killed them with a shotgun, Skagget was quoted as saying that he'd "wanted people to think

388

someone crazy had done it." No mention had been made in the article about whether law enforcement agencies were still questioning him in connection to the Fausen family's disappearance. *No one's talkin about Emilio an Rainbow Rick as people anymore, either,* he'd noticed after finishing the story. *They're beside the point.*

At eleven this morning, Zane finally dropped a cinnamon/raisin bagel in the electric toaster he'd gotten for five bucks at the J-Ville Thrift Store and poured milk on his bowl of Gone Nuts granola with fresh blueberries. Lately he only ate when forced to by hunger pangs, or dizziness. Crazy, he knew, having taken such care to fill the kitchen shelves with food. Carrying breakfast into the living room, he raised the volume on the FM for the news. More of Ford justifying the pardon, meandering explanations in response to reporters' questions. Assuring the country his people were doing everything possible to address the oil shortage. Calling on God for help. *An whose God would that be, Jerry? Jehovah? Allah? Vishnu? Yahweh? Jesus's dad? Buddha's breath?* He went from there to Richard's latest rant about how the new president had only ever been elected by a few thousand people in Michigan's 5th congressional district on the lower peninsula, a thin sliver running through several counties which had been gerrymandered by Republicans out of the southwestern edges of Saginaw Bay. Decidedly more rural than urban, Richard stressed, as if the ridiculousness of that spoke for itself.

By the time he focused on news again, it was already over. Quivering strains from Cream now filling the room. After finishing what passed for sustenance, he dispensed his bowl to the sink, grabbed his smokes and headed for the open door before making a U-turn to the frig, opening a beer to take out with him. Back on the porch, he watched cattle milling in the pasture on the downstream side of the driveway, feeling the slight breeze coming up the river, musing for no apparent reason about the absurdity of the Trojan Horse story. *So the Greeks had laid siege to Troy for ten years supposedly.*

What'd Troy do for food an water all that time? No one's supposed to ask. Then, one day Odysseus decides Greeks should build this wooden horse big enough to carry thirty elite swordsmen. Story says it took three days to build. Ok. So where were the Trojans durin those three days? They didn't look out one of their portholes, or over the edge to watch this thing bein built? All the Greeks took off in the night, leavin the horse outside the gates. How'd it get there? I mean, I think this was takin place in a sandy soil. They'd need thousands just to pull the damn thing. An, again, none of the Trojans saw a thing? Just doesn't hang together, this story. I understand they believed in Gods an fairies an all kinds'a flyin creatures, thought they screwed with people in their daily lives, but still... He broke off re-writing mythology to watch, with anxious curiosity, a blue El Camino nose up the driveway toward him. *It's George,* he realized when he could see inside. *Funny, I've never seen his car before. Looks like he's got a woman with him.* Zane had never witnessed George even talking to a woman, unless it was Mickey at the tavern. *Must'a misread a whole helluva lot.* As if a nicitating membrane in his brain automatically filtered his perceptions, he'd never thought of George in any connection to women, hadn't skimmed across his thinking even once.

What he noticed first when they exited the car was that George's white hair was just long enough to be lifted by the breeze—he hadn't seen him in over two weeks—and that the woman was strikingly good looking, fit and shapely with sable brown hair over her shoulders. She was a good foot shorter than George and they looked to be about the same age, he guessed on the slimmest of evidence.

"Zane," George said, as the woman suddenly hung on his arm. "We just went up to the dam," talking while walking, "it's getting taller. This is Jackie." They reached the porch steps and waited a few clearly uncomfortable seconds until Zane woke up and waved them forward. He stuck out his hand, took hers which was soft and warm, introduced himself and led her up the steps, leaving George to trail a step behind. "Come in. You guys want a beer?"

When Zane placed the bottles on the table in front of them they'd set themselves on the couch. He noticed Jackie taking in the room, sweeping her head around, cataloging impressions. Zane saw she found it appealing. "I love the smells," she'd said at no one's prompting. "Ginger and wood smoke. Warm and homey. Lots of books and records, but no TV."

"Can't get any reception," he said stupidly, knowing it wasn't her point, stumbling over himself. "So, George," he tried regaining lost territory, "how'd you manage to get off work on a Monday?"

"On vacation. One more week."

"So whadda you been doin with your time off?" Zane hoped he wasn't over-reaching in the friend department. They'd really only ever talked about mining claims and survivalists. He noticed George catching Jackie's eye before answering. Her cheeks blossoming twin pink patches.

"Uh, I've been moving," dropping his voice at the end, looking sideways out the window above the stereo and receiver.

"In with me," said Jackie, eyes sparkling as she put a hand on George's plaid shirted arm. "My boys wanted to live with their father in Ashland, so…," she hesitated. For effect, he thought. "…we've been hauling stuff, cleaning his old place."

Zane was clearly stupefied, in unknown territory. Not knowing where to go from here. Beginning to feel uneasy that he was learning more about their lives than he needed to know. But she seemed friendly, kind, and George was suddenly displaying sides of himself he'd never seen, giving way, deferring, adoring. Zane felt drawn to them despite his reticence. The two generating warmth and a welcoming openness. Well, mostly Jackie, but George didn't appear to be minding. Quite the contrary. George's expression suggested he could burst into giddiness in a heartbeat, like it took all his effort to control himself. George was smitten. *Is that the word for someone his age? So now I'm single, while solitary lonesome George has found love? It's an upside-down world.* It was clear they were together. The ringing implications of that word cutting deeply, though he worked not to show it. George already knew about Sasha's departure, and Zane assumed he'd surely told Jackie as neither of them made the slightest mention about his living alone, for which he was thankful.

He was slouched in Sasha's chair by the window smoking, with the cigarettes, lighter and ashtray on one flat wooden arm, beer on the other. Door still open, ambient sunlight, FM low. George and Jackie sat, hips touching, having difficulty keeping their eyes off each other. Afraid they might start nuzzling soon, Zane squeezed in.

"Richard tells me he heard talk at McKee that Wade Perkins' brother Jed plans to open a marina on the lake when the time comes, that he already had an *Evinrude* franchise."

"Sounds par for the course. You know, I keep wondering about Wade. What's he getting? Can't help seeing him as the runt of the litter, sort of the Fredo of the bunch.

"So who's in charge? Any idea?"

George glanced out the side window again. His tell, Zane filed away. Before he could answer, Jackie piped in happily. "George thinks that fake cowboy Sheriff Willets is in it up to his neck."

Jesus. He tells her everything.

George found his voice again. "I do think that, in fact. But Ed Scott is a big player, too. Brereton doesn't have his name on anything, but they're all his people. It's quite a group, I think. With direct connections to law enforcement, though that's the part of the story that needs the most attention. Without it, there's no way to proceed, no case to make."

"I told him he had a responsibility to follow through," Jackie said matter-of-factly. "Too many people stay silent when others are made to suffer."

"So what can I do?" He asked George directly.

"Don't really know yet. Let me sniff around some more. Soon as I finish this moving and cleaning." He smiled down at her over his left shoulder. Zane could see her fingers squeeze his arm. He knew the sign of intimacy, or at least he thought that was it. Aware he only understood intimacy as physical, prelude to sex. Didn't have a sense of any other kind, or a clue about what else it might mean. How he'd act. *Like I'm missin some vital part. The old man might be dead, but I'm still staunchin open wounds.*

"My money's on Wade Perkins to crack first." George offered this as though it were part of an on-going dialogue. "He's the weak link. I'm gonna give him a good look."

Zane watched as George put a hand on her thigh. Not patting condescendingly. Just resting, being there. Decently, he thought. "I gotta do somethin, George. Can't just sit out here communin with cattle." He got up abruptly. "Another beer?"

"Naw. I'm driving and we gotta get back to work."

Not knowing exactly what he was doing, standing there, Zane watched as Jackie slid open the large box of Diamond stick matches, fiddling around, only to find it full of grass, stems and seeds clinging. "Oh, look," she said. "Herbal remedies."

"You want some?" Without waiting, he disappeared into the kitchen, returning with a small plastic bag. As if on cue, the two of them stood, Jackie smoothing down her jeans.

"Gonna be strange not meetin at the tavern anymore," Zane said as he shook half the box of weed into the baggy, handing it to her. He swore she curtsied, but it could have been otherwise. As with most things, he was slowly coming to understand.

"We can still do that. I'll drive over to meet you there, just not this Saturday." George stuck out his hand to shake. A first, in Zane's memory. "We'll keep at it, don't worry. I doubt we can do anything about Perry, it's impossible to prove. But Brereton's part in moving the claim is something that might stick. And the Fausens. Can't shake the notion that whatever happened to them is connected to these people. As I said, I think with the right pressure, Perkins might cave on Brereton, try to save himself. Just a matter of finding the right lever to press. He's really not that smart. As for the other land stuff around the lake, I'm afraid that unless there's a reason to justify searches for stockpiles of weapons or explosives, and absent some smoking gun about the Fausens, we just have to keep our eyes and ears open. I'm not giving up," he nodded toward Jackie. "She's not going to let me. If Richard finds anything new, you can get a hold of me..." He pulled his wallet from his left back pocket, slid out a business card. "You got a pencil?"

"Upstairs. Hang on a second." Zane didn't wait for a response.

When he returned and handed George a ballpoint pen, Jackie was smelling the pot, smiling as she re-rolled the bag. Using his wallet as flat surface, George wrote a number on the back of his card. "Jackie's phone, when I'm not at the office."

Jackie waved as she got into the El Camino. George stuck his hand out the window, gave it a couple tilts back and forth. Zane watched from the porch as their car turned onto the highway and disappeared behind the painter's pallet of riverside colors. He was struck by ever-so-faintly hearing heavy machines banging and screeching at the dam, that muffled sound sporadically overshadowed by clanging dump trucks and earthmovers spewing black diesel fumes as they sped toward town. Their noise drowning out the sounds of the river splashing over and around channel rocks. *My new reality.*

Back in the house, he stuffed his cigarettes into his pants, thinking about he didn't know what, caught in cognitive dissonance as Jimi Hendrix sang "All Along the Watchtower." Then Zane remembered drinking too many beers in a tented enclosure at the Mt. Angel *Oktoberfest* in '70, listening to that song when he was told Janis had just OD'd, and he'd wondered who'd be next since all the good ones seemed hell-bent on killing themselves. Turned out to be Hendrix himself died next. Today, the song spoke of too many lost hopes, echoed of all those voices now stilled.

He walked through the house and out the back door, aiming for Sasha's hillside. He called it that to himself, like he called her favorite place by the beaver dams Sasha's meadow, had thought that way since he first watched her cross the creek and climb. He'd followed her up and into the woods to see where she was going, relying on stealth developed as a kid at the lake to stay hidden. Once she'd stopped and spread her blanket on the grass, he'd slowly backed away, beat a silent retreat so he wouldn't feel like a sleazy voyeur.

He didn't know why he was going there now, but felt impelled to climb up, change perspective perhaps. Or emotionally scourge himself in expiation for a multitude of sins. If only it were that easy. He made it to the cleft of the hill, where it flattened out into a wide ledge that led back to the creek. Standing in a low thicket of young madrone and crawling vines, about to lose sight of the river and highway miniaturized by distance, he hesitated. Blips of colored lights blinked through trees downstream. At the corner of his vision, but coming up river.

Emergency lights, he guessed a couple seconds before he actually saw them. Like slow motion, burning into his consciousness, two white Coroner lab trucks, a state police cruiser, and three 4 x 4s belonging to agencies he couldn't identify. Flashers on full, no sirens. Followed by a handful of state vehicles without lights. He immediately knew what it meant. *Looks like they've found the Fausens. Knew from the get-go they were dead. George an Jackie must'a seen them on the road. They would'a put two an two together.* He found a weather-eaten stump to sit on, cold cramping in his gut as he saw his future becoming irrevocably complicated in a soon to be re-energized search for answers.

Act Locally. What else can you do? Join the headlong rush to squeeze every last penny from the world? Believe in God and gettin ahead? We're only around for a fraction of a cosmic millisecond with soulless eternity beckonin. Doesn't matter what we find about Brereton or the Sheriff. Maybe George is right that Perkins will crack eventually, but that wouldn't bring anybody back. Perry an Emilio an Rainbow Rick are still dead. Gary and Clarise Fausen, young Gary Jr. and baby Eva. Say their names. Now probably nothin but chewed bones and bits of clothing.

395

A significantly growing piece of him wondered how any of his personal traumas could possibly matter in the big scheme, when global powers on belligerent alert stood ready to hurl flotillas of ICBMs through the ozone-depleted, hairspray atmosphere, threatening whole continents with imminent, indiscriminant destruction? *It's the nature of life in the 20th century, isn't it? Truth up for grabs, uncertainty everywhere you turn. While most passionately held beliefs an attitudes preach exactly the opposite, build their structures on what they claim are absolutes. Right an wrong. Us an them. We got a serious problem here. But no one's listenin. Patty Hearst is still on the run an Nixon's gone. We can say that much at least. An I'm still above ground, lookin for more windmills to tilt at.*

He was alive, of course, which was more than he could say for some, for millions of the uncounted, like the water-softened carcasses floating belly-up every spawning season. "I never meant to hurt you, Sasha," he wished he could say to her face, look in her eyes, re-establish. *Not a chance. You blew that.*

He knew that in a few weeks the fall runs of Chinook and Coho would begin surging inland, in fewer numbers year by year perhaps, but still coming nonetheless. Coherent rhythms and cycles, assuming patterns held.

In his mind's ear he could hear them thrashing through foaming white rapids, their open jaws straining against a constant current, their eyes wide and frantic, driven insane by instinct. As he watched even more official vehicles sweep past on the road below, he momentarily fantasized himself struggling through clinging vines and thorny brush to find the shallow, stagnant pools of the salmon's last dead. Seeing the end of the line. Made perfect sense, given his track record. Give up. Move on.

"But not this time," he countered, cropping out the negative images, surveying the narrow, pastured valley and the quilted stands of timber that blanketed every hill and ridge in sight. *Been hidin long enough. If George an Richard are gonna keep fightin, then it's the least I can do. Hold the bastards accountable. Make their crimes known.* As he talked himself into combative resolve, he once again toyed with Pascal's existential questions of why he was alive now rather than in some other time, why he was born in relative plenty rather than in the raw misery common to most of the world.

"Why not?" He said firmly, decisively. Finally seeing himself at home in this best of all possible worlds.

Epilogue

Big Dave blew out the back half of his head with the Browning "Sweet Sixteen" he'd inherited from his dad, who'd checked out a couple years earlier amid Alzheimer tirades and spit bubbles. The water-frayed, ramshackle and slouching old house they'd briefly shared was hidden by a wild tangle of vine maple and blackberries at the end of a private, cat-track driveway. When alive, his father had been known around town as something of a recluse. Which was saying quite a lot, considering the near-to-the-coast community's habitual distrust of anyone not related by blood. So few noticed when Big Dave moved back to Myrtle Point right after 9/11 and parked his Dodge Ram next to his dad's rust-pitted International.

After he'd had the old man cremated on the GI bill and unceremoniously dumped him into the south fork of the Coquille, Big Dave stayed in the moldy house, repainting his duck decoys. He gave some time as well to cursing all those "baby California spawners" who were to blame for everything from thinning salmon runs to the fact that his 401K had lost over half its value.

In an act of supreme irony, when he mouthed the shotgun, Dave was wearing the nearly faded away purple "Gooned Again" t-shirt Moe had given him on one of their runners. Caricature of a Daffy Duck with eyes agog and lop-sided stars swirling around its head. I can't imagine how it still fit.

Of course, I learned all this later by phone from Win a couple of weeks after the suicide. I'd lost track of Big Dave somewhere in the eighties, only heard that he'd gone to ground, cut himself off from most everyone he knew and talked about being a "native patriot" in a low whispery voice. That's how Win told it, explaining that Cecilia had kept intermittent touch with Dave over the years through a gyppo logger out of Roseburg who'd known Dave from his time pushing high interest loans for Household Finance. I got the stories from Win, who got them from Cecilia, who got them from the logger. Not exactly the horse's mouth. More like the finger streams that feed the river, the stories blend colors. But Big Dave was gone, regardless. I don't know why I'm telling you all this; it's not really part of the story. Win had to go on oxygen, which dropped a leaden veil on his conversation, so I didn't call him often, or even rarely.

A few days before he died, Win phoned. I got him to tell me what ducks ate when they dove underwater. I started to apologize for not calling him more often but he cut me off, saying he had another long time friend on the line. Last words I ever heard from him.

About the Author:

After retiring as Director of Rhetoric and Writing Studies at Chapman University in Orange, California, Doug now lives in Eugene, Oregon with his partner, Jeanne Gunner, and more cats than they'd ever admit.

Made in the USA
Middletown, DE
13 September 2020